Trisha Telep is the editor of the bestselling Mammoth romance titles, including *The Mammoth Book of Vampire Romance, Love Bites, The Mammoth Book of Paranormal Romance* and *The Mammoth Book of Time Travel Romance*.

Recent Mammoth titles

The Mammoth Book of Undercover Cops
The Mammoth Book of Antarctic Journeys
The Mammoth Book of Muhammad Ali
The Mammoth Book of Best British Crime 9
The Mammoth Book of Conspiracies
The Mammoth Book of Lost Symbols
The Mammoth Book of Body Horror
The Mammoth Book of Steampunk
The Mammoth Book of New CSI
The Mammoth Book of Gangs
The Mammoth Book of One-Liners
The Mammoth Book of Ghost Romance
The Mammoth Book of Best New SF 25
The Mammoth Book of Horror 23
The Mammoth Book of Slasher Movies
The Mammoth Book of Street Art
The Mammoth Book of Ghost Stories by Women
The Mammoth Book of Unexplained Phenomena
The Mammoth Book of Futuristic Romance
The Mammoth Book of Best British Crime 10
The Mammoth Book of Combat
The Mammoth Book of Covert Ops
The Mammoth Book of Dark Magic
The Mammoth Book of Zombies
The Mammoth Book of Hollywood Scandals
The Mammoth Book of the World Cup
The Mammoth Book of The Lost Chronicles of Sherlock
Holmes
The Mammoth Book of The Western

The Mammoth Book of

Southern Gothic

Romance

Edited by Trisha Telep

RUNNING PRESS
PHILADELPHIA · LONDON

ROBINSON

First published in Great Britain in 2014 by Robinson

Copyright © Trisha Telep, 2014 (unless otherwise stated)

1 3 5 7 9 10 8 6 4 2

The moral right of the author has been asserted.

A CIP catalogue record for this book
is available from the British Library.

ISBN 978-1-47211-063-3 (paperback)
ISBN 978-1-47211-077-0 (ebook)

Typeset in Plantin Light by Hewer Text UK Ltd, Edinburgh
Printed and bound by CPI Group (UK) Ltd, Croydon, CR0 4YY

Robinson
is an imprint of
Constable & Robinson Ltd
100 Victoria Embankment
London EC4Y 0DY

An Hachette UK Company
www.hachette.co.uk

www.constablerobinson.com

First published in the United States in 2014 by Running Press Book Publishers,
A Member of the Perseus Books Group

Books published by Running Press are available at special discounts for bulk
purchases in the United States by corporations, institutions and other organizations.
For more information, please contact the Special Markets Department at the
Perseus Books Group, 2300 Chestnut Street, Suite 200, Philadelphia, PA 19103,
or call (800) 810-4145, ext. 5000, or email special.markets@perseusbooks.com.

US ISBN: 978-0-7624-5472-3
US Library of Congress Control Number: 2014937357

9 8 7 6 5 4 3 2 1

Digit on the right indicates the number of this printing

Running Press Book Publishers
2300 Chestnut Street
Philadelphia, PA 19103-4371

Visit us on the web!
www.runningpress.com

CONTENTS

Acknowledgments vii

Introduction ix

1. Shiloh Walker	The Haunted	1
2. Sonya Bateman	The Devil Went Down	39
3. Dianne Sylvan	Sweet the Sting	79
4. Erin Kellison	Wylde Magic	101
5. Jill Archer	Dream, Interrupted	141
6. Laurie London	Enticed by Blood	180
7. Bec McMaster	The Many Lives of Hadley Monroe	211
8. Angie Fox	Date with a Demon Slayer	247
9. Elle Jasper	Return to Me	273
10. J. D. Horn	Pretty Enough to Catch Her	296
11. Tiffany Trent	Love, Sugar	332
12. Shelli Stevens	Savage Rescue	357
13. Jessa Slade	If Only Tonight	393
14. Shawntelle Madison	Cursed	425
15. Amanda Bonilla	Waerd Awakenings	457

About the Authors 495

ACKNOWLEDGMENTS

"The Haunted" © by Shiloh Walker. First publication, original to this anthology. Printed by permission of the author.

"The Devil Went Down" © by Sonya Bateman. First publication, original to this anthology. Printed by permission of the author.

"Sweet the Sting" © by Dianne Sylvan. First publication, original to this anthology. Printed by permission of the author.

"Wylde Magic" © by Clarissa Ellison. First publication, original to this anthology. Printed by permission of the author.

"Dream, Interrupted" © by Black Willow, LLC. First publication, original to this anthology. Printed by permission of the author.

"Enticed By Blood" © by Laurie London. First publication, original to this anthology. Printed by permission of the author.

"The Many Lives of Hadley Monroe" © by Bec McMaster. First publication, original to this anthology. Printed by permission of the author.

"Date with a Demon Slayer" © by Angie Fox. First publication, original to this anthology. Printed by permission of the author.

"Return to Me" © by Elle Jasper. First publication, original to this anthology. Printed by permission of the author.

"Pretty Enough to Catch Her" © by J. D. Horn. First publication, original to this anthology. Printed by permission of the author.

"Love, Sugar" © by Tiffany Trent. First publication, original to this anthology. Printed by permission of the author.

"Savage Rescue" © by Shelli Stevens. First publication, original to this anthology. Printed by permission of the author.

"If Only Tonight" © by Jessa Slade. First publication, original to this anthology. Printed by permission of the author.

"Cursed" © by Shawntelle Madison. First publication, original to this anthology. Printed by permission of the author.

"Waerd Awakenings" © by Amanda Bonilla. First publication, original to this anthology. Printed by permission of the author.

INTRODUCTION

The states of the Southern USA have a bad reputation for great drama. Just ask fans of Charlaine Harris's Louisiana-set, Southern-fried vampire fest that became TV's *True Blood*. And although Southern literature has a respectably long and storied history, it's essentially the creepy, dark, ghost-ridden, crocodile-infested roots of Southern Gothic that we're interested in at present.

It's always fascinating to see what fifteen feisty romance writers will get up to when you ask them to write in a subgenre they may never have written in before. It's plain to see that the Southern Gothic elements of menace, mystery, and magic aren't more than a stone's throw from the fantastical, creature-loving paranormal romance that we know and love. So, when issuing the challenge to the writers featured in *The Mammoth Book of Southern Gothic Romance*, I was pretty sure they were going to take to the subject matter faster than a knife fight in a phone booth. And you know what? They did.

Some writers have transplanted their series to a Southern milieu, like Angie Fox, who's moved her merry band of biker witches into a field off Route 11 in Georgia, and Laurie London whose Sweetbloods may or may not have a dirty weekend planned in New Orleans. There are grim reapers, ghosts of every size and shape, including Civil War fiddlers, pirates and time travellers and more wrought iron than you ever thought possible. It's a well-known fact that the thin veil between the living and the dead, the present and the past, and the possible and the impossible just doesn't exist in the South.

Paranormal romance is right at home down South. Hunky Southern shape-shifters, elegant vampires in crumbling mansions, werewolves under ancient curses and little girls in lonesome graveyards who can see the dead fit effortlessly into Southern climes. And you'll find writers having a little fun with the genre too – "Southern" becomes southern California, and bright summer days can prove just as sinister and mysterious as the darkest swamp.

So grab your umbrella and your Tarot cards and return to the honorary birthplace of paranormal romance, where the living is easy and the handsome ghosts are too.

THE HAUNTED

an FBI Psychics story

Shiloh Walker

There was a child in his graveyard.

Gabriel Tallant Tallman stood in the shadows, staring at the small figure. It was a cool evening. Fog had rolled in, the wisps of it winding in and out of the monuments, clinging to the ground. The girl was almost motionless as she bent her head over whatever it was that held her so fascinated.

She sat with her back pressed against one of the family vaults. Either she wasn't concerned by the fact that there were bodies inside that structure or she just didn't know. It could go either way. He knew from experience.

There was a look to her face that unsettled him. One that spoke of an age beyond her years. Some sort of wisdom that didn't suit her youth. As the mist thickened around her, he had the strangest sense that perhaps she was one of the spirits that so many people came to the cemetery hoping to find.

Of course, he knew better.

If a person wanted to find a real ghost, you didn't come to a place of rest. The people who ended up here were just the empty shells of the dead. Their spirits would linger on in other places, unless of course somebody had actually *died* in the graveyard.

Nobody had.

That's why Gabriel liked it.

It was quiet.

Ghosts didn't bother him.

But that girl did.

She didn't belong here.

He debated between ignoring her and asking her why she was here, but in the end, the lateness of the day decided it for him. It was coming up on seven and the sun was already kissing the horizon. Soon, this place would be shrouded in darkness and it wasn't a place for children.

When he moved out from behind an obelisk, she lifted her head. If his presence surprised her, she didn't show it. Her gaze bounced off him and then returned to her notebook.

He had to amend his earlier observation. Maybe she wasn't as wise as he'd thought. Those eyes, as old as they'd seemed when she looked at him, might be more naive than he'd assumed. A smart kid wouldn't ignore a total stranger like that. She should be more careful.

Abruptly, Gabriel felt angry. Where were her parents? Didn't they think to teach her about strangers and crazy people?

Why was she here in a cemetery?

She shot him a look, a quick flick of her eyes. She had pretty eyes, he noticed. Absurdly so. They actually reminded him of somebody. A woman. Before that thought could become an ache, he blocked it out. Thinking about her never led to good things. How much good could come of it when all of it had led to heartache, anyway?

Instead of letting his mind wander down that long, painful path, he focused on the here and the now.

The young girl with her blue-green eyes and her café au lait skin sure as hell shouldn't be out alone this late, so far from anybody.

Almost as if she could sense his thoughts, she looked back at him and her chin went up. "You got a problem, mister?"

"It's getting late," he pointed out. "Not the best place to be at night."

She wrinkled her nose and looked around. "Why? Is the boogey man gonna get me?"

Frowning, he shoved his hands in his pockets. Mouthy, arrogant bratty girl. "If you believe in the boogey man at your age, then somebody needs to have a talk with your folks."

"It's not my *folks*. It's just my mom." She shrugged and looked back at whatever she had in her lap.

Craning his head, he caught a better look of it. It was a notebook, the spiral-bound kind, and she also had a pen clutched in one hand. "Well, when you talk to your mama about the boogey man, maybe she should explain to you about why you shouldn't be messing around in cemeteries this close to dark. Or . . . at all."

"What's wrong with cemeteries?" she asked. "They're quiet. Not like there's anything dangerous here."

They're quiet. Those words hummed through his brain. Thoughtfully, he narrowed his eyes. Gabriel studied her closer, but this time, she kept her gaze locked on the notebook in front of her. "What do you mean, quiet?"

"Is the word foreign?" She shrugged, her voice self-conscious. "You know. *Quiet.* It's the opposite of loud."

He had a feeling that his idea of *quiet* and her idea were two very different things.

"Quiet or not, that doesn't make it safe. You can still run into dangerous people, get hurt. Your mama know you're here?"

There was a pause and the girl finally glanced up at him. "She probably knows." She pursed her lips, giving him the same thoughtful study he'd given her. "Don't tell me *you're* dangerous."

Honey, if only you knew.

But he kept that thought tucked safely inside his head. "You should get home. The graveyard locks its gates at dark."

"You sure are paranoid about this. You act like you own this place or something." She paused, one eye squinting thoughtfully. "You don't, do you?"

A reluctant smile tugged at his lips. "No. I don't own this place." That didn't mean it wasn't *his*, though. When he was in town, he spent more time in this old garden of stone than the actual groundskeeper, walking the paths, caring for the overgrown weeds and leaving the plots alone where the families had left such requests in place. He knew this place so well, he could walk it in the dead of night with no light to guide him. Especially lately.

This was his haven and he wasn't going to share it with some mouthy child.

"You should leave," he said again, looking around. It was full dark now, and if somebody didn't know the way, it was easy to get lost in the shadows. "Can you find your way out?"

She sighed and pushed herself up, clutching the notepad to her with skinny arms. "Yeah." She plodded off past him. "I liked this place better before you saw me."

Jonni Hart was calling the cops.

That girl had less than five minutes to walk through the door before she made the call. Pacing back and forth, she gnawed on her left thumbnail, a habit she'd tried to kick so many times over the year.

Up until she'd been forced to come back to Golgotha, Mississippi, she'd actually managed to do it.

Thanks to losing her job in Nashville, thanks to the damned economy slump, thanks to a lot of things, she'd been forced to do the one thing she'd never wanted to do – move back into the house where she'd grown up. It had been left to Jonni – Jonquil on her driver's license and birth certificate but she'd hurt the person who called her that – and her brother, Royce, after their father had died two years ago.

Royce, a cop on the minuscule Golgotha police department, had been fixing the house up over the months. They wanted to sell it, rid themselves of the place, of the memories, of a time when their lives had consisted of long, tense nights, of days with little food, and a drunken bastard who had barely managed to hold a job. The only way they'd been able to keep the bills paid was because Royce was smart enough to swipe money out of the old man's wallet once a week come payday.

It was cleaner now. Quieter. The walls no longer echoed with the sound of his drunken bellows. *Keep the noise down, you little brat . . .*

She cast a look around the small living room, painted a smooth, easy shade of pale green. Quieter, yes. Cleaner, yes. But it wasn't the place where she wanted to raise *her* kid.

"Damn it, Tally, where are—"

The door opened.

Hurling down the cell phone she'd been clutching like a talisman, she whirled on her daughter. "Where the *hell* have you been?"

Big, blue-green eyes, the same shade as her own, stared back at her as Tally heaved out a sigh. "I was just out, Mom," Tally said, shrugging out of her coat and hanging it up.

"Out. Out *where*? We've been here for less than two weeks and to my knowledge you haven't told me about any friends, which means disappearing with any of them is a big, fat *no* in the mom book of rules." She propped her hands on her hips and waited.

Tally shot her a look that managed to crush Jonni's heart. *Oh, baby . . .*

"I haven't made any friends," Tally said, her voice soft. Then it turned sulky. "So don't worry. I just wanted someplace . . ."

She stopped and looked around, while her smooth, light-brown skin went white. "I needed it to be quiet."

Quiet.

Jonni refused to think about how much it worried her when Tally talked about needing things *quiet*. The last few months before they'd left Nashville, Tally had looked for *quiet* places a lot. She'd found them, too. Usually in weird places. Jonni had hoped moving would help whatever had taken her normally happy child and turned her into this worried, truculent shadow. Even as much as she herself had hated to come back to this tired old river town.

"Quiet." Jonni smoothed her hands down her jeans. Blowing out a breath, she settled down on the couch and stared at the wall in front of her. In her mind's eye, she saw the wall as it had been the day she finally left. Royce had packed up and moved out the same afternoon.

That wall had once borne the marks of a fight between Royce and that mean, old son of a bitch – a hole in the plaster where Jimmy Hart had thrown him when Royce had stuck up for her, yet again.

"It's quiet *here*," Jonni said. *Please talk to me, baby.* "Why do you have to leave to find quiet when it's just you and me? It's not like there's an apartment next door or sirens blaring down in the street or a baby crying upstairs. How much more quiet do you need, Tally?"

Tally didn't speak for so long Jonni didn't think she *would* answer.

But, finally, the girl sat down on the couch next to her. "It's not that kind of quiet, Mama." She leaned her head against her mother's arm. "It's hard to explain. If I can figure out how, I will."

Wrapping an arm around Tally's thin shoulders, she said, "You've been needing this kind of quiet for months now. How much longer you think it will take?"

"I don't know." Tally turned her face into her mother's embrace, the way she'd done since she was a baby. "There's just so much noise in my head, Mama."

Silence fell between them and Jonni squeezed her eyes shut. "Is this because of how rough the last year has been? I know it's all kind of sucked. I'm getting more work coming in with my freelance stuff, but . . ."

"No." Tally looked up and shook her head. "It's not that. I mean, sometimes I miss Nashville and yeah, I didn't like it when I had to quit piano, but it's not like I can't practice on my own. It's just other stuff."

Jonni caught a fat, soft curl in her hand and wound it around her finger as she studied Tally's face. "Other stuff. Listen, baby, I'm trying to respect the fact that you're growing up, but whatever this is, it's bothering you and I want you to trust me enough to tell me."

Something scared flitted through Tally's eyes.

Jonni bit her tongue. Tally was a good kid, and a smart one. But that didn't negate her fear. If she didn't start talking soon, Jonni was going to have to take desperate measures.

"I will, Mama," Tally said, almost as if she'd read her mother's mind.

They were back, insistent questions and voices pressing at him almost from the time he woke. The voices of the dead chased him, but he'd learned to ignore them.

Gabriel was on vacation – more like a sabbatical really, and there was only so much he was required to do.

Maybe it made him a jerk, but if he didn't take time away, he'd go insane.

So he ignored everything that wasn't absolutely necessary.

Well, very little *was* absolutely necessary – he took care of those things, and some of his email. If he didn't take care of email, certain people would start to call and that would kind of negate the whole point of being on sabbatical.

He hadn't logged in to check his email in nearly a week and the sheer number of flagged messages had him wanting to gouge his eyes out. He grabbed another cup of coffee, tied back his dreads and bent over the laptop. Sunlight shone in through the window, the only light he chose to work in. His dark hands moved over the keyboard and he opened what he figured would be the easiest ones first.

Several from an old contact, Desiree Jones. Beautiful woman, married to a bastard whom Gabriel personally didn't like and it had nothing to do with the fact that Taylor Jones ran the spook squad with the FBI. Gabriel didn't like him on principle, because the man was an asshole. An efficient one, but still an asshole.

Several emails were related to cases connected to said asshole. Yet another reason that Gabriel didn't like him. He'd hoped to sever any and all contact with Jones once he'd left the squad. If he wanted to work with the FBI, he'd still be there, instead of working for a freelance group.

The next batch of emails came from that group. He grimaced and mentally bitched his way through those. His former boss, Elise Oswald, had died recently. While the Oswald Group wasn't going away, it was being restructured.

Gabriel was taking some time to decide if he wanted to be part of it any more.

He was losing interest if he was honest. It wasn't like he could turn off the need he had to work, but did he want to keep chasing the jobs?

He was debating that very question when the subject line from Taige Morgan – the woman who may be his new boss – had him freezing.

Possible newbie near you.

Gabriel's hands hovered over the keyboard, his jaw going tight.

Part of him wanted to delete the email.

If there was somebody out there, it wasn't really his problem. Taige had plenty of people she could send out. Or, hell, Jones could do it, too. Yeah, it was sort of a necessity because some things weren't best left alone – nobody knew that better than him.

That didn't make this *his* responsibility.

Except if he wasn't connected – or meant to be connected – he didn't think Taige would have emailed.

He wasn't one of the altruistic sorts who stayed with the unit out of some innate need to *serve* and *protect*. That, in his mind, was the surest way to drive yourself insane. Half the people he'd tried to protect in his life either hated him or had abandoned him. The rest weren't even aware of the things he'd done to help.

But Gabriel also knew that some things were just connected.

If he was connected to this, then he was connected to it.

"I need this like I need a hole in my head," he muttered as he clicked on the email and started to read.

Within five seconds, he slammed the top of the laptop shut. It only took him another twenty to hit the stairs.

He had to get dressed. Get out of there. Find that girl.

It didn't dawn on him until nearly three hours later that he'd have some trouble finding her, for several reasons. He didn't know her name or where she went to school, and his cemetery might not be the only one she hung out in.

The biggest concerns were the first two. Namely because if she was anything like him, if she'd hit his spot more than once, then she'd developed a liking for it. He knew how that worked. He'd done the same thing. Once a person developed a connection, they just weren't as comfortable elsewhere.

Prowling around Golgotha First Baptist Cemetery, he kept an eye on the front gate as he noticed signs that she'd been spending some time there. It had been a while since he'd had to do any major investigative work – he used a different skill set in his line of work now – but he could see where somebody had been spending time at several different spots. Namely, the family vault where he'd found her last night. And down by the little pond.

The grass was tramped down in both places, and by the pond she'd left a scarf. He picked it up and grimaced as his skin came in contact with it.

Well, if he'd had any question, it was all gone now.

"Hey!"

He turned around and saw the girl coming toward him, a grin on her face. "You found my scarf!"

He looked down at the bright bit of pink in his hand. "This ain't yours."

"It is, too."

"No." He jammed it into the pocket of the hooded sweatshirt he'd pulled on. "It's not. I found it. Makes it mine. You want it, then you have to earn it back."

"That . . ." She crossed her arms over her chest and glared at him. "That's stupid. You want to take a *girl's* scarf?"

"I don't really want it. You can earn it back. Easy."

Something skittered across her face. She backed up, finally showing some of that wisdom he'd wanted to see. Her hand went to her back and although he never saw it, he had a feeling she had pulled out a cell phone. "Fine. You keep it."

He chuckled and turned around, staring out over the water, smooth as a mirror under the sun. "Don't worry, kid. Nothing like what you're thinking. I just want you to answer a few questions."

She was quiet a moment. "What kind of questions?"

"Well, for starters, how about you tell me when you started to see them?"

He looked back at her as he asked and, judging by the way she'd gone ashen, he knew he'd hit the mark. But she played dumb. "See who?"

"Ghosts, kid. How long have you seen them?"

Jonni finished up work and checked the time. She'd made some serious headway on several of her projects. One of them was going to bring in a nice sum of money – nothing to write home about but she could pay off some bills.

Best of all, she'd finished at a decent time.

Decent enough to know it was past five and Tally wasn't home. She'd been home, checked in after school, spent thirty minutes on her homework and then disappeared.

Jonni had asked where she was going and Tally had glibly said, "For a walk."

"A walk my ass."

Tally wasn't spending an hour, an hour and a half outside because she'd developed a fascination with her health. She wasn't out there wandering around and looking for social interaction.

Abruptly, Jonni pulled up Google maps and searched the area around the little house they now called home. She'd lived here for the first eighteen years of her life so she knew the area well, or had.

Where would Tally go for her *quiet* time?

The pond. No.

The old park where Jonni had used to go, even when she'd been too old to play . . . ? Her heart shied away from thinking about that spot for too long because that had been the place where she'd spent a lot of time with one particular person.

But the park was gone.

Out of a need she hadn't been able to define, she'd driven by there a few days ago, and it had been torn down, replaced by a skate park. Tally had once expressed an interest in skating but the board had been sitting around unused for going on two years now.

So that was a no-go.

Her eyes skipped over it twice. But then she found herself staring at it, and her heart wrenched.

She knew. Just like that. She knew where Tally was.

"I don't know what you're talking about."

"Sure you do," Gabriel murmured. He cocked his head, his heart twisting a little at the defiant, frightened look in the girl's eyes. He'd been there. "What's your name, sweetheart?"

She darted a look around. "I . . . I should go home."

"You don't wanna do that, though. You come here because there aren't any of them here. The dead don't haunt a place like this. They're drawn to the living – the places they knew in life. That's why it's quiet here." He watched as her eyes rounded, understanding lighting them. "You wondered, didn't you? Why they don't bother you when you're at a graveyard?"

She licked her lips, moving forward a step. Gabriel doubted she even knew she'd done so. "How . . . how do you *know* that?"

"Because I see them, too." He held out a hand. "Come on, sweetheart. Let me help."

"Why do you think I need help?"

"Because I did, too. I started seeing them when I was a little older than you and I didn't have anybody to help me. For a good long while, I thought I was going crazy." Gabriel continued to stand there and wait, hand outstretched.

Seconds passed and then she moved closer, lifting her own hand. When she put her smaller hand in his, something rushed over him. A wave of recognition that almost over-whelmed him. It didn't make sense.

For now, he couldn't let himself think about it.

All that mattered was helping this girl get a handle on what was happening in her head.

She was a lot younger than he'd been, and chances are, she was every bit as scared. Maybe even more so.

He didn't understand why, but the longer he looked at her, the more intolerable it became for this child to be afraid.

"Now. Let's try this again." He squeezed her hand gently, his big, dark hand all but swallowing hers. "What's your name, kid?"

"It's Tally," she said softly.

"I'm Gabriel." He smiled at her. "Nice to meet you."

"When did it start, Tally?" Gabriel asked. They'd found a bench near the pond, a spot sheltered from the wind by a copse of trees.

"Sometime last year." She scraped her nail over a small brown smudge on her jeans, the notebook she'd carried sitting untouched next to her. "I thought I was just freaking out at first. Mom . . . she, um . . ."

Her voice tripped, faded away. After a moment, she tried again. "She was seeing this guy. We both liked him. Seemed really nice. Then one night, when she was out late cuz of work – she was a reporter for a paper in Nashville – Neil was watching me and he . . ."

She bit her lip and looked away.

Gabriel rose from the bench and moved away. He layered up his shields as he moved. He didn't know just how strong her abilities were, or what she could do other than see the dead. He couldn't take the chance of her picking up on what he felt. "Did he hurt you?"

"No." Her voice was small. "But he scared me. Talked about how pretty I was, how much of a woman I'd be soon. He touched my hair and . . ."

She stopped, and when he looked back at her, she was staring at her hands, knotted in her lap so tightly her knuckles were bloodless. "Mama called. I answered the phone and he tried to stop me. She knew something was wrong because of the way I sounded. Neil tried to make out like I was just in a bad mood, said he'd fussed at me because I had an attitude but she came straight home and I told her. He started yelling. Mom hit him."

"I like your mama already." Gabriel moved back to the bench and knelt in front of Tally.

She gave him a nervous smile. "He acted like he'd hit her back and she said she'd bury him. My mama is scary when she wants to be. Neil believed her. He left. We never saw him again, but I started having nightmares. And . . ."

"That's when you started seeing the ghosts." It made sense. Puberty often brought it on and any kind of trauma could precipitate it, force the ability on sooner.

"I thought I was going crazy. Mama's daddy was sick. She never said how but I know he wasn't right up here." Tally tapped her head. "I thought maybe I was the same way. But then our neighbor died and I started seeing her . . ."

Gabriel reached out and caught her hand.

Her fingers closed over his with startling strength and he squeezed back gently. "I can tell you that you're not crazy." He hesitated and then asked, "Have you told your mother?"

"No!" The word burst out of her, sharp and startled.

"Why?"

Tally shot up and started to pace, her movements erratic and uneven. "Because I . . . I . . ." She bit her lip.

Gabriel could practically see the words trapped inside her and his heart ached for her. "Are you afraid she won't believe you?"

"Not exactly." Tally wrapped her arms around her body, huddling in around herself.

In that moment, she reminded him so much of himself, it was surreal. It was almost like looking through a warped, twisted sort of mirror. The uncertainty, the fear.

"She might believe me," Tally whispered, staring at the ground. "My mom's wonderful. She might believe me. But I don't want her to look at me and know I'm some kind of freak."

"You're not a freak, Tally." He crossed to her, cupped her cheek and made her look up. How many times had he worried that same thing, and wished somebody would give him reassurance?

It hadn't happened. Not for him. But he could maybe offer that reassurance for this child.

"Listen, I think you need to trust your mom," he said, searching for the words to make her understand. Tally needed people around her to support her, to help her. "I think you—"

"Tallant Marie Hart, where are you?"

That voice, clear and steady, rang through the cemetery. Tally's eyes went wide as she jerked away and looked around. Gabriel felt it echo right through him. He felt it echo all the way to his very soul. That voice.

But then the name hit him, and it hit hard. *Tallant* . . .

"Tallant," he murmured. "Sweetheart. What's your mama's name?" She didn't answer, but he didn't need her to. Jonni Hart was behind her.

Time warp. That was all she could think. Time warp, and a dream come true, all at once.

How many times had she wished for just this, to see the two of them side by side like that?

But it wouldn't ever happen, not after he'd disappeared off the face of the planet the summer she was eighteen. She'd gone to his parents, time after time, tried to find out where he was, but the Tallmans hadn't exactly approved of their only son's relationship with her.

If she'd been a little older, a little more confident, she would have pushed harder, fought harder.

But she'd been eighteen, scared and pregnant – a poor girl from the wrong side of the tracks, her father an alcoholic who could barely hold a job. Gabriel Tallman had been the only son of one of the wealthiest families in town.

That wealth hadn't exactly translated to *respectable*. They lived in Golgotha, Mississippi, a backwoods Southern town. And the Tallmans might have money, but more than a few people in that neck of the woods were still trapped in an era where the white folk and the black weren't supposed to *mingle*.

I have a better future in mind for my son than seeing him with some white trash child like you, Rochelle Tallman had snapped. Her husband had intervened then, his words kinder, his eyes kinder. But the message was the same. They wanted different things for their son, and no, they wouldn't help her get a message to him.

Jonni's father hadn't kept his disapproval to words.

Rochelle Tallman had called her father, and when Jonni got home, Clyde Hart had unloaded his fury, and his fists, on her. That was the day Royce almost killed him.

That was also the day she'd left, promising herself she'd never come back. She never would have, except her daughter mattered more than a promise.

Now . . .

Her mouth went dry as she stared at the man who still haunted her dreams, and the child he'd never known they had.

"Gabriel."

Fury flashed in his eyes as he stared at her, but when he looked down at Tally, he just smiled. "Well, sweetheart. It's a small world."

He looked back at Jonni, and the warmth was gone from his voice as he said, "We need to talk."

Gabriel's head spun with so many thoughts, he almost couldn't handle it. So instead of letting his mind wander down any of the twisted avenues open to him, he focused on the girl.

She walked along between him and Jonni and he could already see the easy love between them. That, and that alone, kept him from losing the slippery grip he had on his temper.

He had a daughter.

Tallant. Jonni had given her his name.

But not *his* name – she had her mama's last name and he had a feeling she didn't know a damn thing about him, either.

Now that he was looking, he could see it, too. She was going to be tall, like him. Jonni was five foot five and Tally was easily that already. He did the mental math, tried to figure out how far along she'd been, but those last few months . . .

He shoved it back.

Those last few months were a blur to him. He'd barely been able to distinguish the line between reality and nightmare at that point. Ghosts, too many thoughts and the pain of it all had threatened to crush him. All the things he'd hidden from Jonni hadn't helped.

She'd been pregnant. When he'd finally gotten himself back together, when he'd come back to find her, she had gone. Questions boiled in the back of his mind, but now wasn't the time.

As they left the graveyard behind, Tally paused to look at him. He could see he wasn't the only one with questions – hers burned in her eyes, but for now, he ignored them. His had to be answered first, and he had to know how Jonni would react. If she wasn't going to be able to handle what Tally was going through, then he'd take the decision out of her hands.

His daughter wouldn't suffer the way he had.

"Where are you staying?" he asked flatly. There was no way in hell she was getting out of answering his questions.

She dampened her lips, a nervous look on her face. Her eyes slid away.

He prepared himself for whatever excuses she had, and how he'd deal with them, because this was going to happen. Whether she liked it or not . . .

"I'm in my old house," she said, surprising him.

He shot a look back at her. Despite the fury that still choked him, sympathy bloomed inside. Both of them had been all but desperate to escape Golgotha and the chains that bound them. And her chains cut deeper. The ghosts, even if she couldn't see them, clung to her even harder.

But he kept that to himself. "We are talking."

Her nod was shaky. "You can just follow me over."

The drive lasted minutes. As the crow flies, less than a mile separated Jonni's place from the graveyard. More than once, he'd been out here, thinking about her. Thinking. Wondering.

All this time, they'd had a child together.

One he hadn't known anything about. That sent a spike of fury pulsing through him.

He was going to lose it. At some point during the night, he was going to lose it. He knew it. How he could have had a daughter . . .

Unwittingly, his gaze slid to Tally and his heart did a crazy little flip as the two of them stepped out of the car onto the busted-up sidewalk.

They looked so much alike. Now that he was standing side by side with her, he wondered how he'd missed it.

The woman he'd loved— No. He didn't know the *woman* in front of him. She'd been a girl then. The similarity to the girl he'd loved was so clearly echoed in Tally, so clear that he had to wonder how he'd missed it.

Any softness he might have felt died when he remembered that Jonni had kept her hidden.

"You want to come inside?" Her chin angled up ever so slightly. Almost in challenge.

Lifting a brow, he said coolly, "Yes."

This sure as hell wasn't a conversation he was going to have out here on the sidewalk.

She nodded and then looked over at Tally. "Uncle Royce had plans to pick you up for dinner. That's still happening."

Gabriel narrowed his eyes. Oh, he didn't think so.

"But—"

"No buts." Jonni shot him a look, too. "Gabriel and I both need to talk and it's not a talk that will happen with you here. We . . . ah, we've known each other a long time and there are things we need to talk about. Royce is just going to take you to McDonald's. You'll be back soon."

Gabriel didn't care if she was going for a walk around the block. He'd just discovered what was going on and he didn't want to let her out of his sight for even a minute.

But Jonni was right. He barely had his fury under control. This wasn't a talk he could have with the kid here.

"But . . ." Tally looked from him to Jonni.

"I'm not going anywhere," he said, pitching his voice low.

She looked at him, her eyes darkening to jade. "You won't?"

"No."

"You made fast friends with her." Jonni watched as Royce disappeared down the street, Tally in the passenger seat of his squad car.

"I wouldn't call it fast friends," Gabriel said. "I'd call it . . . kindred souls. The two of us met at the cemetery and we just felt a connection."

"A connection." Jonni slid her hands into the back pockets of her pants, her voice slow and lazy. She'd always had a voice that did the worst things to him but it was worse now; it was like honey and whiskey and velvet, stroking over him like an audible caress.

Despite himself, his skin went tight. He wondered what she'd do, how she'd react if he moved to her, tangled his hands in the shortened strands of her honey-blonde hair and tasted her again. She'd always tasted sweet, far sweeter than she should.

"Just what kind of connection could a grown man feel to a kid her age?" Jonni asked.

"Considering the fact that she's my daughter, I'd imagine a man could feel a pretty strong connection." Closing the distance between them, he leaned in until he could smell the teasing scent of whatever soap she'd used. Subtle, soft, erotic. It clung to her skin. He wanted to have it clinging to his own as well.

Stop. Don't go there. He pushed the thought away as he pressed his lips to her ear. "You might want to think about asking me in now. You don't have a lot of neighbors, but as mad as I am, if I start yelling, I'm going to attract a lot of attention, baby. You really want that?"

She flinched at his words, but when she pulled back, her eyes were level, her face unconcerned. "You think this will be the first time I've ever had somebody yell at me? Yell at me *here*? Wow. You went and forgot a lot, Gabriel."

She turned on her heels and made her way up the sidewalk.

The impact of her words didn't hit until a minute later. He'd been too focused on the nearness of her, the scent. Then her words sunk in and he wanted to punch himself in the head.

As she mounted the steps, he looked around, searching for signs of the ghosts she'd fled from. Of course, Jonni wasn't running from literal ghosts, but memories could be just as devastating.

It didn't take a heartbeat for him to realize that whether she saw them or not, Jonni had some very, very real ghosts. Pale, ephemeral forms drifted all over.

It was little wonder that the girl wanted to escape the place as often as she did. The place was lousy with the restless energy of the dead.

Sucking in a breath, he braced himself and started to follow. Because it was a much more pleasant thing to focus on, he locked his eyes on the plump curve of Jonni's butt and just how good it looked in those blue jeans. She'd been pretty as a teenager. Now, she just about stole the air from him.

Jonni studied the small living room. She'd done this before, back when she'd first brought Gabriel Tallman into her life. His father was one of the family doctors in town, his mother a popular author of Southern fiction. They were one of the wealthiest families in the area, while the Hart kids barely managed to keep clothes on their backs.

Gabriel had never made her feel anything less for being Clyde Hart's daughter, never made her feel anything less because she didn't get to dress in nicer clothes, or even *new* ones. He hadn't cared about the fact that her father drank away the money. Hadn't cared about much of anything – except her.

The house looked better than it used to, but she didn't know if anything could erase the stain of memories. She didn't see what *was*. She saw what had been. She probably always would.

"Did you ever see him after you left?" Gabriel asked, his voice soft.

She didn't have to ask who. There was only one person he could be talking about. Chilled, Jonni wrapped her arms around her mid-section. "No. I didn't want to."

Her father died alone.

He'd never sobered up, had never attempted to mend fences with his kids, although every now and then, Royce had reached out to him.

"I didn't want to." Jonni shook her head. "I can't even be sorry about it."

"You have no reason to be sorry. I . . ." His words trailed off. From the corner of her eye, she saw him shrug. "I don't know what happened between you two at the end, but he never had any kindness in him. Why should you regret not giving him any more tears?"

A nice way to put it.

She eased a little farther into the house, swallowing the knot in her throat. Turning, she faced him. She had given *this* man tears, a lot of them over the years. Especially that summer. But she'd never let him know.

"How long have you been back in Golgotha?" she asked.

Gabriel shrugged. "A couple of weeks. On a work hiatus. I don't leave the house much. I've got a woman who comes in and cleans, does my shopping for me."

She slid him a look, then jerked her eyes away. Licking her lips, she tried to mentally brace herself, mentally steel herself. It wasn't happening, but if she had a few more minutes, she could figure out how to tell him. She'd had reasons. Rationales. Explanations . . .

"Why didn't you tell me?"

Gabriel wasn't going to give her that time. Of course.

"Why . . ." The question fell from her lips as she raised her face to the ceiling, staring up. The answer was easy. So easy. But was he ready to hear it?

She moved farther into the room and stood in front of the window, as memory streamed through her mind, an endless reel that alternately taunted and infuriated her.

"Well?" he demanded, his voice edged, angry.

"How old do you think she is?" Jonni asked, her voice thoughtful.

When he didn't answer right away, she turned and leaned her hips against the windowsill. Arching an eyebrow, she asked softly, "Well?"

"Seeing as how I don't remember seeing you pregnant the last few times I saw you, I'd have to assume it happened one of the last times we were together, baby." His eyes glinted, hard and sharp, like broken glass glittering in the harsh summer sun. "That puts her at about twelve."

Shoving her hands into the pockets of her jeans, she

balled them into fists. "The last time we had sex was after the Valentine formal, Gabe. The condom tore. Remember?"

His lids drooped over his eyes, a slow, lazy blink. Then he shook his head. "No. That's not right."

"What the hell ever." She laughed bitterly and turned back to stare out the window. "I remember it pretty clearly. You . . ."

Her heart turned to ashes as she remembered that night. They'd only slept together a few times and up until that night, it had been only remotely pleasant for her. She *enjoyed* it, but it wasn't the act itself that she enjoyed. It was being with him. Knowing he loved her. Needed her. Wanted her. Having him hold her when it was over. But that night . . . something had been different. Heat had bloomed where before there had only been a slow warmth. Then, after the condom had torn, they'd been starting to dress in the awkward silence. She'd looked at him, her gaze lingering on him, muscles gliding under dark, smooth skin, and her mouth had gone dry.

Seconds later, his hands had been on her and she'd been pressed between him and the wall. That was the first time he'd brought her to orgasm and she'd come screaming against his mouth while he drove into her.

Then, the next day, he'd started to pull away.

"I what?" His cold voice brought her back into the present.

Swinging her head around, she met his eyes. They were icy, hard. Maybe it was the memory of the way he'd looked at her that night, with need and love and desperation, that made it so much more painful now. That anger was like a lash across her heart.

It hurt.

It hurt and it tore open the wounds that had never fully healed. With nothing else to fall back on, she reached for the pride that had gotten her through everything else in the past twelve years.

"You were there," she said with a lazy roll of her shoulders. "Don't you remember?"

★

Her eyes had gone from that surreal blue-green, warm as a tropical sea, to ice. She stared at him and lifted her shoulders, shrugging as though whatever had hurt her hadn't really mattered at all.

But he *felt* it.

Despite the fact that he had his shields up, layered and solid against the ghosts that swarmed in the air, he could *feel* that pain.

You were there . . .

Except he hadn't been.

Not entirely.

Bits of pieces of him had blinked in and out of existence as he struggled to cope with everything rushing through him. Sometimes he'd existed – usually when he was with her, and only her. Other times, he'd shut himself away until he was only a shell, the *real* him locked in the depths of his mind.

"Why don't you explain it to me?" he said, keeping his voice flat, even as a hollow ache spread through him. Was this . . . he shoved the thought away before it could form. "I'd like to see your side of things."

From the corner of his eye, something white glided over, settling near Jonni as she started to speak. He focused on her words even as his concentration split.

Son of a bitch.

It was her father. Her father's ghost clung to this place.

Little whore. Clyde Hart sneered at her. *You think I'm going to take care of you and that brat? You went and spread your legs like a whore. You can fix the problem on your own . . .*

The words faded and Clyde drifted out of existence.

Caught, Gabe realized. Clyde wasn't exactly here. He was one of the remnants, caught in a loop.

Shaken, he forced himself to listen, to concentrate on Jonni. She had words to say that mattered.

". . . old history and all. I don't see what it matters if I go through it again."

She had an odd look in her eyes and he turned away, walking aimlessly around the room. It had a naked, empty look, unfinished somehow. Stopping by the couch, he stared at it, hands hanging loose at his sides, feeling useless and impotent.

"It matters because I need to understand." That was all he could say, for now.

"Look, this is done and we both lived through it, so I don't see why I need to relive it just for your amusement—"

"Tell me!" he snarled, spinning around as the threads of his control snapped and splintered.

Jonni snapped her jaw shut, her eyes glittering in the pale circle of her face. Slowly, her chin angled up. "I didn't know you any more," she said starkly, coldly. Ice all but dripped from her words. "I don't think half your friends did, either. You'd been getting moodier all the time, but after that night, it was worse. There were rumors that you were doing drugs – if you were, fine. But if you are *now* then don't expect to spend any time around Tally. She doesn't need that in her life and don't think for one *minute* that your family and your money will change a damn thing. Not this time."

Those words tugged at something, made a warning start to murmur in his mind. He couldn't follow that whisper because she was already talking again.

"I didn't know how to handle it – you'd been my world for the past five years. Then you just cut me out. I got depressed and wouldn't talk to anybody at school. Then there were days when you'd show up and act . . . fine." Her gaze fell away and she sank listlessly into a nearby chair. Hands clasped together, she sat there with her shoulders slumped, her eyes empty. "You'd come here, talk to me, or just sit on the swing and hold me. I'd think everything was okay. Then the next day at school would roll around and it started all over again."

Unable to look at her confused, drawn features, he strode to the far end of the small living room and just stood there. When she started to speak again, he closed his eyes tightly, as though that would shut out the sound of her voice, the memory of the misery on her face. "It kept up for more than two months – I lost weight, figured it was because I was so miserable, didn't think about it when I never wanted to eat. Then in April, I was at my locker, grabbing some books and Matt Cole came up, asked me if maybe I'd go to the prom with him. You . . ." Her breath shuddered out of her.

Dread grabbed him by the throat.

Matt.

The guy had been one of his better friends. He'd tried to talk to him when he'd come back to town a couple of years ago, but the man had taken one look at him and then turned and walked the other way. Gabriel didn't even know why.

Just how much had Gabriel forgotten from that time?

How much had he been *made* to forget?

"You were at your locker a few feet away. I heard you say Matt's name, then you two were on the floor."

What . . .

He turned and stared at her.

Her eyes burned into his. "Why do you look like you don't remember any of this?"

"Because I don't," he rasped.

Jonni scowled, a thousand comments trembling on the tip of her tongue. How could he forget that? "You don't remember."

"No." He looked around, his gaze lost, distracted. He leaned against the wall and slid down, knees drawn up. The thick, dense dreads shielded his face as he stared down. "I don't remember. There are flashes of you. Me, being here. Touching you."

"You came here. You kissed me a few times. But you didn't really touch me, not once, after Valentine's Day," she said woodenly.

"That's . . ." He shook his head, swallowed, a queer look in his eyes. "That can't be true. I *remember*—"

"It is true," she snapped, cutting him off. "You beat the shit out of one of your best friends. It took four teachers to pull you off him and when I tried to see if he was okay, you went half crazy, but you don't remember that. You never came back to school after that. Hell, Gabe, *were* you on drugs?"

He started to laugh. It was bitter and ragged, echoing on and on, until she wanted to cover her ears just to block it out.

"No." The word came out in between jagged peals of laughter. "No, but it would have been better, easier, if that was the reason."

Abruptly, he was on his feet, striding toward her.

"I got better. I came back, almost a year later. I got better, and I came back. For you. Where *were* you?" His hands closed over her arms.

There was no cruelty to his grip, but she couldn't escape him either. As he hauled her to her feet, her heart jumped up into her throat. Outside, there was a clash of thunder and it made her breath hitch, then catch in her throat.

"Where *were* you?" he demanded again.

"I left," she said simply. "I was five months pregnant. You'd been gone since April. By May, I'd figured out I wasn't just depressed. I knew I was pregnant, and part of me kept hoping you'd be back, but you weren't. I went to your house, time and time again, hoping to find you, but the servants would either refuse to open the door or they'd refuse to tell me anything. The last time I went, they actually let me in and I thought, maybe, just maybe, they'd tell me something. But it was your mother – she was in her office and when she saw me, she took one look and she knew. She offered me money – I could either get an abortion or she would find somebody to adopt the baby. Either way, she'd give me five thousand dollars as long as I never tried to speak to you again."

He let go of her so abruptly that she nearly fell. Catching her balance, she watched as he spun around and roared, the sound of his rage flooding the small house.

The muscles bunched in his shoulders, his arms. His hands clenched into tight fists and she could hear his breath coming in ragged pants.

"No," he rasped, shaking his head. "No."

There was no point in responding.

Rochelle Tallman was all about protecting the family. Jonni was a threat to the family, in her eyes, a threat, a distraction. Gabriel was smart, belonged in college, had a chance at one hell of a life.

While Jonni was . . . nothing.

Rochelle had been more than happy to point that out. A child would only make matters worse.

"I left. I didn't want her money. I didn't want to see her or speak to her." Jonni stared out the window.

The heat of his rage flooded the room. She shivered, painfully aware that he'd turned back to look at her. "I was afraid. She could make things rough and I knew it, so I left. She called my dad. When I got home, he was throwing my stuff out on the porch and he . . ."

Gabriel tensed as the white form solidified, once more coming into view near Jonni. *Little whore . . . You think I'm going to take care of you and that brat?*

"Shut up," Gabriel said, unconsciously dropping his shields and flooding the words with the ability that connected him to the dead.

The shade flinched, his form blinking in and out as the words connected.

But Jonni heard him, too.

She jerked around, her mouth falling open as she stared at him.

He wasn't looking at her, eyes focused on her father's wavering form. *You don't belong here any more*, he thought. It wasn't enough to do it, enough to snap Clyde's connection to this place, but the man's time here was at an end. He'd see to it, and soon.

Tearing his eyes away, he severed his connection to the dead and blanketed himself so thick with shields, he wouldn't see or hear them. "Sorry," he bit off, shaking his head. "That wasn't . . ."

"Shove it. I'm not going to listen to this bullshit from you again."

She went to push past him and he caught her arm, whirling her around when she would have tried to keep walking.

She crashed into him. The feel of her, after so many years of *not* having her close, threatened to erase whatever control he had left. Gabriel savored every second, even as he fumbled for some way to explain.

But there was only one.

There was only ever one.

"I see your father," he said softly.

Jonni stared at him, uncomprehending.

"He's stuck here. Or part of him is."

Blood drained out of her face, her eyes glowing, dark and stark against the pallor. "What are you . . ."

"You know what I'm talking about," he said gently. "I started seeing ghosts in the fall, that last year. It wasn't often, not at first. But it got worse, and fast. Then it wasn't just ghosts. I was picking up on . . . more."

Physical contact always made it easier and an intimate connection doubled it. So it was little wonder he caught that one, clear thought as it cut through her mind.

Oh, man. I really hope he is *on drugs.*

"I'm not on drugs," Gabriel said. "I'm not crazy."

She jerked away with a strength that would have surprised him, if he hadn't already been prepared for it. Catching her against him, he spun her around and locked her arms against her body in a bear hug.

"Calm down," he whispered against her ear even as she started to cuss and swear. "Calm down, Jonni. I'm not going to hurt you. I'd never do that."

Minutes passed before the words sank in. Or maybe she realized the futility of it.

"Let me go," she said, her voice trembling slightly, but otherwise calm.

"No." Turning his face into her hair, he breathed in the intoxicating sense of her. Honeysuckle and rain and lazy summer nights. He'd missed it, more than he'd realized. Her being gone had been an ache he'd never let himself feel. "I can't."

"Why not?" she demanded. "You did it before easily enough."

"I didn't *let* you go." He nuzzled the soft skin below her ear. "Do you know where I was those months? Why I wasn't there?"

The tension remained, but she no longer fought him.

He rubbed his cheek against hers and felt her shiver. Awareness sparked between them. It was still there, he realized. That need. Was it too little, though? Too many years of silence, too many years of hurt on both sides? Too many secrets?

"My parents thought the same thing everybody else did. I was on drugs. I was going crazy. But they had even more reason to think it, because I tried to tell them. About the ghosts. About how when I touched somebody, I could hear what they thought."

He slid one arm around Jonni's waist, braced her against him as he slid his free hand up her arm. She was tensed, ready to bolt. He lowered his shields, focused on her and just her. "Right now, you think I *am* crazy, but that's pretty obvious. You also think you're crazy, too. Because you still feel it. Feel the want, the need. You're standing there, trying not to move because when you do, it makes it worse."

He slid his lips up her cheekbone to catch her ear lobe. Nipping her, he felt a shudder rock her body. "Baby, it doesn't matter if you move. I'm already dying of want."

A weak moan escaped her. It took everything he had not to turn her around, make her face him so he could kiss her. But if he did, he wouldn't stop there. "You can see the clock. You're counting the minutes until Royce gets here. He's never late and you think you'll be safer, able to think more clearly with him here. Do you believe me yet?"

Her breath hissed in as he slid his hand under her shirt. Her words were shaky as she said, "None of this tells me where you were that summer. I *needed* you."

The words broke his heart and he bowed his head, pressed it to her shoulder. "I'm sorry."

Those words weren't enough. He knew they'd never be enough.

Because he needed to look into her eyes, he let her go, prepared for her to bolt, but she didn't. She just stood there and when he turned her, she moved, docile and unresisting. That alone was enough to tear at him. "I'm sorry," he said again, but he didn't know entirely what he was sorry for.

"Where were you?" she rasped.

Closing his eyes, he lowered his head. Shame, frustration and rage pulsed inside him. He'd thought he had put all of that behind him. All it took to bring it all to the fore was this woman. And the child who looked so much like both of them.

He lifted his head and the look in his eyes had her trembling.

Unaware she'd done so, she lifted her hands, curled them in the nubby weave of his shirt. The heat of him reached out to taunt her, to warm her.

He lifted a hand and when he cupped her cheek, she turned her face into it without thinking. Eyes closed, she let herself take comfort in him, even if it was just for a second.

"My mother and father had me committed to a mental health facility," he said softly.

She jerked back, so hard and fast, she practically fell over her own feet. "*What?*"

He studied her with calm eyes, as though he'd just told her what the temperature was. Lifting one straight, black brow, he said it again.

The words didn't change.

Jonni tried to wrap her mind around what he'd said. Tried. Failed. "*Why?*"

"Because they feel like you do. That I'm crazy. That I don't see the things I do, hear the things I do. They think I'm crazy."

She flinched in shame and wrapped her arms around herself. Twelve years ago, he'd frightened her. Badly. He'd be like an automaton in the day, then almost normal when he'd seek her out. It wasn't often, maybe once every week or two. On those evenings, he'd be like he used to be.

Then when she looked at him the next time they saw each other, she was looking at a stranger once more.

Something had been wrong. She'd known then, but she just hadn't understood what.

"What happened when they . . ."

She couldn't finish. But he didn't seem to need her to. "You mean once I wasn't having drugs pumped me into me night and day to control the *psychosis*? I learned how to control it, somewhat. The quiet. Being away from others. I spent most of my time locked away in my room because I got violent around others and they would have to sedate me. Once they learned that I was better when I was on my own, they just left me alone. Eventually they lowered the doses of the drugs and I could think. But I didn't really learn to control it until . . ." His voice trailed off.

"Until what?"

"You'll think I'm even crazier," he said softly.

"You might as well finish."

"Ever heard the name Taige Morgan?"

"Ah, I'm a journalist. So that pretty much means yes." The woman was something of a legend – or a con artist. She saved countless children and was reputed to be . . . "Shit," Jonni whispered. "Oh, shit."

He inclined his head. "She was there to talk to one of the patients. She felt me. More or less."

"You know her."

"Yes."

Feeling sick, Jonni stumbled over to the couch and sank down on it. Now, she had to decide. Yeah, she'd heard of Taige Morgan, the psychic of the South. That was what she was being called these days. Some thought she was the real thing. Others assumed she was a con artist or just really, really clever.

Jonni had followed some of the cases the woman had taken on, oddly fascinated.

"She found you. Because you . . ." She swallowed. "You're like her."

"Not exactly. She connects with children. I see the dead. I hear thoughts – usually only those connected to strong emotion, which was why school had gotten so hard. Nobody has more strong emotion than teenagers." He shrugged and looked away, his jaw set in a hard line. "Now you get to go back to telling me I'm crazy. Don't worry. I'm used to it."

"I don't think I can." The words escaped her in a hush.

Gabriel looked back at her, head cocked to the side, his hard, dark face set in unreadable lines. "Why is that?"

Before she could answer, the door opened and Tally came in, Royce at her back. Her brother had his hand on the kid's shoulder and he looked between Gabriel and Jonni, eyes narrowed slightly.

Tally bit her lip, but she wasn't looking at Jonni. Her eyes were all on Gabriel.

"Did you tell her?" she whispered.

Gabriel could have turned the air blue. Tally's question, innocent and unsure, couldn't have come at a worse time.

Jonni frowned, confused. "Tell me what?"

Tally eased farther into the room, or tried to. Royce kept a hand on her shoulder. The look in the other man's eyes had Gabriel studying him closer.

Abruptly, he realized, Royce *knew*. Somehow – no, not somehow. The son of a bitch was a cop. He could have easily checked into Gabriel's background. There wasn't much publicized, but the man was smart. He could connect two plus two, especially since more than once Gabriel had worked with Taige.

Royce knew.

Now, with a thoughtful look, the man studied him, before shifting his gaze to his niece. His features tightened and then he looked at his sister.

"What's going on?" Jonni rose from her chair.

"Tally-girl, I think we should go outside," Royce said.

"No." She pulled away. "I should have already done this. I have to do this. I'm tired of hiding it."

Tally stared at Gabriel for a long moment before she turned and looked at her mother. "Mama, I have to tell you something."

The dark, strained look in Tally's eyes made Jonni's knees buckle.

"Tally, sweetheart," Gabriel said, his voice gentle. "Wait. Just—"

"No!" Tally took another step toward her mother. "Mama, I don't know how to say this, but I . . . um . . ."

"Tally. Wait." Gabriel's voice was sharp, slapping at the air so hard both Jonni and Tally flinched.

It didn't silence Tally, though. "I can see ghosts. Like really."

Jonni closed her eyes.

"They kinda scare me. I . . . I go to the cemetery cuz I can't see them there. It's like the dead don't like it much."

"Tally. Please." Jonni pressed the tips of her fingers against her temples. "Just stop for a minute. Give me a minute, okay?"

But the words continued to pour out of the girl like they'd been trapped behind a floodgate and now nothing could hold them back. Spinning around, Jonni wrapped her arms around her mid-section, desperate to keep herself from falling apart.

Bits and pieces fell into place. The look on Tally's face over the past months as she withdrew farther and farther inside herself. The calls, the notes from her teachers – *withdrawn, almost like a different child . . . concerned . . .*

Withdrawn – a different child.

"Tally, give her a minute." Gabriel's voice was like a punch to her stomach.

Jonni remembered how he'd been that last year. Withdrawn. Like a different person.

No wonder he'd felt such a connection to Tally. It wasn't just that he'd felt drawn to the daughter he didn't know he had. This went deeper; it was something Jonni couldn't even fathom.

"Mama. What . . ." Her daughter's voice broke.

Jonni turned to look at her. Tears glittered in the child's eyes and Jonni felt her own start to burn.

"Sweetheart."

"You don't believe me. I can tell." She shot Gabriel a wide, hurt look. "She doesn't believe me."

"Yes, I do." Jonni took a step forward, but Tally flinched and backed away. Her gaze bounced around the room. "I can't . . . I can't . . . I *hate* this place and you won't ever understand because you don't believe me."

Abruptly, she turned and bolted. Royce caught her.

Tally started to scream, peals of terror clogging in her throat and choking her.

"Let her go."

Gabriel couldn't believe how completely *wrong* this had

gone. Straight to hell in a handbasket. Royce still gripped Tally by the forearms, his intentions nothing but good.

That was all it took to push the girl into overload.

Gabriel caught her in a bear hug, his gaze skewering the other man. "Let her go. You can't help her."

Royce's eyes bore into his as he slowly let go. "After twelve years, you think you can come back in and make everything better. Just like that."

"No. Not just like that. But you don't understand this. I do."

After all, he was the son of a bitch who'd passed this on to her.

Cut off from whatever she'd been picking up from her uncle, Tally went limp in Gabriel's arms. Carefully, he scooped her up and took her to the couch.

"Listen, Tally," he murmured, his voice low and soothing. "You need to listen and you have to calm down. I know that's not fair. You just want to retreat, but if you go too far away, you won't come back. Trust me, baby. I know."

My fault. The words were a refrain inside his head. He stared down at his daughter. *This is my fault.* He'd been so caught up in his own pride, his own hurt when he'd come back and realized Jonni was gone.

He hadn't let himself reach out, hadn't let himself look for her.

The table shifted, wood creaking in front of him. He looked up, even as he continued to murmur to Tally. Jonni sat on the coffee table, her eyes haunted. "What's going on?"

"Overload." He looked back at Tally, his dreads falling over his shoulder. Impatient, he shoved them back, focused on the child's face. Her face was still ashen, her mouth drawn tight in pain, muscles rigid in fear.

But when he said her name again, she turned her head, almost as if she heard.

From the corner of his eye, he saw the white forms gathering closer and closer. If he could have sent every last one of them from this world, he would have.

Instead, he cracked open his shields, well aware that their

cold touch would snake through. Tally already felt it, shivering in his arms like nothing would warm her.

She couldn't form her own shields yet, so he'd just take her inside his.

Bit by bit, he lowered them. As the chill of the dead settled inside his bones, he took the frail, faltering essence that was his daughter inside his own shields. She gasped, her eyes flaring wide, locked on nothing. "It's okay, sweetheart. I got you. I got you."

Bit by bit, he started to rebuild.

"You knew about him." She stared at her brother, trying to decide if she was furious or just too tired to feel anything.

Almost two hours had passed since Gabriel had settled on the couch, cradling their daughter in his arms, his gaze locked on hers. Nothing and nobody else existed.

Royce didn't say anything, just stared into his coffee. But he didn't deny it. That was answer enough.

She turned her head and stared out the window into the dark of the night. "How long?"

"Well . . ." He drew the word out as though he was unfamiliar with it. Then he took his time before he said another damn thing. "I suppose it's been about six or seven years."

"Six or seven years." A hollow ache settled in her chest. She shoved away from the counter, crossing the bright, cheery blue tile he'd put down in the kitchen. "You've known about him for six or seven years and never bothered to tell me."

"You never asked," Royce pointed out.

Swearing, she shoved her hands through her hair and spun away, all sorts of nastiness building up inside. But even as she thought about letting it spill out, she caught sight of the man in the doorway.

Gabriel stood there, hands hanging loose at his sides. He stared hard at Royce before slowly shifting his gaze to her. "She's sleeping. She'll be okay in the morning."

"Sleeping." She sagged, all but collapsing against the small dinette as the strength drained out of her. "What in the hell *happened*? What happened to our daughter?"

The word slipped out and she realized what she'd said about the same time he did. Jerking her head up, she met his eyes. A heavy moment passed.

"I assume Tally will be okay." Royce's voice came from behind.

Gabriel flicked him another flat look. "She needs to learn how to control what she has, how to protect herself. But she'll be fine. I'll make sure of it."

The protectiveness, the possessiveness in his voice might have bothered some. But Jonni was a woman who'd grown up without knowing the love of even *one* parent. That her daughter might have two parents who'd go to the wall for her made her heart clench. Even if there was so much left unresolved between her and Gabriel.

"I'm going to go then." Royce paused beside her.

She looked up at him, the frustration still tearing at her. But she leaned into him, hugged him. For the longest time, they'd only had each other. "I'm not done being mad."

"Never expected otherwise, sis." He dropped a kiss on her cheek and left.

Alone with Gabriel, she looked up and found herself lost in the dark brown of his eyes. Her heart slammed hard against her ribs. Shaken, she turned away. "This is only going to get harder for her, isn't it?"

"For a while."

She jumped at the nearness of his voice, then shivered when he stroked a hand down her spine. "I'm sorry," he whispered, his mouth so close to her ear she felt his lips brush against her skin.

"For what?"

"I should have been here. I should have . . ." His head fell onto her shoulder. To her complete shock, she felt a ragged breath shudder through him.

Turning, she smoothed her hands up his chest until she could cup his face. "Gabe." She urged him to look at her, felt his stubble rasp against her palms. Just that light sensation sent a jolt of need racing through her. She had to lock her knees because her thighs started to melt. *Focus. Have to focus* . . . "What are you sorry for? Look, we both screwed up. If I'd known what your parents were up to, I would have done something."

"Like what? Nobody faces the Dragon." He caught her hand in his, pressed a kiss to her palm as he tossed out the word they used to describe his mother.

"I would have. If I'd known."

His eyes came to hers. The air inside her lungs evaporated, singed right out of her as need slammed into her. His pupils flared and she braced herself.

Yet Gabriel only stood there. Softly, he said, "I should have tried to find you. I came back here. I faced them. I was ready to find you, ready to tell you everything. But you were gone. I was too stupid, too arrogant. Too hurt and proud. I missed all this time with her."

With her. Pain dug hooked claws into her heart and she swallowed, forced herself not to let anything she felt show. She was good at that, if nothing else. With a fake smile in place, she nodded. "No reason you can't make up for it. She'll need you."

She went to pull back. He crowded in, his arms coming down to cage her between his long, lean body and the table. "She'll need me, yeah." He dipped his head, pressed a kiss to her neck.

Jonni gasped in shock, her hands clutching at his shirt.

"What about you, Jonni?" Gabriel's lips moved along her neck, upward. "Do you need me, too? Because I sure as hell need you. I always have. That's becoming pretty damn clear."

He pulled back to stare down into her eyes.

Sucking in a breath, she struggled to find the words.

There were none.

She couldn't articulate the years of hurt, of loneliness or the hope that suddenly burned inside her.

So she didn't try. She reached up and fisted her hands into the long, dense locks of his hair and pulled him to her. He met her halfway and heat slammed through them both as their mouths connected.

Yes. She needed him.

That had never, ever stopped.

★

Dawn came.

She went to slide from the bed, trying not to wake him, but his hand closed around her wrist, his thumb stroking against the sensitive skin. "Where you goin'?" Gabriel asked, his voice a low, sleepy drawl.

"I need to check on Tally. I don't want her waking up to find us like this. We should talk to her first."

He cracked one eye open. "She won't wake up without me knowing. Not right now."

She frowned.

Gabriel rolled onto his back, a sigh spilling out of him. It distracted her for a moment, the way his skin played over the muscles in his chest. He'd been built, seriously, in high school, but now . . .

Mouth dry, she tore her gaze away. He watched her, a faint smile curving his lips. That mouth. It was made for sex and sin and soulful kisses.

"She's in my shields right now." Gabriel sat up, the sheets pooling around a waist ridged with muscle.

"'In your shields'?"

"That's how people like us survive, baby. Shields. It's like . . ." He paused. "There are different kinds of psychics. Some are precogs – they pick up on future events, although those are fluid and can change. Others, like Taige Morgan, pick up on events connected to children. Some are telepathic and sense thoughts. Then there are people like me and Tally who see the dead, feel them. Now picture those things that we pick up as an element, like rain, but not regular rain. More like acid rain, because it can be dangerous, especially until we learn to protect ourselves. We use our shields as an umbrella, in a way. Or a full body slicker – because they come at us from everywhere, all the time. Tally has no shields. So until I can teach her, I took her inside mine."

Jonni blew out a ragged breath. "This is so crazy. I can't handle this. I don't know if I can handle any of this."

"You can." He leaned in and pressed his lips to her shoulder. "We're going to handle it together."

Turning her face to his, she kissed him. "Together."

It was, after all, all she'd ever wanted.

An hour later, Tally started to stir.

Mixing up the hot chocolate her daughter loved, she looked at Gabriel, the man she'd never expected to have back in her life.

"Are you ready?" he asked softly.

"Yeah. Come on, there's a lot we need to tell her."

Side by side, they went to join their daughter. There was so much they needed to talk about.

THE DEVIL WENT DOWN

Sonya Bateman

Chapter 1

By the time Julie Walker drove the ten miles from the Greens' place to the DA's office, her thighs were sticking to the seat of her car. Normally, she wore pants while she worked, but it'd been ninety degrees already at the crack of dawn this morning, and shorts just seemed like a better idea. Until she remembered her car's A/C was dead.

Of course, it had to conk out on her just before the peak of the Georgia summer. She couldn't afford to get it recharged unless she got an actual client real soon, or at least a bigger assignment from Coop than these damned process server gigs.

She parked at the curb in front of the county building, climbed out and gave her shorts a couple of quick tugs to unstick them. She wasn't really looking forward to this. Serving yet another summons to Bobby Green and his best friend, Mr "Get Offa My Property" Winchester, hadn't been her idea of a fun morning. And unless Coop had something else for her, the afternoon wouldn't be much better.

Climbing the polished stone steps to the front entrance in this heat felt like scaling a mountain, and her shirt clung to her back by the time she pulled the heavy door open and stepped into the cool utopia of central air conditioning. The lobby was deserted except for the day security guard. She raised a hand in passing and said, "Hey, Wyland."

"Miss Julie." He touched the brim of his hat. "Gonna storm a pisser pretty soon. You get mud tires for that Yankee car of yours yet?"

"I've been here five years, Wyland," she said with a smirk. "When do I get to stop being a Yankee?"

He laughed. "I guess when you get yourself some proper tires," he said, and shook out the magazine he'd been reading. "You just watch yourself with that storm comin'. It'll break any day now."

"I will."

She waved again and took the elevator to the second floor, surprised at the sting Wyland's comment had caused. No Yankee was Julie Mae Walker. She'd been born right here in Flower Springs, and it hadn't been her choice to leave. She was only five when her mother and Gran Walker had a falling-out – over what, she'd never been told – and she was whisked off to Pennsylvania. They hadn't even gone to her grandmother's funeral a few years ago.

Mom hadn't been happy about her decision to come back, but something she couldn't explain had practically compelled her down here. She still didn't understand it fully. But she suspected it had something to do with her secret – the one that made her good at her job.

She'd learned to keep that little bonus to herself.

Inside Coop's suite, the front desk was conspicuously missing Maddy. Maybe the receptionist had taken an early lunch. Shrugging, Julie hit the buzzer under the desk and let herself into the district attorney's private office – where she stopped short and barely managed to hold back a gasp of shock.

It was like walking into the depths of hell.

Julie didn't know much about her gift, or curse, whatever it was. She could see things around people or places in a different way – sometimes a gleaming explosion of light, other times a blasted landscape of horror, but mostly things ended up somewhere in between. It was some kind of aura she thought of as simply the Dark and the Light. Usually she had to concentrate to see it.

But this was in her face, impossible to ignore. Charred walls, cracked and blistering, tendrils of smoke curling from jagged floorboards. A pot of fire standing where the end table by the window should've been. The stench of things burning and dying, and the faint sound of screams.

"Jules?"

The friendly, slightly concerned voice made the illusion vanish, and she was looking at plain old Cooper Boyd, District Attorney for Barlow County. Across the desk from him sat a stranger in a dark suit, who was currently pinning her with a suspicious stare.

"Sorry, Coop." Julie shook herself and moved fully into the room. "Maddy wasn't out front, so I let myself in. Didn't know you were busy."

A slight frown marred Coop's brow. "We're about done," he said. "Jules, this is Detective Roth out of Atlanta. Detective, this is Julie Walker, the best LPI in Georgia."

"LPI?" the detective drawled.

"Licensed private investigator." Julie didn't offer her hand, and Detective Roth did her the favor of not offering his.

Instead, his cold black eyes shifted to Coop, and he stood abruptly. "You just let me know if you hear anything about what I mentioned," he said, tossing a small white card on the surface of the desk. "I'll be in town a few more days. Call my cell any time." He turned and left the office without sparing Julie another glance.

"Christ on a crutch," Coop said when the door closed behind the detective. "Cops with grudges. Don't they ever watch movies? This shit never ends well." He rubbed a temple briefly and looked up. "What've you got for me?"

"I served Bobby," Julie said. "He didn't take kindly to it."

"Never does." Grimacing, Coop pulled a drawer open and stopped midway. "You don't think he's . . ."

He didn't have to finish the sentence. "No, he's guilty," she said. "I have a hunch." Bobby's place had been blacker than midnight's asshole when she looked at it in her special way – an experience she didn't want to repeat anytime soon. Hopefully, he'd be put away for good this time. There had to be a special spot in hell for people who killed other people's pets.

"That's my girl." Coop handed her a Proof of Service slip. "You know what to do with that. Stop back and I'll have Maddy cut a check for you."

She took the paper slowly. "Thanks," she said. "Hey, Coop . . . I hate to ask, but do you have any more jobs for me? I'm a little short on work this month."

"Yeah, I know. It's just too damned hot to break the law right now." His mouth firmed for a second, and then he held up a finger. "Hold on a minute. I've got a complaint here, just filed, which might need some investigating. Let me find it." He opened a few more drawers, and finally extracted a folder. "Here we go," he said. "Mrs Alma St Clair has reported criminal fraud in the matter of one Zephron, no last name, psychic adviser—"

"Oh, come on," she said. "A psychic?"

"Psychic *adviser*," Coop said with a grin. "Seems this Zephron told Mrs St Clair that she would hear from an old friend who'd gone away, and she suffered 'severe emotional distress' when said old friend failed to materialize." He raised an eyebrow. "She offered to pay a two hundred dollar investigation fee."

"Done." Julie snatched the folder. "So, what am I supposed to investigate? The fact that psychics aren't real, and Mrs St Clair must be short a few marbles to believe one?"

Coop shrugged. "It's probably harmless enough," he said. "I'd advise the psychic to offer Mrs St Clair a refund, and maybe an apology. That oughta do her. The address is in there."

"All right," she said. "I'll be back soon, with one genuine apology."

Julie headed back outside, already imagining the blessed relief of cool air pouring from her car's vents once she collected on the job. This one would be a breeze.

Zephron, the psychic adviser, operated out of a trim white cottage on Buckeye Drive, at the fringes of the west side of town. A stone walkway lined with pansies, rose trillium and bellflower led to a cosy screened porch flanked with fragrant lilac bushes. The pink-white riot of a late-blooming dogwood tree stood to the left of the house, raining petals on emerald green grass. Nothing about this place said "spooky lady with a crystal ball and a bad accent", except that it was a stone's throw from the back end of the Flower Springs Cemetery.

Julie parked on the street and rechecked the address. This was the right place – at least on paper. She headed up the walkway, expecting to encounter black curtains or strings of beads, maybe wind chimes made from bone. But everything looked normal, even cheerful.

The porch door was unlocked, so she went to the entrance and found the only confirmation of her target – a hand-lettered sign above the doorbell reading *Zephron: Advice & Guidance*. Maybe all this down-home charm was the psychic's attempt at authenticity.

Her finger hovered over the doorbell. Before she could press it, the door opened. And the figure on the other side was no scarf-wearing gypsy drowning in costume jewelry.

This was a man. And he was beautiful.

Julie stared for way too long. Finally, she ventured, "Zephron?"

Concern swept his fine features. "Oh, poor Alma," he said. "Her letter is caught in the rosebush. If she doesn't find it soon, it'll get ruined."

Astonishment made her head whirl, but she caught herself quickly. It had to be a trick. A lot of self-professed psychics could spin a few snippets of fact and deduction into a plausible-sounding statement. This guy probably knew Mrs St Clair would complain about him. And Julie's profession wasn't a secret – she had her own office, with a sign out front and everything.

Zephron smiled. "Such a logical mind for someone with your gift," he said. "Well, come in. I'm sure you have questions for me."

Okay. That one was a little harder to swallow. Likely just a wild guess, and he'd gotten lucky. Still, she wasn't sure about going inside. It would be easier to unsettle her in his work area, where he probably had a bunch of mirrors and hollow panels or something set up to freak people out. "This won't take long," she said. "Why don't you come out here?"

"All right." Still wearing a faint smile, Zephron stepped onto the porch. "What can I do for you, Miss Julie Walker?"

She had to forcibly remind herself that he could've found out her name anywhere. "Well, obviously you know I'm here about Alma St Clair," she said. "So why don't you start by telling me what you did to her, since you knew she'd complain about it?"

Zephron sighed and shook his head. "Would you like to sit down?" he said, gesturing to a pair of charming wicker chairs at a charming wicker table.

"No." Was there anything not charming about this guy? "Like I said, it'll only take a few minutes."

"Suit yourself. But I'm going to sit." He settled in the farthest chair and leaned back. "Alma," he said, with nothing but fondness in his expression. "Where to begin? I could bore you with the details, but I'll just tell you right out. She's cross with me because I can't contact her dear, departed husband."

Julie raised an eyebrow. "Isn't that what psychics do? Commune with the spirits?"

"Not always." His smile was a little sad this time. "Alma came by yesterday and asked about her cat. She thought Horace was getting depressed, but it's just the heat. Anyway, one thing led to another, and when I told her she'd hear from an old friend, she was a bit disappointed that it wouldn't be her husband."

"Wait a minute." Julie had barely realized she'd been edging closer to him, and now she sat in the other chair without quite knowing why. "Mrs St Clair – Alma – consulted a psychic about her *cat*?"

Zephron laughed. "Alma doesn't consult me," he said. "She stops in every Wednesday at three, just to say hello. She doesn't even know she keeps to a schedule."

"Oh. Well, I suppose that's sweet . . ." Julie shook herself, remembering she had a job to do. It was too easy talking to this guy – like a best friend she'd just met. Whatever he was, he had charisma. "Look, I came here to address a complaint," she said. "Mrs St Clair wants you charged with fraud. The DA's willing to drop the charges if you issue a refund and a formal apology. Do you agree to this?"

"Charges, huh?" The smile resurfaced. "I'm happy to apologize, Miss Walker. I really am sorry I'm unable to help Alma contact her husband. But I'm afraid I can't give out refunds."

"And why is that?"

"Because my services are free."

She blinked. "What, *all* of them?"

"Yes." Zephron leaned forward and clasped his hands. "Julie, I wasn't sure I should tell you this—"

"I think we'd better stick with Miss Walker." Suddenly, she was cold all over, and she didn't want to know what Zephron wasn't sure he should tell her. She tensed to stand, and said, "Don't worry about the refund."

"You call it the Dark and the Light."

She froze. "No."

"You see things most people won't. Take a look around, Julie."

"No. You can't . . ." But she was already looking. And what she saw stopped her breath.

Pure, golden light bathed everything around them. It transformed every detail, elevating the mundane and ordinary to impossible beauty. She could barely stand to look at it – much longer and she'd fall to her knees and weep. "Okay," she whispered, squeezing her eyes shut. "I'll listen."

"Thank you."

When she opened her eyes, the world was normal again, though she could still feel the echoes of the vision. "You said most people won't see it," she said. "Does that mean you can?"

"Of course. But that's not a conversation for today." Zephron looked serious for the first time since she'd met him. "Tomorrow you're going to be offered a job, and you won't want to take it."

Julie snorted. "Some psychic. Right now, I'll take any job I can get."

"You won't want it," he repeated. "But you must take it."

"Didn't you hear me?" This time she did stand, knocking the light wicker chair over in the process. "I'm not about to turn down a job. I need the money. And you *are* a fraud." Irritated with herself for believing this guy, she shoved her hands in her pocket before she could do something stupid. "Next you'll be telling me I'm going to meet a tall, dark stranger."

"Actually, you are," Zephron said. "Tonight, when you go to the Whistle Stop with Raylene."

A shiver traveled down her spine. "We're meeting there at eight," she muttered. "Jesus. How much do you know, anyway?"

"Not everything." He stood slowly, like he didn't want to startle her. "Tell you what," he said, "if I'm right, and you do meet a tall, dark stranger tonight, keep in mind what I said about the job. Remember that some things aren't what they seem, and fight your instincts."

Julie let out a shaking breath. "All right," she said, and held out a hand. "It's a deal."

Zephron took it. His grip was incredibly warm and comforting, and she fought an urge to hug him. "Good luck," he said. "Now, I believe I'll head over to Alma's and 'find' her letter. It's a pleasure to meet you, Julie Walker."

"Thanks," she said. "You, too. I think."

She headed back to her car a little dazed, a lot confused, and wondering how the hell she was going to explain this to Coop.

Chapter 2

Back in Atlanta, people said Harlan McKay had the luck of the devil. Here in Flower Springs, he apparently had a rambling monstrosity of a historic plantation house, and the nagging suspicion that he was losing his mind.

Why else would he have bought this place sight unseen, and then cut all of his Atlanta ties to move out to North Nowhere and live in . . . this?

The house had been abandoned for years and looked it. Creeper vines, long dead and bleached out to bone, swallowed the front stoop and climbed crazily up the once-white columns. The peeling front door hung crooked from a single hinge. More than half the windows were boarded over, and those that weren't had thick coatings of filth. Shingles buckled from the roof like jagged black teeth.

He could practically feel his bank account draining.

Shooting a hot glare at the disaster he'd already sunk half a million into, he popped the trunk of his car and dragged out the two-wheeled suitcases. The movers had already dropped off the first small load of necessities – they'd used the side door, since the front entrance was presently impassable. The bulk of his estate would arrive tomorrow.

Where he'd put everything, he had no idea. He hadn't even seen the inside of the place yet. If it was as bad as the outside, he'd probably opt to look for a hotel somewhere in this sorry excuse for a town. And then head back to Atlanta in the morning.

"No you don't, McKay." He winced at the sound of his own voice. Talking to himself – yet another sign he was cracking up. But he was determined to make this a clean break, a fresh start. It wouldn't be easy.

It hadn't been easy building himself up from nothing to millionaire. The sad part was how easy it would've been to make the leap from millionaire to billionaire. Easy, and illegal, and downright evil. He'd resisted that path. What he got instead was a criminal investigation, which eventually cleared his name, but not his conscience. No amount of legal evidence could reverse what happened. The kid was still dead.

And Harlan might as well have pulled the trigger himself.

So he'd closed down McKay's Rare and Antique Weapons for good, and put in a purchase offer on this place based on a hundred-year-old photograph that had given him a feeling. His feelings had always led to deals that made him a lot of money. But it seemed like this time he might've been wrong.

"All right, let's get this over with," he muttered under his breath, and started hauling the suitcases toward the side entrance. The feeling he'd gotten when he first looked at the photo came back stronger with every step. Gradually, he realized it wasn't the same thing he felt when he looked at a piece or talked to a seller. This was an intimate, eerie familiarity . . . déjà vu all over again.

He'd been here before.

It was completely impossible. He'd never set foot in this part of Georgia, and up until three weeks ago he'd never even heard of Flower Springs. But he knew, right now, that the long-gone wooden shutters in the black-and-white photo had been painted blood red. And in the backyard, there'd been a stone courtyard with a black granite fountain, depicting a vengeful angel with great black wings. It held a long, thick sword in one hand. A stream of water arched from the empty, outstretched palm of the other. And by that fountain . . .

The rest of that thought failed to materialize as the sky filled with smoke, and the air echoed with shouts and gunfire.

Harlan jerked stiff. The suitcases slipped from numb fingers – and when they clattered on the hard, dry ground, the visions vanished. He didn't even realize he'd been holding his breath until his lungs started to burn, and he let it out in a rattling gush.

Then a voice behind him drawled, "You look like you've seen a ghost."

"Goddamn it." He knew who the voice belonged to without looking, but he turned anyway. "Ever hear of private property, Detective?"

"Ever hear of probable cause, McKay?"

"I've been cleared."

"Not by me, you haven't." Detective Val Roth, the nastiest cop in Atlanta, cocked his hip and rested a hand on his service piece – a modified Glock with steel sights and an extended mag release. "I'm curious why a . . . gentleman of means such as yourself wants to move to a shithole like this. Do tell, McKay."

Harlan's hands clenched into fists. "I'm slumming," he said. "It's a rich guy thing."

"Planning on opening back up soon?"

"No. Not that it's any business of yours." He forced his fingers to relax, bent and retrieved the suitcases. "Stay away from me, Roth."

"Or what? You'll call the cops?" Roth flashed a withering grin. "You're mine," he said. "One way or another, I'm going to have you."

"Is that a threat, Detective, or are you making a pass at me?"

"No, sir. It's no threat." Still grinning, the detective touched two fingers to his forehead in a bizarre salute. "It's a promise. See you soon, McKay."

Harlan watched him spin on a heel and stride toward the unmarked car parked behind his Lexus. It was all he could do not to race after the bastard. He'd endured enough harassment from Roth back in Atlanta and, damn it, he wasn't about to put up with more. Tomorrow he'd call the Atlanta PD and tell them to leash their guard dog.

Tonight, he'd dump this stuff inside and head into town after all. He wasn't going to run, but he needed a drink or ten before he could even begin to process this shit. And getting drunk alone, in what just might be a haunted house, seemed like a real bad idea to him.

For a Thursday night, the Whistle Stop was packed. All the pool tables had games in progress, and it looked like standing room only at the bar. But there were plenty of tables open, and Julie had seen the place more crowded than this on weekends. Nothing too unusual here.

Still, she half expected a mysterious stranger – tall and dark, of course – to pounce at her the second she walked in.

She finally realized she'd been standing by the door and staring at nothing in particular long enough to draw looks. In an attempt to act casual, she panned a deliberate gaze across the room until she spotted Raylene at a table that was totally free of tall, dark strangers. She made her way over, telling herself to get a grip.

The encounter with Zephron had kept her rattled all day. In the end she'd told Coop to just toss the complaint, because there hadn't been any money exchanged, and left it at that. Of course, it meant that she didn't get paid. He added another twenty-five to her check for the inconvenience of chasing a dead end – which was nice, but not enough to fix her A/C.

Between then and now, she'd replayed the whole conversation with the psychic a dozen times or more. And hard as she tried, she couldn't figure how he'd called her coming here tonight with Raylene. It wasn't like they did this often. Raylene had a four-year-old son, so they usually hung out at her place or took Mikey along to the diner. The Whistle Stop was a rare treat.

Raylene saw her coming and waved like a lunatic. Shoving thoughts of psychics and strangers from her mind, Julie grinned and slid into the seat next to her. "Look at us rebels," she said. "Out on a weekday night."

"Oh, I feel positively sinful." Beaming, Raylene threw an arm around her and squeezed. "So how was your day, honey?"

She rolled her eyes. "Let's talk about yours first."

"That good, huh?" Raylene said. "Well, things were interesting today. We had a hound with a cold, a parrot with a growth, and a horse in the parking lot with an owner trying to figure out how to get him in the door. I did my first solo operation – stitches for Mrs Laramie's German shepherd. And Mikey performed his first criminal act."

"He did not," Julie said. "What happened?"

"He stole a kitten."

She clapped a hand to her mouth, but a laugh burst through anyway. "How'd he manage that one?"

"Marla Granger's cat had a big litter, six weeks old now. She brought them in today for a check-up, and she had eight when she came in. But when she brought the basket back to Doc, there were only seven." Raylene smirked. "We tore the place apart looking for it, and finally I went to ask Mikey if he wanted to help. He was asleep in the playroom with the little kitten curled up on his chest, happy as a clam."

"Aww. Isn't that the sweetest thing?"

"Yeah, except for giving poor Marla a heart attack." She shook her head. "He begged me to let him keep it. Gave me that face. Said she was the best friend he ever had, and she was lonely because she was a different color from the other kittens. Of course, I said no way. Not in a million years. We've already got two dogs."

Julie nudged her. "So you're getting a kitty, huh?"

"Yes," she sighed. "She really is an adorable little thing. Two weeks, and she's ours."

"No one can resist the Mikey face."

"Tell me about it." Raylene smiled fondly. "All right, now it's your turn. Spill it."

A frown tugged at her lips. "Well, you know I served Bobby Green this morning."

"Shit-for-brains bastard," Raylene spat. She and Doc Pullman had worked six hours straight, trying to save Jaime Verger's sweet little spaniel after Bobby shot him. At first he'd tried to claim it was an accident. "I hope you served him right in his baby-killing balls."

"I'm sure they'll have him this time," Julie said. "He all but confessed. Anyway, after that my day got weird. Coop sent me out to talk to a psychic."

Raylene chuckled. "Not the great Zephron."

"You know him?" she blurted.

"By name only. My Aunt Casey swears by him, and I figured there could only be one psychic in Flower Springs."

"Yeah." Julie stared at the table, not sure how much she should say. "Thing is, he kind of freaked me out," she said at last. "He knew my name before I said it. I guess he could've gotten that from anywhere, but . . . he knew I was coming here with you tonight."

"Come on, Jules," Raylene said. "What'd he actually say? Like, you're going to see a friend tonight, or you will have a social encounter with someone you know . . . some fortune-cookie bullshit. Right?"

"No. He said, and I quote, 'when you go to the Whistle Stop with Raylene'."

Her mouth dropped open. "You're kidding."

"Wish I was. Seriously, the man is spooky."

"Okay, so what's the rest?"

Julie's brow furrowed. "The rest of what?"

"When you come here with me . . . *what?* What's supposed to happen?"

"Oh. That." Her face flushed with heat. "Er, I guess I'm supposed to meet a tall, dark stranger. You know. Fortune-cookie bullshit."

Raylene didn't laugh. She was staring across the bar, a look of almost comical surprise on her face. "You mean like him?"

"What . . ." Julie followed her gaze, and for the second time that day forgot how to breathe. The man was definitely tall. And dark – black hair, black clothes, deep Southern tan. He was a stranger, too. She would've remembered seeing him, because he was hotter than a bonfire on an August night.

And he was headed straight for her.

"Oh, my," Raylene whispered. "I think I need to go see the great Zephron."

Julie opened her mouth to reply, but at once the man was there in front of her. He looked stunned – like somebody had just whacked him upside the head with a shovel. "Excuse me," he said in a voice that could've melted an iceberg. "I'm sorry to bother you, but . . . do I know you?"

"Um. I . . . no," Julie stammered. "I mean, I don't know you. I think."

The man smiled, sending a flutter through her. "You think?"

"She'd like to know you, is what she means," Raylene said.

Julie scowled at her, and then turned back to the stranger. God, he had gorgeous blue eyes, and they were staring right into her soul. "I'm sorry," she said, a little more evenly. "You must have me confused with someone else. We've never met."

"Damn," he said. "It's just that you look so familiar, I feel like . . . well, never mind. Maybe we could meet now." The man smirked. "Hello, stranger. I'm Harlan."

She almost didn't respond. For some reason, she felt like "officially" meeting this man would be acknowledging that Zephron was the genuine article, and everything he'd said about tomorrow would come true. But honestly, what could be so bad about a job offer?

Finally, she smiled. "I'm Julie," she said. "And this is my friend Raylene."

"Nice to meet you, ladies." Harlan's gaze didn't leave Julie. "Well, thanks for humoring me," he said. "And now I *really* need a drink. Sorry for the interruption."

"No problem," Julie said. "Nice to meet you, too."

He stared a moment longer, and then closed his eyes briefly. "Goodnight . . . Julie," he said hoarsely. Before she could respond, he turned fast and walked away.

Raylene cleared her throat. "Your tall, dark stranger is escaping. Why are you still sitting here?"

"Hey. Zephron said I'd meet him, not chase him around all night." That fluttery feeling he'd started in her with his smile refused to go away, and she was actually glad the guy had something better to do. Because she might've done something really stupid if he'd stayed to chat. "Besides, he seemed a little weird with all that 'do I know you' stuff."

"Haven't you ever heard a pickup line? It wasn't a very good one, but still. *Whew.*" Raylene waved a hand in front of her face. "He is one fine gentleman. You should go for it."

She shook her head. "I'm here to hang out with you," she said. "And it looks like he's gone, anyway. I don't see him at the bar."

"I think you broke his heart." Raylene gave her a playful shove and slid back from the table. "Let's you and me hit the bar, then, and grab that pool table before somebody else does."

"You're on." Julie was on her feet first, telling herself firmly that she wasn't going to look for the mysterious Harlan. And she definitely wasn't going to pay attention to the small part of her thinking maybe it wasn't a pickup line, and maybe she'd felt the same startled familiarity that had been written all over his face. That just for a second, she *did* think she knew him. It was impossible.

Just like Zephron's impossible predictions, which were somehow coming true.

Harlan stumbled into the men's room and rushed for the nearest sink. Splashing cold water on his face got his hands to stop shaking, but it didn't ease the knots in his gut. The déjà vu at the house had been nothing compared to what he'd experienced looking at the woman out there. Julie. He'd probably scared the hell out of her coming up like that, talking like a crazy person.

Hell, he'd scared himself. He *felt* crazy. He didn't know a soul in this town – besides Roth, who didn't belong here anyway. But one glimpse of that blonde woman he couldn't possibly know, who had the sweetest smile he'd ever seen, had set his blood roaring. He'd felt things he couldn't even name, and most of all that she was the only thing in the world that mattered. That he'd die for her.

Somehow it was all connected to the black fountain. The one he knew was behind the house, though he hadn't brought himself to actually go back and look yet. If it was there, he suspected seeing it would push him right over the edge of insanity.

He gave himself another shot of cold water and stayed bent over the sink for a minute, gripping the sides and staring down the drain like he'd find an explanation for all this down there. Finally, he raised his head and looked in the mirror.

A man in black stood a few feet behind him, staring with cold black eyes. *Roth.*

Harlan whirled around, a curse on his lips – only to find no one there.

"What the hell?" He looked back at the mirror and saw nothing but himself, and an empty stall behind him. "Hey," he said. "Is someone in here? This isn't funny."

No response. He was alone, all the stalls open and deserted. The restroom door hadn't opened or closed, and there was nowhere to hide in here. But what he'd seen hadn't been a shadow, or a hallucination. Someone else had been there.

"Jesus," he whispered shakily. "What the hell's going on in this town?"

He wasn't expecting an answer. So it startled a few years from his life when a voice said, "Nothing that doesn't go on every day. Care to be a little more specific?"

Harlan turned around slowly this time. An actual person stood by the door – a man who looked around sixty, sporting a bemused smile. "Sorry," he said, grabbing a few paper towels from the wall dispenser to dry his damp hands. "Talking to myself, I guess."

"We all do that from time to time." The man came toward him, still smiling. "You're new around here," he said. "Just passin', or here to stay?"

"Staying." At least until he lost the rest of his mind and got tossed into a nuthouse somewhere. "Name's Harlan McKay," he said, extending a hand.

The man shook firmly. "Nate Pullman," he said. "Call me Doc."

"You're a doctor?" he said before he thought about how stupid that sounded.

Doc didn't seem to mind. "Veterinarian, actually," he said. "So, what's troubling you about our little town, if you don't mind my asking?"

"Nothing, really." Harlan wasn't too eager to start babbling about phantom gunfire and recognizing people he didn't know. "I just got here today. Maybe I'm a little homesick."

"Well, that's understandable," Doc said. "Where are you staying?"

He shrugged. "I bought a place out at the north end of town," he said. "Kind of isolated. Needs a little work."

"You're the one who bought the old Webster place?"

Harlan frowned. "Seems that way," he said. "What's wrong with it?"

"The house itself, probably nothing a little hard work won't put to rights. But the history . . ." Doc shook his head slowly. "That place belonged to Hawthorne Webster."

For some reason, the name went through him like a blade. "I take it that's not a good thing," he said.

"Webster was a general in the Confederate Army," Doc said. "He built the place as a command center and clearing house for his . . . extra-curricular activities. He was a brilliant man, a brilliant strategist, and wicked to the core. Killed more soldiers personally than any one man in the entire Civil War – not all of them Union, either."

Harlan felt the blood drain from his face and hoped it didn't show. This might explain the vision at the house at least. "What happened to him?"

"Shot to death. Right in his own backyard, too." Doc offered a brief shrug. "Not that I subscribe to the old notion of antebellum glory, but I believe the South might have actually won the war if they hadn't taken out Hawthorne Webster. The man was ruthless. And right until the end, he had the luck of the devil."

"Well," Harlan managed to say, "it seems I've made a colorful investment."

Doc smiled. "Indeed you have. Good luck with it, Mr McKay. I think it'd do the old place good to have decent folk take care of it."

"Call me Harlan," he said. "And thanks for the history lesson."

"Don't mention it."

Doc went into a stall, and Harlan made himself walk casually out of the men's room, despite his desire to haul his ass out to his car and straight back to Atlanta. He still planned to get drunk, but there had to be another bar in this town somewhere. One without any amateur historians or beautiful women who made his blood burn with a smile.

Tomorrow, he'd learn more about his new home – where he was definitely staying. No matter how many ghosts tried to drive him out.

Chapter 3

Julie had almost talked herself out of opening the office this morning.

The big storm hadn't come around yet, so everybody's favorite weather tag-team of Hot and Humid still dominated the day. Five minutes in her A/C-less car had Julie wishing she could just keep going until she hit water – a pool, a beach, she'd take anything – and spend the day never finding out whether Zephron was right.

In the end, sheer morbid curiosity found her sitting behind the desk at 9 a.m., in the single room she rented from the law firm that owned the Main Street building. It was hard not to keep glancing at the door every thirty seconds. She busied herself by tackling the random files that cluttered her computer's desktop, and thinking about Harlan.

She'd met him for all of a minute, but she couldn't get him out of her mind. The way he looked at her – she'd never seen a stare more intense. And that smile of his had stayed lodged in the pit of her stomach, fluttering away every time she thought on it. But it was more than attraction. A deep, inexplicable sorrow mingled with the butterflies and threatened to break her heart. She couldn't tell whether she felt sorry for him, or herself.

It was almost frightening how powerfully the tall, dark stranger had affected her.

Between the monumental task of organizing her computer and the visions of blazing blue eyes, she didn't realize that someone had come into the office until a shadow fell across her desk. She looked up, startled and breathless – and thought, *No. Oh, hell no.*

"Miss Walker." The man had exchanged his suit for jeans and a T-shirt, but she recognized his chilling black eyes. The badge clipped to his pocket and the gun in the side holster clinched it. This was the detective who'd radiated hell into Coop's office yesterday. "Interesting place you have here," he said.

Julie managed to keep her expression neutral. "Hello, Detective . . ."

"Roth." He flashed a thin smile. "Glad to know I'm so memorable."

She fought to keep from squirming in her seat. Already she could sense the Dark this man seemed to generate, threatening to spill into the world and burn everything in its path. "What can I do for you, Detective Roth?"

He gestured to the client chair beside him. "May I sit down?"

"Feel free," she heard herself say, though every instinct in her wanted to throw him out of her office.

Roth pulled a folded piece of paper from his pocket before he slid into the chair. "I'm not sure how much your boss told you about why I'm here in your quaint little town," he said.

"Coop isn't my boss. And he didn't tell me much."

"Well, that's just fine." He tossed the paper on her desk. "I'm investigating a killer who's moved in with you people," he said. "I want to hire you for a little undercover work, to gather me some evidence."

"A killer?" She didn't touch the paper, though she could see it was a page from a newspaper. Somehow she knew exactly who Roth wanted. She tried to tell herself it was an educated guess – small town, everybody knows when a new person moves in. But it was more than that. She could feel the shape of his name wrapped up in this. *Harlan.*

Damn Zephron for being right. She absolutely did not want this job.

"I'd appreciate you taking a look at that." There was steel behind Roth's laid-back drawl, a suggestion that turning him down was not an option. "You should know who you're dealing with here."

"Fine. I'll look." She reached for the paper and unfolded it slowly. Her heart dropped as she read the headline screaming from the clipped article: MILLIONAIRE GUN DEALER CLEARED IN SHOOTING DEATH OF TEEN.

There was a picture of Harlan wearing a small, cold smirk that was miles from the breath-stealing expression he'd given her last night. Next to it was a school photo of a sweet-looking boy who couldn't have been more than fifteen. She scanned the article, and the tightness in her chest eased a little. "He didn't kill anyone, Detective," she said. "The killer used a gun bought from his store."

"Yes. A gun Mr McKay sold to a convicted criminal on parole. Which, as I'm sure you know, is illegal here in the great state of Georgia." Roth leaned forward a little. "The man is a menace. I have reason to believe he's acting with criminal intent, and I want you to find me some evidence. Any evidence. Get close to him, find his secrets. And I'll pay you triple your usual fee." He extended a hand. "Do we have a deal, Miss Walker?"

Julie's throat went dry. She hadn't wanted to touch this intensely cold man before, and she sure as hell didn't want to now. Not even the offer of a tripled fee made this job attractive. He really was a cop with a grudge. Whatever he thought Harlan had done, the law had already declared him innocent – at least, all the law except this detective. If she worked for him, wouldn't it be trying to prove an innocent man guilty?

You won't want it. But you must take it.

Zephron's words echoed through her mind, and she wanted to scream. Why? Goddamn it, *why* was she supposed to take this job? If there was any chance Roth was right, she'd be helping to catch a man who'd slipped through the cracks of the justice system. But she just couldn't believe that. So what was her involvement going to accomplish?

"Well?" The hand hadn't moved. "Miss Walker, you're not in a position to turn down my offer. I know it, and you know it." Roth's black eyes practically glittered. "I can change your life," he said. "You'll have money. Job offers – more than you can handle. You'll be very successful. I'll see to it . . . if you just make the deal."

She stared at the outstretched hand. And once again, her mind whispered, *You must take it.*

"All right," she finally said. But she still wasn't about to shake his hand. It felt too much like making a deal with the devil. "I have a standard contract you can sign, and—"

"No contract." Roth lowered his arm, and a slow grin spread on his face as he stood. "We'll just call it an old-fashioned verbal agreement. You hold up your end, and I'll hold up mine."

Julie frowned. "What's your end?"

"To pay you, of course." His upper lip curled slightly. "And to bring McKay back where he belongs."

The statement froze her blood. All at once she caught a whiff of sulfurous smoke, like a freshly struck match . . . and heard a faint chorus of screams.

"I'll be in touch, Miss Walker." The visions, or whatever they were, vanished as soon as Roth spoke. He stared at her a little too long, seemed about to say something else, and then turned and left the office.

Julie shuddered. Her hands wanted to shake, but she refused to let them. There was something far from right about Detective Roth – besides the obvious grudge and the bizarre offer to make her rich and successful. She'd never seen anyone carry so much of the Dark around with them, enough to bleed through in places they'd never been. He was like the anti-Zephron.

But she'd taken the job. Now it was time to find out what she'd gotten herself into, and how she was going to get out.

Harlan woke up cold, sore, and gasping for breath. The fountain. He'd dreamed about that damned black fountain – backed up against it, no way to escape the advancing shadow bearing a gun. It was an old piece, the type that had been his specialty. A Civil War-era musket. Not much of the dream had been visually clear, but he'd felt helpless rage and biting sorrow as the faceless figure raised the weapon and fired.

A single shot rang out. He'd turned, in that soupy-slow way of dreams, and saw the fountain spewing not water, but blood.

His own hoarse screams snapped him into consciousness.

It took him a few minutes to get oriented. Last night, he'd been too drunk to drive back here. He'd left his car at that other bar and started walking. Drunk logic suggested that it was a small town, and therefore no place was too far from anyplace else to walk. Eventually he'd ended up at a cemetery, utterly lost. Some guy had offered him a ride home.

He hadn't said where he lived, but the guy drove him straight to the house anyway. He'd stumbled in through the side door where he'd left his stuff, spread a blanket on the floor, and promptly passed out.

So he was cold and sore because he'd basically slept on a stone slab in the mudroom all night. A man he'd never met knew where he lived, which meant maybe the whole damned town did. And where he lived was the former home of a ruthless killer.

Oh, yeah. This was a great fresh start so far.

He managed to stand without groaning too much, grabbed his small bag of essentials, and headed for the inner door. He knew from the real estate agent that the most recent attempt to renovate this place had been around thirty years ago. They'd gotten as far as updating the plumbing and electricity before the project was abruptly abandoned. No one had ever said why. But after last night, Harlan suspected it was the ghosts.

Well, the ghosts would just have to get used to him being here. This was his place.

The first actual room was the kitchen. It wasn't much to look at, but he soon realized that was mostly because it lacked appliances. The floors and cabinets could use sanding and staining, and the countertops would need replacing. But everything seemed pretty solid.

He headed for the sink. The power had been turned on a few days before he came out, and the place was on a spring-fed well, so technically it should work. He wouldn't be surprised if it didn't, though. Standing well back and half holding his breath, he turned the cold tap.

A grinding shudder sounded from somewhere deep inside the house. The faucet hissed and stuttered a few times. He was about to turn it off when a brief burst of water sprayed into the sink, then another. After a slightly longer, groaning pause, there was a steady stream.

Red. The water was red.

Harlan's throat clenched. He fumbled for the tap, unable to stop staring at the bloody rush, and noticed the color was fading. Now it was a dirty pink, and he could make out a few flecks of grit in the stream.

Rust in the pipes. Not blood, not a ghostly omen. Just a bunch of perfectly natural, oxidized metal sludge.

He laughed aloud and let the water run itself clear while

he took a few things from his bag. Once he was reasonably sure it was safe, he washed up as best he could and brushed his teeth. He could use a shower, but it'd have to wait. The movers would be here soon.

And before then, he was going to look at the backyard. He had to know. If the fountain was there, he wasn't sure whether it would make him less crazy, or more. But he had to see, one way or the other.

With a quick stop in the mudroom to change his clothes, he headed outside before he could change his mind.

The heat slammed him first, and the brilliant morning sun followed up with a glare that spiked straight into his aching head. Of course, he'd left his sunglasses in the car. He stood blinking and squinting until his eyes reluctantly adjusted to the light, and set off at a fast stroll around the house.

He saw the courtyard first. And then, with a dull lack of surprise, the fountain.

His steps slowed as he approached. The piece was disturbing, even without considering that he'd somehow known it would be here. An angel ready for battle – flowing black robes, massive black wings outstretched, great black sword pointed ahead. Ageless and genderless, its features the picture of wrath. No water arched from its open palm. But he thought that if it did, it would be red as blood.

The reality of the fountain failed to drive him insane, and that disturbed him more than anything. Why did it seem normal that he'd known things he couldn't possibly know?

And why was this impossible fountain tied to the woman he'd met last night?

Julie. Blonde, beautiful, sweet as cane sugar melting on your tongue. It had always been her. But that hadn't been her name, not the last time . . .

Harlan was barely aware of the thoughts pounding through his head, or the fact that his arm was stretching toward the fountain, his fingers nearly brushing the angel's empty hand. He heard shouts and guns thundering, the distant crackle of flames. The air thickened with smoke.

"Harlan?"

The voice came from behind him. He whirled around and there she was, wearing that knowing little smile. Alive. Relief poured into him, and he went to her like a man dreaming – to kiss her, to claim her.

It wasn't until his lips met hers that he realized he'd been having one hell of a crazy hallucination . . . and he was passionately kissing a complete stranger.

Chapter 4

Julie hadn't been sure what to expect when she headed to the old Webster place, after Doc tipped her to where the new town resident was staying. But it definitely was not this. Harlan had taken one look at her, smiled like the sun, and without a word strode over and kissed her. Hard.

Damned if that kiss hadn't taken her breath away.

He stopped just as abruptly as he'd come on, and pulled back with horror stamped on his face. "Oh, God," he said, taking a step back. "I'm so sorry. I thought you . . . Christ, I'm an idiot."

"No, it's fine." She managed to sound normal while her pulse raced in her throat. Obviously it was a case of mistaken identity, but for a few seconds there, she would've given anything to be the reason for that smile. Which would be a huge mistake, considering she didn't even know him, not to mention why she was here in the first place. "That's how everybody greets each other in Flower Springs," she said. "Now you'll have to say hey to all the ladies like that."

He offered a wry smirk. "Great. Well, thanks for not slapping me. Julie, right?"

"That's me." She was absurdly touched that he'd remembered her name. "And you're Harlan."

"Afraid so."

There was something so sad behind those words, they almost hurt to hear. She looked away – and her gaze landed on the sculpture he'd been looking at when she came around the house. It was a fountain, she saw now, or it had been once. A warrior angel carved out of black stone. It held a terrible beauty, and something more. A sense of familiarity.

The same quick spark she'd felt at the Whistle Stop last night when she first saw Harlan

"Don't touch that!"

Julie gasped as Harlan grabbed her wrist. She hadn't even realized she'd been reaching for the fountain. "All right," she said unsteadily. "Let go of me."

He swore and jerked his hand back like she'd burned him. "I'm sorry," he said. "It's old, and . . . not safe. That's all."

"Right," she murmured. Truth be told, she was feeling pretty burned herself. Whatever fascination she held with him was only growing, and it didn't help when he touched her. Or kissed her. This was going to make it real hard to do her job.

He frowned. "What are you doing here, anyway?"

"Oh." She had to stop acting like a flustered schoolgirl. The plan was to get friendly with him, make sure he really wasn't a killer, and report back to Roth as quickly as possible so she could get this over with. "I just came to welcome you to town," she said. "And to see if you were busy tonight."

The frown slid into surprise. "Are you always this forward with strangers?"

"Only when they're forward with me first."

He laughed. "Fair point. What did you have in mind?"

"Well, I . . ." Damn. She hadn't really thought this far ahead. "How about a drink?"

Harlan shot a glance past her and sighed. "I'm afraid I have to regretfully decline," he said. "Very regretfully. Believe me, I could use a drink . . . and the company. But I've got movers coming, and cleaners, and I'm putting in a full day and then some on this monstrosity. I'll be too exhausted to go out." A smile quirked his lips. "Don't really want to sleep on the floor again tonight, you know?"

"You slept on the floor?" she said. "In there?"

He nodded. "An experience I don't care to repeat."

Julie averted her gaze from the intensity in those blue eyes. She knew she had to look at him in her "special" way, but something held her back. Not that she believed the detective for one second. It was the odd little pricks of recognition, the instant connections – first with Harlan, then with the fountain.

She didn't want to find any of the Dark around him. If she did, it just might crush her.

"Tell you what," she finally said. "I'll bring the drinks to you."

His eyes narrowed just a touch, and his mouth opened. Before he said anything, the rumble of big engines filled the air and his expression smoothed into neutral. "That'd be the movers," he said. "Look. Thanks for being neighborly, but I'm real busy up here. Maybe I'll see you around town or something."

Julie frowned. This guy shifted gears faster than a NASCAR driver – hot to angry to laughing to cold. The first simmer of suspicion rankled the investigator in her, and she wondered if maybe there wasn't a grain of truth to Roth's claims. There was one way to find out.

She let out a breath and looked at him, allowing her gaze to relax. The best she could explain her special sight was like looking at one of those Magic Eye pictures – just random colors and patterns, until you stopped looking and started *seeing*.

What started coming into focus was like nothing she'd ever experienced. Dark and Light at war, shadow clashing against electric brilliance. The space around him looked like a roiling thunderstorm.

"You need to leave."

The vision vanished as Harlan put a hand on her arm and started steering her around. She pulled away so fast she almost stumbled. "Sure," she managed. "I'm leaving."

Somehow she got herself walking away, and didn't look back. She wasn't surprised that he didn't try to stop her. Usually she could hide her reactions to the visions, but that one, brief as it was, had been powerful.

She had no idea what it meant, but she knew someone who might. Someone who'd convinced her to take this job in the first place.

And Zephron was going to explain a few things, right now.

★

Harlan watched her hustle to the beat-up little car like all the demons of Hell were at her heels, or maybe just one. He couldn't blame her, really. But it still hurt when she'd looked at him like that, and all the color drained from her face. From her point of view, he was crazy and probably dangerous.

He was starting to agree with that idea. Crazy was a definite possibility, and dangerous . . . well, he just might be. At least to her. The feeling that she was better off staying away from him had tangled itself up in the impossible notion that he knew her. And it started the instant she tried to touch the fountain.

So he'd driven her off intentionally. Julie, who his fracturing mind had decided was someone else. That alone was a good enough reason to stay away – although his aching heart said otherwise.

He wasn't going to listen to that, either. It was just as crazy as the rest of him.

With a heavy sigh, he started for the driveway to meet the moving trucks. Today was going to be a long damned day.

Julie drove to Zephron's in a weird kind of daze. She couldn't stop seeing that ethereal storm that surrounded Harlan like a shroud, almost obliterating him from view. Whatever was happening with him, it was intense.

She pulled up in front of the little cottage and sat there for a minute. What, exactly, was she here to demand? Zephron said he could see the Dark and the Light, but who said he'd know what it was? Maybe he really was psychic. He'd been damned convincing so far. But that didn't mean he understood it any better than she did.

Well, she could at least find out why he'd been so insistent that she take this job.

She got out and started up the picture-perfect walkway with its profusion of flowers, and not a petal out of place. Apparently the man was a master gardener in addition to being a psychic. Probably communicated with the plants or something, too. She'd gotten halfway to the house when the porch door opened and Zephron stepped out. He nodded at Julie, and then held the door while a little old lady with stark white hair made her way past him.

"You watch that storm tonight now, Alma," Zephron said. "Remember to get your back window closed. You don't want Horace getting out."

The lady beamed up at him – she was five foot nothing, and Zephron well over six feet. "Ain't you just a treasure," she said, in an accent thick enough to paint walls. "And after all the fuss I raised, too. You are a dear, dear boy to help an old woman out."

"Always a pleasure, ma'am."

"Bye, now."

Julie stood there awkwardly as Alma St Clair came her way. The woman finally noticed her, stopped and broke into a fresh smile. "You must be Miss Julie Walker," she said. "Just a child last I saw you, but you're the spitting image of your grandmama now, God rest her soul."

"You . . . knew Gran?"

At that, Alma burst into rich laughter. "Course I did, honey. I live in Flower Springs, don't I?" She reached out and patted Julie's hand. "A good woman. Had a touch of the sight, too. Not as much as that one," she said, motioning back toward Zephron, "but she could see farther than most."

Something in Julie's stomach clenched hard. "My grandmother was a psychic?"

"Oh, but she never called it that. Wouldn't have truck with such things. She always said what she saw was—"

"The Dark and the Light," Julie rasped.

Alma tilted her head a bit. "That's right, child," she said gently. "And since you know that, I'd say you have a touch of your own."

"Yeah," she said. "I guess I do."

"Well, then Zephron is just the man to see." Alma smiled again. "Y'all have a nice chat, now. I've got a window to close, before that rascal cat of mine slips out." She nodded smartly, and kept going down the walkway.

Julie watched her for a minute before turning her attention to Zephron, who stood just outside the porch door. His expression revealed nothing. But as she approached, he shook his head and sighed. "I'm sorry, Julie," he said. "I can't tell you what you want to know."

"You damned well can." She stopped in front of him. "What's the deal with Harlan McKay, and why it is so important that I take this job?"

"That's not what you really want to ask me."

"No, but it's what I *am* asking you," she said. "And I want an answer. The truth."

He frowned. "It's not that simple."

"Isn't it?" She closed her eyes for a moment and once again saw the roiling storm, Dark and Light clashing around Harlan. "You were right that I didn't want the job," she said. "I took it because you said I should. So who am I working for – Roth, or you?"

"Julie . . ."

"My God." At once she made the connections she hadn't seen before. Roth, with his powerful Dark aura infecting everything around him, and Zephron, with enough Light to banish shadows. She didn't understand it, but she knew it was the right general idea. "You're fighting over him," she said. "Why? I mean, I know what Roth wants, but you . . ."

"Can't fault him for doing his job, Miss Walker."

The voice behind her was a thunderclap, jolting her breath away. She half turned and stumbled back as Detective Roth strolled up the walkway. Something about his sudden arrival was very wrong, and it took her a moment to put it together. Hers was still the only car on the street, and there'd been no one out there a minute ago. He'd just appeared out of nowhere.

"Zephron." Roth stopped and leveled a chilling grin at the psychic. "It's been too long. Fort McAllister, wasn't it?"

"You're out of line." Zephron's features blazed with fury. "Keep your mouth closed, or I'll close it for you."

"Oh, yes. That worked so well for you last time."

"Hey." Julie shook herself out of the shock and crossed her arms. "You two know each other?"

Roth swung his cold gaze to her. "We're acquainted."

"Don't listen to him, Julie," Zephron said. "He's delusional."

Roth laughed. The sound sent shivers down her spine. "So bold," he said. "I must admit, I'm impressed that you got to her first. But that won't matter in the end."

"What the hell's going on?" Julie tried to sound demanding, but it came out a hoarse whisper. "Who *are* you two?"

"You wanted to ask Mister Good Side here about your visions," Roth said with a sneer. "Well, he's not going to tell you. His kind doesn't believe in giving straight answers. They think you should figure things out for yourself – as if you could possibly comprehend anything."

"Enough," Zephron said. "You know the rules."

"There is *one* rule. And I'm not breaking it, even though it would be quite satisfying." Roth shrugged and turned back to Julie. "What you see is Citadel, the light of heaven, and Shade, the darkness of hell. I'm sure you can guess which sides we're on. Simple, isn't it?"

"It is *not* simple." Zephron stepped forward, his features etched with sorrow. "Julie, please. Your heart knows the answer. Don't listen to anything else. You've got to reach him."

Julie shook her head and started backing away. This was all just too much. "You're crazy," she said. "Both of you. I don't know what you're trying to prove, but you're not using me to prove it. I don't know you, I don't know Harlan, and I quit."

She spun and strode for her car, fighting the urge to look back with her special vision. Heaven and hell, if that's what it was, could kiss her ass.

Chapter 5

Julie spent all day trying not to think about psychics and detectives and tall, dark strangers. She especially tried not to think about the implications behind what Roth had said about heaven and hell, and which side they were on. But despite her best efforts, she kept returning to the bizarre confrontation, turning it over in her mind.

His kind. She was pretty sure Roth hadn't meant psychics when he said that. Whatever they were doing, they had rules. And there was the crack about how long it had been since they'd seen each other last, at Fort McAllister.

A national park, yes. But also a major battle in the Civil War.

The idea was ridiculous. Still, no matter how hard she tried she couldn't get rid of it. Heaven and hell . . . angels and demons, with psychic powers and the ability to materialize out of thin air. Carrying light and darkness with them through the ages. But why Flower Springs, why Harlan – and how did she fit into this mess?

Finally, as the last rays of the setting sun dissolved behind a thickening bank of clouds, she called Doc Pullman. When it came to town history, he was faster and more thorough than Google any day.

"Evenin', Julie," he said when she identified herself. "Did you find your young man this morning?"

"Right where you said he'd be." She ignored the little twinge at the idea of Harlan being hers. "Doc, I've got a question for you, and it's going to sound strange. So bear with me, all right?"

"Okay. Shoot."

She drew a quick breath. "It's about General Webster," she said. "Did he . . . ever fight at Fort McAllister?"

"Indeed he did," Doc chuckled. "It was his last great victory, before he was killed."

"He died in the battle?"

"Oh, no. The man was shot to death in his own backyard," Doc said.

At once, Julie knew that Webster had died at the black fountain. "Who killed him?"

"Well, some say it was his second-in-command. He was power hungry and wanted to open up a position as a general for himself. That's the story the history books accept. But there's a lesser-known account claiming it was all because of love."

"Love?" she whispered.

Doc paused. At last he said, "Hawthorne Webster was said to have fallen in love at first sight with a woman who was dead set against slavery, and war in general. In other words, a sensible human being." He coughed once. "She'd thawed his cold heart, they said. Made him see the error of his ways. But she was too late – he'd already made a deal with the devil, and his soul was lost."

Julie shivered. "What happened to them?"

"As the story goes, it was a murder-suicide," Doc said. "Some say he shot her because the devil made him do it, and then killed himself out of remorse. Others think she shot him to save the world from the devil's plans, and took her own life so she could join him in hell." He laughed a little. "The rest of the story is even crazier."

"What is it?"

"Legend says that Webster and his love keep meeting the same fate, lifetime after lifetime. That heaven and hell fight over their union – and hell keeps winning. It's always love at first sight, because they've loved before. And it always ends in tragedy."

Her head spun, and for an instant she thought she'd faint. That couldn't be true . . . could it? Crazy as it was, it still felt more right than anything. "Well," she managed at last. "This is fascinating. Thank you, Doc."

"Any time."

She hung up, already headed for her car. One way or another, she had to know if Harlan felt the same connection, and how much he really knew about Detective Roth.

After the crews cleared out, Harlan was surprised to find the inside of the place wasn't that bad after all. It still needed a lot of work. But the front door was back up, the great room and the guest bedroom suite were serviceable, and the kitchen was more or less functional. At least he had a fridge – even if there wasn't any food in it.

He'd moved furniture and cleaned alongside the crews all day. It kept him busy enough not to think about Julie and how awful he'd acted toward her. How stupid he'd been. Well, he wasn't about to let the ghosts, or whatever it was about this place, dictate his life. He'd find her and apologize – and maybe try again for that date, if she'd ever speak to him again.

But right now he was filthy and exhausted, and would've happily dropped into bed and called it a night if he wasn't starving, too. He decided on a long, hot shower before anything else.

The first rumblings of thunder sounded in the distance as he undressed and got in. By the time he finished, it was coming down so hard that he could barely tell he'd shut off the water. He dried off and pulled on a pair of jeans, and tried to remember whether he'd seen any restaurants in town where he could grab something quick to eat. The drive down was going to suck.

Then he realized he'd never made arrangements to get his car back. So unless Flower Springs had a taxi service – or he decided to walk five or six miles in the downpour – he was stuck out here with no food until the crews came back in the morning. Or . . .

"Delivery," he said aloud. "They've got to have a pizza place or something." He headed back to the great room, fished the phone out of his jacket pocket, and unlocked the screen.

No service.

"Oh, come on!" He tossed the phone on the settee with a grunt. Of course, he didn't have cable or internet service hooked up yet, so he couldn't use his laptop either. With a sigh, he wandered toward the front door. "What's it gonna be, McKay?" he mumbled. "Walk, or starve?"

Just to see how bad it was out there, he opened the front door – and his heart stopped when he was greeted with the face of an angel. A soaking wet angel with one hand raised to knock, looking just as surprised as he felt.

Julie held a damp pizza box in the other arm, and a plastic bag with what looked like a six-pack looped on her elbow. "Um," she said. "I know you told me to leave and all, but . . . well, I did leave, actually. And then I decided to come back."

"Oh. Well." He couldn't help grinning. "Looks a little rainy," he said. "Do you want to come in?"

"No. I like it out here." She grinned back and shoved the pizza box at him. "Of course I want to come in," she said. "I figured you wouldn't have gotten around to stocking your kitchen yet, if you have one that works, so I brought dinner."

"You read my mind."

She gave him an odd look. "Really?"

"The food." He nodded at the pizza. "Not only are my cupboards bare, but my car's still in town and my phone isn't getting service. You're basically saving my life here."

"Well, you're welcome, then." She glanced back at the rain. "So . . . can I come in?"

"Absolutely." He stepped back to let her pass, and closed the door behind her. "You're soaked," he said. "Make yourself comfortable, and I'll go get you a towel."

Her mouth opened slightly, and she stared at him with wide eyes. "You're . . . not exactly dressed."

"Oh. Er, right." He turned away fast, headed for the coffee table and put the pizza box down. "Make that a towel and a shirt. Be right back."

He rushed out of the room and headed for the bathroom before he could do anything really stupid, like accidentally kiss her again. Not that it would be an accident this time. The things she made him feel were unbelievable. He'd spent a grand total of fifteen minutes with her so far, and already he wanted to spend the rest of his life with her.

Do that, and the rest of your life is going to be real damned short.

He froze halfway to grabbing a towel. Where did *that* come from? Like the hallucinations weren't bad enough, now he was having phantom thoughts.

"No more of that," he muttered aloud. With a quick stop in the bedroom to pull on a shirt, he went back to the great room and found Julie standing behind the red velvet settee, running a slow and appreciative hand along the polished wood of the top edge.

She looked up and smiled as he approached. "How did you find time to furniture shop today?" she said.

"I didn't." His brow furrowed. "This stuff is from my old place."

"Really? It all looks so . . . perfect here. Like it was made for this house."

Something deep in him shivered. Back in Atlanta, he'd bought furniture pieces whenever the mood struck him, not really caring how they went together or where he'd put them. Now, he looked around and realized she was right. It all belonged here.

He'd been subconsciously preparing for this move for a long time. Years before he ever laid eyes on the pictures of this place.

"Are you all right?"

"Sorry. I'm fine." He squeezed his eyes shut briefly, then held out the towel. "Here. You're . . ."

"Soaked." Her gaze met his, and he saw fire in her eyes. "You already said that."

This time the shudder went down to his bones. Like a man dreaming, he reached out and brushed the towel lightly against her cheek. "I'll help you," he murmured.

She responded with a slow nod, her eyes not leaving his.

Biting back a moan, he stepped closer and stroked her dripping hair with the soft terrycloth. He shook the towel loose behind her back, then brought his other arm up to enclose her while he gently rubbed away the remnants of the storm still raging outside.

Touching her only quickened the storm within.

"Harlan," she whispered. "Do you feel . . ."

He dropped the towel. Without thought, he cupped her chin and ran a thumb along her silky-soft lips, knowing every contour of them. Remembering. "Can I . . ."

"Yes."

The taste of her filled his mouth just before his lips met hers, sweet and warm and Southern sultry. His arms tightened around her as her hands slid over his waist and sent ripples of heat through him. She was everything – then, now, forever.

Then the haze shattered abruptly when a deep voice behind him said, "If I had a heart I might be touched."

Julie broke away with a gasp and stumbled back. "No. You can't be here."

"Son of a . . ." Fury poured into Harlan, hotter than fire. He whirled with a glare, ready to tell the detective exactly where he could shove those brass balls of his – and stopped cold when he saw what Julie must have realized right away.

There was Roth, standing not five feet from him in the middle of the room, gun at his side . . . and dry as a bone. The front door hadn't opened. And there were no wet footprints leading from the side entrance to the spot where he stood. As if he'd just appeared from thin air.

Roth grinned without a trace of humor. "Well, not *thin* air," he said. "It's actually pretty thick in Shade. All the brimstone, you see."

"You . . ."

"Read your mind?" The grin dropped like a stone. "I'm tired of chasing you," he said. "It's boring me. Time to come home now, McKay . . . or would you prefer Webster?"

Jagged pain coursed through Harlan's head. He could practically feel the fabric of his mind tearing as memories forced themselves up from the depths – from this life, and the one before, and before. She swam through them all, her clothing style regressing, her face unchanging. He felt death again and again . . . and the pain of betrayal that made death sweet by comparison.

He remembered Roth. His keeper, his tormentor, his personal demon. The bastard had barely tried to disguise himself – he'd only shortened his true name.

"Vassaroth." Harlan's voice rang out in accusation. "You promised I wouldn't remember this time."

Roth laughed – an awful sound, like endless nails on endless chalkboards. "I thought you were smarter than most mortals," he said. "Did you really expect a demon to keep a promise?"

"Harlan," Julie said in shaking tones. "Did he say what I think he said?"

He forced himself to focus through the thunder in his head. "It's all right," he said. "He can't hurt us."

"Can't I?" The demon's slow smile was more sinister than the grin. "Miss Walker," he said as he advanced toward them, drawing the gun from his holster. "It's time to do your job."

Once again, Harlan found himself unable to stop the inevitable. He could only watch as the woman he loved sent him back to hell.

Julie could barely breathe.

If Roth had shown her a glimpse of hell before, he wasn't holding anything back now. The world around her was a shimmering, blackened husk, zigzagged with fiery cracks that billowed smoke. The stench of sulfur and blood coated the air, and even Roth himself had warped with the landscape. He was taller, thicker. And his eyes gleamed red.

The only thing unchanged was Harlan.

"That damned rule." Roth's voice had deepened to a booming baritone that shivered through her gut. "Things would be so much easier if we could just kill you mortals. But this should be easy for you, Julie Walker. You righteous types are so much more eager for blood than the worst of your criminals have ever been." He held the gun toward her, butt first. "Kill him."

The words were a vicious imperative, and she was reaching for the weapon before she realized what happened. When her fingers brushed cold metal, she snatched her arm back. "No," she said. "This is not happening."

"Oh, but it is." Hot, dry flesh gripped her wrist, and the gun was shoved into her hand. "You have to kill him," Roth boomed. "He's evil. A ruthless threat to humanity, and only you can stop him. Send him to hell where he belongs."

Julie looked from the gun in her outstretched arm to Harlan. His features were pale and drawn, his blue eyes brimming with sorrow. He made no move to stop her or defend himself. "Please," he rasped. "Not again."

The cloud in her mind lifted instantly. She saw him . . . she *knew* him. And she knew what she'd done. Not once – over and over. She could always see the Dark and the Light. And every time they were pulled together, the Dark had already taken him. It was too late.

Tears spilled hot from her eyes, and the gun shook in her hand. "I went after you," she whispered. "Every time you went to hell, I was right behind you. I couldn't live without you." Her breath hitched. "I always wanted you to know that."

"This is all very touching." Roth grabbed her arm and steadied it. "Now end it."

"No." The bare whisper scratched from her throat. Fighting the urge to pull the trigger took everything she had. "Something's different this time," she said, a little stronger. "He's . . ."

Glowing. It wasn't the right word, but it was the closest she could come to the way Harlan seemed to dispel the Dark around him. He'd made mistakes. They both had, but every lifetime, they got a little better. A little closer to the Light.

With tremendous effort, she lowered her arm and let the gun fall to the floor. "I'm so sorry," she said. "Please . . . forgive me."

A hesitant smile touched his lips. "Only if you forgive me."

"I do."

A sound like a thunderclap filled the room, and the darkness vanished. "Mortals," Roth spat. "You were so much more tolerable before the Crucifixion. Your ancestors could really hold a grudge, you know."

Julie stared at him. "What are you talking about?"

"Love. *Forgiveness.*" The demon sneered. "Now I have to wait for you to tarnish your souls again. And Lucifer knows how many lifetimes *that* will take."

"So . . ."

"You're off the hook. For now. And since you actually managed to make me feel just a sliver of guilt over that whole broken promise thing, I suppose I can give you this." Roth sighed. "It wasn't your fault, McKay. I influenced one of the actual detectives to suppress the record of the man you sold that gun to. Enjoy your clear conscience while you can."

Harlan raised an eyebrow. "Are you allowed to be nice?"

"Believe me, my motivations were entirely selfish." Roth took a step back. "Zephron is going to gloat about this for centuries, the angelic bastard," he said. "But when you fall, I'll be waiting."

In a blink, he was gone.

Julie let out an explosive breath. "That was—"

Hot, hard lips pressed against hers, cutting off whatever she'd been about to say. She couldn't remember what it was. Every inch of her was focused on Harlan, and the sensations that swirled through her blood at his touch.

It was an eternity before he drew back. "We're still here," he rasped. "Both of us."

"Yeah. I'm probably stuck here until it stops raining. I don't have mud tires, and your driveway is all dirt." She was babbling. She didn't care.

"Stay the night." He kissed her again. "Stay forever. Marry me."

"Right now?"

"Before he comes back."

She laughed. "Let's start with the night. We have a few lifetimes, remember?"

"I don't want to wait that long."

Butterflies of anticipation shivered in her stomach. This time, the tinge of sadness was gone. "Neither do I," she said.

As they walked hand in hand toward the bedroom, the storm blew over as fast as it had come in – and the light of the stars banished the dark clouds from the sky.

SWEET THE STING

Dianne Sylvan

You must see the Beekeeper.

I first hear the whispers in Dallas. I'm in the middle of
nowhere, in what might as well be a circus tent whose
flaps are snapping back and forth in the wind, which
brings in bursts of dust from the drought-abraded plains.
There are three-dozen people packed into that tent,
bodies braising in the 97-degree heat, but I'm the only
one who seems to notice how miserable we all are.
Everyone else is focused on the man up at the podium
and his thundering voice.

I don't have to look at him to know what I'd see. Balding,
a little paunchy, with wild eyes and a pasty complexion.
He'll be wearing a suit, maybe with the jacket off and the
sleeves rolled up to emphasize he's an ordinary man, even
while everything else about him tells another story.

For weeks now I've followed one story and another, one
flyer after another. Most of these men set up shop outside
of a small town for a few months before local law enforcement decides they're a menace and they vanish to reappear
one county over. They leave behind a trail of awed, hushed
voices and tales so fantastical they make even my own cyni-
cal heart clench with what I know must be hope.

I join the line snaking up toward the podium. I have no
faith, but I'm willing to find some. I don't believe in this
crap, but I need it desperately . . . and what besides desperation would send a college graduate into the land of
barbecue and brimstone looking for something as prosaic
as a miracle?

I watch them with my heart pounding. One by one, he puts his hands on their heads, or chests, or whatever, and his voice rises over the noise of the crowd and the clichéd organ music. Up to a minute later, the person falls to the ground, usually twitching violently, only to stand back up – no, *leap* back up, renewed, claiming this pain is gone or that the leg can suddenly move again after twenty years of lameness. Wheelchairs are pushed away, canes cast aside.

Every time it seems I get closer to the front of the line, only to have the Reverend Brother Something-or-Other fall back into the waiting arms of one of his attendants, usually his wife, the last of his holy load blown on the person right in front of me.

Later, in the only coffee shop in town, I choke down a handful of opiates and hold my mug in cold hands. The coffee in these places is always fantastic, as is the lemon meringue pie. That's one thing about small-town Texas I've missed: the food.

Someone joins me at the bar. "I saw you out at the Reverend's place," she says. She has a beautiful drawl – almost elegant, even though it's not the upper-crust variety you find in Atlanta.

I look over. A pretty young woman, maybe twenty-five, dishwater-blonde hair pulled back, floral dress. Church clothes. She's got sparkling hazel eyes and freckles.

"Yeah," I say.

"My cousin got to the front of the line once. Took care of his legs. The doctors said he'd never walk again."

"They always say that, don't they?"

She smiles. "Are you gonna try again tomorrow?"

"I have to. I have to keep trying." I stir sugar into my cup absently. "I've been to half a dozen of these guys and none of them ever has time for me. One of them has to."

The usual response is to ask what's wrong with me. This girl doesn't. She looks around, leans a little closer. "You know, I heard about somebody down Austin way . . . somebody people go to when nothing else works."

"Another faith healer?" Maybe that's why I can't get through to them. I'm so damned sick of Jesus and the lepers, of the Kingdom of Heaven. Western medicine may be woefully inadequate in some respects but at least it doesn't demand belief in fairy tales. I can practically hear my Sunday school teacher asking why God would help someone who looked down her nose at Him . . . but I can also hear my grandmother saying Jesus would heal anyone, without prejudice. You catch more flies with honey, after all.

"No . . ." the girl is saying quietly. "This one isn't a preacher. In fact some people say his power comes from the devil."

Maybe the devil heals without prejudice too. "What's his name?"

"I don't know," she says. There's a crowd of men I recognize from the tent coming into the coffee shop, so her words become hurried, and just before she hops off her stool to leave she says, "They call him the Beekeeper."

It takes weeks to find out more. I find hints on the internet, but nothing more than rumor, and not much more than what the girl told me already. There are a few accounts of people going to the Beekeeper on death's door and leaving the picture of health.

Something about this vague idea pulls at me as I lie awake in one motel bed after another, tears leaking from my eyes from the pain, trying to keep my mind fixed on something besides the slow decay of my body. Six months, they said. I've wasted half of that looking for a free pass back to the land of the living. What else could I have done with all that time? I could have been to Europe. I could have had all sorts of sex. I could have had all sorts of sex in Europe.

I am about to give up when one afternoon in the library of a suburb of Austin I find a book of local legends produced by a tiny publisher whose doors had closed years ago. There are all sorts of ghosts and cryptids in Texas, but buried in amongst the tales is a chapter on miracle workers, and, in that chapter, a few paragraphs that make my heart hurl itself from one side of my ribcage to the other.

The author claims that the story of the Beekeeper is what inspired him to write the book; almost nothing was known about him outside this one area of Texas, but within that region everyone claimed to know someone who knew someone who had been to him. There was a debate over what exactly he was – a man, a demon, some sort of angel?

Two things are certain, the author says: one, when you find the house on the edge of town, nestled in the forest's hemline like a child in its mother's skirts, you knock on the door and wait, sometimes for hours. If you bring an offering of fresh flowers, you'll be seen sooner. And two, the people who go into that house come back healed, yes, but they also come back . . . different. The book isn't more specific than that.

It does however give the town where the author is from: Frisch, Texas. As the girl in the coffee shop said, it's a small town to the west of Austin. Six thousand people, not a single Starbucks. Just like where I came from.

By the time I get to the motel in Frisch I'm so tired I fall onto the bed with my clothes still on and don't move for twelve hours. That happens to me more and more as I get closer to the big deadline. Pretty soon, the doctors said, I should be blacking out from the pain, and come crawling back to them for help.

Not yet. As weary as I am, as heartsick as I am under my Strong Southern Woman bravado, I want so badly to give up and just accept the inevitable, spend the last few weeks I have on this Earth out of my mind on morphine. But first . . . first I have to try this. Just this last phantom to chase.

Again I find myself in the library. I find a copy of the book and take it to the librarian to ask if she can tell me how to find the author.

But he's been dead for three years.

"Well, do you know anything about the stories in the book?" I ask.

The librarian, a heavyset woman in her fifties with curly hair and knowing eyes, looks me over a second before saying, "You mean you're looking for the Beekeeper."

My fingers clench the book so tightly they shake. "Yes." I

had a whole story rehearsed about research for the University of Texas, but she would see right through me, and I can't muster the conviction to stand behind a lie.

"Well, you know, Bill Myer was a folklorist, not a historian," the librarian replies. "He didn't really believe in all those ghosts and goblins."

"This one's real," I say, louder than I should, given where I am. "It has to be real."

"You don't strike me as much of a believer," she points out, politely ignoring that I might become hysterical any moment. "And you don't strike me as a small-town girl. How did Bill's old book get you here?"

I don't know how to explain it. "I just . . . I'm looking for a healer. Not a doctor, a healer. None of the other ones I've found has wanted to help me."

"And you think the Beekeeper might."

"I don't know. I have to ask."

She's silent for a moment, and in the meantime a kid comes up to check out a huge stack of books, so I fall back and wait, holding Bill's old book against my chest like a plate of armor. The answer has to be here.

Finally, she looks back over at me and I return to the circulation desk.

"You know, you're the first pretty young woman I've ever seen looking for him," she says. "It's usually sick old men or mamas with ailing babies."

"Does that mean I'm special?" I ask weakly.

She looks me over again. "Maybe." She continues with, "He's not what you think, you know. Whatever you need fixed, there'll be a price."

"Unless it's higher than my life, I'll pay it."

"What if it is?"

I don't understand the question, and I don't pretend to. "Can you tell me how to find him?"

Another pause. Then, "If you take the main street out of town, about five miles out you'll see a little turn-off called Apia Road. It comes up quick, so watch for it. You'll have to park your car just inside the fence – the rest of the way you'll need to walk."

"Is there anything else you can tell me about him? Anything else I should know?"

She gives me the oddest look. "Just do me a favor. Tell him nine makes us even."

Before I really know what I'm doing, I am standing on the Beekeeper's front porch, clutching a bunch of something purple the woman at the florist's assured me are native to the area and not the usual bouquet bloom. I'm hoping that being memorable will help, and the purple things, whose name completely slipped out of my mind on the drive over here, are supposed to smell amazing.

I can't smell them. My sense of smell has degraded over the last few months. I can still smell coffee, roofing tar, skunk and gasoline. Delicate scents like flowers have left me completely. Most of my favorite foods are nothing more than a memory. I miss roses, and soap. I miss that fire-and-wax smell when you blow out a candle.

They come back different, the book said. I don't care. I knock on the door and wait.

And wait.

To stave off panic, I look around. The house is small and very old. Vines cover entire walls, the woods trying to reclaim their land one tendril at a time. The grass around the house is tall, heavy with wildflowers, but the brick path I'd followed from the road isn't overgrown at all. Huge oaks stand sentinel over the house, so the sunlight is dappled and muted. The wind in the leaves and grass sounds almost like the ocean. Everything is soft, drowsy, even the flight of a few butterflies flitting over the flowers.

I feel something on my hand, and look down to see a honeybee perching on my finger. A city girl's automatic fear hits me and I almost swat it away, but at the last possible second my poor battered brain reminds me that I am here to see someone called the Beekeeper, and starting things off by killing a bee might not be wise.

The bee looks up at me. I swear it does. We stare at each other for a second.

"Go tell your friend someone's at the door," I whisper to it.

The bee flies away.

Not five minutes later, I hear something moving in the house.

I turn back to the door and wait, heart pounding.

The locks clank back, the door shudders slightly under the effort required to open it. A gap of a few inches opens up.

A deep green eye fixes on mine, looking up at me. "Yes?"

I almost don't hear the voice. "Um, I must see the Beekeeper," I say, my own voice hushed as well, out of some instinct I can't name. "I need his help."

The door opens a little further, and I get my first surprise.

A little girl no more than ten years old stares up at me through big, green eyes. Her dark ash-brown hair is working its way out of a braid that goes all the way down her back. She is barefoot, and her skin is baked nut brown from the sun, the way mine always used to be during summers. My grandmother lived in a house on the outstretched palm of the woods, and I spent long days running through grass and climbing trees.

The similarity ends there, however, for I don't think my eyes ever looked like hers. She's staring at me unnervingly, almost through me, like she can see all the pretense and the lies I've told myself about how scared I really am.

I hold out the flowers wordlessly.

She takes them wordlessly.

Then she gestures for me to follow her into the house.

Serial killers. Rapists. Axe murderers. All the reasons I shouldn't go in begin to clamor in my head. I ignore them – I have to. But I know once I step over the threshold there's no going back.

The house is surprisingly empty. The few furnishings in the living room are covered in white sheets against the dust. Some of the vines from outside have found cracks in the window casings and crept in, and there are cracked shutters and panes that let in a flood of that same golden light from the yard.

The girl takes the flowers into the kitchen, one of the few rooms that feels like it's been occupied recently. There's a large vase sitting in the middle of a huge, heavy table; it's full of dead flowers. She plucks them out and replaces them with mine, adding water from the tap with a cup. She brings the dead stems with us as she leads me on toward the back door.

"Do you live here?" I cringe – my voice is cracked and blasphemously loud.

She pauses, turns to look at me. That's when I notice there's a bee on her shoulder, just sitting there like it's going for a ride. I wonder if it's the same bee I talked to on the porch.

"Sometimes," she says. Her voice is much older than she looks. It's like she's a hundred years old, walking around in a young body with bare feet and a grass-stained eyelet dress.

"Are you the Beekeeper's little helper?" I ask.

She tilts her head to the right slightly. "I'm his sister."

"Oh."

She is, apparently, done with the conversation, and turns to walk again. I take the hint and don't say anything until we've left the house, emerging onto a winding path just like the one that had led me here, old red brick meandering downhill through tall grass and into the trees. The girl tosses the dead flower stems into the underbrush. I guess birds will like them for nest building.

Once again the sleepy afternoon soothes the edges of my mind, and I fall into a sort of trance, walking deeper into the woods. I see deer trails cutting through the underbrush, hear a squirrel chattering in vociferous complaint at my presence. I wish that I could smell the dirt, the flowers, decaying wood. The memory of all those things is over-whelming. I have to stop and put my hands on my head – dizziness and pain hit me at the same time.

For the first time the girl shows a hint of actual human emotion. "Are you okay?"

I nod and try to get myself together.

"You want to live," she says.

"Everybody wants to live," I murmur.

"Then why should he help you?"

The question shakes me back to reality. "Maybe he shouldn't," I say. "Maybe other people deserve it more."

She shrugs. "Are you nice?"

I smile. "No. I'm a mean old lady."

For a second, she looks like a little girl – a tiny giggle escapes her. She turns and keeps walking.

We round a curve in the trail before I become aware that I can hear something. I start to feel like I'm being watched. There's a faint hum in the air growing louder and louder as we walk, and I get the sense of the entire forest turning its eyes on me.

Something touches my arm. I look down and see another bee. There's another on my shirt, and I hear buzzing around my head. Again I have to fight not to panic.

"They won't hurt you," the little girl says. I look down and gasp: there are dozens of bees on her, a few walking around on her arms but most of them just sitting still like the ones on me. "They just want to live too."

The shadows covering the path begin to give way, the trees thinning until we reach a small clearing. The humming – buzzing – is loud now, and I immediately see why. The clearing is full of beehives.

There are ten, in two rows: sturdy white boxes that look like filing cabinets. Unlike the house, the hives show no sign of disrepair. They are freshly painted, meticulously maintained.

The air is full of bees, but they seem to avoid me almost entirely. The ones that have landed on me flit away after a moment and apparently tell the rest that I'm not a threat. The little girl, however, is still playing bee chauffeur.

Slowly, she raises her arm and extends her finger, indicating the far side of the clearing.

That's when I see the other hives. There are three of them under the outmost hanging branches of the tree, and there's someone over there, moving among them.

"These are the ones that give us regular honey," the girl says. "We sell what we don't eat to a store in the next county."

"All you eat is honey?" I ask, teasing.

She fixes her big eyes on me. "That's all we need."

I decide it's best not to ask. "And those three hives?"

"Go and see."

I approach one step at a time. I try to focus on something less terrifying than what I might be about to meet. I think about the bees, how the ones landing on us were infertile females who, this time of year, would only live for a few weeks until dropping from their labors. I think about how most of the time a bee would die from stinging. Her stinger has its own musculature that will continue pumping venom after being detached, but since their stingers are barbed, "detached" is more like "having your lower gastrointestinal tract ripped out". I couldn't remember how I knew that – a documentary, maybe?

I think about how the male bees are only useful for mating. I'd have to agree with the bees there – most of the males I'd known hadn't been good for much else either. For the first time in a long time I think about Will, the supposed love of my life, whom I caught in the shower with our neighbor two days after my diagnosis. Drone bees die because they literally shag themselves to death – the convulsions kill them. Would that have been appropriate for Will, or too enjoyable a death? It was better than the one I was going to get.

Thinking about my love life, however, is less appealing than thinking about where I am now, so I banish the thoughts and pull my attention back to the present. I am almost across the clearing now, and the hum of the bees has become almost relaxing, white noise like an ocean or the wind in the trees above.

I am about fifteen feet away when the figure at the hives turns to look at me.

I stop.

"Hello." I feel like there is some language I should be speaking other than English, but I don't know it yet. I don't know how to speak bee. I have to rely on clumsy and overloud words.

There are, however, no words for what I'm looking at. At least, not words that suffice.

A young man, no older than myself, is watching me, his eyes the same dark leaf green as the little girl's. Indeed they have more than a passing resemblance. Both have high cheekbones, wide eyes, tanned skin. Both have that same dusty brown hair. Both are slender and have a strange, wild grace.

I was expecting an old man – a seer, a sage. Bearded, wrinkly maybe. Scraggly like one of the sadhus of India who leave society and live as homeless beggars in the name of their gods.

He is not that.

My grandmother would have called him "Fae". She was full of stories about the hidden world in the woods – ghost lights that called travelers away from the path and into darkness; tree spirits whose roots tangled in your hair; shape-shifters who took the form of wolves, deer, birds. Were there bee spirits too? I don't remember her saying so.

His scrutiny makes me feel exposed, and I wrap my arms around my chest. I wish he were looking at me flirtatiously, even covetously – that I would understand. Back when I wasn't a wraith and I still had long hair I was damn near gorgeous. The first round of chemo, the one that had made me realize I'd rather drop dead, had destroyed that. So had not being able to properly taste my food.

He continues to watch me, but his hands are occupied, and I see that one of his arms is inside the first hive; its lid is propped up nearby. He withdraws his arm, revealing it covered nearly solid with bees. He holds on to a small jar.

He looks away from me long enough to murmur something to the bees, who immediately take wing en masse and pour back into the hive. When the last of them has done so, he carefully screws a lid onto the jar and then replaces the cover of the hive.

"You're the Beekeeper?" I ask. Even as the words leave my mouth I want the ground to swallow me. Who else would he be, the Plumber?

A faint smile touches his lips. Apparently the same thought crosses his mind. "Yes."

Just like the little girl's, his voice is quiet, nearly a whisper. That single syllable hits me between the eyes but sinks warmly down into my hips. How long has it been since I felt any actual interest in another person and not just in my own pain and fear?

"I heard . . . I mean, they say . . . they say you can heal people."

He doesn't reply, merely waits.

"I need help," I say. "I'm . . . I'm dying."

His eyes travel from my face down to my feet, then back up again. "Yes."

"Can you help me?"

He looks back up into my eyes. "Why?"

I think about what I told the girl. "I don't know," I say. And I don't. Why do I deserve a miracle when millions of other people don't? Hundreds of people will die today. We all will eventually. Maybe he'll heal me now, but what good will that do in fifty years? Will I have earned it? Done something with myself? Or will I go back into my little normal world, never quite feeling like I spoke the language there either?

I remember that day I was driving home from the oncologist. I had to pull over – I couldn't see the road around my ragged sobs. I sat in my car on the side of the road for nearly an hour, screaming, crying. Since then I had shoved that feeling away. I didn't have time to cry. I was on a quest, a quest for the impossible.

I feel weak again like I did that afternoon. I'm so tired of doing this alone.

Still, I fight not to cry in front of this strange, and strangely beautiful, man. I wipe my eyes and run my hands back through the inch of hair that's grown back.

When I look back up I nearly jump. While I've been fidgeting he's come closer. He walks slowly around me, evaluating something. My worthiness maybe? My condition? Again his gaze is penetrating, and I feel laid bare.

Finally, when he returns to where he started, he holds out the jar in his hand: amber glass, with a handwritten label. Based on what he'd been doing when I arrived, my guess is it's honey.

I take the jar gingerly. The edge of my hand touches his, and a weird humming runs through me – a low vibration, just like the bees.

"Take one tablespoon per day for nine days," I read. "Then return for further treatment."

I want to yell that it's going to take more than honey to save me, that he must be out of his mind, that this is insane and I'm leaving. But after standing in circus tents for weeks watching people fall down and flail until Jesus made them walk again, I can do nothing but accept whatever this is at face value. I've been prescribed a jar of honey. Okay.

Apparently done with me for the day, the Beekeeper turns back to the hives, and the little girl takes my hand and leads me back the way we came.

I hadn't anticipated staying in Frisch for over a week, and am at a loss for what to do with myself. I'm a writer, so my job can travel with me, but to say I felt uninspired is an understatement. I haven't put a word on paper in weeks.

I explore the town in less than a day. Frisch is the sort of place that people romanticize when talking about small-town life, and it is a nice town – everyone is friendly, even to the stranger wandering around in a daze barely speaking. The beautification committee keeps the historic shops and other businesses along the main road in fantastic shape. But it's also the sort of place some people will do anything to escape. I'd been one of those people as a teenager. I was too depressive, too weird. I loved my family but I could never shake the feeling I'd been an egg dropped into another bird's nest.

That feeling has been a step behind me my entire life. I was never really unhappy before, but I've always felt a second out of synch, like if I turned my head too quickly I'd see an entirely different life playing out – my real life, going on without me.

The first night, sitting down in the motel room's chair at the Formica table, I stare at the jar for a long time before opening it. I don't know how exact I have to be. I have a bottle of Nyquil in my suitcase, so I pour the honey into the dosage cup with its graduated markings for one, two and three tablespoons.

The honey is dark, almost red. I hold it up to the light and admire it for a while. Then, I knock it back like a whiskey shot, or at least I try to. It runs so slowly that I end up sitting there like an idiot, with it hovering over my mouth, for a couple of minutes.

I expect cloying sweetness, but it tastes as dark as it looks, almost like molasses. My stomach lurches. It tastes more intense than anything has in months. I end up licking the inside of the cup until no more is left, and wishing I had a big plate of pancakes to pour the rest on.

Two days later, I have an episode. They've happened more and more frequently as things have progressed. First comes dizziness, then comes pain, intensifying until I can knock myself out with painkillers. Once or twice I've had seizures. When that happens I can't see, can't hear, and the fear is worse than the pain. Unconsciousness is the only remedy. At least, the only one besides death.

I get back to the motel and collapse, groping for the bottle of pills in my bag. As I'm trying to get a glass of water with hands gone uncooperative, I bump the honey jar with my elbow and in my mad state become determined to take my nightly dose. My vision is spotty and blurry, but I can remember how much to pour into the dosage cup, and suck the dark syrup down while I can still swallow.

Then I pass out.

I wake up free of pain. I didn't take any pills, only the honey, but the agony has ceased anyway. Was it the honey, or a coincidence? I don't know how to tell.

Midway through the week I return to the library. The woman I'd talked to before is there again. This time I notice her name tag says "Molly".

When she sees me, she doesn't look surprised that I'm still in town. I hover near the circulation desk until the knot of patrons she's tending to has gone.

"Thank you for the directions," I tell her.

She sighs. "So he agreed to help you."

"I don't know – I guess. All I have so far is a jar of honey."

Something unpleasant flickered in her eyes. "Oh."

"Does this happen often?"

"No, not often. There aren't that many people who believe he exists. And even fewer who'd be fool enough to go to him."

"Why not? If he's such a miracle worker. What's the price?"

Molly frowns. "I honestly don't know," she says. Whatever it is, she thinks it's bad, but she can't be more certain than that.

"So there's not a basement full of skeletons or anything like that?"

"Not that I know of. Everyone I've ever known who went in came back out again. But they don't come out the same. Just be careful."

Her words are echoing as I take the path back to the house at the end of the nine days. She's right, of course; I have no reason to trust this guy or believe he has good intentions, and I have no idea what the consequences of this could be. But what do I have to lose?

It's a cloudy day, the wind grown still ahead of a storm. Everything feels ominous as I wait on the porch. There have been a few brief showers and the air is thick with the scent of rain on dry earth.

I'm inhaling the smell with my eyes shut when the door opens. This time it's not the little girl but her brother who answers.

In nine days the power of his presence had worn off, but it comes roaring back nearly hard enough to knock me over. I don't know if it's magic or just charisma, but I have twin urges: to run screaming, or to pin him against the wall and kiss him. My body can't decide which urge to give in to, and I waver on my feet, weak.

Hands take my arms and hold me up. I gasp and stare at him, less than a foot away. A chord of scents – herbs, dark earth, beeswax.

I realize suddenly that I can smell him – just as I could smell the rain a moment ago, out of nowhere after weeks of nothing. This time my knees give out completely and I fall against him hard.

He doesn't seem surprised, but holds me up, and I draw in as much of that scent as I can, gulping it into my lungs.

After letting me get my feet back, he guides me into the house, this time into the kitchen where he sits me down on a bar stool. I am holding the empty honey jar in my hands and staring at it. Several minutes must pass, because a cup of tea slides into my view.

"Thanks," I say vaguely and hand over the jar.

I don't know how to be around someone who doesn't talk. I want to ask a thousand questions but I know I won't get answers. What do we do then, stare at each other?

The house creaks around us. I take in the room with curiosity. It's not exactly cosy, but has a warmth to it I wouldn't have expected. The flowers I brought last week are still in the vase, still alive. In fact, they don't look like they've wilted at all.

The house is old and doesn't look long for this world, but it's clean.

He's been sitting there watching me, and it's driving me crazy. "Where's your sister?" I venture.

A pause, then: "With the bees."

"What's her name?"

Green eyes lower to his cup, then lift back up to mine. "Melissa."

"What about yours?"

I'm not sure if he's deciding whether to tell me, or deciding what name to give. "Kieran."

I start to ask for a last name, but before I can, he says, "Mead."

I nod slowly. "Beekeeping isn't a very common career for young men these days."

A slight smile. "It's a family business."

He intercepts the conversation before I can come up with another question. "You have a brain tumor."

I sit back. "How . . . how did you know?"

"You have, perhaps, three more months to live."

I nodded. I had been trying not to think about the math,

but there it is. "Yeah. I won't see this Christmas. Unless you can help me." I try to pick up my teacup again but my hands are shaking so hard it rattles on the saucer.

A hand closes gently over mine, stilling the tremor. I stare down at his fingers. He turns my hand over, palm up, and runs a finger down my lifeline. I get another tremor, but this time through my entire body.

I did safe things before. My life was not exciting or notable. I worked, I shopped, I had drinks with friends, I dated uninteresting men. I certainly would never have gotten the tickle from a stranger who stuck his hand in a beehive without gloves and has barely spoken a full sentence to me.

"You're not ready," he murmurs, continuing to stroke my palm. "Not yet."

"What do you mean?" My mouth is dry, but that's the only thing that is.

Our eyes meet. Next thing I know, there's a jar in my hand. I look down and see a container slightly larger than the last one, with similar instructions, but on the fourth day I'm supposed to double my dosage. Without really thinking about it I open the jar; I can tell the honey inside is different. "Why the change?"

"It's from a different hive," he replies. "Every hive's honey is subtly different. Even when the bees harvest from the same fields. Most of the time it doesn't matter but this work is delicate. We have to be precise."

I would ask for clarification but he's still touching my hand and my command of the English language has unfortunately flatlined.

Shortly thereafter, before I walk back to my car, he takes my hand again and kisses it.

I wander up the path in the gathering dusk like a sleepwalker, holding the new jar with one hand and pressing the other to my chest.

This jar is definitely not the same. The honey is cloudy, and it separates after sitting. I notice that on the label it says I'm supposed to stir it before consuming. The thicker layer looks like condensed milk, and I have the distinct feeling I shouldn't taste it on its own. Even mixed together it's not the tastiest thing. I miss the dark amber honey from last week, and don't end up licking the cup.

Still, after a couple of days it grows on me. By the time I have to double the dose, I'm almost looking forward to it.

I'm feeling better, as well. It could very easily be a placebo effect, but who cares? Better is better. I have more energy and, looking at myself in the motel mirror, I don't feel as horrified. For months I've been chasing my miracle, merely existing, but I finally feel a little bit alive again.

To my dismay, when I return to the house, I am met not by the Beekeeper himself but by Melissa and her big strange eyes. Her brother, she says, is busy, but she takes my empty jar and gives me a new one. Seven days, she tells me, then come back.

It's less time than before, which pleases me. I have been thinking about him a lot this past week. Aside from being garden-variety attracted to him, I keep wondering, questioning. I think about writing a story about him. Not a biography or collection of legends, but almost a fairy tale. A man and his sister living in the woods with all those bees. How had they come to be there? If it really is a family business, where is the family? Is it the solitude that makes them so weird? Constant exposure to bee stings? I long to really know them both.

I've never been all that much on children, but Melissa is hardly a normal child. I want to hear her story, to know how she feels about her unusual life. Does she go to school? Does she have friends – human friends? If she doesn't go to school, why hasn't Child Protective Services snatched her?

I start writing down all of these questions and filling in what little I know of the answers. While I'm trying to pass the week, I ask around, but everyone in Frisch is tight-lipped about the Mead family. One older gentleman claims he knew the father, but that father and mother both had "up and left" one day. No one has any direct knowledge of the two younger Meads, and no one can give me the name of any of their clients. No one even knows where they sell what Melissa called the "regular honey".

I am beginning to think they are figments of my imagination.

The only reassurance I have is the honey itself, although once again, it's different – there's almost none of the sweet honey from the first week, almost all the milky substance that turns out to be bitter, yet again strangely compelling. It coats my tongue and makes me gag the first night, and I have to wash it down with an enormous Coke, but after that it's not so bad.

Finally, finally, the jar is empty, and I'm ready. I pull up to the path and climb out of the car, stretching, enjoying the fragrant summer air and the light wind causing a pattering noise from the trees that sounds like they're applauding Nature's job well done. I grab my bag and head toward the house.

Funny, I don't remember bringing my bag. I'd left my bigger suitcase at the motel, but had packed my really valuable things and some clothes. I shrug. Not a big deal.

Melissa answers the door. This time, when she sees me she actually smiles. The expression is almost alarming. It's so rare, but it makes her haunting eyes look sunny and, for once, her age.

She leads me through the house but stops at the door. "At the hives," she says. She takes my bag. "I'm not to go down there today. You know the way."

I do.

I've only been to the hives once, but the sight of them is comforting, as is the chorus of buzzing. The minute I enter the clearing the bees begin to land on me – five, ten, dozens. They don't stay long, but the oh-so-light touch of their tiny feet and the vibration of their little bodies is, I imagine, their way of saying hello, of declaring me welcome in their parlor.

This way, they seem to say. I walk along the closest row of hives to the three that stand apart. It occurs to me that each of the three jars I'd been given might have come from each one of these hives.

Their music is making me feel sleepy, a little drunk. I stand there enjoying it for a moment, eyes closed.

A hand takes mine.

I open my eyes. We stare at each other. There's nothing I can think to say right now, nothing either of us needs to say.

Just inside the edge of the woods is a sheltered little area curtained with vines – honeysuckle, no surprise. Their scent is heady and sweet, and it surrounds me as I sink into the bower and his mouth finds mine.

Everything is slow and delirious, not quite real and yet completely crystal clear. I feel the cool shade on my skin, balancing the racing heat of one body merging with another. I can hear the trees above, and my own panting little cries, and his breath in my ear, and, underneath it all, the bees, distant but under my skin.

He kisses my throat, and a second later I feel a sharp pain. I cry out and start to struggle, but it's gone as quickly as it came. When he looks down into my face again I notice a smear of blood on his lip.

Before I can really make sense of the fact that he bit me, and that it didn't feel like any other love bite I'd ever been given, it feels like something scalding hot is rushing through my veins, searing me inside like acid. The pain is as intense as my episodes, but spread through my whole body, and I go rigid, back arching, and scream.

"Be still," I hear him murmur with a kiss on my ear. "Try to relax."

I remember a feeling like this, when I was a kid, but only a thousandth of this agony. I'd been out in the woods and . . . been . . .

Stung by a bee.

My body is full of venom, and it should be killing me, but he moves harder against me, and soon one kind of scream gives way to another. I'm still in agony, but I no longer care. My veins run with venom, but my flesh is suffused with honey.

I feel a hand gently opening my mouth, and sticky sweetness drips in – the dark amber again. I take it in greedily. Melissa's voice echoes in my mind: *That's all we need.*

He kisses my honeyed lips, and the taste mingles in both our mouths. I am sticky and sweaty and have leaves in places no one should ever have leaves, and a man I barely know just poisoned me, and I never, ever want to leave this bed.

We stay there in the bower until the night has cast its veil over the forest. I listen to the music of the hives and, as the hours pass, I begin to understand their song. Hundreds of thousands of voices, all joined together to create what we needed to survive. And in return, these little creatures, a sacred line unbroken for thousands of years, are protected, the survival of their race assured. We care for each other.

I can hear them, I can understand them, and moreover I can feel them. The great unity of a hive, all those cells of a single body, connected to me, to us, to the Earth herself. No one could ever feel alone with a family this big.

I turn over to face him. When I speak my voice has become as quiet and feathery as a bee's. "You're not going to drop dead now, are you?"

He smiles. It's a real smile, like Melissa's earlier, and it makes me feel warm, alive. "We are still human . . . mostly."

"Your parents hived off, didn't they?"

"Yes. As you and I might one day, or even Melissa, if she chooses to become a queen and finds a suitable mate."

"So I'm a queen." I shake my head, smiling. "This is utterly insane, you know." A thought arises. "And all those people who say you healed them . . ."

"Some received honey and went on their way. Some joined us. There have been other drones here over the years. The males can only sting once; the women once, unless they become a queen and can then sting as often as they need to in order to keep our family going. I'm the last male in our line, at least for now."

"Does that mean I have to have lots of babies?"

At the unease in my face, he chuckles. "You don't *have* to do anything. And each pair of us may have one, perhaps two children the old-fashioned way, but to keep the gene pool healthy, we have to make the rest from outsiders."

He draws me into his arms and begins kissing me, hands curving around my hips. "How did you know?" I ask softly. "How did you pick me?"

"I didn't. They did. But I agreed."

"And what if I'd said no?"

His green eyes are practically glowing in the moonlight. "You would have gone your way, gone back to normal life, and always wondered what you had missed by leaving."

"Molly," I say abruptly. He raises an eyebrow. "The librarian. She said to tell you nine made you even. What did that mean?"

"She didn't mean me, she meant the family. We nearly died out a generation ago. When Molly's daughter was on the verge of death, my mother went into town and healed her at great risk to us all. They struck a bargain that Molly would help nine people find us, in the hope that the hives might choose at least a couple to join us."

"I have the bees to thank for this then," I say, shifting so I'm underneath him, biting his neck lightly in the same place he'd bitten mine. Would my bite feel like a sting to an outsider now? One day would I feel called to pass venom on to a normal human, feed her honey? "Like you said, they picked me."

I know I will offer that sweet sting when I need to. There are only three of us. I don't know all the rules, but I know three isn't enough for the number of hives we have. I'll be careful whom to trust, whom to declare worthy. Only a few people deserve such a gift.

He's smiling, as if he knows where my thoughts are headed. "Of course they picked you," he says, kissing me softly, reverently, on the lips. "They know a queen when they see one."

WYLDE MAGIC

Erin Kellison

Chapter One

Sergeant Evangeline Renard's gaze lingered a moment on the mud-splattered Maryland license plates of an unfamiliar Chevy truck. Heavy tools and buckets had been dumped in the back, along with random building debris.

Contractor?

Unlikely. The Wyldes hadn't had that kind of money for a long time.

Had they sold the old family home at last?

Huh. She hadn't heard a thing.

An odd pang of loss made her frown, but she proceeded up the porch stairs. Like the tall Corinthian columns, the large double doors of the plantation's main residence had once been grand, though the paint had now worn to dusty off-white specks stuck in the wood grains. There being no knocker or bell button, she rapped sharply. The thickness of the door muted the sound of her knuckles.

She gave the ghosts a minute to stir.

While she waited, wind hissed through the surrounding oak trees, and branches did a clacking bone-dance that was out of place in the afternoon summer steam which made the vegetation dark, fragrant and lush green. The humidity clung to her skin like a second set of clothes, but as she'd been born to it, she put it out of her mind. The house itself was void of sound – a dense, impenetrable stillness, full of sad history and dissolution.

She held her breath a few more moments. No answer.

She almost took herself down the front porch steps to her police SUV – it'd been silly to come, she knew that – but, on instinct, leaned in to knock again, this time with the flat of her hand. Harder.

Soon one of the doors cracked, and then opened partway. In the tall, dark rectangle it made stood the younger Wylde brother, Jackson, also tall and dark.

Jack. Back in town.

Well, wasn't this interesting.

A week's worth of beard crowded the lower half of his face, but his amber eyes were as arresting as always. Dirty jeans said he was still poor, or that he didn't care if he looked poor even though she knew for a fact that he now had a few university degrees tucked in his pocket. His T-shirt reconfirmed her best teenage fantasies about his chest and arms.

Well, she wasn't a girl any more, but an officer of the law. And someone had been killed.

"Yeah?" His drawl had deepened from the insolent, fighting tone he'd had when they were kids. Now it was a rough, masculine stroke of irritation.

"What an unexpected pleasure." They'd been inseparable friends once, so in spite of the sad and worrisome business of the day, she grinned. "You here to stay?"

"Not if I can help it."

Still rude though. "Fixing up the place?"

"No."

Her smile mellowed. "Selling?"

"No."

Friends once, but apparently no longer. The sense of loss compounded, the pang sharper, but like the heat, she had no choice but to put it aside. On to the matter at hand.

"This is a courtesy stop. Your brother around?" Her hand went to her hip, an old cheap bid for authority and a habit she thought she'd broken. She dropped her arm again. She didn't need to look big; she'd earned her badge with hard work.

"Gus can't come to the door." Which meant she wasn't welcome and should get to the point.

Fine, damn it, she would. "I wanted to make sure your brother, and now also you, have been warned, considering how far you are from town. There was an animal attack last night, just a couple miles north." It was baffling, actually. Witness described a big cat like a jaguar, though it would be a thousand miles or more outside its range. "Young girl dead."

His gaze remained flat and cold. "Consider us warned. You can leave now."

His mamma had died too soon after his birth to teach him manners. Surely he'd had to learn some elsewhere by now? Or did he occasionally get stuck in old habits too?

Something in the dark over his shoulder moved, but she couldn't make out what with the glare of the day behind her. "Is that Gus?" The older brother, current owner of the ruined plantation. Why they hadn't sold the place and moved on had stumped town gossipers for generations. The brothers weren't without buyers. Even recently, one of those planned community developers had been interested. "Might I have a word with him?"

"He's not fit for company."

"Everything all right?" A hunch told her no.

"Fine."

"Well okay." If he didn't want help, she wasn't about to force it on him. "Be careful. Especially at night." She turned to navigate the porch's steps. Top one was splintered.

"What are you doing about the animal?" he said to her back.

She looked over her shoulder. "Getting together with some people from Fish and Wildlife. Hunt it down. Won't be safe until we do."

"You won't go after it alone, will you?"

She raised a brow. "If it weren't for the meanness in your voice, I'd think you almost cared." The path from the porch to the dirt drive was pitted with holes and lumped with roots. She didn't stumble once. Yanked open the SUV's door.

He called after her. "Don't track that thing alone."

She wasn't an idiot. "Can handle myself, Jack. Been doing it for years."

★

Jack shut the door only after Eva was safely inside her SUV.
A police officer? He never would've guessed, except . . . it
seemed right. And what had she said?

Animal attack.

His brother was indeed prowling behind him, but Jack
needed a moment before facing him. Bracing his hands on
the closed door, he hung his head. "Is she talking about
you?"

When Jack got no answer, he lifted his head and turned.
What he wanted to know would be plain on his brother's
face, not that Jack would believe it.

He couldn't. It was too soon.

Every Wylde was born a jaguar shifter, but the bloodlust
didn't overcome them until they were middle-aged. Gus
wasn't even thirty-five.

His brother had an arch expression of civility stretching
his features, but it was a mask. The heaviness in his eyes and
the sick pallor of his skin made him look like their father.

"Have you been hunting?" Jack didn't mean with a
permit and rifle and hunter orange vest. He inhaled through
his nose, searching for that telltale dark, rich, metallic scent
that had the power to drug the soul. A Wylde soul,
specifically.

Gus smelled sour, though not of blood, but then he
could've showered early this morning. And those weren't
the clothes he'd been wearing yesterday.

"I've been trying to tell you." His brother's voice had
lowered to a chest growl.

"It's not possible." The bloodlust of the curse had overcome their father a full decade later, and Nana in her fifties.

And this was *last night*? While Jack was sleeping in the
same house? No.

"I warned you that it was coming. I could feel it." Gus
bared his teeth in a smile that wasn't a smile at all. "And I
was right. I had bad dreams last night. Bloody dreams."

Eva had said a young girl. A young girl killed by a wild
animal.

Jack's throat went dry, breath shallow. He was too late.
What to do?

Of course, there was an obvious answer.

No. He shook his head to refuse the inevitable. Maybe that was why believing was so difficult, because if he believed, then he'd have to . . .

His brother was already nodding. "You're going to have to do it."

"It doesn't have to be like that." Jack's mind raced. He'd come home to find the *answer*, not perpetuate the bloodshed. Once overtaken, the cursed couldn't take their own lives. The animal side of them wouldn't allow it. A family member usually did the deed.

"Yeah it does. After last night, it absolutely does."

"How long . . . ?" Before it happened again.

If only chains could buy time. But once a Wylde shifted, the curse allowed them to slip through anything as if it were made of shadow. There was no containing them. No saving them. Of course they'd tried on their father, but that just made the old bastard angry later.

"How long did our father last after his first kill?"

Jack flinched to hear it put so starkly. Their father, easily the weakest and most angry of the Wyldes, went a few days between his first and last attacks. "That's not enough time to find the answer."

Two days. Maybe three.

Gus staggered toward what had once been the study, from which the man of the house reigned. It'd also been their father's favorite den. He paused and turned in the doorway. "There's no answer for me, not any more. I tried to tell you. We need to do this as soon as possible."

Jack shook his head no.

A feral yellow gleamed through the natural golden brown of his brother's irises. "Eva sure smelled good."

A threat to Eva. To force action.

Then Gus shut the study door behind him.

Jack was left to look after him, stunned by a blunt-force shock not unlike the smacks and falls that had knocked the air out of him as a kid at the hands of an equally unhappy father.

Jack was a grown man now, but his lungs still screamed

for oxygen. He couldn't breathe in this house – and not because of the stifling heat or the earthy smell of mold slowly eating at their legacy. The house was a cage that couldn't quite confine the wildness of its inhabitants. And yet, if anything, running free was worse.

A sledgehammer leaned against the stairwell wall, one of the tools Jack had brought to make sure his search exposed every last secret the house kept. Rage had him hefting it over his shoulder and swinging it like a baseball bat, taking out several of the graceful banister's wooden supports.

The crash raised a cloud of fine dust to float in the sullen air.

A couple of days. That's all he had. And then he'd have to kill his brother.

Jack tossed the sledgehammer to the side. It thumped heavily against the entry doorjamb and clattered to the scarred floor.

He looked up the sweeping stair to the open landing above. Afternoon shadow disguised the dinginess of the walls and indulged his imagination in a timeless sense of how the house must've been once. Silk wallpaper and gleaming wood. Everything beautiful, elegant, the hope of prosperity within reach. Had his ancestors known that a kernel of hatred had been hidden within? Well, if they hadn't, they learned soon thereafter and again every generation since.

The answer *had* to be here: all his research into curses, voodoo, witchcraft, his fieldwork studying what was left of the old ways, and his travels into dark and horrifying places had told him that there would be a talisman, something innocent-seeming even, that would've secured the curse. Once found, its power would be self-evident to a Wylde. He had but to find and destroy it.

So simple, except it seemed there was no time left. In fact, they were *past* time if Gus had . . .

No. His *brother* hadn't killed. Not the brother who'd stood between him and their father too many times to count. His brother was innocent, was even now trying to do the right thing. It was the curse at fault – the animal side could be controlled, until one day it couldn't.

Work. It's what Jack had come home to do. Now he just had to do it faster.

He returned to the cluttered office he'd made of a wasted bedroom and forced himself to sit shaking in front of the pile of papers he'd exhumed from thick dust in the attic. The early household accounts, half ruined by dampness and thoughtless discard, were stacked in one pile. If a clue had been written within, it was now black with mold.

He shoved aside the ledger in which he was creating an inventory of Wylde household items. Why had he been wasting time on records? Well, he'd thought he had a decade to search, that's why.

The angry rummage through the next trunk yielded bits and pieces of the past: shattered china, a stack of yellowed, embroidered handkerchiefs, a pair of porcelain dolls with time-crusted dresses and hollow eyes and a smaller case holding heavy iron figures of soldiers braced to fight the War of Northern Aggression.

All the objects felt mundane. No talismans here.

Jack looked up to the window as the edges on his desperation eased. The air was doing that intoxicating velvet thing, the summer heat softening. Night was approaching, making him careless.

It was shifting time again, and he resisted it better as a man than he had as a boy. But *goddamn* the sensation had the power to seduce. His body heated with an insistent basic drive, and it took all his concentration to pull out of the draw. One day his mind would darken too.

Jack picked up a random scrap of paper and forced his concentration into the sharp, forward-leaning old-fashioned script.

This was pointless. Work was pointless.

Jack squeezed his eyes shut – the blackness behind his lids pricked with white – then opened his eyes to glare at the paper. The note was a receipt of funds from an auction of items, dated 1855. The items themselves were not listed, but the receipt had potential. Something to follow up. He paper-clipped the scrap to a fresh folder to pursue the next day.

A paper clip was laughable. The folder so idiotic. This was what they'd been reduced to.

A thump and echo shuddered the house and brought his head up. He recognized the sound of the kitchen door closing, which meant Gus was going out. Jack dropped the folder and went to the window in time to catch a streak of liquid night dashing across the grounds and into the trees.

Jack's throat tightened with anxiety.

He hoped his brother would just run and run and run through the night. Jack had to admit that the wild run was its own kind of pleasure. But, yes, in a couple of days, Gus would get hungry.

What if Eva and her Wildlife people shot him?

Jack's heart beat hard.

And then his heart stalled, as he recalled Gus's threat, "Eva sure smelled good."

He could trust Gus, but . . . Jack wasn't so sure about the animal side with a woman's scent in its nose. And if Gus was succumbing so much younger than other Wyldes, could he really wait a few days between hunts?

Suddenly, Jack felt a little more ready to pull the trigger.

What if Gus found Eva first?

Chapter Two

The sun was setting, the heavy air sweeter, if just as close, as fireflies ushered in the night with a sparkle of magic. Eva walked the narrow park access trail back to her SUV. The animal had been tracked from the attack site to the creek a quarter-mile beyond. Signs had been posted, warnings at every juncture. Traps set.

She'd been up at least thirty-six hours straight. Walters from Humane Enforcement could finish up with Wildlife. Time to pick up a pizza, say a prayer, and catch a few hours of sleep.

The peachy-red sky blushed to deepest violet, and the long shadows of the pine trees diffused into the encroaching earth-born darkness. Twilight.

Either she grew quieter, or the trees grew louder, but a hot shiver crawled down her spine as she came to that uncomfortable awareness that she was less powerful in the dark, and the wildness in the trees more potent. Too soon the fiery warning flare on the horizon burned out.

The fine hairs on the back of her neck lifted. Her hearing grew more acute as whispers filled her mind, but they were just natural sounds – leaves waving, cicadas giving way to chattering katydids.

Nevertheless, she sensed pursuit, and her blood pumped faster.

This of course was only her imagination, fed by fatigue and unforgettable images of violent, bloody death. *That poor girl. Those poor parents.*

Eva forced herself to keep her stride long and steady, but couldn't resist looking over her shoulder.

Not ten paces behind, the trail was swallowed by darkness, which brought to mind that funny game her niece played on her phone where the ground fell out from beneath the runner if they slowed down too much.

Silly game. But Eva walked faster. It wasn't far now.

The trees thinned near a wide, grassy area. On the other side, accessible to the road, her SUV glinted in the dusky light, and if she squinted she could just make out a figure standing nearby.

Male, by the shape of him. Young. Fit.

Armed?

Not that she could see. And anyway, she was.

Upon recognizing him, all the fear dropped out of her.

Jack Wylde. Had he come to apologize? He must've been to the station first to know where to find her.

In spite of him basically inviting her off his property earlier that day, he wasn't a bad man. Bad boy, yes. Bad man, no. That had been his father. And Jack had obviously been troubled about something before she'd arrived.

"I thought I warned you to stay inside," she said as she approached. There were six officers deep in those trees, each with a high-powered rifle under their arm.

Jack was leaning on her driver's side door. If he weren't slightly out of breath, he'd look as if he'd been patiently waiting. "And I told you not to go after the animal on your own."

"I didn't. In fact, I'm on my way home." She waved him out of the way.

He looked at her with those golden eyes, and then shifted to transfer his weight to his feet. The smooth way he moved made her belly flutter.

Yes, yes. Born in hell and bred to sin. Her gran had been absolutely right about Jack Wylde.

Which meant it was time to go home. The constant heat and exhaustion were wearing on her good judgment. Who was she kidding? *Jack* wore on her good judgment. Always had.

"Why are you still here?" he asked, as she unlocked and opened the SUV door. "You could've gone anywhere, done anything."

This was a follow-up to a conversation years old – they'd both pinky promised as kids to leave Bloomfield, Georgia for fantasy futures in big cities or overseas. She effortlessly picked up her place in the dialogue. Everything had been effortless with Jack.

"The Judge needed me," she answered and climbed into the driver's seat. Daddy needed help after the stroke, and, well, she'd also realized that this was home. These were her people. No one understood them better. "You sound bitter. Why'd you return?"

Jack squinted into the trees, then looked back at her. "Blood got to me too."

Eva thought of the shadow behind his front doors that afternoon. Gus, had to be. And she could guess the issue. Their father had been an alcoholic, and his before him.

She heaved a heavy sigh on Jack's behalf. He'd tried to do something different with his life, but history, especially family history, sometimes forces a path. How many "bad boys" took on that kind of long, thankless responsibility? Jack might be rough and rude, but he'd become, if against his will, a good man.

Poor Jack. His teenage self would be mortified.

She cocked her head, smiling. "You remember that day

we first met? When I swore I wouldn't go to church if you weren't welcome?"

She'd been a righteous nine maybe. He, around eleven, hadn't seen a bath in a year.

A little smile played about his eyes, still slightly luminous in the dim starlight. "I'm an atheist now, but yes, I remember."

"And in my defiance, I ran off with you?"

"Lady Justice. Blind to the realities of social status."

Eva warmed from the inside, and hoped Jack didn't see her pleased blush. Lady Justice had been her inspiration for becoming a law officer. Though not the scales Justice carried, like her father, the Judge. She'd been more attracted to the sword in the icon's right hand.

"I think I was just too restless to sit in a hot, stuffy church on such a beautiful day," she said, "but paint me the hero if you must."

"I think I must."

She grew warmer still. "You remember what you told me that day? It was the first thing I thought of when I heard a big wild cat had attacked someone."

The humor dimmed from his eyes. He shook his head no. He didn't remember.

"You said your family was cursed."

No spark of recognition.

"That you all had a wildness inside, hence your last name?"

Nothing.

"That any born to your line were part wild cat." Jaguar, her memory supplied. The story had burned in her young imagination until more lustful thoughts had taken over a few years later.

"And that's what you thought of when you discovered someone had been killed by a wild animal? You thought of me."

She wasn't apologetic. "The mind does funny things when confronted with senseless death. You don't remember the story?"

"I know I wanted to be special," he said, glancing into the

trees again. "I wanted a reason for the way things were. Times were tough back then."

He was evading her questions, and expertly so since he'd seen fit to include an artful tug at the heartstrings. The unhappy little boy playing pretend.

Yeah, he remembered.

Her pulse doubled as he stepped up close to where she sat at the steering wheel. He put a hand on the shoulder of her seat, the other on her open car door, thereby boxing her in. He smelled like hard-working man, and she didn't mind a bit.

What was he playing at now? Something – she couldn't put her finger on what – but something was still off with him, and *that* she didn't like.

His voice lowered, his Southern drawl thickening enough to drop a "g". "Was wonderin' if you'd have dinner with me tonight."

See? Right there – he'd *never* flirted with her before.

"Thanks, but no." Until she knew what he was about, he could just pick that "g" right back up again. "I've been on my feet since yesterday morning." Curious, she tossed some bait, just to see what he'd do. "I just want to curl up in bed."

His luminous eyes narrowed to eerie twin crescent moons. "I like your idea even better. Let's do that."

Ugh. She couldn't have been more disappointed. She hadn't seen him in six years and he invites himself into her bed? At one time he'd been her best friend, so careful of her desperate crush, so careful not to hurt her. Her friend would never treat her like a fling, not even for a mutually satisfying lay. Even when it had seemed like it was just them against the world, he had not touched her. Who was this person masquerading as Jackson Wylde?

"Girl died last night, Jack," she said to sober him up.

He dropped his arms, his expression smoothing again.

First unbelievably rude, then showing up here of all places and lying to her face when she *knew* he remembered the discussion that was the foundation of their friendship. Then coming on to her?

She grabbed the inside door handle. "I really do need to get home and put the day behind me."

Her tone told him to step back, and he did. She shut the door. Started the engine. Left him standing there.

She was just too damn tired. A young girl had died, but this was the first time that Eva wanted to cry, as if she'd lost someone too.

The night was a deep black soup when Jack sat up in his truck, suddenly alert. Now a few hours into his vigil, he was accustomed to the slow creep of shadow surrounding Eva's little white house, as well as the bright scrape of light when another car passed by on her street.

But this particular low-lying shadow had a distinctly Wylde lurk. And it was circling her place.

Gus. And yes, it seemed he *was* forcing the issue by going after Eva.

First the park, now here. It'd taken his brother a while to find Eva's bungalow. Gus had probably gone to the Judge's big house, from which the Renards had ruled Bloomfield. But of course independent Eva would have her own place, regardless of the comforts and staff available to her at her family home.

Lovely Evangeline Renard, fighting for the light. It hadn't surprised him that she'd declined his invitation to dinner and then – an uncomfortable heat crept up his neck – into her bed. Never mind that his true intent was to protect her. That's not how he'd ever imagined asking her out. He'd imagined bringing flowers and, in all humility, asking her right. Because if she said yes, he intended to keep her close forever.

He got out of his truck and let the door hang open so as not to awaken anyone on the street. Not to awaken her.

Magnolias scented the air. The moon was a hot white haze behind a cloud-swamped sky. This deep into the night, the houses dotting the street were little islands on a primeval landscape of darkness.

There was Gus. Right in front of him. The devil turned its yellow cat eyes on him, head lowering as it braced to attack.

Jack knew it for a feint: Gus had spent the first part of his life *protecting* his little brother. He wouldn't hurt him now.

"You'll have to go through me," he dared his brother back. "Then there'll be no one left to help you."

The devil bared its long sharp fangs.

Jack flashed hot with sweat, the human part of him reacting to the threat of a menace far beyond that of a simple wild animal. He'd lied when he'd told Eva he was an atheist. He did believe in some gods; how could a *Wylde* not believe in the supernatural? He just didn't believe in Eva's God, whom he had never known. Jack believed in Powers spawned by darkest passions. Like his brother Gus, those Powers held the note on his soul and Jack didn't have the currency to redeem it.

The jaguar screamed at him, a beastly sound to rip open the sky. Another feint.

A light went on next door.

Jack shook his head at his brother. *No.* "Go home. I have three days."

The devil screamed at him again.

Jack tried a new tactic. "I found something tonight – a fresh lead." That scrap of paper, the receipt of a sale. Jack had no hope of it yielding an object that could possibly end the Wylde torment, but he had to try. "Give me the time."

The click of a lock turning. A neighbor stepping outside to see what was causing the racket.

Jack lifted his hand in hello. "Sorry for waking you. Engine belt." If he didn't look at Gus, perhaps the middle-aged lady in her flowery robe wouldn't either.

The neighbor's gaze flicked from Jack to Eva's house – nothing like fuel for gossip – and to Jack again. But no expression of fear crossed her face. She shut herself back inside. Turned the lock again.

When Jack looked back, the devil had gone.

"No missing persons either?" Eva held the phone to her ear with her shoulder, reaching in the closet to grab a fresh set of clothes for the day. She wasn't due at work for a couple of hours, so she was going to forego the uniform, but she still wanted to look professional in case something happened and she didn't have the chance to change. She went with black slacks and a simple sleeveless blouse. Blue, her best color.

"No," Lynn said in her ear. "We had a quiet night, thank the Lord."

"Well, all right." Eva would be happier if the animal had been caught, but she'd settle for no new attacks.

"County Records called with that information you requested. It's waiting at the front desk." That'd be the reports of other animal attacks in the area. Eva had been shocked to discover that this wasn't the first. Apparently the area had a history. How curious that she had not known about it.

"Then that's where I'll be this morning. See you later this afternoon."

Eva got ready. Checked herself twice in the mirror. Didn't think about Jack and how he'd propositioned her last night. Didn't think about the old recurring dreams she'd had of him holding her close, what it would be like to kiss him. Hot, she guessed. Very hot. She didn't think about any of that, but she did acknowledge that it was time she started dating again. Not Jack, she told herself, but someone. And soon.

She grabbed her keys and purse. The screen door was just clattering shut behind her when she noticed Shirley Madsen out on her porch.

"Morning!" Eva called, a Renard's duty to always be friendly. Her place in the community.

"Evangeline," Shirley said in return, but drawn out slow and with purpose.

Hell. The woman had appointed herself a surrogate parent, having known Eva's mother in school and being a retired nurse and so apparently an expert on strokes like the Judge's.

Eva found a sunny smile. "Are you well this morning?"

"After last night? Hrmph. The racket your *guest* made?"

Eva triple blinked. She'd been so tired last night she'd slept like the dead, but she sure hoped she would've remembered if she'd had someone over. "My guest?"

"It's none of my business who you pass your time with, but you just be sure not to shame the Judge."

Eva shook her head, at a total loss. "I don't know what you mean." But the wheels had started turning in her mind. By Shirley's disapproving tone, the guest had to be male.

"Next time I see that truck loitering out front, I'm going to call the police."

"I am the police."

Shirley shrugged and gave her a lie-piercing glare.

Well. Eva looked at her for another few seconds, and then took her confusion to the SUV. Apparently, she'd had a guest of the objectionable male variety and he drove a truck.

Not much to go on, but she had a feeling she could guess the man with some accuracy.

He'd come over – to try again, perhaps? – and Shirley had scared him off.

In which case, Eva owed her nosey neighbor an apology and a thank-you, a debt she knew she'd never repay.

Something was going on with that man. And she was going to figure out what.

Chapter Three

Wait. 1855.

Jack looked from his scrap of a receipt to a line of scrawl in the records on the screen before him. It'd taken him hours to find, but there it was. Same date, same forward-leaning handwriting. The records office was decades behind the times, so he was going old-school microfiche.

He checked the dates again. The dates gave him the name of the buyer to whom the Wylde items had been sold.

He shook his head as he printed the page to deny the possibility. *Someone* had to have already checked. He couldn't believe that he was the only Wylde in well over a hundred years to attempt to find the source of the curse. Someone either had to have made very sure when they'd sold that nothing in this particular lot could free the family – wouldn't they have *felt* it? – or they had to have followed up later to discover what exactly had been sold and then tried to retrieve it.

Jack went online on his phone and searched the name. It came up right away in connection with a collection at a museum in Savannah. He made the call, posing as a historian out of the University of Maryland, and asked if he could come down to view their records. No, they couldn't accommodate him today – *shit* – but the curator would be in tomorrow morning, nine o'clock. He'd be there.

The slight brain lag from lack of sleep evaporated. He hadn't lied to Gus about a lead after all. He'd show him the receipt of Wylde items sold and the printout of the matching entry in the ledger. It might be enough for Gus to give him hope. Could hope combat the darkness to buy more time?

No, Jack wouldn't let himself be fooled. Hope was a joke. This receipt was a lottery ticket at best, odds of a million to one. At stake was either his brother's life or someone else's, like—

"Done yet?"

He startled and turned in his seat. Eva?

The blue of her blouse made her eyes that much more captivating.

He stood up. "Are you stalking me?"

"Hardly. I'm waiting for my turn, and you're just sitting there talking on your phone."

Oh. He stepped around the chair and pulled it out for her. "Apologies. I'm done here. What are you researching?"

She hesitated, and then shrugged. "Seems that the area has a history of deadly animal attacks."

Jack felt the blood drain from his face, but he faked surprise. "More than just the one?"

"I'm about to find out." She waved a little slip of paper with a list of references. "Last one was in the nineties."

That would be his father, who'd killed two people before Gus had taken care of him, though his father had been a monster a long time before being overcome by the curse.

"Mind if I join you?" Early that morning he'd searched the Wylde house again, attic to cellar, and had found nothing. Then he'd been waiting at the records office when it opened at ten. Now he was curious what other public records might hold. Maybe he should've started here in the first place.

"If you want," she said, with a heavy undercurrent of distrust.

Well, he'd probably earned it.

He pulled up a second chair to her side, just behind her. One breath of the air near Eva and his baser nature flared into awareness, just as it had last night. Her sweet, clean fragrance, with just a hint of sweat; the warmth of her bare shoulder; the luxurious flowery fall of her thick hair – he wanted to scent her all over, get past the shower soap to the woman underneath. The Wylde darkness was in him too, beating his blood like a drum. With difficulty, he stopped himself from leaning forward and tasting.

She was tracing over magnified old newspaper pages to find the article she wanted, and then abruptly turned to him, cocking her head to ask, "Were you at my place late last night?"

Yes. At the moment he was regretting not going inside.

"Your neighbor?" he guessed to cover his distraction.

He couldn't afford to look at Eva's face – her mouth was so close – so he flicked his gaze up to the article, headlined CAMPERS FOUND DEAD. He cooled slightly, even though he could feel Eva's warm breath on his cheek.

She raised her eyebrows with her smile and nodded. "That'd be Mrs Shirley Madsen. She told me not to shame the Judge."

Jack scanned the top paragraph, and then went stone cold. His father hadn't been responsible for just two deaths. There'd been four. Gus either hadn't known, or he'd lied to his little brother.

"For being with a Wylde?" Jack didn't blame the neighbor. *Four.*

"For having a man over at all. But that's not the point." Eva looked him up and down. "What the hell were you doing there? And did you actually ask to join me in *bed* last night?"

Suddenly, as if self-conscious of what she'd said, Eva glanced around.

The archivist was looking at them.

Chastened, Eva turned back to the screen. In a lower voice, she said, "You still look like Jack – well, an older version – but I don't recognize you."

When she'd refused dinner, Jack couldn't think of a way to keep close to her. Not that he wouldn't be happy curled up with her in bed. He thought of Eva, pale and soft against him, and the darkness within stirred his blood again. Though he'd never want such a casual and offhand way to get there. If he ever ended up inside Eva, it would be absolutely deliberate.

"I'm sorry," he said lamely.

"Fine." She didn't sound fine.

"Eva . . ." But he couldn't explain, couldn't locate the right words to make something up. Not now, hot as he was and yet also staring at the proof that his father had killed four people. Not to mention Gus's paltry hope for salvation clutched in his hand.

Jack forced his mind to clear.

Eva was disappointed in him. If he lost her friendship, he'd lose hold of himself too.

She enlarged the text of the article and leaned in to read.

"I've been an asshole since you first knocked on my door," he said. "Can we start over?"

"Doesn't matter," she said to the screen. "You're just going to go away again anyway. And you know what? I'll be glad when you do. This place has been nothing but hell on you. I want you to be happy. Congrats on the professor thing."

His new job, how he'd planned to make enough to live and keep his sanity while researching his family history. She'd been checking up on him.

"Eva. I *am* sorry. It's me, I promise." If she cut him out of her life, the animal inside would take him soon too. He knew it. She was the reason he'd finished school and then gone on to more. She was the reason he'd thought he might have a chance to end the darkness and have the power to leave this town behind.

"I'm just a little . . . stressed," he explained. "I haven't seen you in six years, and it doesn't feel like time has passed at all to me. I'm still your friend. And I . . . I don't have to go away again, not even for the job. I moved away before in order to . . . survive." She'd understand that much. "But you have only to say the word 'stay' and I will."

He'd stay here if she asked. The plan before last night had been to go back and forth from the university during breaks and weekends. But he'd find another way to live if she said so.

Eva turned her head, slanting a shocked look at him.

He gulped. Yes, he meant what she thought he meant – though he hadn't intended to make a declaration today or any other day. A Renard did not consort with a Wylde; the Judge had been very clear with him on that point one sunny and terrible afternoon. But Jack's feelings couldn't be a surprise to her, the one person in the world who understood him without knowing the worst. "You *had* to know."

She shook her head no, the shock still freezing her face.

He frowned and tried to make a joke. "And here I thought you were so smart."

If possible, her eyes got wider, and then she laughed. She brought her hands up in frustration. "Who the fuck are you?"

"Language," he chided, imitating the Judge. He'd been falling down a dark, dark hole when she'd come up behind him to use the microfiche today. Now here he was flailing for the light.

"Law enforcement," she shot back as an excuse for her vocabulary.

Her color was up and she didn't seem like she was looking for the words to gently let him down. Which meant what . . . ?

His hell was getting darker. He shouldn't have said anything. His hell could only get *worse* with the knowledge that she might have been his if not for the curse.

She shrugged her shoulders. "That's all it takes? Stay?"

He nodded, wondering in horror if she was going to say

it. All this beauty . . . that he couldn't have. The curse had been so beautifully crafted.

"Good to know," she said and turned back around.

He was left looking at the back of her head, disoriented, a buzzing in his ears.

And then, on cue, she proceeded to disassemble the darkest, most violent parts of his family history. His father had killed four people, and there were three additional missing persons from that year. And as far as Jack had known, Nana had never attacked and killed anyone. But the records testified to God and Bloomfield otherwise. Three. One of them a young child.

So, in a way, Eva did know everything about him. By the time she was done, he had no more secrets left and was so numb with powerlessness that the auction receipt he'd found and the matching printout had fallen from his fingers to the floor. His stupid lottery ticket.

Eva, angel that she was, picked them back up for him.

If she'd been blind to his feelings for her, what was she going to do now? She had all the pieces. He'd given her the first when they were children, and she admitted that it was the first thing she'd thought of when they'd found a body.

She *had* to know.

Facing the screen, she said, "First things first. You asked me to dinner last night."

All he could manage was a low grunt. It was actually a kind of sob.

"You should ask again."

He closed his eyes and shook his head. His sweet Lady Justice was indeed blindfolded.

And he was so greedy for light and beauty that he would take her up on her offer. A little light. Wyldes never got second chances. Or was he a devil already?

"Evangeline Renard," he heard himself say, "would you do me the honor of dining with me tonight?"

She winced. "Can't tonight. Working. Tomorrow's good though."

"Tomorrow?" Was this happening?

"Wear a tie."

★

"Are you going in to the station now?" Jack had his hand at the small of her back as he opened the door into sunshine. From that one spot on her body, the rest of her hummed, nerves jangling as if they each had a little quivering bell attached. She couldn't imagine what it'd be like to have his hands on her bare skin. Jack as a hot and angry teen had been tempting. Jack as this dark and troubled grown man?

She bit her lip to ground herself in the moment. "I'm not due for a while, but yes, I want to catch Walter and hear how the search went last night before he goes home for the day."

"I'd like to hear about that search myself, if you don't mind."

"Sure. Come along, though I'm going to stop by the Judge's place on the way to check in on him. Won't take a minute." The walk wasn't far – her father had preferred to preside over the town from its center.

She glanced at Jack to find his expression had tensed, but wisely he said nothing. The first time she'd invited him home years ago, she'd had to dare him to get him across the threshold.

They skirted the small central park, a burst of greenery surrounded by both historic and utilitarian buildings. A low wrought-iron fence bounded the perimeter.

"How is he?"

Eva smiled at Jack's attempt at polite conversation. The Judge had been very vocal about his disapproval of the Wylde boys.

"He can't speak or move well, especially on his left side." From the park she could cut through to the back of her father's house. "But he understands what's going on around him."

"You see him every day?"

She looked over. "I try. Missed yesterday because of the attack."

They entered via the kitchen door, and Jack followed behind her. Every surface was polished, not a speck of dust on the floor. The quiet, refined perfection had been a source of constant anxiety all her life. She was not a neat person.

She passed through the swinging door and crossed the prep pantry to the dining room. A long mahogany table, with seating for twelve, dominated the space. A sparkling chandelier cast rainbow drops of light on one wall. A small display to one side exhibited a couple of tintype photographs of soldiers from the Civil War, her relatives, as well as a Southern Cross of Honor at the center.

"Exactly as I remember it," Jack said behind her.

Down the main hallway, they came to the sitting room where her father now rested or watched TV. A burst of floral fragrance greeted her as she stepped inside – a huge arrangement of fresh flowers gave the room color and life. The Judge was dressed, sitting in his wheelchair, and listening to an audiobook. A thriller by the sound of it, with screams in the background while the narrator read.

Lettie, the nurse, rose from a chair and touched a button. The book paused, and she excused herself from the room.

Eva went over to give the Judge a hug. "Hi, Daddy."

But her father's gaze had found Jack, and there it stayed.

"You remember Jackson Wylde, don't you?" Eva knew he did, or he'd have disregarded the person accompanying her and given her a kiss, or at least tried to. As her father had not attempted to kiss her, she knew he was displeased with her as well. Too bad.

"Nice to see you again, Judge," Jack said.

Eva pressed on. "Turns out you share a common interest. Jack's received a doctorate in history. He's going to be a professor now." Maybe they'd have something to talk about.

Her father's mouth was working, but the downturn of his expression told Eva that no university degree could redeem a Wylde. The Judge finally said, "Animal," but the sounds of the letters and vowels had slurred together so that for a second she hoped Jack might not have understood.

"I'll be just outside," Jack said gently, which meant he had and was being respectful anyway.

A few minutes later she joined him on the sidewalk in front of the house.

"Some things just don't change," he said, seemingly not angry, but resigned to the fact.

"Some things don't," she agreed as they started back toward the town square. And to prove it, she wrapped her hand around his bent elbow to make the two of them a joined pair.

Chapter Four

Jack couldn't concentrate on what Officer Walter was saying about the search for the jaguar last night – it seemed they had at last positively identified the species of wild cat. Jack could do them one better with its actual name: August Rainier Wylde.

Eva leaned in to Jack's ear to note that the other animal attacks had also been jaguar. How very interesting.

He was spared answering by another officer joining the group.

And yet, all the while, Jack's mind was preoccupied with the Judge and his rejection. Not that he cared any more that the Judge thought he wasn't worth the air he breathed. Jack was used to feeling like scum every time he met Eva's father, and had often wondered how the man could've had a daughter like her.

The Judge had called him animal.

Which could be an insult, yes. Not too many years ago, Jack would've left it there. But maybe the Judge was simply speaking what he knew to be true. Jackson Wylde *was* an animal.

Eva tended to speak her mind just as directly. Maybe she was more like her father than Jack had considered.

Which meant someone outside his family knew the secret.

The Renard family had settled in Bloomfield a long time ago, not as far back as the Wylde family, but soon enough thereafter to be present for generations' worth of Wylde torment. And the Renards were in a position of authority. They knew everyone's business.

But then, why hadn't they hunted the Wyldes down with torches and pitchforks? Why had the Judge let his little girl near him at all?

The contradiction was too much for Jack to riddle while listening to Walter go on about tracks and hair.

Maybe Gus knew if anyone was aware of the curse. Maybe he might remember something that Jack, years younger, did not.

He should check on his brother anyway. This morning Gus had shouted, "Go away!" from behind the library door.

Jack whispered back to Eva. "I've got to go."

Her brows went up, but she nodded, and he left her.

When Jack pulled up in front of the Wylde plantation house, he was more bothered than ever. If someone like the Judge did know, and knew the origins, and had let them all suffer . . .

The thought made Jack's throat burn. The fragments were like shrapnel, tearing him up and slowly inching toward his heart. No wonder his father had drunk himself numb and struck out at his sons. He couldn't save them.

The front door hung open – a bad sign – but once inside, Jack saw that the study door was shut. Gus would be in there, stewing in his misery.

Jack didn't knock. When he entered, he almost staggered back out because of the sour alcohol and body stink clouding the room.

Gus had collapsed on the floor.

Jack knelt to take his pulse. It was strong and steady – hangovers couldn't kill a Wylde. He stepped through the accumulated trash and discarded bottles to toss aside limp curtains and open a couple of windows. Light burned through a billion dust motes.

Gus grunted his protest.

"It's past two," Jack said.

They'd both been up all night, each in his own way.

Gus drew an arm over his face to block the streaming sun. "Get out."

"I need to talk to you."

"There's nothing left to talk about." His brother's voice was full of gravel. "Just fucking kill me."

"Soon," Jack promised. "I need you to answer some questions."

Gus opened his eyes to slits and Jack saw that his brother still had the wide yellow iris and black pupils of the devil.

Sweat slicked Jack's skin in the space of a blink. "Tomorrow afternoon," he said, compromising.

"Won't last another night without a kill," Gus breathed. "And you know it."

"One more." *Please.* Because Jack had an appointment tomorrow to follow up on the auction receipt. He needed another day even if his lottery ticket had the worst odds ever.

The preternatural yellow in his brother's eyes didn't lie.

Jack was looking at a beast. Only the sunlight held Gus in his own flesh.

Did he only have hours?

The realization of the end was almost enough for Jack to slump to the floor beside his brother and pick up one of the half-empty bottles to numb himself too.

But he had to do *something.* He had to at least try.

"Does anyone outside the family know about the curse?"

"Did you tell Eva?" His brother smiled, or tried to. "They'll come for us both then."

"No, I didn't tell her." Well, he had as a kid. "But our family can't have gone this long without someone learning about it."

"If somebody knew—" Gus tried to lift his head, and then gave up and let it hit the floor with a dull thump "—we'd be dead."

"That's what I thought," Jack answered. "But that's not the impression I got today. Someone called me an animal." He'd never say who, or the devil might go after the Judge.

Gus laughed silently. "A woman, I hope."

"I'm serious, damn it." Jack bit back. "Does anyone know? Has anyone threatened to tell or hinted at our history?"

Gus closed his eyes and shook his head. "That's how you'll have to go, you know. A mob hunting you down. After I'm gone, there'll be no one left but outsiders to take care of the devil in you."

"I'll think of something," Jack said offhand. His mind

was already racing ahead, his feet pointing in the direction he had to go.

Out the door. Not to Savannah – no time for that – but back to the Judge's house, this time without Eva. Ask the old man the same damn questions.

Jack was losing his brother.

The drive back into town was both interminable and shockingly brief, the traffic slow but sparse, the stoplights red, but few. He parked out front of the ornamental gate that laced the entry path of the big stone house, and proceeded up the stairs to knock on the door. The crisp moldings, crosshead, and pediment all spoke to the refined wealth of the owner. They were all original to the house, Jack was sure.

Eva would be angry and demand to know why he'd bothered her father. He wouldn't tell her, of course, so she would shut him out of her life. Well, it had been a nice dream anyway, the idea of dinner with her.

When no one answered, he rang the bell, and then knocked again, until at last the nurse he'd seen earlier came to the door.

"Did you leave something here?" she asked through an opening big enough for only her head.

Jack pushed the door open, the woman stumbling back. "Yes, I did. I'll just be a moment."

"You can't just barge—" she said behind him, voice raised with alarm.

"Just one minute, and I'll be on my way." Except, it might take more than a minute.

"Sir, this is an inexcus—"

Jack grabbed her by the arm tightly, and then whipped it back to restrain her.

What the hell was he doing? These were the kinds of moments when madmen were born, when desperation overrode good thinking. This was a crime; not his first, not his last. And yet, it was too late to stop now.

She screamed as if he were murdering her. Well, he really hoped it didn't come to that. He was a Wylde after all. Looking around, he caught sight of a closet – storage, he remembered from way, way back – and dragged her toward it. She started trembling horribly, strength going out of her with her fear. He felt badly for the scare she was getting, but it was nothing compared to the torment his family had lived with year after year. She would recover at least.

Into the closet she went. He slammed the door behind her.

The closet door opened a little – valiant of her – and he pushed a heavy piece of furniture across to force it closed.

The woman's body might have gone weak, but her scream was just as shrill.

He wouldn't have much time. When he entered the Judge's sitting room he found that the nurse's screams had brought the old man to his feet on his own. The Judge stood there, wavering in place. Either he couldn't decide what to do or where to go, or his legs wouldn't obey him.

"I just want to ask you some questions," Jack said, holding up his hands to seem friendly.

The Judge glared at him with all the condemnation in the world.

"Why don't you sit back down? I'll stay right here if you do."

The Judge said something, but Jack couldn't understand what it was.

"Frustrated?" Jack asked him. "Me too."

And still that woman screamed. Maybe he should've gagged her, but now it was too late. It was too late for everything. And here he'd backed himself into a corner. Eva would find out. She would demand an explanation, and nothing he could tell her would save him.

"You said I was an animal," Jack told the old man. "And I am."

The Judge's head bobbed slightly – or was it only a tremor? His gaze was as fixed as ever.

"And my brother Gus is an animal, and my father. We are cursed."

With a precarious kind of wobble, the Judge dropped back into his seat again.

"But if the curse can be broken, my family has forgotten how. We don't even know why any more. Each generation has become more and more ignorant of how it came to be. I just want to know how to break the curse. Do you know how?"

The old man's lips moved into a half-smile, but whether friendly or contemptuous, Jack had no idea.

Had he lost his chance with the Judge too? The man's garbled speech meant speedy communication was impossible. He waited, hoping for something, anything from the old man.

This was madness.

"My brother went after Eva last night," Jack said. "He wants to end the curse too, just not the same way I do."

The sound in the room was different. The woman had stopped screaming. Was someone here? Was he found out?

"Can you help me?" Jack asked the Judge one last time.

The Judge merely trembled in his seat.

It had been idiocy to come. Idiocy and desperation. Jack had been counting on taking a good ten years to carefully research and unpick the tapestry of Wylde history. Interviews with founding families in the area had actually been part of his plan, just not like this. All his plans had been ripped away with the death of the girl the night before last.

Why was Gus so different from their father? Gus was by far a better person. Maybe the devil sensed the end of the Wylde line? Or maybe the curse went into effect when it would most torment its victims?

Jack checked the hallway just in time to see a shadow pass by a front window. No time left.

If the Judge had the answer, he wasn't telling. Or maybe he couldn't.

Which left Jack with one last thing to do. It had always been inevitable. Gus had been right all along.

Jack crossed the hallway to the back pantry. The nurse was creeping in the other direction toward the front door. She'd managed to get free and had called for help. A worthy nurse for the illustrious Judge.

Jack could thank Eva that he knew the back way out of the house, via the kitchen, to the small yard and beyond to the park.

The humidity clutched at him, the day smothering him with miseries.

A surreptitious glance told him that a police car was moving down the street toward the Judge's house. His truck was still out front – he couldn't go back for it now – so his identity was obvious. There was no hiding for him.

The sun had passed its zenith. He had a very long walk home, backstreets and fields to the woods, to prepare. He'd kill his brother, and then Eva would come for him.

Chapter Five

Eva didn't understand.

"Jackson Barrett Wylde," the officer was saying, "you know from up—"

"Yes, I know who Jack Wylde is." She glanced again around her father's pristine entryway. The only thing that had been moved was a piece of furniture. As far as she could tell, nothing had been taken – none of the memorabilia, and some of it was worth quite a lot. So they could just drop the robbery charge right now.

Furious. That's what she was with Jack. If he wanted to speak to her father, he could've damn well done it when she was present.

And Lettie was carrying on as if Jack had cruelly manhandled her, which wasn't him at all. Though he had been skulking around her place in the middle of the night and that was out of character too. Another odd thing – his truck was out front, and he'd run off without offering an explanation, like someone who was guilty of something.

But she *knew* him. Jack was not dangerous, not violent. He just looked it.

Well, her patience was at an end. It was time she talked to Gus, the constant shadow in Jack's life. It'd started yesterday, she thought, when she'd first knocked on their door.

Jack's older brother had been behind him, and Jack had acted so cold. Gus had to know what was wrong.

She went back to kiss her father goodnight. The paramedics had come and gone – nothing for them to do – but her father's doctor was in there chatting up the Judge to satisfy himself that there'd been no harm done.

The doctor nodded the all's well when she stepped back into the room.

"Nothing like a little excitement," she said, playing along. "An officer will be posted outside, just in case."

The Judge mumbled something. Again Eva recognized the word "animal", even as the doctor chatted right over her father's words. "Nothing to worry about here. The Judge has nerves of steel. It's the nurse that needs a sedative." Chuckle.

"I have to go, Daddy." She rarely called him that, but she'd been very scared for a few minutes today. The emergency call to this house had shown her just how unprepared she was to lose him. "I'll check back in tonight."

Her SUV was double-parked. In two minutes flat she was around the square and onto the wider street that would take her to Oak Grove. From there to the long stretch of Old Highway 23 to the Wylde plantation. She had to restrain herself from racing up the pitted drive that led to the house, oak trees parting the way.

Once again she climbed the front steps – top one still splintered – and pounded on the door with the flat of her hand. Déjà vu, except her heartbeat was up, anger snapping along her nerves.

"August!" she shouted. Jack wouldn't be home yet because he'd left his truck outside the Judge's house. "Open up!"

The vertical line between the doors cracked. She peered into the darkness. "Hello?"

But Gus was hidden behind the right door. "Evangeline Renard. Welcome back."

She'd never liked Gus. He'd always had a sick watchfulness about him that made her want to look behind herself even though he stood right in front of her.

"I was hoping you'd come by again." His voice was so low, breathless. Strange. "Would you like to come inside?"

Jack had never invited her in, and she was powerfully curious. The kind of curious that made stupid people do stupid things. Not her.

"I have some questions I'd like to ask you," she said.

"All the ghosts are in here, and I think that's what you came for."

That voice. It made her belly cold. She'd thought she might encounter Gus drunk, even angry drunk, but he had an absolutely predatory sound to him. She was armed, yet she felt small and weak and hated it. The sun outside was safer than the darkness within.

"I think I'll wait out here. Why don't you come out?"

"I can't. I'm sick," he said. "But I'd like to speak to you too. In fact, I need to talk to you about Jack. He's taking my illness badly. It's terminal, you see, and I haven't got much time left."

She was taken aback. Sick? "What do you have?"

"It's a kind of wasting thing, a gradual loss of control of my body. It's not pleasant."

Sounded a little like her father's stroke, except . . . the Wylde brothers probably didn't have money for treatment, nurses, and doctors' visits to their home. "I'm very sorry."

She hadn't expected anything like this.

Gus was ill. Would the prospect of losing his older brother make Jack a little less himself? She thought of the truck and the building debris in its bed. Had he been renovating the house to accommodate his brother's needs? She'd had to make some changes for the Judge too.

And Jack was alone with the task. Eva felt her heart breaking for him. She understood what it was like to see a loved one lose hold.

He should have told her.

"Here," Gus said, backing up to slowly open one of the double doors wide. He still kept to the house's shadows. "I've got to sit down. You come in when you're ready. Have a look around. Jack's always been ashamed of where he came from, but as you're his friend, you ought to know."

A shadow retreated and Eva was left with one hand ready to grab her gun, the other reaching out to open the door.

Light streamed into what had once been a wide and gracious entryway, now uninhabitable by any standards. Filthy, stained, seeping. Even the stairs were busted, the railing hanging off to the side. And *this* was where a terminally ill person was supposed to convalesce? The mold alone would suffocate him.

She leaned forward to get the layout of the building. Hallway that way. Open rooms beyond, but cluttered with heaping shapes. Furniture, maybe. The smell was . . . not good. No repairs that Jack could make would salvage this place. It needed to be gutted at the very least. Possibly demolished. They should have sold. God, they should've sold long ago.

And the coldness touching her skin, in spite of the hot summer afternoon, affirmed that, yes, the place was full of ghosts. Gus was fast becoming one too, she realized. She wasn't fool enough to go inside. There was no way to go inside without coming out *changed* in some way. The place was bad.

Instinct told her to get away from here, but she descended the porch steps to wait for Jack. She did so with her gun in hand.

Twenty minutes passed while the doors of the house stood open like a big black mouth to hell. Something terrible and dangerous was in there – a strange, prescient sense warned her – so she did not take her eyes off it. Up until now, she'd never discounted the idea that there were unnatural things living alongside the rest of the world. Could be she'd been told too many stories as a child, but she'd always allowed for the possibility.

Jack had grown up there. A child, hiding from his angry father.

It made her angry and afraid for the child he'd been. She was afraid because she'd loved him and would've done anything, gone anywhere he'd asked. But she couldn't have saved him from that house. Not then. She'd been a child herself.

But maybe now.

And for that, she would hear him out and try to understand. The fact that Gus was ill, sad though it was, helped a little to explain.

A flicker of movement to her right. She darted her gaze away from the big black opening to a thicket of pine trees beyond the oaks. A man coming. It was Jack.

He had seen her too and was coming straight toward her, which was a start at least. Honest.

On the other side of the drive he halted. Sweat soaked the shoulders and chest of his button-down shirt.

"You been inside?" he asked.

"Gus invited me, but I preferred to wait for you."

Jack nodded, strong emotion in his eyes. "You know we tried to burn it down?"

"Looks like a single match would do it," she said, her voice too high.

"Poured gallons of gasoline. Used a blowtorch. I'm pretty sure it'll stand until the end of the world."

Another person might think Jack was making the place a metaphor for the unhappiness that it held and his attempts to get free of it. Eva had a small suspicion that he was being literal.

She got to the point of her visit. "Jack, why'd you go to see my father? If you needed something, why not wait for me to go with you?"

He looked at the ground. "I was hoping he'd help me with something. Help me find something."

Find some—? Oh. Now she understood. Jack needed money to care for his brother and he had antiques or historical documents to sell. "Is this about the museum in Savannah? I heard you make an appointment with the curator this morning. They mostly worked with my father, but I know they'll talk to me too. You could've asked me."

Jack put a hand to his face to cover up an expression – laughter maybe? Was he laughing at her? If he was, it was the dark, bitter kind.

"It's a little late for that now," he finally said.

"There's still time," she argued. "The Judge doesn't like you, but if I ask, he'll forgive the trespassing."

Jack had turned to look at the entrance to the house, that big black square hole into darkness.

"No," he said to it. "I promised I'd do it. I'll do it as soon as Eva is gone."

Gus had to have heard and come out.

She followed Jack's line of sight, but had difficulty seeing inside the black rectangle with the contrast of late afternoon light, but yes, Gus was in the doorway. There was a funny reflection of the setting sun in his eyes. It lit them bright yellow. And he was shirtless, pants unbuttoned. Muscle rippled beneath his taut skin. His shoulders were thick, stomach a washboard. This was not the body of a sick man.

She was confused and angry again.

"I figured it'll have to be you," Gus said to her, stepping into the waning light. "Your friendship is a godsend. Because after I'm gone, Jack will have no one to take care of him."

After he was gone? August Wylde did not look ill.

Jack came toward her. "Go home, Eva. If you were ever my friend, go home now."

"I rather think it important that I stay," she said. Gus didn't look sick, but he didn't look right either. *Those eyes.*

"Then give me your gun," Jack demanded.

"I know perfectly well how to use it, thank you." She glanced at Jack, an arm's length away. His eyes too had an odd color, gleaming in the late rays of the sun.

Those weren't human eyes.

Not human. More like . . .

She looked back at Gus, whose very skin was becoming darker, his body hunching.

Oh dear God.

"You're cursed," she said. Jack had refused to talk about it last night. She would've stepped back, cringed farther away from them, but she was already flush against her vehicle.

"Yes," Jack said.

He'd been completely honest with her once, but then children are like that. The whole family, he'd said. Wylde.

She swallowed hard. "Was it you or Gus—?"

"I killed the girl," Gus said in that horrible voice.

Jack held out his hand again. "Can I have the gun now?"

"I think I want it." No way in hell she was giving it up. In fact, she wasn't sure who to point it at.

She was seeing the wisdom of her father's admonitions to stay away from the Wylde boys. She'd thought her father meant that they might take advantage of her youth, innocence or her soft heart. Get her pregnant or hooked on drugs. She'd been offended at the Judge's lack of trust and gone ahead and done what she'd wanted anyway. He'd never known just how disobedient she was.

"What *specifically* did you want from my father?" she asked again.

"He called me an animal, and so I thou—"

Eva finished his sentence. Funny how she could still do that. "—you thought he knew something." She nodded. That made sense. "And the appointment you made in Savannah?"

"Tracing family memorabilia to find the source of the curse. I ran out of time."

Gus stepped forward, an almost serpentine movement. Eva shivered.

"Jack will do his duty by me," he said, "but someone will have to take care of him. My greatest concern has been the thought of him alone and hunted. My prayers have been answered in you."

Eva looked to Jack for a more coherent explanation.

He obliged. "Gus will kill again tonight if he lives. And, one day, I won't be able to control myself either. We're a family of murderers."

While her alarm sharpened her senses, the daylight went rosy, the dappled shadows stretching. The scent of the air was sweeter, richer with dirt and sky and a combination of all green things.

First August Wylde was a man, slowly, if too smoothly, stepping down from his porch.

And then he was a low black shadow with a huge black feline head and the feral eyes of a beast. His black fur glinted as his legs rolled through its joints, prowling silently forward. The jaguar was made of sinuous muscle and coiling violence. And he was coming toward her.

"Eva—" Jack warned, his arm moving to push her out of the creature's path.

"Yeah, I got this." She flicked off the gun's safety, took quick aim, and fired.

Jack was in motion as soon as his brother fell. Eva had fired her gun, but as far as Jack could tell, not one single bullet hit the mark, and he didn't think it was because Sergeant Evangeline Renard had bad aim. It was the curse.

The world had gone silent when she finally stopped, and still his brother prowled forward.

Jack lunged between them; Gus would never hurt *him*.

"Get inside the car!" Jack hoped she'd obey him this time. He didn't dare take his eyes off his brother to check.

Gus coiled to spring, and Jack recognized a feint, just like at Eva's house last night. He'd distract Gus, and if she could just get away, then . . .

But his brother was no longer present. The devil was.

The shadow sprang, like night itself crashing out of the sky, mauling Jack's chest with vicious gouges from its claws. The blunt triangular head came down with its moon-bright fangs chomping for meat.

Jack used all his strength, fists gripping fur at its roots, to keep that maw from clamping down. Simultaneously, he gave himself up to that same promise of blood, and shifted himself into his own jaguar form, a bone-rattling transition that gave him a feral supernatural strength and teeth just as sharp.

The spectrum of color in the world changed with the thump of his heart. He tangled with his brother, rolling in the dirt. His clothes were ripped to shreds during the shift and fight. He didn't care if he bled or died. He couldn't let the devil hunt tonight. If the devil hunted, it would be Eva's blood he drank.

A slippery twist and the bloodbeat of instinct said, *Now!*

Jack darted like black lightning, his fangs finding vein and sinew. With a hearty, raging bite, he tore out his brother's throat. The body in his embrace shuddered and then went slack.

His mouth still filled with flesh, Jack looked up to find Eva.

She'd opened the SUV's door but was only part-way inside. Her blue eyes were wide and unblinking. Her lips were parted, mouth in a shape of distress. But she was alive, and for that, his wild heart knew peace.

In a blistering ripple, he became himself again. But naked and bloody. He gagged against the taste in his throat and spit out the gristle. Wiped his chin with the back of his arm.

Only then did he notice that Eva was holding a shotgun.

He waited for her to lift the weapon and fire. He was strong enough to keep still.

Her blindfold was off now. No illusions any more. *This* was what he was.

Tears spilled from her eyes. She blinked at them. Shook her head, and then put her weapon on the seat inside. "I won't do it," she said.

He understood. The prospect of killing Gus had been hideous to him, though he'd been prepared for it from childhood. How could she fire on someone in cold blood?

"I'll go away," Jack said. "You're not responsible for me."

There were lots of ways to get himself killed when the time came. No need for her to assume a Wylde burden.

Very slowly, he stood. His guts ached to see the dead jaguar soaking the dirt red, but Gus had gotten his wish and had died this day.

Jack staggered back toward the house. It was his place now, but he couldn't live there. Wouldn't. He'd hose off this death, stuff a few things into a bag and be gone. He didn't care where.

His bare foot touched the first of the porch steps when Eva spoke behind him.

"Stay," she said.

He inclined his head a bit. He didn't want to face her

with this gore all over him. "It's okay, Eva. It's over. I'll go far away where I can't hurt anyone."

It was just him now, no more Wyldes to come. A vasectomy had made certain of that. At the moment, he felt lighter by a thousand pounds. Of course that could be blood loss.

"No, you won't," she said.

He twisted his head around a little more. The red stripes on his chest burned, little stars pricking into the edges of his vision.

"You said all it would take was for me to say 'stay'. Well, I just did." She'd stepped out from the cover of the door. The repulsion was gone from her expression, her chin set just as it had been that day they'd met when she was nine and wouldn't go to church if he wasn't welcome.

He shook his head. "You don't know—"

"I think I do. And, rest assured, I'll plug you between the eyes if it becomes necessary."

He had nothing to say to that.

"Get what you need. You're never staying here again. You can crash at my place. We'll patch you up and see if we can't make that appointment in Savannah tomorrow."

Seemed like in the space of five seconds she had it all figured out. Her hands were trembling though. Her body stiff with tension.

He turned back to the house. It was difficult to argue with her while he was covered in blood.

"Don't make me come in after you," she threatened.

His choked laugh broke through his disbelief. He went inside, cleaned the blood off his face, neck and chest. He had a mean cut down one shin too. The long scratches on his chest wouldn't stop bleeding. He put on pants, but no shirt, threw his stuff in a bag and met her back at the SUV.

She was radioing the station to inform them that the jaguar had been found and killed. Could they send someone to pick up the remains?

When she was done, she nodded toward the black shadow on the ground. "They'll be here soon. Do you want to say some words for your brother? You might not get another chance."

Jack shook his head. "That's not Gus."

She nodded. "Okay. We better take you to the hospital to get those gashes treated."

"Fine," Jack said. "You sure about this? You can change your mind anytime. I won't hold you to anything. I've got no right. In fact, I'll probably leave in the morning." He needed some quiet time to think the events of today through.

"I'm sure," she said. "And you promised you'd stay. So you better, or I swear I'll hunt you down."

At the first sign of the dark hunger he'd leave, but she could have her way for now. Maybe they would find the answer in Savannah.

He leaned in, as if to kiss her. She trembled a little, but allowed his closeness. Brave Eva.

She looked at his mouth, a cautious invitation. They were and had always been more than friends. But then he gave her a long, rough lick up her neck to the back of her ear. It was both a promise and a threat. This is exactly what she was getting herself into.

The pulse at her throat leapt, but she swayed toward him, rather than away.

"This is going to be interesting," she said. As she was looking for her keys, she realized she already had them in her hand.

He placed his bag inside the SUV. "You have no idea."

DREAM, INTERRUPTED

Jill Archer

Moonlight, Georgia or thereabouts

10:00
There's an old song by a band called the Black Crowes titled "She Talks to Angels". At first blush, the woman in the song is a liar. She talks about being an orphan but she has a family. She's also an addict and a lunatic. She smiles when she's in pain and she rings her eyes with more kohl than any one woman has a right to use. You may not like her but, if so, it's because you don't really know her. Because a third cousin twice removed whom you see only once every five years doesn't count as "family". And sometimes, addictions are the only thing you have left.
    I'm an addict.
    What's my addiction?
    Sleep aids. Oh, you know, zaleplon and zolpidem, diphenhydramine and doxylamine, tryptophan and turkey legs. Forget about coffee; it's chamomile tea for me. Lately, I've even traded in my nasal strips for a full-on CPAP mask. How's that for laughs?
    Well, don't. Because my addiction is more deadly than you'll ever guess.

I woke up in the dark, legs thrashing, arms flailing. Something was dragging at my ankles, making them feel heavy and wet. I kicked my legs, thigh muscles straining, knees popping, but nothing happened. My feet met resistance, but nothing solid. I was drowning in a vat of gelatin.

Huge gobs of the stuff pressed up my nose, down my throat, and into my lungs. My chest heaved and I panicked. I swept my arm out and – finally – made contact with something solid. A corner. Its hard edge bit into the bone of my lower arm just above my wrist. Faint tinkling sounds pierced the numbed hum in my ears, suddenly shattering my dream like glass.

I was awake.

I blinked, trying to make sense of the green glowing numerals in the round face of my bedside clock, but 0:00 didn't make any sense so I ignored it. My left arm was still throbbing from whacking it against my bedside table so I used my right to disengage from the tangled mess of my sheets. I swung my legs to the floor and hopped down, wincing as something sharp stabbed the padded sole of my foot. I sucked in my breath, but managed not to cry out. I might be awake, but I sure as hell didn't want *them* to be.

Biting my lip in pain, I switched on the bedside light. A circular wash of color swam across the blackness as if searching for something. Once my head stopped buzzing, the circle stopped and steadied, illuminating a small swath of blinking, winking lights. Scattered across the floor in a shallow pool of water were myriad jagged pieces of broken glass, a half-dozen vials and bottles, and a thin trail of bright red blood. Off to the side, a mask spun slowly on the floor. It reminded me of a spinning top or a game piece. I stood, despite the pain in my foot, and wobbled over to it. I reached down and picked it up mid-spin, stopping its rotation.

I stared at it, turning it over in my hands, testing the elastic straps. It would be easy to just slip it on and go back to sleep. This was the thing that was supposed to protect me. This was the thing that was supposed to keep them away. As exhausted as I was, though, I couldn't go back to sleep. For one thing, I had to dig the glass out of my foot.

I set the mask on my dresser, careful not to set it spinning again, and limped in the direction of the bathroom. My long white nightgown swished around my ankles as I propelled myself forward, following the long thin trail of blood to the door.

How many times have I done this?

I ignored the pounding of my heart and focused on keeping my breathing slow and easy. Deep gulps of air were not advisable. I glanced back at the bed I'd just risen from. They'd never appeared in my room before, but I couldn't afford to take chances.

In the round splash of my bedside light, my deranged covers were a choppy, sloppy mess. Waves of black quilt and gray sheet, dotted with tiny circles of sea-foam green and aquamarine, roiled up every which way. My bedside table was empty except for the neon green lights on my clock face. All else had been swept to the floor by my flailing arms as I'd emerged from my dream. Above my bed was a sign. It read:

THE ONEIROI INSTITUTE
REQUIESCAT IN PACE

9:00
Everyone always thinks of the song, "My Darling Clementine" with a smile. Like it's some cheery love song. But you know what? She died. Clementine drowned.

Daylight, thankfully, found me before they did. The exact moment of awakening is always subject to interpretation in my world. Is it when the alarm goes off, alerting you in its screechingly insistent tones that you must act or die – get out of bed *now* before it's Too Late . . . Or is it when you first realize that you are no longer dreaming? When you finally realize that you have left *that* place for *this* one?

Or is it when you first open your eyes?

Frankly, it didn't matter. At least not to me. I didn't give a flying sheep's fleece what the administrators, therapists or doctors thought. I only knew I had two minutes to get to Dr Ambrose's Sunshine Session. One hundred and twenty seconds to dress, race down the hall, and find my seat. Needless to say, my clothing choices were erratic. But then everyone's clothing choices at Oneiroi were erratic. Somnambulists, narcoleptics and parasomniacs didn't wear suits or ties, belts or suspenders. They didn't wear panty-hose or pencil skirts. They wore pajama tops and sweatpants, thick socks and slippers. Bed head and black eyes from lack of sleep were *de rigueur* at Oneiroi.

Still, I had but one life to live. And I wasn't going to live it in fashion purgatory. So, even with only seconds to spare, I donned one of my retrofitted antebellum dresses (along with my money, I'd inherited a trunk-full of gowns, which I'd promptly hacked and dyed), fishnet stockings and thigh-high black boots. The look was somewhat extreme, but since I was the only one here whose snoring woke the dead, I figured I should look the part. My hair – long enough to be truly tangled and amazingly bedraggled from my struggles – would have to wait. I tore through the long, dark, dank hallways of Oneiroi, hairbrush in hand.

Why did I care so much about being on time for Sunshine Session?

Because it was a diversion. A blessed distraction. It was a discussion inspired by the work of talented but troubled writers like Shakespeare, Edgar Allan Poe and the Brothers Grimm. It was dark therapy performed at sunrise, but at least the talks focused on something made up. Something fictional. I mean, look, it wasn't as if it was the Weird Sisters, Roderick Usher or the Big Bad Wolf I was running from.

So, the Sunshine Sessions were half an hour out of my life when I could try to forget the Blackhearts and whether my snoring might summon them later. It was thirty blissful minutes of having a chance to forget whether today might be the day they would catch me, drag me out to sea, and drown me.

8:00
10,000 Maniacs had to have been at Oneiroi. I'm not talking about real maniacs (although that's possible too), but the band. Okay, I might be lying (remember the girl who talked to angels?), but still . . . How else to explain the song "Like the Weather"? Surely, they wrote that song for me. *Gray skies, shivering bones, quivering lips – ready to cry. Why? Because she can't get out of bed, of course! She's tired. She's depressed.*

She forces her lungs to fill, and she breathes. But she never leaves. It's cold and it's rainy and she hears the sound of a bell tolling. She's pulled down, trapped, and yet . . . she hopes, she prays . . . that it will all pass away . . .

Oneiroi is a bit like Alcatraz – if Alcatraz was a centuries-old mansion called "Wailing Rock" instead of just "The Rock", if it was located off the coast of Georgia instead of California, and if the residents there were patients instead of prisoners. But make no mistake. Residents at Oneiroi are still trapped. Our disorders keep us locked in as much as the house – an old, rambling structure built on an island just outside of Ossabaw Sound, south-east of Savannah and due east of Moonlight, the town where my mother was born. The town where I lived last year, my senior year of high school. The town where I met Caradoc Ambrose and he asked me to prom and . . . well, let's just say prom night did not end well.

I left Moonlight screaming, running from the Blackhearts. But they found me. They always do. And so I came back to Moonlight. The only home I'd ever really known. To Wailing Rock – the Ambrose family seat. Ancestral home of the eighteenth-century pirate, Bonny Black, captain of the *Alice Anne*, his forty-cannon frigate flagship that he'd named after his wife, who'd been rumored to be a witch. And to the Oneiroi Institute, the sleep clinic and research facility founded by Caradoc's father. As Caradoc explained to me last year, his father's methods were effective but controversial, so he'd set up shop in his own home, away from the sounds and psychological congestion associated with cities like Savannah. ("Sometimes it's helpful to have an old, out-of-the-way family mansion, Corelei.")

The island that Wailing Rock was built upon is so small, it's hardly ever shown on maps, and even though I lived in Moonlight for a year, I'd be hard pressed to give anyone directions. Let's face it, when I committed myself to Dr Ambrose's care, I was so out of it from the constant stress and sleep deprivation associated with my disorder that I could barely remember my last name.

"*Neverest!*" I chortled bitterly, remembering the varied emotions that raced across Dr Ambrose's face when I'd first introduced myself: disbelief, humor, and then, for the briefest moment, fear. Because he knew then he'd have to cure me. My last name said it all. My last name *was* my file.

ONEIROI INSTITUTE
INTAKE SHEET

Name: Corelei Neverest

Previous Addresses: Superstition Mountains, Arizona; Portsmith QLD, Australia; Charlestown, Nevis, West Indies

Parents: Wilder and Beulahbelle Neverest, late owners of Neverest Quests, Inc., a company specializing in "Exploration, Discovery, and Recovery"

Next of Kin: Gershom Wallace (distant cousin, whereabouts unknown)

Complaint: Claims she suffers from "apnea anima", a self-diagnosed condition that occurs when a person's snoring summons the Blackhearts

Other Alternatives to Consider: Adrenaline addiction, psychosis . . . *Somnicantare?!*

Diagnosis: Unclear . . .

A winter rabbit's fur is white for one reason. And my camouflage was black for the same. As sleep deprived as I was, I just never knew when I was going to cross over to the dark side. And it wasn't Morpheus I was afraid of meeting. Because despite Dr Ambrose's suggestion that I might be making them up, the Blackhearts were real. They were deadly. And they were out to kill me.

My goal at Oneiroi since I'd arrived was based on a simple strategy. Act like the white rabbit. Hide, evade, run.

My rubber-soled boots hardly made a sound on the wood floors of the house. I imagined (hoped) that my long blonde, low-lighted hair and black dressed silhouette

would appear no more substantial in the darkened corridors than a ghost's soul, that wispy residue left behind by
a life already lived. Something no more noticeable than a
fading glow stick on All Saints' Day, one left on a bedside
table, or tossed in the grass, after a long night of blazing
incandescence.

I entered Sunshine Session with exactly two seconds to
spare and tried to ignore the euphoric feeling the successful scramble had given me. One of Dr Ambrose's theories
was that I liked to run. That, even if the Blackhearts
weren't real (which they were), he theorized that I actually *liked* the idea of running from them (which was
insane; I'd like to see what *he* would do if the Blackhearts
were chasing *him*; run like hell was what, if he knew what
was good for him).

I slipped into my seat, nodding to those who were awake,
and saying hi to Rob, who sat to my left. Somnael Robusta,
a.k.a. "Rob", suffered from multiple cataplectic attacks
every day. He would be completely animated and then,
within a matter of minutes, his words would first slur and
then stop altogether. His head would fall against his chest
and then that would be it for Rob for the next half-hour.
Thar she blows and off he goes and all that. I think it scared
him and I felt sorry for him. He was the youngest of us at
Oneiroi and I went out of my way to be nice to him. The rest
of them were okay.

Poppy Mogeneti was a little bit snobbish. She wore sleek
cotton sweatpants and matching hoodies and her hair was
always severely pulled back in a tight ponytail, as if she were
on her way to a jog. But she never went anywhere, except in
her dreams. Poppy was a somnambulist and chewed an
unbelievable amount of gum. I think she did it to try to stay
awake. (None of us were allowed coffee.) Poppy raised an
eyebrow at my unkempt hair, chewing, popping and cracking the whole time. Self-consciously, I gathered my hair at
the nape of my neck and began pulling my hairbrush
through it.

Dr Ambrose finished writing something on the chalkboard at the front of the room:

Should Ophelia have fought back?

Against what? I thought. My recollection was that no one had been chasing her. Shakespeare's doomed maiden had been stupid enough to slip and then hadn't been strong enough to get herself out of the mess she'd gotten herself into. But I doubted Dr Ambrose would appreciate that analysis so I wrapped my hair in a knot and tucked my hairbrush into mȳ bag, thinking hard about what sort of adversary (real or abstract) Dr Ambrose might be referring to.

Suddenly, I felt a sharp pinch in my arm. It was the corner of a small white folded piece of paper. I turned around in my seat and stared at Aisling.

Aisling Liberica was by far the student with the most seniority at Oneiroi. No one knew exactly when she'd come and she alone acted like she never wanted to leave. Aisling was always tired (though who at Oneiroi wasn't?) but Aisling wore her tiredness the way I wore my black camouflage. Everything about her was fleeting: the way she talked, the way she ate, the way she walked, even her hair was gossamer thin and flyaway. She hardly ever completed a full sentence. Her voice always trailed off before she finished. It was like watching someone with Attention Deficit Disorder live their life in slow motion. Someone had pushed fast-forward and pause on Aisling's life simultaneously so her preferred method of communication was pictures and poems . . . snippets, sketches, stills and shorts. That's how Aisling saw our world.

She poked me again with the corner of her note. I took it and turned back in my seat, opening it under the desk. I expected to see a picture of a steaming cup of coffee, with swirls of steam so real they would almost lift off the page, a cup of coffee so lovingly and realistically depicted that my mouth would water in anticipation of its bold bite and hot sting. But instead, there was a poem.

> Hickory, dickory, dock,
> Kore ran out the clock.
> The clock struck zero,

Now he's nearer!
Hickory, dickory, 'doc.

I had no idea what Aisling's poem meant. But then, none of us ever did. I slid the piece of paper under my notebook and made a mental note to ask her about it later. Of course, if she had an answer, I would get only half of it, and then I'd be more confused than ever. But I had to try, right?

The fifth and final patient at Oneiroi was Tristan Gallienii, a huge bear of a boy who had obstructive sleep apnea. He hated me because he didn't believe in the Blackhearts. He thought I was a prissy prima donna who was too embarrassed to admit I had a snore worse than his.

Dr Ambrose rapped the chalkboard with a pointing stick. "Rob, what do you think?"

Rob swallowed hard, his eyes bulging and his Adam's apple bobbling. *Please let him have read the play* ... If Dr Ambrose found out the majority of the group hadn't read today's suggested passages, he might end Sunshine Session early. And then I'd be scrambling to find another distraction to fill my time until breakfast.

"Against who?" Rob said finally. "Her father?"

Poppy's hand shot up and Dr Ambrose nodded at her. "Hamlet," she said, removing the piece of gum from her mouth. She carefully placed it on the center of a clean piece of paper and folded it out of existence.

"Yeah," Tristan snickered, his massive shoulders shaking and his deep lungs rumbling. "When Hamlet told Ophelia to 'get thee to a nunnery', she should have told him to shove it."

"But she loved him," Rob said, frowning in confusion.

"Did she?" Poppy asked, unwrapping a fresh stick of gum. She folded it exactly four times and put it in her mouth. "Where in the play does it say that? In what scene does Ophelia declare her love for Hamlet?"

Tristan scoffed. "Well, does Hamlet really love Ophelia? I don't think so—"

"Who cares if they love one another?" Poppy snapped, chewing furiously. "The play's not about that ..."

"Of course they love one another," Rob said quietly. "It's a tragedy."

"Which requires unrequited love or doomed lovers?" Poppy sneered. "It's not *Romeo and Juliet*. It's *Hamlet*. It's *his* tragedy."

"It's *everyone's* tragedy," Tristan bellowed. "Everyone dies!"

Dr Ambrose cleared his throat. The room fell silent. "Corelei, thoughts?"

Somewhere between Rob's romanticism, Poppy's cynicism and Tristan's apoplexy, I'd figured out the answer to Dr Ambrose's question. I'd been right all along. When he'd written his question on the board, he hadn't meant *who*, but *what*. And no, even though the play was steeped in the supernatural, Dr Ambrose wasn't referring to an adversary like ghosts or the Blackhearts.

Dr Ambrose was a nonconformist and a fighter. The answer, from his perspective, was society. To him, the biggest tragedy wasn't that eight people had perished inside of four and a half hours of stage time; it was that Ophelia hadn't told *everyone* to shove it. I think what Dr Ambrose wanted me to say was that Ophelia should have told Hamlet, Polonius, Laertes – even King Claudius himself – to go to hell with her blessing. Then she could have escaped Elsinore where the whole grim story had gone down and gone off to . . . what exactly? Become a prostitute? Join the gypsies? Work as a seamstress or scullery maid? With what skills?!

No, there was no way I was going to tell Dr Ambrose that Ophelia should have fought back – because I didn't see how she could have. Still, like him, I had a beef with Ophelia.

But mine was somewhat different.

"Yes," I said, nodding. "She should have fought back."

"Against?"

"The river. She shouldn't have let herself fall."

7:00

Remember that song "The Wreck of the Edmund Fitzgerald"? The old folk song by Gordon Lightfoot? It's been spoofed a few times, but the story behind it is no joke. Twenty-nine people

drowned. *(And I dare you to listen to it twice and then pretend
the lyrics and melody don't stick to the inside of your brain like
glue. Do you take dares? God knows, I do . . .)*

The Edmund Fitzgerald *was a freighter that sank just
outside of Whitefish Bay in Lake Superior. She was going
about business as usual – hauling iron ore late one afternoon in
November of 1975 – when a storm-driven wave came up and,
like the devil's fist, grabbed her and pulled her to the bottom of
the lake. Had her crew seen that fist coming? Did they try to
fight it? I don't know. But I do know you can't dive at the
wreck site without a license. It's prohibited under the Ontario
Heritage Act. If the Canucks catch you, it's a cool one and six
zeroes fine. Far less risky to dive the* Andrea Doria . . .

My mother drowned. Diving the wreck of the SS *Andrea
Doria*. Divers used to call it the "Mount Everest of Scuba
Diving". The depth of the water, the fierce currents, and the
intermittent lack of visibility due to heavy sediment all make
the dive highly technical. Added to that, the wreck itself is
collapsing. She sank in 1956 so the cold Atlantic Ocean has
been slowly eating away at her, leaving bits of the upper
decks strewn across the ocean floor as if disgorged from the
maw of the very thing that destroyed her. And then there
are the fishing nets . . .

Draped across her crumbling remains, like giant
Frankenstein sutures, are endless fishing lines. Failing
utterly to hold the decaying ship together, the nets' only
purpose is to ensnare, trap and kill. My mother got stuck on
one of those lines, somewhere near the promenade deck. At
least that's what we think happened, based on their dive
plan and my father's cryptic words once he reached the top:
"They got her." Is it possible he was suffering from the
lingering effects of nitrogen narcosis? Doubtful. What is
certain is that he was suffering from the bends. He died
from it two days later and I've hated the water ever since.

Outside Wailing Rock the rain continued to fall in muted
drum rolls, as if a legion of drummers had capped their
drumsticks with marshmallows and were merrily beating out

a tuneless, unending rhythm. My stomach rumbled in anticipation of breakfast. Thinking of marshmallows made me
want a big bowl of puffed rice cereal. But Dr Ambrose was
writing another question on the board so those lovely little
popping, crackling, snapping sounds would have to wait.

Was Ophelia's death an accident?

"Corelei, you said Ophelia *let* herself fall. Are you saying
she wanted to drown?"

"No!" I said too quickly. *Who would want to drown?!* And
yet . . .

There were all sorts of indications that Ophelia may have
wanted to. Her father had been recently murdered, by her
ex-lover of all people, who had, a mere act earlier, viciously
slandered her, telling her he hadn't loved her, that she
should either take the veil or join the whores (depending on
one's interpretation of the infamous "nunnery" line) or,
alternatively, that she should enter into a cursed marriage
with a fool because "wise men know well enough what
monsters you make of them". Wow. It was almost enough to
make anyone jump the bridge. Or break the bough, as
Ophelia had.

"Of course her death was an accident," Poppy said, jaw
clenching and unclenching. "She was mad, not suicidal."

Tristan scoffed. "That's like saying you're a little bit
pregnant."

"Maybe she was." Poppy shrugged and pulled her hair
into a tighter, higher ponytail. She was itching for a fight.
Passive characters like Ophelia always brought out her
mean streak.

"What? I don't understand." Hurt mixed with confusion
on Rob's face. "How could she have been pregnant?"

I glanced over at Dr Ambrose, wondering what he
thought. The suicide theory was controversial enough
without adding another possible (and highly improbable) motive. Besides, how could anyone ever know the
truth of *Hamlet*? The players themselves didn't even
seem to know.

"Never mind," he said, rapping Poppy's desk with his pointing stick – *Snap!* She jumped and there was a tense moment when I thought she might have choked on her gum, but then she started chewing again . . . *Crackle* . . .

Aisling poked me. This time when I opened her folded note, there was a picture. Amazingly lifelike, as always. Rendered in stark black ink on white lined paper, Aisling had nonetheless managed to create an image that had instant impact, one that hit me like a punch to the gut. In the picture, Ophelia looked radiant, rebellious, *alive*. Her skirts billowed, spreading wide, while her hair whipped in the wind like a flag. Her expression said she was climbing a mountain, not a tree, and her smile, in those last moments, was one of pure bliss.

I knew it was likely exhaustion that made Aisling's drawing move as if I were viewing it through a zoetrope, but the effect was still startling. In the time it took me to blink, Ophelia had climbed ever higher. She clambered out onto the longest, thinnest, highest branch on the tree, clearly reaching for something. A bird? A butterfly? Based on the play, it would most likely have been a flower. But in Aisling's drawing the thing that Ophelia desperately wanted was just out of reach. I realized it then. The subject of Aisling's drawing wasn't Ophelia's desire, or even Ophelia herself. It was the branch. One single, slashing pen stroke. That's all that stood between Ophelia and Death. This drawing was Aisling's way of answering Dr Ambrose's question.

I glanced up at her. Around us, chairs squeaked as everyone else got up for breakfast. Aisling's huge gray eyes stared back at me like two giant full moons. The corners of her mouth quirked up in a sad smile. She pointed to the paper, wanting me to look again. I did.

Suddenly, the branch broke – *Pop!*

The last image I saw before I crumpled up the paper was Ophelia tumbling into the water.

Wailing Rock's dining room was a miserably drab place. Everything about it was dull: the mottled gray wainscoting, the peeling yellow paint and the scuffed unvarnished floor.

The food was bland and tasteless, all mashed potatoes (made from flakes), soft mystery meats, puddings and gelatin. Even the silverware was dull. And no knives! Like Oneiroi was a mental ward instead of a sleep clinic.

I crept along the edge of the buffet table intentionally ignoring stomach-turning selections like chitlins and liver mush. I grabbed a bowl (chipped and cracked) and a spoon (still in relatively good shape) and two small boxes of . . . *What else?* Crisped white rice cereal. I opened the boxes and upended them, ignoring the wet pitter-patter of raindrops on glass in favor of the dry tinkling sounds of puffed rice against china.

I smiled. *Now for the best part . . .* I grabbed the milk and sloshed some into the bowl, waiting to hear . . .

"Corelei Neverest," drawled a voice so deep and low, it seemed to travel at subsonic speed. It crashed into the back of me with a splash, drenching me with emotion, and passing through me like an X-ray. I turned around, knowing my face would be as revealing as a radiograph.

"Caradoc," I whispered. Not for the first time I wished that his effect on me was less intense. That he did *not* make my navel zing and my heart ping and my cheeks burn and my breath hitch. But he *did*. Oh, he did.

Caradoc was, in a word, beautiful. The handsomest man I'd ever seen. One who made my knees wobble and my throat seize. One who made me want to swoon – which I could never, *ever* do. He was all sculpted muscles and lazy smiles. He was brooding bedroom eyes that pinned me to the wall and had their way with me. He was a wolf in wolf's clothing with thick, soft, sandy-colored hair (I knew because my fingers had wound their way through it countless times), eyes that changed color from sky blue to seafoam green to squall gray depending on his mood (you can guess what color they were the last time I saw him, squirming out of his arms just before I ran screaming into the night), and a body that just begged to be touched. By me.

I could almost feel his desire.

How much he wanted me.

How much he wanted me to run to him. To press myself against him and bury my face in his shirt and tell him I'd never leave again.

I could almost feel how much he'd wanted me to stay with him.

How much he wanted me now. To wrap my hands around his back, to glide them up his chest, to clutch the back of his neck, to grab fistfuls of his hair. I could almost feel how much he wanted my palms cradling his face as my lips gently met his. As if Caradoc were a bubble and my kiss might . . . *Pop!*

There was so much electricity between us . . .

Crackle.

I could feel how Caradoc wanted to touch me . . . to kiss me . . . to sleep with me . . . *really* sleep with me.

"Welcome back," he said softly, smiling all the while.

Snap!

I blinked. And backed away.

His smile disappeared. "Where'd you run to this time, Corelei?"

"Nowhere," I said, shaking my head.

Liar!

Why couldn't I just tell him the truth?

I was the girl from Everywhere. The girl from Up Top and All Over the World. And Caradoc? Well, he was the boy from Moonlight. The man from Midnight. He shined like silver and, from the moment I met him, I could barely look away, barely stop listening to his voice. His drawl crawled in my ears, dissolved in my blood, and bored straight into my heart.

6:00
Sometime in the early twenty-first century, the alternative rock band Ivy released a song called "Edge of the Ocean". I love that song. It's slow, but still manages to sound happy. Hopeful even. French singer Dominique Durand's voice is melancholic as she croons about a place where the sun always shines and the sky's always blue. She reminisces about a familiar, faraway place. She sings of mystery at the edge of the ocean . . .

A place where her lover should take her so that they can begin again. So they can start over.

"Corelei, you're focusing on all the wrong things."

Caradoc and I were outside, sitting in the back garden at a glass-topped iron table having breakfast. The rain had been replaced with skies the color of Caradoc's eyes – cornflower blue. He stared at me, first quirking his lips and then parting them in a full-fledged grin. His white teeth gleamed in the sun as I moved my hand to my stomach. As if that would quell the butterflies alighting there. Suddenly, it felt as if my mid-section was Michoacán, Mexico, sanctuary for a million migrating monarchs.

I glanced down, surprised to see that I must have changed as well.

Gone was my short, black retrofitted antebellum dress. In its place was the real deal: a green flowered muslin dress with yards of fabric draped over hoops and topped with a close-fitting basque, which showed ample amounts of bosom. I raised a shaky hand to my hair, which was now knotted in a smooth chignon. I narrowed my eyes at Caradoc.

"What happened to the breakfast I was eating earlier?"

"You said you wanted something different."

I did? When?

I glanced around, my worry over a Blackhearts visit increasing by the second. I'd always run before, but now . . . in this dress? Instinctively, I searched the area for possible weapons. I spotted one almost immediately: the knife resting by the side of my praline-pecan French toast-laden plate. *Great.* Twelve inches of soft metal with a dull blade against creatures that were undead and incorporeal. But it was better than nothing. I grabbed the knife and clutched it in my hand, twisting my torso, craning my neck, surveying the sun-drenched landscape for signs of an impending attack. Seeing none, I turned back to Caradoc.

"Did I . . . Was I . . . ?"

Had I fallen asleep? Had I been . . . snoring? God, I hope not.

I cleared my throat and put the knife down, determined to appear normal. I didn't want to encourage Caradoc's affection, but I also didn't want him to think I was a basket case.

I smoothed my skirts and gave him a tremulous smile. "You're not eating?"

He shook his head. "I came to see you, Corelei. You've been here for a month now and you haven't stopped by once to say hello. I was worried about you. After . . . prom night."

I lowered my eyes. Caradoc might live at Wailing Rock, but he and his father lived in a different wing than those of us who were patients at Oneiroi. What he was saying was true. I hadn't gone to see him since I'd arrived. But what could I really say? It had been a mistake to go to prom with him. And an even bigger mistake to agree to spend the night with him at the Magnolia – Moonlight's one and only inn.

What had I been thinking? How can I explain what I'd done?

"Caradoc . . ." I started and then stalled, letting my gaze wander.

Wailing Rock's gardens were truly magnificent. Our table was situated on a lower stone patio that was some ways away from the house – a colossal white clapboard, black-shuttered, hipped-roof creation with wide, wrap-around balconies, a giant widow's walk, and so many columns, it would take forty days and forty nights to count them all. Directly in front of me was a set of crumbling stone steps. They led to the house's back upper lawn. But all around me, just outside of the perimeter of our little stone patio, were gardens. I could smell the flowers from here: sweet, poisonous yellow jessamine blooms, white bursts of Confederate jasmine, lovely wisteria vines, dripping with low-hanging lavender-colored clusters, and lush, intoxicating, ivory-colored gardenia blossoms. There were statues too, amidst the greenery and sparks of color. I could see glimpses of them from where I sat. Bits of wing . . . the tips of horns . . . the tops of tails and sails . . . and more than a few gravestones.

"I didn't come here to see you," I said quietly.

Liar. Liar. Heart on fire.

"I came to see your father."

I looked down at my hands, which were now clenched in my lap.

I didn't know how much Caradoc knew already. From prom night. And from possibly reading my file. *Would he have done that?* I didn't know how much I should tell him now. Part of me wanted to confide in him. Tell him about the Blackhearts. Take a chance that he would believe me. But the other part of me was embarrassed. Embarrassed to be telling such a tall-sounding tale. Embarrassed about the fact that I woke up every night wanting to run. Embarrassed about the fact that I was an addict. That there was a mountain of drugs on my bedside table. I was embarrassed about the fact that I snored, but I was way more embarrassed about what happened when I did. And, let's face it, even though avoiding the Blackhearts was Priority #1, my CPAP mask was decidedly unsexy. It was embarrassing enough that it – and the memory of prom night – had me banning Caradoc from my bedroom forever.

"I have trouble sleeping," I said finally, looking up and meeting his eyes.

There was only one word for a green like that, I thought. *Ardent.* I stared and swallowed as Caradoc pushed back his chair. The grating scrape of iron across stone made me jumpy and I suddenly pushed back my chair too, nearly bolting, but Caradoc closed the distance between us and leaned toward me. He placed his hands on the sides of my chair and brought his face within inches of mine. My eyes widened and I licked my lips. My heart raced and . . .

Oh. How. I. Loved. The. Thrilling. Zing. Of. Him.

Experiencing Caradoc was like biting into a lemon wedge while jumping off a cliff.

"Trouble sleeping, huh? Darlin', you are so full of it."

I pressed my lips together, shifting nervously in my seat. I turned away, feeling my cheeks burn. A moment later, his fingers touched my chin, trailing along my jawline. Gently, he turned my face back toward him.

"I've missed you," was all he said, but it was enough.

5:00

Pink Floyd is a rock band whose popularity peaked sometime in the late twentieth century. Their music is trippy and psychedelic and, needless to say, it made a lasting impression on me. One song, in particular, is an earworm that constantly plays in my head, like an echo, over and over and over again. When David Gilmour sings "Wish You Were Here", you can feel his sincerity and it's hard not to get swept up in the emotion of it. He lays it all out there, infusing Roger Waters' poetic lyrics with sharp, heartfelt sorrow. And yet, the song still feels restrained. Patient somehow. Resigned. As if Gilmour knows his sense of loss and longing will last forever.

The song wasn't written for a lover, but that's how I've chosen to interpret the words. And they are glorious! Each and every line of that song seems profound. He sings of blue skies, green fields and smiles, and then compares them to pain, steel rails and veils. He sings of two lost souls doing the same damn thing over and over and over again . . . the way the song plays in my head over and over and over again. But the opening idea is the one that sticks.

Is there a difference between heaven and hell?

I leaned toward Caradoc and pressed my lips to his. Before I really thought about what I was doing, and what might come of it, I reached my hands up and clasped them behind his neck. He immediately deepened his kiss, capturing my mouth with his, sliding his hand from my cheek to the back of my neck. His tongue slid across the center of my lips. Suddenly, a few bites of puffed rice and sweet toast felt like ignited titanium and potassium nitrate. Caradoc's tongue met mine, lighting sparklers in my stomach, as he pulled me up out of my seat and into his arms.

He crushed me to him as if I'd been gone for centuries instead of months, making me breathless. I stiffened – swooning was simply *not advisable* – and Caradoc relaxed his hold. But he didn't let go. Instead, he broke off the kiss and rested his forehead against mine, his body tense with bridled restraint. His hands slid slowly down my back, finally stopping at my waist, his thumbs pressed into my abdomen. My breath hitched and my bosom heaved and he couldn't resist. He pulled me toward him and lowered his face to my décolletage, raining soft, slow kisses over every exposed inch of my skin. His fingers pressed into my back, keeping me close. I tipped my head back, sighing.

I have to stop this.

But I didn't. I couldn't.

Caradoc traced the skin along the top of my bodice with his tongue, dipping into my cleavage and I nearly cried out. I arched my back and squeezed his sides, finally letting my hands go limp where they rested on his hips. *Would he just rip the basque from body and get it over with already? God, why was breathing so hard?*

But sanity prevailed and Caradoc released me from his embrace, keeping hold of just my hand.

"Let's walk," he said.

"You're overcomplicating what's happening here because of your background, Corelei. You've been everywhere. So you're thinking like someone from Everywhere. You need to start thinking like someone from Moonlight."

"But I'm not from Moonlight."

"Do you want to be?"

I'd agreed to the walk, of course. Suddenly, it seemed as if letting go of Caradoc's hand was as out of the question as taking it had been only an hour or so ago.

So we set off. On a tour of the gardens. It was a diversion. A blessed distraction. Because I had nothing scheduled until lunch and that left far too many moments to accidentally nod off.

Along the way we ran into everyone. Rob was sleeping on a bench under an oak tree. Poppy was running. The first time we spotted her pink sweatshirt and swinging ponytail, I started, instinctively wanting to follow her. But Caradoc squeezed my hand, leaned in close and whispered words of assurance. Soon after, he let go of my hand, but only so that he could tuck my arm through his elbow. Our hips would have touched as we walked but for my hoops.

After that, we spotted Poppy three more times, but always in the distance. Tristan, thankfully, we saw only once, while we were walking through a particularly dense forested section of Wailing Rock's grounds. I expected him to sneer at me, but instead his eyes widened at the sight of us and he bowed his head as he passed, saying nothing.

We walked on.

Eventually, we found Aisling standing under a vine-covered archway holding another folded piece of paper. She pressed it into my hand as we passed and Caradoc shook his head and sighed.

"Would talking about what happened on prom night make you feel any better?" he asked.

Yes. No! I shook my head violently, shoving Aisling's note into my pocket, and pulled Caradoc deeper into the forest.

"The manager of the Magnolia thought you were psychotic, you know," he said a few moments later. I tensed, but Caradoc shook me gently and planted a big kiss on my forehead. "But I know you're not."

He did? Well, that made one of us.

"I also know Gershom Wallace, your no-good third cousin twice removed, was quoted in the *Savannah Sentinel* as saying he thinks your problem is that you have an adrenaline addiction. He believes you developed an addiction to epinephrine and your own endorphins in childhood because your parents dragged you along on all of their globe-spanning, treasure-hunting trips. Wallace's theory is that you were forged in the fire of mountaineering, wreck diving, spelunking, and the like. According to him, you can't get enough of your body's natural fight-or-flight response. But you've climbed too high, fallen too fast, and dived too deep. Now you're exhausted and scared. But you're still addicted to adrenaline and that's why you caused such a scene at the Magnolia last year."

"I don't dive, Caradoc," I said in a quiet, steely voice. "Not any more."

"I know that."

Walking here was like swimming through a giant coral reef, but one in which the sun had bleached all the warm colors of the rainbow out, so that everything was now some variant of jade, sage, moss, or olive. The oak trees grew up out of the sandy soil, quickly branching, twisting, curling, waving, and rolling over one another. And draped over it all was Spanish moss, which swayed in the wind like seaweed caught in the surf above us.

"Do you think what Gershom said is true?"

"No," he scoffed.

"Then what *do* you think?" I asked as Caradoc took firm hold of my waist and lifted me over a limb that had fallen across our path. He held me aloft just a moment longer than necessary, gazing at my face. *Could he even see me?* I imagined I was backlit by the sun since Caradoc's face was completely shadowed. He set me down and we resumed walking.

"I think if you have to choose between fight or flight, Corelei – *fight*. And I'll fight with you. Hell, I'll fight *for* you. Just don't leave again. Okay?"

"I don't think I'm addicted to adrenaline," I said. "I'm addicted to something else."

Caradoc's eyebrows shot up and he gave me a wide grin. His teeth were so bright and white against the dark green of the island's maritime forest he looked like the Cheshire Cat from *Alice's Adventures in Wonderland.*

"An' who would that be, darlin'?" he asked, unhooking my arm from his. He slid his hand across my lower back, skimming the area just north of my derrière, finally resting it on my hip. He gave me a light squeeze and we stopped walking. I turned toward him and he clasped me around the waist with both hands. But he did nothing else.

He didn't pull me toward him.

And he didn't try to kiss me again.

He just looked at me with one eyebrow cocked. Waiting . . .

"Not who," I said, turning. "What." I slipped from his grasp and started walking again, thinking of the pills that waited for me later. And that damned mask.

Caradoc caught up to me immediately, sliding his hand back into its place at my side. He easily matched his strides to mine, but when I glanced over at him, I saw that his eyes had turned stormy. And they shone with what looked like St Elmo's fire. I crossed my arms in front of me and doggedly walked on.

"And you, Corelei," Caradoc snorted. "*You* think you've got apnea anima. You think you snore and that your snoring is loud enough to wake the dead."

"You read my file?!" I pulled away from him, using indignation to mask my embarrassment as I waited for him to laugh.

But he didn't.

"There was nothing in there that I didn't know already," he said. "We talked a lot last year. Don't you remember?" His face looked hopeful, but when I slowly shook my head (memory lapses are often associated with sleep deprivation), he just appeared resigned.

"Your file's not important anyway. It's full of red herrings: your various possible diagnoses, the facts surrounding your parents' life and death, your preoccupation with old, sad songs about angels, death, drowning, bad weather, loss, or loneliness. Even my father's Sunshine Sessions and Aisling's poems. They're *all* distractions. I get that you have problems, Corelei. Who doesn't? But I want you to start focusing on the true story here."

"Which is what, exactly?"

"Us, darlin'. *We're* the story. You and me. And I think it's fairly clear who you're really afraid of."

I stepped back from him, not wanting to hear his hypothesis. Caradoc seemed too well informed. If the Blackhearts were real, I didn't think it was a good idea to be talking about them. "Speak of the devil" and all that. I shivered and glanced around the forest. Nothing yet. And if the Blackhearts *weren't* real . . . Well, I didn't want to hear that either. Because that meant that the Magnolia manager was right. I was psychotic.

Or worse.

But Caradoc continued speaking, either unaware or uncaring that his words might bring on the Blackhearts.

"You know what's happening here? You are seeing ghosts, Corelei. The ghosts of Southerners past. Specifically, the Blackhearts – the drowned crew of the *Alice Anne*. You're not psychotic. And you don't have an adrenaline addiction. Nor do you have apnea anima." And then he did laugh. "You have a gift. It's called somnicantare. You're a sea witch, Corelei. Just like Alice Anne. And you're able to summon the souls of the drowned in your sleep."

4:00

In 1987, The Cure released "Just Like Heaven", a rousing celebration of love, desire and dizzy kisses beside a deep, dark ocean. The song opens with a girl promising her guy she'll run away with him . . . so long as he shows her a trick. A trick that makes her laugh.

And scream.

They kiss, and it's a swooning kind of kiss. The kind that makes her feel as if she's spinning like a top . . . dancing, twisting. As if she were caught in a maelstrom. She disappears from the beach about midway through the song and he is left alone, lamenting. His girl is now lost, stolen by the sea.

Or by him.

Just before the end of the song, he casually mentions she drowned.

But, it's okay, right? I mean, she's okay. Isn't she?

Because he only means they're so in love, they're drowning in it. In each other.

Right?!

Please tell me that's what he meant . . .

"They say Alice Anne used to stand at that very spot and wait for Bonny Black's ship to appear on the horizon."

Automatically, I glanced down at my feet, but couldn't see them. They were hidden beneath the black-laced trim of my trailing skirt. The green flowered muslin dress, hoops and chignon were gone. My loose skirt and hair streamed in the wind as I turned my face toward the sea. It smelled of salt and storm. One was building on the horizon where a band of black clouds was rolling toward the shore. Every few minutes the darkness would crack, split open by a forked electric bolt.

After dinner, we'd decided to climb to the top of Wailing Rock's Widow's Walk. It wasn't quite the 178-step climb to the top of Tybee Island's lighthouse, but it was darn close. Caradoc seemed fine, but I was out of breath. I stood clutching the railing, desperately wanting to loosen the black bodice that seemed to be squeezing the life out of me. *If I'd changed to make climbing easier, why couldn't I have donned shorts and a T-shirt? And how had* this *dress managed to escape my cutting shears?* I didn't recall bringing any floor-length dresses to Oneiroi.

Caradoc stood behind me. I could feel his presence, prickling the back of my neck. His words tickled my ears, giving me goosebumps. I shivered and turned around to face him.

He was leaning against the opposite railing, dressed comfortably in worn leather boots, an unbuttoned vest and a loose-fitting white shirt. There was also a sword at his side. My eyes widened.

"Where did you get that?" I asked, suddenly alarmed.

He raised his gaze to meet mine, making no secret of the fact that he had not been visually feasting on the sea, storm, or setting sun, and pushed himself off the railing toward me. Instinctively, I maintained the distance between us and began nervously pacing the walk. He moved to where I'd been and gave me one of his lazy smiles. It was a smile that said he could weather anything: our earlier exertions, any possible future threats, even my continued flights, so long as, at the end of them, I ended up with him.

"It was my many-times great-grandfather's, Bonny Black's."

"Your ancestor was Bonny Black?" I stopped for a moment, surprised. But my pause was enough of a delay for Caradoc to almost catch me. He reached out, his fingertips brushing my skirt as I sprung to a spot beyond his reach. I resumed my pacing.

He nodded. "That's why we came up here. You said you wanted to know more about him and Alice Anne."

I did? When had I said that?

At dinner, I guessed, eyeing the position of the sun. Dusk wasn't exactly my favorite time of day.

"How did they meet?" I asked, hoping that continued conversation would forestall more intimate diversions and take my mind off the approaching night.

"Folks in Moonlight say he spirited her away from wherever it was she'd been before."

I scoffed. "'Spirited away?' Bonny Black was a pirate. Don't you mean he abducted her?"

"Such a mean term for something motivated by love."

I arched an eyebrow at him. *Uh-huh.* "Do you think she loved him as much as he loved her?"

"What do you think?"

But I ignored his question in favor of another. "So if Alice Anne wasn't from Moonlight, where was she from?"

"Everywhere."

Something about Caradoc's tone made me think he might be toying with me somehow, teasing me. I waited for him to grin and add, *She was from Up Top and All Over the World*, which was how I often glibly described my globe-spanning origins, but instead he gave me a sad smile and stepped closer.

"Her father was a smuggler and her mother died in childbirth. She was buried beside the sea, just like those souls there." He pointed to a group of headstones down on the beach that I hadn't noticed before. There were two rows of them bleached white like driftwood, half buried in the sand. A few had fallen over and the rest were crooked, making the whole of it look like a giant's mouth with sandy gums and rounded teeth. But that didn't mean it looked less dangerous.

I leaned over the edge of the rail, peering at the gravestones, watching for signs of the Blackhearts. In the distance, low thunder sounded and, nearer to me, a zing of electricity crackled in the air. Caradoc stepped up beside me and placed his hand over mine. Even after all this time the feeling of his skin against mine sent a ping of pleasure from my fingers to my toes where it splashed back up like the exhilarating spray from the bow of a boat. He raised my hand to his mouth, but instead of chastely grazing my knuckles with his lips, he flipped my hand over and pressed his mouth to my palm in a lingering kiss that made all sorts of promises about what might happen later. I snatched my hand away.

And cleared my throat. "What about Alice Anne?" I asked, gesturing toward the headstones. "Was she buried there too?"

Caradoc gave me a cryptic look, but then said:

"No one knows where Alice Anne's final resting place is. There was a mutiny the night her eponymous ship sank. Bonny Black had decided to sail back during a storm. He missed his wife." Those last four words Caradoc uttered *sotto voce* while leaning close to my ear. I leaned back and he continued in a more matter-of-fact tone. "He'd've made it too, if his crew hadn't lost their nerve. By the time their mutiny was under way, the ship was too far inland to turn back. Bonny Black couldn't fight both his crew and the sea. The *Alice Anne* foundered and went down. Everyone drowned. Alice Anne, poor girl, watched the whole thing from here."

I stared at Caradoc, aghast. What a horrible story! I didn't know who to be angrier with – Bonny Black for being reckless, his crew for being cowards and traitors, or Caradoc for telling me such a sad, sad tale. As if I didn't have enough to worry about. But he wasn't finished.

"When the ship started sinking, Alice Anne ran down the stairs, raced through the house, and swam out to sea. Some say she was trying to save Bonny Black, but others say she knew he was gone and that she willingly gave herself to the sea because she didn't want to live without him." He paused then, as if he were waiting for me to say something. *But what? How?* My mouth was dry and my throat was tight; speaking seemed impossible. So he continued. "Others say she survived. And that Alice Anne lived the rest of her life at Wailing Rock, trying to summon Bonny Black."

When Caradoc finished, my eyes were wide and I was shaking. There was something about the story that sounded so familiar. But it was probably just that it was a tale of love and loss, of stormy seas and drownings, which, as Caradoc had pointed out earlier, I seemed to have an unhealthy attraction to. I shook my head, determined to clear it of morbid tales, but I couldn't seem to shake the ache the story had roused in me.

What if I lost Caradoc the way Alice Anne had lost Bonny Black? What if the Blackhearts came and I was forced to watch them drag him out to sea and drown him?

Caradoc might laugh at my apnea anima diagnosis, but I was fairly certain that's what was wrong with me, even if my file was full of other possibilities. I gripped Caradoc's shoulders, suddenly worried about him. Suddenly, frightfully, alarmed for him.

"You have to stay away from me," I said, shoving him. But the look of anguish on his face was so heartbreaking, a moment later, I was back in his arms, my cheek pressed up against his chest, my arms wrapped around his middle.

How messed up was I? Pushing a guy away one moment and then rushing back into his arms the next? I was seriously screwed up.

"Corelei . . ."

Caradoc breathed my name as if it were both cure and curse. He moved his hands feverishly up my body, squeezing my hips, cupping my breasts, and then cradling my face as he bent to taste me. I opened my mouth before his lips even met mine, realizing then why he'd said my name the way he had. Cure and curse. That's what *he* was. I wanted him – all of him, in every way – immediately and always. And yet I knew if I let this go too far, it would be the end. Of him. Of us. So I clutched at him like I was drowning, running one hand up his back and into his hair, clenching it into a fist while my other hand pressed against his chest, ready to push him away again.

"I don't care how damaged you are," Caradoc said, his voice hoarse with unshed emotion. "Or how many problems you have. I don't care if you have addictions, Corelei. Or neuroses. Or even psychosis. I only care that you want to be with me. Because I want to be with you." His words came out in a rush, as if he knew I might stop him at any moment and he couldn't bear to let me get away again before he'd had his say. He hoisted me up onto the railing and I wrapped my legs around his waist, leaning against him, taking deep gulps of air, trying not to panic.

Would he let me go after this? Did I want him to?

"I've wanted you since the moment I first saw you, Corelei. I knew then that you were the only girl for me. I may be from Moonlight but you, darlin', *you* are made of sunlight. Underneath all that dark camouflage you love so much, you glow like the rays of spring. You're sweet as honeysuckle and fresh as a buttercup. And you shine like life itself. How could I ever let you go?"

He pulled me from the railing and into his arms, spinning me faster and faster as the storm grew closer. Lightning blazed across the sky and thunder cracked as the first raindrops fell. Despite our gray surroundings, I laughed. Caradoc's ebullient description of me was beyond flattering and his confidence was catching. Maybe together we could beat my diagnosis.

Wait a minute . . .

I dropped to my feet, stopping our spin. I narrowed my eyes at Caradoc, glancing down at my long black dress and then back at his leather boots, vest, sword and white shirt, which had looked decidedly *puffy* and *pirate-like* before it started raining. In fact, it wasn't a stretch to say that all Caradoc lacked was a tricorn hat and me a pointy one to round out our costumes as Bonny Black and Alice Anne.

"You said earlier that you thought I had a 'gift' – the ability to summon the souls of the drowned in my sleep," I said. "You said I was a sea witch like Alice Anne. And then you told me Bonny Black was your ancestor. What are you *really* trying to make me believe, Caradoc? That *we* are Bonny Black and Alice Anne reincarnated?"

Caradoc shrugged and looked sheepish. But he also looked wary – like I hadn't yet guessed everything he'd been up to. The rain fell in sheets, thoroughly drenching us. My dress clung to my body, no doubt revealing every curve Caradoc had been imagining beneath its folds earlier. The lightning strikes and accompanying thunder grew faster and more furious. Standing on Wailing Rock's Widow's Walk was courting disaster, but for once, I didn't feel like running.

I spat rainwater out of my mouth and demanded that Caradoc declare his intentions.

And then he said it. What I'd been afraid of all along.

He wanted to sleep with me. *Really* sleep with me. He didn't care what was wrong with me, whether I was a witch or a psychotic or a necromancer with an unbelievably loud snore. All he wanted was to watch over me while I slept.

And maybe do some other stuff before that. If I wanted to.

Did I? Want to?

3:00
During the first year of the new millennium, Irish pop rock band, The Corrs, released a song called "Breathless". It was a lively romp about how falling in love makes you feel. You know, that weak and out-of-breath feeling you get when you're with the person you love?

The song starts at dusk, as the two lovers are heading into night. Andrea Corr, the lead vocalist, sings about waiting. And wanting. It's not profound as much as it is fun. The way she unabashedly begs her lover to tempt her . . . to tease her . . . Well, who wouldn't want that?

Until she gets to the part where she admits the whole thing is like a dream that she never wants to wake from . . .

We tore down the steps of Wailing Rock's Widow's Walk at breakneck speed, hand in hand, happy we didn't actually break our necks tripping over my skirts or slipping in our wet shoes on the way down. One hundred seventy-eight stairs (give or take), plus another 1,923 steps (plus or minus) to my room when we couldn't *wait* to get our hands on one another was A LOT.

I raced into my room, pulled Caradoc in after me, and shut and locked the door. A locked door wouldn't stop the Blackhearts, but it made me feel better. Caradoc wasted no time getting back to where we'd been when the storm had struck upstairs. He pressed me against the door, kissing me wildly as he unfastened the front hooks of my basque and dropped it on the floor. I gasped for air, exhilarated as much by Caradoc's passion as by the liberation of my lungs. But the feeling was short-lived and that breathless feeling returned. I stood before Caradoc in my sopping wet, black shift, shaking as I peeled his vest off, discarding it. Caradoc moved his mouth from my lips to my neck, trailing soft kisses down my throat, across my collarbone, and down to that dip in my décolletage that he loved so much. The warmth of his lips on my wet skin was exquisite. But my shivering only increased.

Unable to resist any longer, I slipped my hands beneath Caradoc's shirt. *Divine* and *mine* were my only coherent thoughts as my fingertips traced hard muscle all the way up his stomach and chest. I slid the shirt off his shoulders, kissing him where he'd kissed me, down his throat, across his collarbone, toward his navel . . .

His shirt fell to the floor, freeing his hands, and he reached for me, gently lifting my head so that I would meet his gaze. His eyes glowed with a color I'd never seen before. It was beyond squall gray or ardent green. It was beyond mad-about-you, head-over-heels, or crazy-in-love. *This* color was everlasting and eternal. I could tell then that Caradoc had meant every word he'd said earlier. That he didn't care what was wrong with me; he wanted me regardless. That he'd fight with me – or for me. Still, I glanced over at my bedside table, at the mountain of meds and my mask, and bit my lip. Caradoc frowned and, an instant later, I heard scratching at the door.

I jumped back, my arousal completely dashed and replaced with fear. I looked around for a weapon, immediately spotting Caradoc's sword. But he got to it first and tried to push me behind him. I wasn't about to let him die defending me though, so I ran to my dresser drawer and got the knife that I'd managed to steal at breakfast. Caradoc chuckled when he looked at it (it looked positively paltry beside his sword), but he didn't try to stop me from wielding it. In fact, he looked pleased.

Until he saw the note being slid under the door.

Aisling. Even after hours she was determined to pass on a poem or a picture.

Realizing the threat was less severe than we'd thought, Caradoc groaned in frustration and reached for it. But I beat him to it and grabbed the note before he could stab it with his sword or tear it to bits. The romantic mood had been broken.

"I'm going to change," I told him, my teeth chattering. "There are some spare blankets in the closet."

"*Corelei . . .*"

I shut out the anguished sound of his protest and bolted the bathroom door behind me.

2:00

Jamie Walters released his song "How Do You Talk to an Angel" in October 1992. Less than a month later it became a #1 Billboard hit. The lyrics were written by the late Stephanie Tyrell. They are simple but memorable, perhaps in part because Tyrell asks questions that are difficult to answer.

When your loved ones are gone, how do you keep them alive in your mind and your heart? How are words ever enough to describe the dearly departed and how much they meant to those left behind?

And – most importantly, but also most impossibly – how can you hold on to them when it's their time to go?

Inside my tiny bathroom, my breath became even more labored.

What had I been thinking?! Allowing Caradoc to come into my room? Had I learned nothing from prom night?

I was no longer worried about my meds and mask. I only wanted to keep him safe. What did it matter if I was a sea witch *or* a snoring necromancer? The Blackhearts were real and they were coming for me. And if Caradoc was sleeping next to me when they came, he'd be dragged out to sea as well.

I slipped out of the wet shift and pulled on one of my dresses. There was no way I was going to sleep with Caradoc tonight. I laced up my black boots and then, almost as an afterthought, I unfolded Aisling's note.

And lost my breath entirely. I stood at the sink wheezing, clutching the unfolded note against my middle, having what felt like a severe asthma attack.

It wasn't a note. It was a newspaper clipping. It was an article from the *Savannah Sentinel* with an accompanying picture. Of me. *In a diving suit.* The caption read:

ADRENALINE JUNKIE CORELEI NEVEREST
PREPARES TO DIVE
THE WRECK OF THE *ALICE ANNE*,
SCUBA DIVING'S NEWEST "MOUNT EVEREST"

I didn't read the article. I couldn't. I couldn't do anything but stand there looking at the picture, gasping for air like a hooked fish that had been reeled into a boat.

What did this mean? That I was having a psychotic break?

Because I couldn't remember preparing for that dive. I *hated* the water. *Hated* the sea.

But another glance at the picture provided an even darker theory. My dive mask in the picture looked eerily similar to the CPAP mask on my bedside table. And on my wrist was a watch that looked exactly like my bedside clock. Only its glowing green numerals read "90:00" – a full ninety minutes' worth of oxygen. I began to feel light-headed as I realized how surreal and distorted my memories of this place were.

I burst out of the bathroom, slamming the door into the wall, and ran over to the clock on my bedside table, which still read 0:00. I stared at the sign above my bed, my sight dimming as I grew fainter, but I could still make out the Oneiroi Institute's prime directive: *Requiescat in Pace.* Rest in peace.

Oh . . . Oh, no . . .

Caradoc was shouting at me, but I couldn't hear him because of the ringing in my ears.

I wasn't . . . I couldn't be . . .

Was I dead? Had I drowned during the dive?

★

1:00

*Do you remember the song "My Immortal" by the American
rock band Evanescence? The 2003 version from their album
Fallen? There are differing interpretations about its meaning.
Some say it's a ballad about a deceased loved one. Others call
it an angry break-up song. But really, does it matter? Because
sometimes death feels like a break-up. When vocalist Amy Lee
wails about the pain of loss, she sounds sad. And pissed off.
Because losing somebody you love sucks.*

*I always wonder how much angrier that song would sound if
it were sung by a man whose eyes were the color of everlasting
and eternal . . . if that man lost the woman he loved and it
turned out she* wasn't *immortal . . . if she died . . .*

I woke in Caradoc's arms, startled by a sound.

We lay on top of the quilt, still dressed, with me in my
short, black antebellum dress and my big ass-kicking boots.
But no mask. It was on the bedside table – beside my clock,
whose glowing green numerals still showed 0:00. I ignored
it and swung my legs over the side of the bed. At least this
time the floor wasn't covered in blood and shattered glass. I
frowned.

How many times had I done this?

I slid slowly off the bed, not wanting to wake him. I'd
recognized the sound. It was both frightening and familiar.
And waking without my mask had confirmed my suspi-
cions. I slipped out the door, hoping to lure *them* far away
from here.

At night, the hallways of Oneiroi were even darker than
they were during the day. Shadows draped the unseen edges
and corners like charred Spanish moss. They even seemed to
flutter and follow me as I walked past. I quickened my pace.

Outside, the daylight's earlier cheerful colors were
completely shrouded in shades of black, gray and silver.
The night seemed to have been sculpted out of charcoal
and then dusted with shards of sharp, glistening moonlight.
The storm had subsided but the ocean still raged, its
midnight blue waters crashing along the shore. The tide was
coming in.

And it was bringing something with it.

In between me and the shoreline was the old seaside graveyard. I crept among the headstones, my boots squishing in the wet sand, waiting for the Blackhearts I knew were coming. Here and there were oyster-colored statues, which were so weathered they looked like pillars of salt. But I could tell what they'd once been: weeping widows and grief-stricken guardian angels. They wept over their loved ones' graves or stared out to sea – the biggest grave of all.

An unholy shriek rolled in with the next wave, sending chills up my arms and across my shoulders. I only had to wait until they saw me and then I could lead them on a chase through the gardens. I turned toward the house, toward Wailing Rock, that big, black, crumbling box that somehow had managed to outlive everything around it, hoping Caradoc would be safe in there. But when I turned back to the sea I knew I'd made a terrible mistake.

The Blackhearts were here. Now. All around me. They hadn't come in with the tide. They'd just materialized on shore.

Instantly, I regretted not bringing a weapon. One by one, they opened their mouths and screeched. It was the loudest, quietest, most terrifying thing I'd ever heard. Their high-pitched gasping screams would have raised even Cerberus's hackles. And they smelled horrible, like decaying meat and dead fish stewed in bilge water. My stomach lurched, my muscles tensed, and I stuffed my fist in my mouth to keep from adding my shriek to theirs. They were truly ghastly . . . grisly . . . wet . . . grotesque creatures. They were ghoulish skeletal automatons hell-bent on drowning me. They started closing in and I started looking for an escape route. A way I could break through their ranks. I couldn't bear the thought of touching them.

Or of them touching me.

But there was no escape.

I threw myself at them, attempting to bust out of the gathering horde. Two of them grabbed me by the arms and started pulling me through the graveyard toward the sea.

I screamed then. I couldn't help it. My scream was a

shriek to rival theirs. Which meant it sounded just as loud in my head – and just as quiet in the dark. It was as if I were already underwater. There were no loud noises coming out of my mouth, just air and a gurgly yelp. I thrashed in their arms, desperate to get free. My arms flailed and my water-logged boots dragged at my ankles. They pushed me under the surf. I kicked at them, thigh muscles straining, knees popping, but nothing happened. My feet met resistance, but nothing solid. I was drowning . . .

I swept my arm out and – finally – made contact with something solid.

Caradoc.

A battle roar pierced the splashing and thrashing sounds as I stood up in the water gasping. Caradoc stood beside me holding the Blackhearts at bay with his sword. He swung it around us in a wide arc while he held my mask out to me.

I stared at it.

I had a feeling if I put it on, all of this would go away. At least temporarily. But I resisted. Tucked into Caradoc's belt was my breakfast knife. I shifted my gaze from the knife to the sword to the mask.

"You think you've woken them with your snoring," Caradoc shouted, while thrusting my mask toward me again. "Then get rid of them by putting this on. Let's get some sleep, Corelei. Aren't you tired?"

Was I ever! I could sense our story was coming to an end. But I didn't want it to end the way Caradoc thought I did. I took the mask from him . . .

And threw it out into the sea.

"I'm not going to run this time, Caradoc."

"You're not?"

His face split with a grin as big as the moon. I shook my head and grabbed his sword.

"I'm going to fight."

I raised the sword tip to sky and its blade glinted in the moonlight. *Perfect,* I thought. *I always wanted to be a pirate. Let's see what the Blackhearts do with cold steel for them to gnaw on instead of my fear.*

Caradoc raised his eyebrows at my boldness, but he let me keep the sword. He pulled the knife out of his belt and together we turned to face the Blackhearts.

We were still fighting them at dawn. Something was wrong. This ending wasn't the one I'd wanted either. I was getting weak and winded again. Each and every time we cut one down, another would come at us. *How many crew members had Bonny Black had?*

Just before daybreak, I recalled Caradoc's theory. That, somehow, improbable as it was, I was Alice Anne and I had a gift – somnicantare. Caradoc thought I could summon the souls of the drowned in my sleep. *Was that what I'd done?*

Only one way to find out. I needed to try to send them back to wherever it was I'd summoned them from. In the loudest voice I could muster (the waves, the rush of blood in my ears, and the clang of steel were nearly deafening at this point), I shouted: "*REQUIESCAT IN PACE!*"

And, with that, they were gone.

The Blackhearts dissolved into sand and salt, blown back to shore and sea.

Sunny side up. Those three words summed up the weather, our moods, and my eggs. Of course, my plate was also loaded with grits, hushpuppies, country ham and buttermilk biscuits. I honestly didn't know how I'd manage to stuff it all in, but I was determined to try. I placed a hand on my stomach. I was wearing another cropped dress, but this one wasn't black. It was a green, yellow and white one sewn from cheerful, flower-patterned fabric. My hair had been braided into a crown, which was threaded with flowers – narcissus, I think. But I still wore my big black boots. I grinned at Caradoc, who was sitting across from me and he grinned back, his eyes reflecting the bright, blue sky.

Once again we were having breakfast in the back garden of Wailing Rock. But things were different. In addition to the menu and my clothing, we had company. Seated around us at other glass-topped tables were Poppy, Rob, Aisling and Tristan. They all looked well rested, even Aisling. And Tristan actually smiled at me. I smiled back and waved at Dr Ambrose, who was reading the *Savannah Sentinel* on a bench not far away. I recalled how pleasant this morning's Sunshine Session had been. Instead of troubled writers, we'd focused on happy couples like Odysseus and Penelope and Queen Victoria and Prince Albert.

I picked up my knife and a biscuit, searching for butter or jelly on the crowded tabletop. Caradoc handed me the jar. It was full of ripe, red, lush-looking jam. I couldn't wait to taste it. After last night's fight, I was starving. Luckily, Oneiroi's food had gone from dull to delightful overnight. I slathered my biscuit with the crushed fruit, raised it to my mouth, and took a huge bite.

Pomegranate. Caradoc had handed me a jar of pomegranate preserves.

As soon as I tasted the seeds, I knew. I remembered who I was and what I was doing here. I put down the knife and my half-eaten biscuit and narrowed my eyes at Caradoc. I should have guessed earlier. Everything about this morning had been just a little too perfect.

"Was *any* of it real, Caradoc?"

"My love for you, Kore. That's as real as it gets. Do you know how many times we've done this? We've been vampires and werewolves, princesses and knights, zombies and aliens, demons and angels . . . This year I figured I'd try a Southern Gothic role-playing game for us. How'd I do?"

I gave him a dubious look. "Pirates, ghosts, and witches south of Savannah in a big, old rotting mansion?" I glanced down at my retrofitted dress. "Eh. You did okay, I guess. I like the outfit, but a lot of it—" I made a sweeping gesture that encompassed the whole of Wailing Rock "—felt . . . off. So you may have missed your mark on this one."

"But did it work this time? Did I convince you? To stay?"

I shook my head and stood up. He stood up too and came over to meet me, taking my hands in his.

"I didn't mean to scare you," he said, resting his forehead against mine. "I don't want you to leave. Kore, I want you to stay with me forever. Always."

We stayed like that for a few minutes, our foreheads touching, our hands clasped, our bodies close. But then I pulled back, saying:

"I can't, Caradoc. I love you, but I can't spend all of eternity with you. I need a break. Loving you wears me out. I'm not sure it's good for me to want to rush back into your arms all the time. I think . . . I think . . . Well, it's just time for me to go."

"No . . . Don't say that," Caradoc said softly, pulling me close again. He let go of my hands and wrapped his arms around my waist. "Please, Kore," he begged. "Don't go."

I raised my hand to his cheek.

"Persephone," he whispered. "Can't you at least call me by my real name?"

I smiled. "I think I like Caradoc better. 'Dearly loved'. You are, you know."

I traced his lips with my thumb, conflicted, regretful, but resolute in my decision to return to Up Top and All Over the World.

"You won't recognize me next time, Kore," he promised with a wink. "Last chance to tell me you love me. *Me*. Not Caradoc."

I shook my head again.

"One last kiss then?"

"Only if you promise to call me 'darlin'.'"

0:00

> *Oh my darlin', oh my darlin',*
> *Oh my darlin' Corelei.*
> *Are you lost and gone forever?*
> *Oh my darlin' Corelei.*

ENTICED BY BLOOD

A Sweetblood World short story

Laurie London

Chapter One

Juliette Bishop wished she could turn around and go home. Although New Orleans was a beautiful city, it was the last place on earth she wanted to be.

She stepped through the wrought-iron gates of the restaurant courtyard, where twisted branches from several trees formed a canopy overhead. If her hands weren't full, she'd brush a wisp of hair out of her eyes. She tried blowing it away, but the strand clung stubbornly to her damp skin.

After her flight, she'd had just enough time to shower at the hotel, change and take a taxi to the French Quarter. Little good that did, because the back of her silk tank felt as if it were already covered in sweat. The locals were probably used to this humidity, but by San Francisco standards, it was almost unbearable.

She glanced around. Only a few tables in the courtyard between the two buildings were occupied. Maybe there were more people inside.

With a heavy portfolio in one hand and a handbag in the other, she headed toward the hostess station. The brick footing was uneven, so she had to walk on her tiptoes to avoid catching a heel.

"Welcome," said a young woman with sleek black hair. "Will you be joining us for dinner?"

Nodding, Juliette set her things on a nearby chair, relieved to be rid of the weight for a moment. "I'm meeting someone, but I'm a little early. I doubt he's here yet."

She pictured herself sitting inside an air-conditioned bar for fifteen or twenty minutes, sipping a tall cool drink. One with an umbrella and lots of ice. That would give her time to cool down and collect her thoughts.

Under her breath, she cursed her father's alcoholic business partner for putting her in this situation. If it hadn't been for Henry's drinking problem, she wouldn't be here right now, taking time off from her job at the brokerage firm, trying to salvage her father's biggest customer – her former lover. A man she despised.

She'd met Andre Lescarbeau last New Year's Eve in San Francisco. Fueled by one too many peach Bellinis and his delicious French accent, she soon found herself in his hotel suite having the best sex of her life. He was dominant and demanding, and although she considered herself a strong, confident woman, she'd willingly submitted to him.

He wouldn't let her take any time off from work, insisting that he had important business matters to attend to during the day. But every evening like clockwork, when she stepped out of her building on Market Street, there he was, waiting for her at the curb in his vintage Aston Martin convertible. How he managed the parking mojo night after night was beyond her.

Andre had asked about her family, so she told him what her father did and all the awards his vintage woodworking company had won, including the articles in *Architectural Digest*, *Traditional Home* and *Southern Living*. Unbeknownst to her, Andre later contacted her father to do some work for him. He'd inherited a string of old boutique hotels in the South – New Orleans, Mobile, Savannah, Charleston – and was planning to renovate all of them one by one.

Then one night, without warning, Andre wasn't waiting for her. She tried to reach him, but he didn't answer her calls or texts. Worried that something bad had happened, she finally went to his hotel, where someone at the front desk remembered he'd left for the airport at dusk with a beautiful young woman in tow. His wife.

It felt as if she'd been punched in the gut. She'd been having sex with a married man. Had actually been falling for him. No wonder he'd been so secretive, sharing little about his personal life. She wasted no time erasing his name from her contacts and vowed never to be so gullible or naive again.

But here she was, less than a year later, getting ready to meet with him.

She had to forget their past, shove it behind her and do what she needed to do – convince Andre not to cancel his contract. A contract big enough that it would secure her father's retirement.

If her father hadn't taken ill, he'd have flown down and handled things himself, so when he asked her to take his place and smooth things over, what could she say? Tell him to send his unreliable business partner? Or tell him she couldn't go because she'd banged his customer, a married man who had lied to her?

So she'd sucked up her pride and said yes.

"Let me check for you," the hostess said, jerking Juliette's thoughts back to the present. "What is the name on the reservation?"

Juliette lifted her hair off the back of her neck, hoping a cool breeze would be kind enough to find its way there, but the air was stagnant. "Andre Lescarbeau."

The woman looked up without consulting the book. "Mr Lescarbeau?"

"You know him?" Juliette asked. He must come here a lot.

"He owns Café Sur La Rue. Would you like to wait in the bar for him? I'll have Jeffrey grab your things."

He owns this place?

Juliette glanced around again. Tiny lights were strung in the overhead branches of the courtyard and twinkled against the dark sky. The wrought-iron gates and railings were exquisitely ornate. The atmosphere was dripping with Old World charm. Just like Andre.

Had he chosen *his* restaurant because he wanted to seduce her again? Well, she was smarter now. And much more informed. She wouldn't sleep with him again if he were the last human male on the planet.

"Juliette."

The sound slid down her spine like melted chocolate. She'd told herself she wouldn't let him affect her like this.

Remember. The guy's married. You're only here because Dad asked you.

Taking a deep breath, she turned to face him and her heart nearly stopped. Although she hadn't forgotten how hot he was, time had a way of blurring the specifics.

His dark hair was tousled and he had a slight scruff on his jaw, making him look as if he'd just rolled out of bed. He wore a *Mad Men*-inspired light-gray suit, impeccably tailored to accentuate his broad, powerful shoulders and narrow waist. With no tie and camel-colored Italian shoes, he had an air of casual elegance. A man like him would be equally at home dining in the fanciest hotels or walking between rows of grapevines in a vineyard.

"Andre," she said, curtly, trying to ignore the urge to offer him her hand. She didn't want to make any physical contact with him. There'd been something strangely magical about his touch, so she needed to avoid it at all costs. "Will your wife be joining us?"

"My wife will not be joining us," Andre said, ignoring the look on the hostess's face. "I trust you had a good flight, no?"

Juliette nodded and reached for her things. He brushed her hand aside and grabbed the briefcase.

"What do you have in here?" He chuckled. "Bricks?"

She didn't smile. It didn't surprise him. American women had long memories, and she'd once been in love with him.

As they were led to his regular table, he couldn't help but notice the way her light-blue skirt clung to her hips. Her legs were long and shapely in those heels, too. And, unfortunately, he remembered all too well how it felt to have them wrapped around his waist.

They'd been flirting all night at a New Year's Eve party and had shared a passionate kiss at midnight. When he got her up to his suite, he couldn't contain himself any longer. With the door barely shut behind them, he pushed her against the wall, dropped his trousers, shoved her thong aside, and thrust into her.

Mon Dieu. The sweet moaning sounds she'd made had nearly driven him mad with desire.

With little warning, his dark nature had taken over. Normally, he had better control than that. His fangs emerged from his gums and, as he climaxed, he sank them into her jugular vein. She gasped, of course, digging her nails into his back as he drank. "Shhh, *ma chérie*," he whispered, projecting soothing thoughts into her mind. "*Un peu plus.*"

When he had finished, he healed the tiny punctures and erased her memory. If he'd been smart and had followed the laws of his people, he would've driven her home at that point and never seen her again. But like many French men, he let passion guide his actions.

Although he'd temporarily slaked his thirst for her, he was still captivated by Juliette in every other way. Her intelligence. Her confidence. The sound of her laughter. Her kindness and devotion to her father. She was a remarkable woman.

As they'd spent time together, he'd found himself falling deeply, madly in love with her. It felt like home when he was with her. Like they were two very different pieces that fitted together perfectly to make one complete whole.

But he couldn't allow that to happen. Relationships between humans and vampires didn't work. He'd seen that first hand with his childhood friend, who had fallen for a human woman who killed herself after learning the truth about him. The man had never been the same since. Andre couldn't risk the same thing happening to Juliette. His broken heart wasn't worth that.

After things were over between them, maybe he shouldn't have contacted Bishop Millwork, but the moment he'd seen their work, he knew he couldn't hire anyone else.

Their attention to detail and beautiful craftsmanship were unlike anything he'd seen in hundreds of years . . . and certainly never in the New World. Renovation on the hotel had been halted for reasons other than a few ill-fitting cabinets, and he tried telling that to Mr Bishop, but the man had been distraught about the faulty pieces he'd supplied. Andre assured him the cabinetry would still work, but Mr Bishop insisted that since he couldn't come himself, he would send their best person to assess the situation.

Except that Andre had no idea that person would be Juliette. He would never have guessed she had anything to do with her father's business. She worked at a brokerage firm, *pour l'amour de Dieu*!

Holding her chair for her now, he caught a faint whiff of her scent – jasmine – and drew it into his lungs. His gaze dropped to her throat where he saw the flicker of a heartbeat. Her blood. It still called to him.

Although she wasn't an actual *sweetblood* – a human whose rare blood is highly addictive to vampires – she was plenty addictive to him.

No. He wouldn't succumb to her again.

Ignoring the ache in his gums where his fangs were hidden, he took a long drink from the Tanqueray and tonic Jeffery had waiting for him. He would take Juliette to the hotel where she could see for herself that everything was fine, and then he'd put her on the next plane back to San Francisco.

After he ordered for them, Juliette cleared her throat. "Before we start talking business, I want to make one thing perfectly clear."

"And what is that?" he asked, even though he had a pretty good idea what she was going to say.

She dropped her voice. "I would never have slept with you, let alone spent all that time with you, had I known you were married."

"I know, and I'm sorry."

"*Sorry?*" Her eyes flashed with anger. "Sorry is something you say when you accidentally step on someone's toe. Or bump into someone while waiting in line. It is *not* what you say after getting caught in a lie of that magnitude. Does your wife know you do that sort of thing when you're away on business?"

"I . . . uh . . ." He wasn't sure what to tell her. Activity on the other side of the room drew his attention. A couple was getting up from their table and looked to be in a hurry to leave. He frowned and turned back to Juliette. "Does who know what?"

She made a sound of exasperation. "Your wife. Does she know?"

He glanced around the room in an effort stave off the guilt rattling around in his gut.

Diners at another table were leaving quickly as well. And they hadn't touched their dinner either. *How odd.*

Juliette frowned. "What's wrong? Or am I boring you?"

He gave her a pointed look. "You are never boring, Juliette." He raised a finger in Jeffery's direction and, a moment later, the man was by his side.

"What can I get you, sir?"

"Do you know why so many people seem to be in a hurry to leave?"

"The news is reporting that the storm out in the Gulf is gaining momentum."

Juliette's eyes widened. "Storm?"

"Not a hurricane, ma'am," Jeffery answered with a reassuring smile. "Just heavy wind and rain. But they're predicting it'll hit landfall in about an hour, so the tourists are going back to their hotels."

"But I thought the storm was heading toward the Florida gulf coast," Andre said. At least that's what he'd heard before he retired for the day. He hadn't thought to check again when he got up.

"It was, sir, but it shifted. It's heading our way."

Chapter Two

Juliette stared through the windshield wipers at the gridlock in front of them. And she thought traffic in San Francisco was bad. At this rate, the drive to her hotel was liable to take hours.

"I don't mind taking a taxi." She wasn't exactly comfortable spending that much time with Andre. In such tight quarters. Alone.

He flicked his hand as if he were pushing her words away. "Why did you choose that flea-bitten place out near the airport? I thought my assistant made arrangements for you to stay at one of my properties."

She'd hardly call the Rosemont a flea-bitten hotel. "Because I didn't *want* to stay at one of *your* properties."

Andre started to reply, but a car cut in front of them. He swerved and blasted the horn. "*Quel idiot!*" Then, without skipping a beat, he said, "When you are in town, you stay with me."

"Oh, really?" What a pompous asshole. "You assumed incorrectly, Mr Lescarbeau. *I* decide things myself. No one else." Her cheeks heated at the memory of their sex play, where they'd had an opposite arrangement.

He raised an eyebrow as if he remembered, too. "Better service. The finest accommodations. And, uh, how do you say . . . ? On the house. No charge. Why wouldn't you?"

Okay, time to get real here. She shifted in her seat. "Because I don't like owing favors to married men who are liars and cheaters, that's why." She felt a twinge of regret for insulting her father's client but she couldn't stand any more of his arrogant attitude. She hoped the storm wasn't going to screw up her plans.

He hit the brakes again, this time so hard that her body would've slammed into the strap of her seat belt if he hadn't thrown out his arm to brace her. Another car had cut in front of them.

"Enough of this," he growled. "Hold on."

Before she knew it, he jerked the wheel, pulling the Aston Martin onto the shoulder, and then slammed it into reverse and gunned it. With his neck cranked around, he propelled the car backward at top speed.

Holy crap.

The barrier to the left and the line-up of cars to the right were a complete blur. Her hands gripped what they could find – the door handle and his right knee. She was sure they were going to die.

He whipped the car around, its tires skidding on the wet pavement, and slammed it into drive. "I should've taken this exit in the first place."

It took her a minute to catch her breath and thank God that she was still alive. "Then why didn't you? You could've gotten us killed."

"Because I *had* been taking you back to your hotel."

"Who drives like that anyway? You're not a stunt man." Wait. She glanced over at him. His profile was hard and angular. "Does that mean you're *not* taking me to my hotel now?"

He had a smug look on his face. "Even *I* can't get you through this traffic, *ma chérie*. No, you are coming back with me."

"What a worthless piece of *merde*." Andre pulled out his earpiece, tossing it and his cell phone to the floorboards behind him. A huge live oak, ripped from its roots, lay across the road, blocking their path.

"No coverage?" Juliette asked, breaking her silence. She'd hardly said two words to him since they'd left the expressway and worked their way down a multitude of side streets and alleys.

"I keep getting an 'all circuits are busy' message."

"Too many people using their cell phones with this storm, I guess. If you need to get hold of your wife, you can use my cell. Maybe I've got better coverage."

She just loved twisting that knife.

Andre gripped the steering wheel tighter and stared at the downed tree in front of them. Even though the wiper blades were on the fastest setting, they weren't very effective.

If only he could tell her the truth, but it was better for both of them if she continued to believe he was married. Thinking he was a cheater was the simplest solution. It wasn't like he could tell her why he'd really left.

"I'm trying to get hold of someone at the hotel to pick us

up from the other side. Otherwise, we'll need to get out, skirt the tree on foot, and walk the rest of the way."

Her eyes widened. "In this rain? In the dark?"

He wasn't crazy about it either. He could throw her over his shoulder and sprint with the super-human speed of his kind, but then he'd really have some explaining to do. He could go faster by himself, but there was no way in hell he was leaving her alone.

"Do you have a better idea?"

"How far away is your hotel?" she asked.

"Another mile or so."

"A mile?" she muttered under her breath. "Here, use mine." She tossed her phone to him.

He dialed the hotel again but got the same message.

"Not good, I take it?" she asked, a curious expression on her face.

"Looks like we're on our own. This fucking storm doesn't look as though it's letting up anytime soon." Putting the car into reverse, he backed it up and parked as far away from the other trees as he could, then grabbed the door handle. "Ready?"

She wore a sleeveless top and no coat. And those heels of hers were going to be a problem. Not only would she be too cold, they'd both be sopping wet by the time they dragged their sorry asses to the hotel.

She nodded and reached for her briefcase.

"Leave it. I'll have someone retrieve the car tomorrow."

Wind and rain tore at him as he exited the vehicle. Sprinting to the other side, he made it there before she'd even opened the door. He reached in and helped her out, but the moment they made contact, a jolt of her energy shot up his arm.

Damn.

He quickly put up a mental barrier to keep from absorbing more. It would make her too tired and they had a long walk ahead of them.

He could go for weeks without blood if he had to, but human energy was another story. Since vampires couldn't go out in the sunlight, they needed to absorb the UV energy from their human hosts. Which was why living at the hotel had worked out so well. He had an endless supply of both blood and energy. A few of the Yelp reviewers mentioned how tired they'd been during their stays, but the beds were very luxurious. He could live with that.

He drew Juliette in close and draped his suit coat over their heads. Her arm remained stiff between them as they ran, and she couldn't move very fast in those heels. When she stumbled, he grabbed her waist, but she shook him off. She removed her shoes and tried running barefoot, but the rocks underfoot were too sharp so she put them back on.

"Climb on my back. We'll get there much faster."

"No," she said, raising her voice above the howling wind.

"Why not?"

"I'm not climbing onto your back. If you want to go on ahead of me, that's fine."

Leaving her alone to walk the rest of the way by herself in this storm was not an option. "Why must you be so stubborn?"

"I wouldn't exactly call it *being stubborn*," she said, laughing bitterly.

"Then what is it?"

"It's having higher moral standards than you and refusing to compromise them. This," she said, elbowing him in the ribs, "is bad enough."

"Sharing my coat because you don't have one isn't a gentlemanly thing to do?" No matter how many centuries he lived, he would never entirely understand women.

"You're right." She moved out from under his suit jacket and shielded her head from the rain with her arms.

What the hell?

"Juliette," he barked. "Get back here."

Ignoring him, she tried walking faster, although she wasn't having much luck in those shoes. She looked like a drenched long-legged bird on a goddamn tightrope.

"Juliette!"

A crack of thunder followed a bright flash of lightning and then the rain came down even harder.

It was ridiculous to argue in the middle of a storm. He lunged forward and scooped her into his arms.

"Andre, what do you think you're doing? Put me down!"

"We'll get there faster this way."

"I don't care. Now put me down."

He ignored her protests and quickened his pace.

She pushed at his chest and squirmed in his arms, but when one of her feet came dangerously close to kicking him in the balls, he had enough. He threw her over his shoulder like a sack of potatoes and started jogging.

She pounded on his back, but he didn't stop.

It wasn't until he turned onto the driveway leading to the small hotel that he realized her protests had turned into sobs. He stopped underneath an old oak and set her back on her feet.

"*Ma chérie*, what is wrong?" he asked. "I am only trying to help."

She swiped a hand over her eyes as if she were mad at herself for crying. "Don't be an idiot and insult me like that. You're married. It's not right. I can walk. Myself. Without your help." Her tone was as sharp as a knife blade and it sliced clear through him.

This rejection was of his own making. It was working perfectly. Wasn't this what he had wanted? For her to hate him and not want anything to do with him?

Time and distance had made it easier for him to pretend that they hadn't shared something incredible back in San Francisco. Hell, he'd even considered buying property up there. There was a beautiful old hotel on the coast that he'd had his eye on before he'd come to his senses.

He reached for her, but she jerked away. Her rejection tore at him, cracking his resolve.

"Juliette, please."

"Do not touch me," she said through clenched teeth.

He couldn't stand it any more. "I'm not married," he blurted.

"What?" Her head snapped up.

"I'm not married," he repeated. It felt so good to finally

tell her the truth, like a heavy yoke had been lifted from his shoulders.

Unimpressed, she narrowed her eyes. "And you expect me to believe that?"

"No, which is why you can ask any person on my staff. Any of them. They'll confirm this. You don't need to take my word."

"So, was that a girlfriend in San Francisco then? The bellman saw you leave with someone."

"I know, but he was . . . mistaken. There was no girl."

"But—"

He put a finger to her lips. "I am not married, nor have I ever been married. I do not currently have a girlfriend, nor did I have one when you and I were together. Although," he said with a smile, hoping to drag one out of her, "I would be a liar to say that I've never had one."

She wasn't impressed and continued to stare at him through humorless eyes. "Then why?"

He sighed. "It's a long story, Juliette, but I swear to you on my *grand-mère's* grave that I am telling you the truth."

Another crack of lightning briefly illuminated their surroundings.

And that's when he saw them.

Three shadowy figures on the other side of the road.

Watching.

Chapter Three

The instant Juliette's feet touched solid ground in front of the hotel, she doubled over and tried to regain control of her roiling stomach. Andre had been telling her he wasn't married, and then, without warning, he'd swept her into his arms and ran so fast it had made her head spin. She couldn't even say how they got through the wrought-iron gate surrounding the courtyard because, suddenly, they were just here.

"What . . . happened?" she gasped.

He stared into the darkness as if he expected the boogie man to jump out, and then he jerked open the leaded glass door and shoved her inside.

A shiver ran down her spine when she noticed his eyes. They looked so . . . strange. Unlike most people when they move from the dark into the light, his pupils were huge, eclipsing all but the thinnest ring of his golden irises.

"Andre, please, you're scaring me. What's going on?" Something out there had spooked him and she wanted to know why.

"I'll explain later, but I have to take care of a few things first."

As he spoke to a guy behind the front desk, she stood there, dripping wet and numb. Overhead, a large crystal chandelier hung from the second-story coved ceiling. A baby grand piano stood opposite a small women's boutique, and high-backed chairs were scattered around the brocade carpet in several seating groups. Plastic railings blocked off the arched hallways on either side of the front desk, reminding her that the place was undergoing renovations. She wondered if there were even any guests here.

Andre soon disappeared, leaving her to follow the hotel clerk upstairs.

A few minutes later, she stood in the middle of a suite located in a private wing on the third floor. Somewhere along the way, she'd been given a thick towel. She absently blotted her wet hair.

Given the running shoes in the corner, the copy of *Le Monde* on the bed and the faint hint of Andre's cologne in the air, this was not a normal guest room. It was his own personal suite.

He expected her to stay with him.

Before she could decide whether she was okay with these arrangements or not, a woman from housekeeping showed up at the door with toiletries and several changes of clothes, including pajamas.

"That was fast," Juliette said, reaching into her handbag for a tip.

The woman shook her head. "Thank you but Mr Lescarbeau has taken care of everything. He left instructions saying if the clothes don't fit to please call down and we'll send up something else."

It sounded like he expected to be gone for a while, which was hard to imagine in this storm "Did he say when he'd be back? I didn't get a chance to ask him."

"No, ma'am." The woman reached for the door and hesitated. "When Mr Lescarbeau goes out like this, he doesn't come back for quite a little while."

Juliette wanted to know if he did this often, but she was struck with a different thought. "How long have you worked for him?"

The woman had a faraway look in her eyes. "Oh, let's see. About ten years, I suppose."

A long time. Juliette nodded and bit her lip. "Can I ask you a question that may seem a little . . . unusual?"

With a grin that lit up her whole face, the woman crossed her arms over her chest, lifting her ample bosom. "I've seen a lot of *unusual* in my day. Both my grandmother and mother practiced the voodoo arts. Nothing surprises me."

The housekeeper's demeanor was non-judgmental, so Juliette continued. "Has Mr Lescarbeau ever been . . . married?" She hoped to God the answer wasn't, *"Oh yes. In fact, he's married now."*

"Not to my knowledge," the woman replied, shaking her head.

Relief rushed over her. So he had been telling the truth. But why had he left San Francisco without even a goodbye in the first place? And tonight, when she'd made several references to him having a wife, why had he not corrected her?

The housekeeper was looking at her with an expression Juliette could not decipher. "That is not such a strange question, dearie."

Juliette waited for the woman to say more, but she didn't. "How about girlfriends?" she asked.

"Ah, well, he's brought a lady friend or two here but not for quite some time." It looked as though the woman was going to say something else but, instead, she reached into her pocket and produced a flattened lump of silver roughly the size of a dime. "Here, take this."

"What is it?" Juliette asked, examining the piece. It had a cross stamped in the center.

"It's an amulet blessed by the priests at the St Louis Cathedral."

She remembered the taxi driving past Jackson Square where vendors sold trinkets and psychic readings right outside the church. She wondered if the woman had actually gotten it there. "What is it supposed to do?"

"Gives you protection," the woman answered.

Juliette frowned. "Why would I need a protection amulet? Protection from what?"

"To ward off evil spirits. They're all around us, you know."

Clearly, this woman's voodoo roots were showing. She decided to humor her. "What do I do with it?"

"Keep it with you at all times and hold it if you get scared. It will drive away the darkness."

"The darkness?" Juliette had an odd feeling that this had something to do with Andre.

The housekeeper opened the door and stepped into the hallway. "Be careful. The nights here are often filled with more than just shadows."

It was well after two before Andre headed back to the hotel.

He'd circled the property multiple times, but had found no trace of the three vampires who'd been watching them. Melding with the shadows to move faster, he'd expanded his radius, combing the nearby cotton fields, the banks of the river and even to the edge of the bayou. A few times he thought he'd picked up their scent in the wind, but by the time he got there, it was gone.

Less than a week ago, he'd tracked the same small group – two men and a woman – to their den, an old cabin in the bayou, where he found empty vials of Sweet littering the rotted floorboards. Unlike most vampires today, they were *reverts*, choosing to live like their ancestors did by killing and feeding from humans.

Knowing his neighbors, employees and guests were at risk from these killers, he'd kicked out several boards in the siding to allow in sunlight the next day. Upon their return, if there wasn't enough time to seek shelter elsewhere, they'd be weak and miserable once the sun hit their skin. Like having an infestation of rats, if you made their current home unlivable, they'd have to find somewhere else to go. At least, that was the hope.

He hadn't heard anything from the reverts after that, so he'd assumed they'd left the area.

He pulled out his phone. At least his texts to his friend in the local field office had gone through. Mateo was a *Guardian*, tasked with enforcing vampiric law as set forth by the Governing Council. Reverts praying on people was never tolerated. Mateo was wrapping up a few storm-related issues on Canal Street but would come as soon as he could.

Andre pocketed the phone and trudged up the driveway.

So Juliette knew the truth now . . . or at least part of it. In an odd way, he felt relieved. This whole time, she'd thought he was the kind of man who would cheat on his wife. That, alone, had been almost unbearable. Honor and respect were very important to him.

But she was going to ask why he left, and he had no idea what he was going to tell her.

Chapter Four

Juliette awoke with a start in a pitch-black room. She bolted upright, unsure of her surroundings, and then everything came back to her in a rush.

New Orleans. The storm. The hotel. Andre.

She slid a foot over to his side of the bed. He wasn't there and the sheets were cold.

Had he not come back yet or had he decided to give her this room and sleep somewhere else?

She groped the nightstand for her phone. Two thirty.

Reaching for the light, she turned it on, but nothing happened. Just the empty clicks of the knob. Maybe that had woken her – the sound of a blown transformer or a tree hitting an electrical line.

She got up, found the robe she'd used earlier and threw back the heavy curtains on the window. Even though it was dark, she could see outlines of huge branches littering the grounds. Had one of them caused the power to go out? The wind and rain had subsided. Maybe the storm had finally passed.

Curious, she unlatched the window and pushed it open a few inches. A fragrant ripple of air whispered across her face. Jasmine and something else. She loved the smell after it rained. Her mother had too, saying it was the trees and flowers celebrating being alive.

She opened the window wider and inhaled again. As she thought about her mother, her heart grew heavier. It had been four years since she died, and it had rained then, too. It was when the world was quiet like this that she missed her the most. And then she thought about her dad. His chemo treatments were going well and the doctors were hopeful, but she still worried about him. Maybe when he was feeling better, she'd bring him down here. He'd like New Orleans. The culture. The food. The beautiful architecture.

Movement beyond the wrought-iron fence caught her eye. Under a huge, live oak was a small gray structure that appeared to be made of stone or cement. Its open door was banging against the frame in the dying wind. A rhythmic, lonely sound. Somewhere in the distance, a dog barked.

Squinting, she saw other low-lying structures organized in rows behind it and realized she was looking at a cemetery. She shivered and pulled her robe tighter.

And then she heard voices.

Glancing around, she spotted three dark figures off to the left. One was gesturing wildly and pointing at the other two, who were wearing long coats that flapped in the wind around their ankles. Although she couldn't be sure, the first person looked like Andre.

What was he doing outside in the middle of the night during the storm? Were they trying to figure out how to restore power to the hotel? According to the guy from the front desk who showed her to the room, there weren't many guests on account of the extensive renovations. Just a few people on the first floor. "You'll have the whole place to yourselves," he'd said with a smile.

Looking out the window, she couldn't tell if the three of them were arguing or if Andre was giving them instructions.

She shoved her hands into the pockets of her robe, and her fingers touched the amulet there. She thought about what the housekeeper had said and how worried Andre had seemed earlier. A chill ran through her body and lodged at the base of her spine.

Something wasn't right. The conversation looked too heated.

As if on cue, one of the figures lunged at Andre, who shot a hand up and moved out of the way so quickly that he was practically a blur. If she blinked, she would've missed it.

Then there was a flash of something metallic. With a stabbing motion, the same figure lunged at him again. This time, Andre wasn't fast enough and he staggered backward.

"Oh my God," she gasped. Had he been hurt?

She grabbed the hotel phone, intending to call security, but the line was dead.

Andre held his arm as the two figures circled him.

"Get away from him!" she screamed, swinging the window wide.

She didn't wait to see if they'd heard her or if it had any effect. All she knew was that she needed to get help.

As she spun toward the door, something stirred in the darkness behind her. The little hairs on the back of her neck stood up.

She was not alone.

Andre jerked his head in the direction of the scream. The third revert – a woman – the one he'd been asking these two about, was clinging to the side of the hotel. On the ledge, right above his window.

His blood ran cold.

Juliette.

She was in terrible danger. He needed to get to her.

A surge of anger shot through him like a drug, making the pain from the silver blade all but disappear.

With a growl, he launched himself at the nearest revert, the one who had stabbed him and knocked the guy off balance. After unsheathing his own knife, Andre was on him in an instant, slashing and jabbing. The instant the blade struck home, he pushed it to the hilt and twisted. With his heart muscle pierced by silver, the vampire would soon turn to dust.

Andre pulled out the weapon and jumped to his feet, ready to take on the next asshole standing between him and Juliette.

To his surprise, the other revert held up his hands and backed away. "I don't want any trouble, okay? These two aren't—" The guy grimaced as he glanced at the body withering at his feet. "Aren't my friends. I just met them a few weeks ago."

He was young. Probably only a few years past his Time of Change, when a born vampire's cravings began, which would put him around the same age as Etienne. His brother had made some poor choices, too.

"Then get out of here." Andre hesitated just long enough to ensure that the boy was indeed leaving and not planning to double-cross him the minute his back was turned, and then sprinted to the hotel and Juliette.

Not wanting to waste time using the door and the stairs, he scaled the wall, just as the other vampire had. He'd reach Juliette faster this way.

The muscles in his injured arm cried out with every movement, and energy drained out of his system.

He needed blood. A lot of it. But he couldn't stop. Not until he got Juliette away from that monster. It would only take a vampire a few minutes to drain a human, so he didn't have much time.

He reached for the ledge and his hand slipped. "Fuuuuck!"

Hanging on by only the fingertips of his other hand, he willed himself to keep going. Juliette needed him. And he needed her.

With a loud grunt, he pulled himself up and swung inside.

But the room was empty.

Juliette's sweet scent was mixed with that of the revert's

– the putrid, rotted meat smell of a vampire who only drank human blood,

Heart hammering in his chest, he dragged himself to a locked cabinet in the closet and punched in the code. Grabbing the gun, he jammed in a clip with silver bullets, chambered a round and headed out the door.

On the far side of the hotel's center staircase, the plastic film sealing off the north wing of the hotel had been torn away.

The revert must have taken Juliette there. Half running, half staggering, he headed in that direction, each step harder than the last.

He'd been fooling himself, pretending he never loved her. That he could go on with his life and forget about her. Once you fall in love, it's hard to go on without it, no matter how much you try to convince yourself otherwise. And now that she was in danger, he'd risk everything to save her.

Chapter Five

Once they were deep inside the area being renovated, the woman shoved Juliette down to the ground.

"Much better," she said, taking a deep breath. "It didn't smell right in that room. Made me sick to my stomach."

Juliette couldn't believe what she was seeing, but there was no other possible explanation for the fangs and superhuman abilities. The woman was a vampire.

Rubbing the abrasion on her elbow from hitting the sawdust-covered floor, she glanced around, looking desperately for another way out. There was none.

Maybe if she could keep her talking . . . "What do you want?"

"Isn't it obvious?" the woman asked flatly. "We're hungry."

"We?"

"My friends. Your boyfriend was arguing with them."

Juliette's heart tightened with dread. Those men were vampires, too. That explained what she'd seen out the window. They'd hurt Andre. Had they killed him?

Bile rose in her throat and she choked. "What did you do to him?"

The woman shrugged, advancing closer. "I'm too hungry to care."

Juliette scrambled away from her, trying to put as much distance between the two of them as she could. In her haste, she hit a pair of sawhorses and knocked a toolbox to the ground, scattering tools everywhere. She grabbed an awl and held the point out like a knife.

Tilting her head, the woman just stared at her like a hawk examining the prey it was about to shred to pieces. Her eyes were almost more frightening than her fangs. Emotionless black holes with no irises. Even the whites were dark.

"Are you scared yet?" the vampire asked. The curiosity in her tone was genuine, as if she truly wasn't sure.

What a sick freak. "Why? Do you want to hear me beg?"

"Blood tastes best when the host is frightened." She talked like she was reading from some kind of vampire manual.

Instinctively, Juliette wanted to cover up as much exposed skin as possible. As she pulled her robe tighter, her fingertip brushed against the amulet in her pocket.

What had the housekeeper said – that it was supposed to ward off evil? Talk about an epic fail.

She rubbed it with the pad of her thumb anyway. Maybe at the very least, it would give her a sense of peace. She said a silent prayer, hoping Andre had managed to get away.

Footsteps pounded on the wood floor.

A rip of plastic.

And there was Andre, stepping into the room. He was still favoring his arm, but now he had a gun. And from the looks of it, he was ready to use it.

"Get. The fuck. Away. From her."

"Andre, no!" Juliette yelled. "Go back. She's a monster." She had no idea if a gunshot would kill a vampire, but she couldn't assume it would.

The woman turned her head from Andre to Juliette then back again, as if she couldn't decide whether biting Juliette would be worth the risk of getting shot.

Too late. Andre fired, and the shot echoed in the empty space.

The vampire fell in a heap. Juliette watched in horror as the body began to curl in on itself.

Dropping the awl, Juliette jumped up. "Andre, are you—"

"Stay away." With the gun at his feet, he doubled over in pain.

He must be delirious from blood loss. Ignoring his protests, she flew to his side and tried to examine his injury.

"Juliette, no," he said, turning his head away.

"You're hurt. You need help."

"You need to . . . stay away. Please. It's not . . . safe."

His eyes looked like they had when they first arrived at the hotel. The pupils were huge. Only a thin gold ring of his irises remained.

"In this condition . . . I'll . . . hurt you."

"What are you talking about?" The man was clearly going into shock.

"I am . . . like her."

Putting a hand gently on his back, she leaned in close. "You're in shock, Andre. You've lost a lot of blood. Let me—"

Then there was a sharp, stabbing pain in her neck and her world went black.

What have I done?

Andre crawled away from Juliette, collapsed to the floor and covered his head with his hands.

How could he have been so stupid?

He should have forced her to get away from him. Showed his fangs to scare her. Then she would've known what he was, that he was no different than the vampire who'd attacked her.

But no.

A part of him – a very dark and deadly part – had wanted her to come closer. He'd wanted to taste her rich blood again – mouthfuls and mouthfuls of it – until his energy had been replenished and his hunger sated.

He'd taken too much. And now she was gone.

He wasn't sure how long he spent on the floor. It felt as if time both stopped and sped out of control. Five seconds? Five hours?

"Are you okay?" A male voice echoed somewhere nearby. Mateo.

So the Guardian had finally arrived. Well, he was too fucking late. The guy was asking something else, but Andre tuned him out.

He wasn't okay. He'd never be okay. Not after what he'd done to the woman he loved.

"Leave me alone," he started to say, but then a soft, quiet voice answered Mateo's question.

"Yeah, I'm . . . a little woozy, that's all. But I think I'll be fine. Can you check on Andre?"

No, it couldn't be. He'd held her in his arms. She was limp. He'd drained her.

"Juliette?" He lifted his head from the floor.

She was sitting on the ground with her back against the wall.

He choked, barely able to speak. "You're alive."

She flashed him a weak smile. "Yes, and so are you."

"But I thought you were . . ." He looked at Mateo. "I don't understand."

"Did you think you'd drained her?" his friend asked.

He pushed himself up. "Yes, I—" Pain stabbed at his shoulder, and he groaned.

"If you had," Mateo said, "you'd be healed by now."

Andre bristled as his friend moved closer to Juliette. He felt his pupils expanding with anger.

Mine.

"I don't think you took much," Mateo was saying as he bent down to examine her neck.

He couldn't stand to see another male's hands on her. Leaping to his feet, Andre grabbed his friend by the shoulder and shoved him away from Juliette. "Get away from her."

She's mine.

"Whoa, calm down." Mateo brushed the sawdust from his muscular arms and adjusted his glasses. "I was just trying to help."

Andre dropped to his knees in front of Juliette. "You were dead, *ma chérie.* In my arms."

"I must've fainted. I'm one of those people who passes out when it comes to blood. When I get my blood drawn, even if they only take a little, I have to do it while lying down otherwise I think about it too much and . . ." She gave an embarrassed smile. "Well, you've seen what happens."

It hadn't happened when he took her blood in San Francisco. Was it because they'd been making love at the time and he'd quickly wiped her memory afterwards?

Overcome by a fresh wave of emotion, he started to move away from her, but she put a hand on his knee, stopping him.

"I must admit, I'm surprised, but I'm not scared of you," she said, pointedly. "You're completely different from them."

He searched her eyes, but didn't see a sliver of fear. She had to be in shock. Either that or she was crazy. He'd almost killed her. "But—"

She shushed him. "I would like someone to explain this new reality to me, though. I think I deserve that much."

Andre darted a glance at Mateo. The man shrugged.

So Andre gathered his thoughts and told her about their kind. Only Darkbloods and other reverts still killed humans. The majority of vampires today lived peacefully and secretly within the human population, staying out of the sunlight and needing blood only occasionally.

"Which is why it's against our laws for humans to know of our existence," Andre said. "If someone finds out, we must wipe their memory."

He started to explain about the Van Helsing groups, a small but secret society that tracks and kills vampires whether they're reverts or not, but she interrupted him.

"Have you wiped my memory? Are you *going* to wipe my memory?"

He looked down and brushed the sawdust off his hands. "I have wiped your memory, yes. I took your blood in San Francisco and—"

"And did I pass out?"

"No."

She nodded thoughtfully. He could almost see the cogs turning around in her mind. "So no humans know about you, except for these hunters?"

"There are others," Mateo piped in, "but they've been sworn to secrecy. I know a few other Guardians who are with human women. They seem to make it work."

She stretched out her leg and touched Andre's ankle with her bare foot. "I want to make it work between us. Now that I know the truth."

"Listen," Mateo said, clearing his throat. "If you two are going to play footsies, I've got some clean-up work to do."

Andre glanced over at the female vampire's body. A pile of ash and some metal rivets from the clothes she'd been wearing were all that was left.

"Thanks for handling things," he said.

Mateo grinned. "What can I say? It's my job. I'm here to serve."

Andre helped Juliette through the construction site to his suite of rooms in the other wing of the hotel. After making sure she got something to eat, he tucked her into bed then turned to leave.

"Where are you going?" she asked.

"To my study. I need to catch up on some reading."

"Why can't you do that here?" She patted the mattress beside her.

He wanted nothing more than to climb into bed with her and pull her into his arms. "Probably not a good idea."

She propped herself up on one elbow. "That's why you left San Francisco, isn't it? Because you were afraid that something like this would happen?"

He nodded. "I implanted a memory suggestion with several of the staff so they thought I'd left with a woman who was my wife. I knew you'd go there to find me. I thought it'd be easier if you hated me."

"Easier?" she choked. "Easier for whom? I hated that I hated you."

He rubbed a hand over his face and thought about the nights he'd spent on Bourbon Street. The absinthe bars.

The women. "The truth is, I've been miserable, too. I've done everything I could think of to forget you."

"And did any of it work?" she asked, softly.

"No."

Chapter Six

It took forever for Juliette to convince Andre that she was okay. She couldn't talk him out of sleeping on the couch in his study the first night, and he waited on her hand and foot the next day. After that, he caved in but slept on the far side of the bed with his back to her, refusing to touch her.

She understood that he was afraid of hurting her, but she found it harder and harder to stay away. She craved the intimacy of a physical relationship with him, and yet she respected him and wanted to honor his feelings, too. She just hoped he'd come around soon. Although her whole world had been turned upside down with the revelation that vampires actually existed, she'd come to terms with it because her love for Andre superseded everything.

During this time, she examined the cabinetry her father had made and where they were to be installed. Turned out, the contractor had made some minor adjustments to the space that caused them not to fit. All that was needed was some trim. Although Andre had tried to explain the situation to her father, he hadn't listened to him. He did listen to his daughter, however, milling the trim pieces one day and overnighting them the next.

Juliette also helped Andre and his staff clean up the mess from the storm, clearing branches and debris, and raking leaves. No one seemed to question their employer's strange hours, having accepted the fact that he was a night owl and slept late. This gave her a chance to email and get some work done online.

It was after midnight and Andre was still at his desk, pouring over the financials of a new deal when Juliette came up behind him.

"When will you be finished? Let's go to bed."

"If you're tired, you can—"

"Who said anything about being tired?" She rotated his chair around so that he was facing her and then dropped her robe. She'd gone to one of the lingerie shops in the French Quarter and bought black lace panties, a matching bra and high heels.

His gaze roamed slowly over her body, making her nipples tighten. She wanted his hands all over her, exploring every inch.

"*Ma chérie*, what are you doing?" he asked huskily.

"What does it look like I'm doing?" She loosened his tie and straddled his lap. "I need you, Andre. I want you to make love to me."

He shook his head. "No, I may not be able to control myself."

She reached for his belt and started to unbuckle it. "I've got that covered."

He narrowed his eyes. "What have you been up to?"

"While you were sleeping, I made a trip into the city. Let's just say there are some very interesting shops on Bourbon Street."

She rose from his lap, grabbed his tie and pulled him behind her like a dog on a leash into the bedroom. Though he protested, he followed her willingly. She then pushed him down on the bed and stood between his legs.

"Juliette," he said softly.

"Shhh. You don't need to do anything. I'll do all the work."

She put her hands on his shoulders to push him onto the mattress, but he grabbed her wrists instead. "Why must you be so persistent, Juliette?"

She shrugged. "Because I want you inside me and I'm not going to stop till that happens."

"Really?" His devilish smile sent shivers through her body and made her panties wet.

She needed to stay focused. She was in charge here. "Yes. Because you've been so stubborn, you're going to have to do what I say."

"This should be interesting."

He took off his socks and shoes and allowed her to push him backwards. She rummaged in a plastic sack and pulled out a pair of novelty handcuffs.

He laughed. "And what do you plan to do with those?"

"I'm going to cuff you to the headboard. You won't need to worry about losing control, because *I'll* be the one in charge. You need to do what *I* say."

"You think those will hold me?"

She raised an eyebrow. "Then humor me."

As she cuffed his wrists to the headboard, he lifted his head off the pillow and rubbed his tongue across her nipples through the thin fabric of her bra. She hissed in a breath and arched into him.

"You're supposed to be doing what I tell you," she said.

"Then give me an order."

She turned her attention back to what she'd been doing before that little diversion and finished cuffing him. She tried to remember some of the orders he used to give her. "Okay, lift your hips. I need to undress you."

He laughed. "I feel like a doll."

"Good. Because you're going to become my plaything tonight." She hooked her fingers under the waistband of his slacks and slipped them off, springing free his thick erection. A drop glistened on the smooth tip, so she bent forward and took him into her mouth.

He groaned and rolled his hips, driving deeper inside her mouth.

She produced a condom from the bag and started to tear it open.

"That's unnecessary," he said. "A vampire can't get a human pregnant. I only used them earlier to make you think I was human."

She pulled away from him. She'd always assumed there'd be children one day, but if she couldn't have them with the man she loved, they'd figure out something else.

Heat pooled in her lower belly at the thought of feeling his flesh directly against hers. After unbuttoning his dress shirt, she smoothed her hands all over his well-defined chest and abs. She knew he could break free from those cuffs with a simple twist of his wrist if he wanted to.

Straddling his hips, she reached back, grabbed the base of his erection and positioned the broad tip at her center.

She looked into his face for signs that he was stressed, but saw only the incredibly sexy man she was madly in love with. "Are you okay, Andre?"

His smile was tender. "Yeah, love, I'm doing just fine."

And with that, she lowered herself onto him.

Andre struggled to keep from breaking the handcuffs. All he wanted was to have his hands on her, but he realized how important this was. For both of them. The handcuffs represented his ability to control his dark nature as well as her ability to feel safe around him.

"When are you going to free me?" he asked, thrusting his hips. Although he had the ability to make a mental suggestion, he didn't. Having her come to her own conclusions was very important to him. He wanted her to do this of her own free will.

"When I feel like it's time."

He groaned. She was slick and tight around him. He wouldn't last much longer. "Then move the lace of your bra aside and lean forward. I want your breast in my mouth."

She did as she was told, which excited him more. Even restrained like he was, she obeyed him.

He ran his teeth gently over her nipple and began to suckle. She hissed and he felt her inner muscles tighten around him. He would never tire of pleasing her.

"It's time, Juliette. Remove the cuffs."

Without a protest, she reached up and pressed the unlocking mechanisms, freeing his hands. He wrapped his arms around her and tangled his legs around hers. She'd done exactly as he told her and that totally turned him on.

Without breaking their connection, he rolled over until she was beneath him. Her blonde hair spread out on his pillow like a halo. His angel.

"I love you, Juliette. I don't ever want to leave you."

"I love you, too," she said, her baby blue eyes looking up at him. "So much it hurts."

"Then stay with me forever. Let's build a life together. Here or in San Francisco. It doesn't matter to me. The only thing that matters is that you're happy."

Her legs went around his waist and she ran her fingers through his hair. "Being with you forever will make me the happiest girl in the world."

The pressure in his lower belly increased and his balls tightened. He was almost there and couldn't hold back any longer. His mouth crashed over hers, taking her. He made one more powerful thrust, seating himself deeper and then the pressure exploded.

She was his. She loved him. And this was the start of forever.

THE MANY LIVES OF HADLEY MONROE

Bec McMaster

1

Because I could not stop for Death,
He kindly stopped for me;
The carriage held but just ourselves
And Immortality.

Emily Dickinson

The storm came in low and boiling; purple-black thunder-clouds that cast an eerie light across the cane fields. The kind of storm that had sprung up when her granddaddy got taken, rest his soul. Hadley grabbed the bag of groceries off the passenger seat of the Chevy and kicked the door shut behind her as she ran towards the porch of her grandmother's house. Fat raindrops spattered down, a blast of wind sending the cane rippling in the paddocks on either side of the house, like waves on the ocean.

Or what she imagined the ocean to look like.

Though she'd spent the first few years of her life out West and shifted from town to town with her mama, she'd rarely been further than a day from Copeland, GA, since she arrived at the age of six. All she had were faint memories of her mama taking her on up to Nashville as a little girl to see Garth Brooks. Sitting in the front of her mother's old powder-blue Cadillac, with her heels on the dashboard as a popsicle melted down her arm faster than her attempts to eat it. Hot sun. Songs on the radio. And her mama, long dark hair tumbling over her shoulders as she grinned down at Hadley and clapped a hand against her thigh as though she were playing the tambourine. Faded memories. Like looking at old photos that had been left too long in the sun.

That was before her mama up and left her here in Copeland with Gramma Monroe. The last she'd seen of Lily June Monroe, Hadley had been standing on this porch, with her tiny hand wrapped in her gramma's, watching the dust trail of that old Caddy dissipate over the lane.

Three steps from the porch the downpour hit. "God damn—" Hadley bit her tongue instinctively. Gramma Monroe didn't approve of that kind of language from young ladies.

The run left her breathless and perspiring, her ribs squeezing tight in her chest. She'd been working too hard lately to keep her fitness up and it showed. Too many long hours working double shifts at the library in town and then the diner.

A black streak shot out of nowhere, sending her heart tripping along 'til she realized it was Grams' cat, Jethro. Hadley nearly tripped on him as he tore through the door the second it was open an inch. The screen door banged shut behind her, rain thundering on the tin roof as she made it to safety.

No sign of the darned cat.

"Hadley? Is that you?" Gramma called from her sitting room.

Of course it was. Nobody else ever visited them any more. Hadley scraped her wet hair out of her face as her grandmother shuffled into the old war-torn kitchen, leaning heavily on the timber dresser where the Strasbourg silver service was kept. A faded nightgown hung around her gramma's narrow shoulders and Hadley's heart fell a little. As a young girl, she'd never seen her grandmother not get dressed. Each morning was a ritual of sweet-scented powders, heated rollers, a matching dress and shoes and the ever-present pink lipstick. Gramma didn't go anywhere without putting her face on.

Or hadn't.

"Did you lie in?" Hadley asked, pressing a kiss against her grandmother's parchment cheek. That squeeze in her chest grew and she turned away, rubbing at it. Hating the thought of her grandmother's decline.

"No. No, of course not."

But Hadley knew she lied.

It's just a matter of time for her, the doctor had said, in that gentle voice she hated so much. *The shock of Mr Monroe's death . . . Sometimes it takes older people that way. They just stop . . . livin'.*

"Looks like the angels are weepin', Hadley May," Gramma said. She made the sign of the cross then coughed, her thin frame jerking as though an invisible hand slammed her between the shoulder blades.

Hadley put the groceries down and caught her grandmother by the shoulders. "Why don't you go sit on down? I'll fetch you some tea and fix up some fried chicken."

"I ain't that hungry."

"You need to eat," she replied. The sink was clean enough for her to suspect her gramma hadn't touched the plate she'd left for her that morning before work. A glance in the fridge confirmed it.

Once she got her grandmother settled with her sweet tea, Hadley returned to unload the groceries. The storm was coming in thick and fast, rattling the roof.

Black skies, thunder like a brass band. That was when I saw him comin' for me, Miss Hadley. The silky-soft pitch of her granddaddy's voice whispered through her memories. His story-tellin' voice, she liked to think it.

Saw who, Grandpa?

His eyes would get that faraway look. *A young man. Like me. Tall and pale, with a shock of black hair. Solemn and grim. Ain't like no man I ever seen before. Somethin' otherworldly about him. Then I realized. He ain't got no shadow.*

Hardly the sort of stories the girls in her class listened to.

But Hadley would lean forward, her breath catching. *No shadow?*

No shadow, her granddaddy confirmed. *He came for me, Hadley May.* A shudder. *An' I cheated him then, but knew he'd come back for me one day.*

Hadley stared out through the window as she washed the greens in the sink. A whole lot of foolishness, as her grandmother would say, but it had been Hadley's favourite story. The time old Lewis Monroe cheated Death.

For another forty years at least. The faint smile on her face died, clouding over. What was she going to do? Her two jobs didn't afford them any health insurance and Gramma was fading every day, like a tablecloth hanging on the line too long.

The lights chose that moment to flicker and die, with a mighty crash of thunder. The sudden surge of darkness made her heart race and she dropped the colander.

"Hadley?" her gramma called. "Hadley?"

"I got it, Grams." Wiping her hands dry on her jean cut-offs, she started for the door to fetch the generator. The faded light through the window was just enough to see by.

Stillness weighed heavily in the air in the hallway. The old longcase clock had fallen silent, its brass pendulum quivering. Hadley frowned as she passed it by, sweat springing up along the back of her neck.

No clock would tick. No electrics would work.

Lightning flashed. For a second she thought she saw a man-shape in the glass of the door and clapped a hand to her chest. When she blinked, there was no one there.

"It's just a story," she muttered to herself as she fetched the shed keys down from their hook by the door.

The clock started ticking again; like a bomb.

"Shit." Hadley dropped the keys. Scrambling for them on the floor in the darkened hallway.

Timber floorboards creaked and she looked up. There was nothing there. But suddenly she didn't want to leave the house.

Clutching the fist of keys, Hadley peered into the kitchen. "Grams, you okay?"

There was no answer. Only a weird, throat-curdling sound from beneath the dresser. Jethro. His back arched and his green eyes locked on something behind her.

Hadley snatched the broom out of the corner and spun. Nothing. Her heartbeat thundered in her ears. Thick spears of yellow lightning lashed through the indigo skies outside the window, outlining a figure in the reflection.

"I know you're there." She clutched at the charm around her throat – her grandfather's. "You might as well show yourself." Swallowing hard, she tipped up her chin. "It'd be rude not to."

The answering stillness seemed like the aftermath of the enormous church bell of St Mary of the Angels; the air quivering, sound hovering just on the edge of hearing . . . Movement shifting *through* the particles of air until she was almost cross-eyed.

Between one blink and the next, he was there.

Jethro tore away through the house, leaving her alone to face the intruder. Hadley staggered backwards, her grip firming around the broom handle, though her mouth parted in shock.

He couldn't have been much older than she. The hood of his black coat hid most of his face. All she could see were a pair of firm lips and the faintest of clefts in his chin. As he lifted his head . . . those eyes . . . they weren't human. The blue of his irises was the only colour about him, the rest of him seemingly made of shadows, or like an old black-and-white movie. Faint curiosity gleamed there, though his expression held only resignation.

He lifted scarred hands and dragged the hood of his coat back, revealing thick black hair that raked over his forehead and a whorl of tattoos vanishing up the side of his neck and into his hairline. No. Not tattoos, she realized. More like scars that had been rubbed with ash. Something vaguely primitive.

No shadow. Her breath came hard and fast. This wasn't happening. Just a story. The way her granddaddy always told it. But the grip of the broom felt heavy in her hands. If she pinched herself she had no misgivings that she'd feel it.

"You're n-not having her." Hadley sidestepped between him and the door behind her. Grams was the only thing tying her to this godforsaken town, but the idea of losing her . . . She was all that Hadley had left.

Death glanced sidelong beneath his lashes, surveying the kitchen. *"If I wished to take her, you could not stop me."*

Truth. "Please," she whispered. "Please don't."

"I do not have a choice. Death is claiming the body and I must do my duty."

She shot a nervous glance towards the living room. "She'll hear you."

"No, she won't." He cocked his head. *"Can't you feel it?"*

There was no lightning, no thunder. Just an ominous silence, thick with brewing intensity. The clock had stopped ticking again, the world weighted with heavy expectation. Perhaps it was the darkness, but she almost thought the world had grayed out, colour leaching from the edges of her vision.

Not her world. Hadley shivered. "What did you do?"

"This is the Between, where I exist. No time here. No sound."

"It's awful," she blurted.

His gaze sharpened. *"Some say it is peaceful."*

"What did you do to me?" Panic tripped over her tongue. "Can you take me back? Am I trapped here? Why can I see you when I couldn't before?"

"You are not trapped here forever. And only those caught between worlds – such as mediums – or those on the verge of death can see me. Or if I allow it." His gaze dropped to the charm at her throat and sudden intensity tightened his expression. *"That is your grandfather's, yes?"*

Hadley clutched the charm. "Yes."

Death cast it a wary glance and Hadley's heart fluttered. Something about the charm disconcerted him. Damn her grandfather, for never telling her how he'd tricked this man.

Black shadows slithered through the corners of her vision. Hadley tilted her head, but they were gone again.

Focus. Everybody wants something. Even Death.

"Perhaps we can reach some kind of compromise? What

d-do you want?" Hadley backed away, holding the broom in front of her.

"It is not a matter of want, so much as what I must do."

"You can't have her. It's not fair! She's not ready to go." *And I'm not ready to let her.*

Death's eyes slowly narrowed. *"They always say this. What makes you any different to the others? Why should I grant you this boon, when I do not for others?"*

"You did it once," she replied.

That made his face harden. *"So he told you then."*

But not the how of it. Hadley squeezed the broom desperately. Her granddaddy would never speak of how. Just trail off, staring into the distance . . . Eyes growing a little sad. If he told her the truth, then Death would come for her instead, he'd said.

"It doesn't have to be forever. Just . . . a little more time."

"No."

"Even Death must want something."

There . . . a flicker in his eyes. His face tightened. *"Only to perform my duty."*

Yet he didn't make a move towards her. Hadley let the broom lower, a certain suspicion filling her. If this were about duty, then he'd have reaped his soul and moved on. Instead . . . he was letting her speak.

Hadley leaned the broom against the wall. Not like it was going to stop him. "One more year," she said, knowing she gambled with her grandmother's life.

"You're bartering with me?"

"Is that not how it works? We play a round of poker or two—"

"No." The sudden echo of his voice in her ears made her wince. *"I do not play games."*

"Then tell me what you want."

"Nothing," he repeated.

"If you didn't want anything, then you wouldn't have shown yourself to me," she shot back.

That made him pause. Hadley's breath caught; she was *right.*

Standing silently in her kitchen with his hands clasped

behind his back, he examined the silver service, lovingly polished by her grandmother. *"I do not understand why you are all so desperate to stay here,"* he said.

Here? "To remain among the living?"

"Those that see me always beg for more time." His eyes grew distant. *"Why?"*

What kind of question was that? But her grandfather had always taught her not to give away the goose for free. "And if I can answer it? Will you leave her be?"

This time he turned to face her, his eyes focusing sharply. Dangerous eyes. She had the feeling that if she stared too long into them, she'd see something she wasn't certain she was ready for. *"A week."*

"A year," she repeated promptly, though her palms were damp.

"Two weeks."

"Six months."

It went on, Hadley's nerves giving way to the surge of desperation. Death wasn't quite so terrifying now. His eyes were bluer by the moment, the stark gray world of the Between seeming just a little brighter. Even those lingering shadows that haunted the edges of her vision seemed to fade away a little.

Finally, Hadley tipped her chin up and stared him in the eyes. "Two months. That's my final offer."

"You act as though you have something I desperately want," he snapped.

Yes, she thought she did. The only question was: what was it? What could she – of all people – have that Death could crave? An answer didn't seem enough. "You gave grandfather longer."

"Your grandfather cheated."

"I cannot imagine you the type to allow that."

His gaze dropped. There was something not quite right here. *"You have a month with her,"* he said finally. *"A month at most, to make me understand. Get the question right at the end of that time and you may have another month."*

"And if I can't make you understand?" Once again she

caught a flicker of shadow, melting down the wall like some slithering Dalí clock.

"What is it?" His voice sharpened.

"Nothing." She focused on him again, forcing herself not to see the shadows. "What happens if I can't make you understand?"

His voice lowered. *"You say your goodbyes."*

The bravado left her. She'd done what she could, though she could feel the sting of heat lash her eyes. It had been so long since she'd cried; only the once since her mother left her behind and that had been over her grandfather's death.

Hadley took a deep breath. "Very well. Do we shake hands or something?" He wouldn't want a blood vow, would he?

Death reached out towards her and she flinched. His hand froze and she could see ancient scars on his fingers. A certain, dreadful kind of stillness masked his face and he tried again. It reminded her of the expression she'd worn during school, when all the other little girls wanted to know where her mama was and who her daddy had been. For a second, she felt a strange kind of kinship.

Only that forced her spine to stiffen; to allow him to press his fingertips to her sternum. Beneath the cool touch, her heart thumped hard and she sucked in a sharp breath. "What are you doing?"

"Two months, so I vow it," he replied in stilted language. *"One for the bargain and two for an answer."*

A hollow pain radiated in her chest. "Stop." She caught his wrist and he withdrew his fingers. The pain vanished, leaving her gasping as she held on to him. He'd grasped her arm with his other hand, those strong fingers digging into her biceps. Hadley looked up at him helplessly. He smelled like burned cinnamon, something inhuman but not entirely unpleasant.

"Tomorrow." His voice softened just the slightest fraction. *"I shall come each day, to ask if you yet have an answer for me. Be warned that once your month is gone, I shall take what is promised."*

With that he was gone. The world erupted back into vibrant colour and noise, the light above her suddenly flickering to life and Gramma's TV blaring. God, she felt heavy, as if she'd stepped from zero gravity back to a world where flesh and bone mattered. The sensation of his fingers still gripped her arm, sending little shivers down her spine.

"Hadley?" her gramma called.

Hadley collapsed against the dresser in relief. One month. Then she would lose the only thing she had left in the world. Unless . . . Unless she could provide Death with an answer to an impossible question.

2

Why do the living always want to stay? Why do they fear death so much? Why do they grieve when their loved ones are taken?

Hadley gnawed on her knuckle as she idly wiped the counter top at the diner. How did you answer that question? *Because they fear death, fear the unknown. Because the death of a loved one leaves a little hollow spot in a person's heart, the way it had done when Grandpa passed on.*

Death wasn't asking for a logical explanation. What he wanted her to do was to make him *understand.*

How did you make a creature who had no concept of what it felt like to live, understand what loss meant? What death meant for people?

To do that, she had to make him understand *life.*

Between one swipe of the rag and the next, the diner was no longer empty. Colour drained from the world and a tall man hunched over one of the chipped tables, his hood pulled up over his head as if he were cold and his scarred knuckles laced together. Silence prickled in her ears and when she turned, Mary-Beth Monaghan – the diner's corpulent cook – was stretched forward on tiptoe, frozen, caught in the midst of hanging her apron up. She had, no doubt, been on her way for a quick cigarette break out back.

Even a fly hung in the air.

Heart racing, Hadley put down the rag. "You could give a girl some warning, you know? How long have you been here?"

"Long enough."

An answer that was not an answer at all. Hadley pursed her lips but said nothing as she poured him some coffee and grabbed a plate of pie. Hospitality around here consisted of fixing up something, no matter what the circumstances. Though all the lessons her gramma had taught her had no bearing on this kind of situation.

What did you do when Death appeared in your life? Offer him refreshments? Iced tea? Set out the Strasbourg?

All she had to fall back on was custom. Tugging her apron off, she tossed it on the counter and crossed towards him, slinging her long legs over the bar stool. "Here." She pushed the mug towards him, wondering if he could hear the nervous patter of her heart. The idea of Death was terrifying, but, up close, he looked like just another man. Albeit, not the sort that you often saw in Copeland. Sneaking a glance at him, she studied the somewhat ragged ends of his slightly too long hair beneath the hood of his coat, thick dark lashes and a firm mouth that gave him a somewhat sober expression. Things that she hadn't noticed about him the night before.

Of course, she'd been somewhat distracted by his impending duty to really take in the smooth honey glide of his skin.

"What is it?" Death peered at the coffee suspiciously. *"It looks like—"*

"Poison. Mary-Beth brews it up each morning. And as it is now—" a quick glance at the clock "—five o'clock—" almost time for her shift to finish. "—I'd guess it has the consistency of river mud."

A faint hint of something warmed his eyes. They were almost blue for a moment. *"Thanks."*

She wasn't sure if there should be a question mark on the end of that. "Can you eat or drink?" The thought hadn't struck her until now.

"I don't require it. Here in the Between, this body does not age or work as human bodies do."

A smear of darkness appeared on the edge of her vision, but when she checked over her shoulder, there was nothing there. Nervousness made her babble. "You sound strange," she said. He was very stiff. Formal even. As though he'd come straight from another time. But how many times had someone said exactly that to her? Growing up outside of Copeland, she'd had hints of the same accent, but everyone at school had made it clear she sounded strange.

Outside meant different. Different meant *not us*.

"English is not my mother tongue. "

"Oh?" A little excitement fluttered in her chest. "You're not American? Where'd you come from?" She could only imagine the rest of the world; glimpses of it seen through the books at the local library and her grandfather's shelves upstairs. Then her excitement died a little. It was almost too easy to forget what he was. "How'd you become what you are?"

Dark lashes obscured his eyes. He even sipped some of the coffee. *So have you answered my question?"*

Her curiosity burned, but she got the message. He wasn't here to play nice. He was here to learn the answer to his question. And if she couldn't answer it . . .

No matter how human he looked, she had to remember that he wasn't. Not at all. "Not yet. But I have a plan."

"Oh?"

She pushed the peach pie closer to him. "A very cunning plan."

Liar. No matter how many hours she'd spent awake last night, she couldn't think of a single thing. Take him to funerals? Show him the mourners? Explain their pain? He wouldn't understand. And no doubt he'd seen enough funerals and deaths in his life that it wouldn't make any difference.

"I thought we could just . . . hang out," she said. "Maybe you might understand, if you knew what Gramma means to me."

Death pushed his coffee aside. *"I'm not the one taking her away from you; death is a natural expiration from living. This is simply a duty. To ensure that none stay behind when they have passed.*"

"What do you mean?"

"*I have the power to reap – and the power to extend the moment of death if I will it . . . But that is not my duty. I simply make sure that each soul passes on, doesn't stay trapped in the Between, where I exist.*"

"Ghosts?"

"*You cling to life, do you not? As you would will it for your grandmother. That urge does not always pass when the body ceases. What is left behind sometimes desires to stay. The stronger, more violent a death, the stronger the urge to remain.*" He tipped his head to her. "*My task is to gather those that hover Between and guide them into the Beyond.*"

That was the kind of talk that would give the minister a heart attack. But who wouldn't want to know what happened after death? "Is that where we go? Is it heaven? What is it?"

"*I do not know.*" He sipped the coffee.

"Bright lights? Tunnels of doom?"

"*Are you always so full of questions?*"

"Are you always so deficient in answers?"

Checkmate. The edges of his mouth curved up.

"Why, is that a smile?" Hadley teased, leaning forward to see more.

Another slow, heated look at her. The hood slipped back from his dark hair, revealing a little more of his face. "*You're not afraid of me.*"

A little. But her fear had lulled to a gentle nervousness and she'd always used humour to make herself feel better. "Should I be? Did you bring your scythe?" she joked, sounding bolder than she truly felt.

A long moment of silence. He picked up the fork and stabbed a piece of glistening peach, staring at it. "*No,*" he said. "*I left my long black robe at home too.*"

Silence fell. "Was that a joke?"

Death popped the piece of peach in his mouth, then blinked and drew the fork out as if it had stabbed him. Hadley's smile reached epic proportions. Even Death wasn't immune to her peach pie.

"I could tell you," he said, the corded muscles in his throat swallowing. *"But then I'd have to kill you."*

Hadley let out a slow breath. "You're possibly the only one who could ever get away with saying that. That was terrible."

The edges of his mouth curled up faintly, but this time she didn't call him on it.

Hadley felt another little flutter in her chest that didn't feel like nerves at all.

3

Death had a sense of humor.

A horrible sense of humor, but it was there.

Hadley slid into the passenger side of the truck, staring out over the field. Yellow stubble stretched for miles, the remnants of this year's cropping. "Well?" she asked, turning her attention to Death. "Please tell me you've driven a stick shift before?"

"No." His knuckles curved around the shift knob.

The last couple of days had been . . . interesting. Every night, after she'd put Gramma to bed, he'd been waiting for her in the kitchen. Peering at all of the photos on the fridge of her and her family as if they were mesmerizing. Perhaps, to him, they were.

Today she had the afternoon off work, and she'd volunteered to teach him how to drive. Despite the way he could move from the real world to the Between, he had very little concept of how things worked. Or perhaps very little curiosity. He had his duty, and from the way he parroted it at her, she'd realized that there was little else in his life. It reminded her a little of the workers at the mill; moving like machines through their day, performing the same routines. They worked their shifts, had a few beers at the same bar as always, followed the same route home to fix up their same mac and cheese, maybe watched some TV and then bed. And the same thing the following morning, all over again.

It was a little scary to realize she'd begun to fall into that rhythm too.

At first Death's visits had been about the question, but when she didn't have an answer for him, he started to spend time with her. He questioned things in her life and when she explained to him how they worked, she saw a hint of curiosity burn in his eyes.

"Okay," she said, "I want you to put your hand on the gearstick . . ."

It took numerous attempts before he could get the old truck moving forward without a jerk. Death revved the truck's engine harder, whips of cut straw streaking past.

The shadows followed them, rippling over the field. Hadley cast a nervous glance behind her and he noticed.

"What is it?"

"Can't you see that?" she asked as he brought the truck to a halt. No matter how much she kinked her neck, the shadows always stayed at the edges of her vision.

Death looked. Then returned his gaze to her.

"Don't look at me like that. I'm not crazy." She settled in her seat, rubbing her arms. "There are these . . . shadows. I can never quite see them, but they've been there every time I'm with you."

His face smoothed of emotion. *"They're nothing to be concerned about."*

"Oh?" Hadley arched a brow. "If you think—"

"Nothing," he repeated firmly and the word rang in her ears for a moment.

"Fine."

If he'd been human he might have understood the connotations behind that single word. As it was, he merely nodded and carefully turned towards the corner at the end of the field.

"You drive like you're chauffeuring Miss Daisy," she said.

"Who is Miss Daisy?"

"Another time." Hadley rolled her eyes. "Here." She reached out and eased his white-knuckled hands on the steering wheel. "Just relax. You don't need to wrestle it."

It was a long afternoon. Death slowly mastered the truck and then Hadley insisted on him shifting over so that she could drive. The second she hit the gas, he grabbed hold of the door, his face paling.

"Hold on," she called, putting the old truck through its paces. Dust circled up behind them.

By the time she spun to a halt, his fingers were clenched in both the upholstery and the door. *"You take too many risks."*

"You don't take enough."

"That's because I know the consequences only too well."

Hadley stared at him. "Do you ever get sad? When you see . . . sometimes . . ."

Death stared out over the field, watching the sun sink toward the horizon. *"I think I used to."*

"Used to?"

"I've seen nearly every way a person can die. After a while, it's easier not to notice. Just complete my task. And sometimes it's a relief, Hadley. Some people seek me out."

He was trying to convince her that Gramma's death would be a release. Hadley sighed. "I couldn't imagine wanting to die," she admitted. "The thought terrifies me."

"Why?"

She gripped the steering wheel a little harder. "What if there's nothing afterwards?"

"Then you would never know."

"Then there *is* nothing afterwards?"

"I told you, I don't know." Death shrugged. *"One day you'll find out. Everyone does."*

"Except you?"

"Except me."

Hadley chewed on her lip. Night was beginning to cool the air. "Will I see you tomorrow?" she asked.

"Tomorrow night."

And then he disappeared.

4

"How did Grandfather cheat you?" Hadley lay along the bank of the creek behind her house, stretched out in the flickering dapples of sunlight and shadows.

Death sat beside her, resting on his hands. They'd picnicked there. It was Hadley's only day off. It felt nice to do something other than work or tend to her gramma. Even if her companion made her a little nervous.

"We played a game of riddles. He asked one that I could not answer. Every year I could come for him and he would ask me again. If I could not answer it, he gained another year."

"What was the answer?"

"I do not know."

"But he died," she said. "After forty years."

"He asked me to release him from our deal. The last time I visited, he had not left his wheelchair and he was gasping oxygen through a face mask. His body was failing him – even I cannot reverse the effects of age."

"I remember," she said quietly. Her proud grandfather hated being confined to his wheelchair, to have to be cleaned and fed and helped into bed. "But he didn't tell you the answer to his riddle?"

"He cheated. The question he asked was not a true riddle. He said that he could not answer it, not in a way that I would ever understand."

Hadley caught her breath. "Is it the question you asked me?"

A long, slow look. *"I would like to know the answer. It has become very frustrating after forty years not to know."*

Despite herself, she laughed. "That's it? That's how he won forty more years?"

Death actually scowled.

"Do you usually make deals with the people you come for?"

"Rarely. Few greet me with such composure as your grandfather – or you."

"I was scared out of my brain," she admitted. It was growing far too easy to talk to him.

"You did not seem to be."

"Mmm." She plucked a daisy and stared at its petals, twirling the stem. "Don't you get lonely? Is that why you occasionally make deals?"

"Of course not."

Silence fell, full of dozens of unspoken words. Hadley
plucked at the daisy's petals. "He loves me, he loves me
not . . ." She finally reached the last petal and sighed, tossing away the stem. "Not, it seems."

"Who doesn't love you?"

"It's a game children play." She explained it to him, but
he couldn't seem to understand the concept – or perhaps it
was the idea of love that he struggled with. "And if you want
an answer to that . . ."

"You've never been in love?"

A careful consideration. "Thought so. Once. I was sixteen
and school wasn't the place for me. He made me think he
cared for me and, you know, I was fool enough to believe it.
Turns out I wasn't quite good enough for his parents." She
shook her head. "That's not love. That's *need*. A need to be
wanted."

"Why weren't you good enough for them?"

Hadley explained gently, "My father – whoever he was
– was the wrong color."

They both stared at her bare feet and the smooth, cara-
mel color of her legs. Death frowned.

She sighed. "When Mama fell pregnant with me, she was
real young. Didn't tell anyone who the daddy was.
Grams . . . Well, things were different back then. They'd
even picked out a name. Hadley May. The type of name you
find round here a lot, in some of the old families. And then,
when I were born – well – it was quite a shock. Things were
said. My mama up and left with me and I didn't see my
grandparents until I was six. Didn't even know they existed
until then." She stared out over the creek. "Sometimes I
don't remember my mama real well. Only little things. Like
other people asking if I was adopted. Mama was good to
me, but it was hard on her. She wasn't meant to be a mother
so young. Sometimes I forget that I'm almost eight years
older than she was when she had me.

"So, she brought me back here. Grams seemed to think
raisin' me was her penance for the things she'd said. She
was real proud at first. Used to hold my hand as we walked
into church and stare any of the other ladies in the eye as if

to dare them to say anything." Hadley shrugged. "She learned to love me. But it didn't mean things were easy growing up. I dreamed of leaving. Getting out, seeing the world. Only Grandpa got sick and passed, and then Grams – you know."

He nodded. Those cerulean blue eyes locked on hers, stealing her breath. Were they getting bluer? *"Perhaps."*

"Not quite white enough for some; not black enough for others. In between." She glanced at him. "Kind of like you."

"People don't like to see me either."

Hadley laughed under her breath. "Thanks," she said dryly. "They don't hate me. Just . . . I know I'm different. Some of the girls that were plain awful to me in school, well, they're better now. Talk to me sometimes. I wouldn't call us friends though."

Painful memories. She took a deep breath. "What about you? Were you born this way?"

"No. But . . . I have forgotten," he said. *"I can't remember much of my life before."*

Hadley lay back on the checkered rug, resting on her elbows. "Before?"

Death stared out over the creek, fingers rubbing on his jeans. A habit. *"I was human once,"* he admitted. *"A long time ago."*

Hadley's gaze dropped to the markings on his neck. There was something ancient about them. Something primitive. "Were these from before?" she asked, rolling onto her knees and reaching out to touch one of the marks.

He was still. He was always still. But this stillness seemed to hint at a trembling within. Like that old church bell, vibrating at a pitch she couldn't see or hear. Hadley glanced down, beneath her lashes, as he met her gaze.

"Sorry," she said, drawing her hand back.

He caught it, pressing her fingers against his neck and clearing his throat. *"I have not been touched for a very long time. Don't feel you have to stop."*

That broke her heart in a million little ways. Here she was dwelling on life without her gramma, but she didn't think she could even comprehend the type of lonely state he existed in. To never feel another's skin against her own To never have known her grandfather's laughter, or the soft press of her gramma's lips against her forehead . . .

She was richer than he in so many ways.

Tentatively, she brushed his collar out of the way. Felt the whisper of his skin beneath hers. The marks marched down his neck and across his collarbone. Dark runes, almost like a child's drawing of bird wings.

"Where were you from?"

"The cold North." He squeezed his eyes shut. *"I have forgotten my language. Forgotten my tribe. It all just seems like shadows, now."*

Shadows. Like the ones haunting her. She looked around, but there was nothing here. Not in her world.

Or perhaps they were here. Perhaps she just couldn't see them when she wasn't Between.

A cold band circled the back of her neck at the thought.

Hadley swallowed hard and forced a smile to her lips. She couldn't help but remain acutely aware that she was kneeling between his thighs, the softness of her summer dress brushing against his jeans. "Tribe? You must be very old then."

The way he looked up at her. Hands resting on his knees as if he were afraid to move. A nervous tension pooled in the pit of her stomach. Something she recognized from that one night she'd spent with Billy Pyke, the boy who'd broken her heart. Yet this was infinitely more. She couldn't tear her gaze away, her fingertips grazing over the stubble of his jaw as though of their own volition. Swallowing tightly against the crazy thought that if she leaned closer he just might reach for her . . .

Death.

Snatching her fingertips away, Hadley lowered herself until she was sitting on her heels, her treacherous hands resting on her thighs. Still far too close to him, of course, but at least now the tension was manageable.

He looked away too and the distance between them seemed to grow, even though neither moved. *"I cannot remember, but yes, I am old."*

"Do you remember how you changed?" Or whatever had happened to make him this way.

"I chose it."

Chose it? "Why?"

That distance echoed across his face. A silent drawing away. *"Perhaps because it was a better option than remaining alive."* Their eyes met. *"I do not remember."*

For the first time, she had the sensation that he'd lied to her. Climbing to her feet, she smoothed her skirt and reached out to help him stand. "Come on."

"Where?"

"I can't think of an answer for you today," she admitted, forcing cheerfulness into her voice and meaning none of it. "But I bet you ain't ever tried a real Lowcountry boil before, huh?"

Back on safe ground.

5

The fair rolled into town that weekend, setting up over by the old school grounds.

"Come on!" Hadley called, catching Death's hand and dragging him down from the truck. "I haven't been to one of these in years!" A little bit of the old childhood excitement lit through her. Sometimes she wondered if she was teaching him about life, or whether she was rediscovering it herself.

Emmie Purnell and her little harem of gossips caught sight of Hadley as she rounded the ticket booth to the Ferris wheel. A false smile froze on Emmie's painted lips and then her eyes widened and her mouth dropped open as she caught sight of Death.

It seemed he could step out of the *Between* when he wished to.

Hadley had made him leave his coat in the truck. People would notice a man wearing heavy dark clothing in the liquid heat of a Georgian summer. What she hadn't expected was just the opposite. Women were noticing him, eyes slinking over his tall, hard form and eyeing the muscles that his rolled-up sleeves revealed.

In Copeland, anything new was interesting. Especially six and a half feet of smoldering blue eyes and dark hair.

"Bless my heart! Why, look at you, Hadley," Emmie called, grabbing her hand and winking. "Who's your handsome stranger? A cousin?"

You wish. Hadley smiled. "This is . . ." Her mind blanked. *"Dean."*

All three women blinked faintly at the sound of his voice. Husky enough to send a shiver through a corpse. Hadley could almost see the subconscious part of them recognize danger when they saw it.

Or perhaps misunderstand it.

"I'm Emmie," the woman said boldly, holding out her hand. Her eyes glittered with interest. "An old school friend of Hadley's. This here is Jo Lynne Hale and Rita Bellefleur."

"How's your husband?" Hadley broke in. Tommy Purnell had once been the running back of the Copeland Sasquatches, but the last she'd seen of him, there were hints his hair was starting to creep back up onto his skull and his muscle was slowly giving way to that six-pack of Bud he drank every night.

And I am not going to take guilty pleasure in that. Hadley linked her arm through Death's. She didn't like the way Emmie was eyeing him.

"Nice to see you girls again," she said, her smile stiffening.

Who's your daddy, Hadley?

Didn't he want you either?

Echoes of the past.

"It's been a real pleasure." Rita's eyes drank in Death's tall frame.

"Hope to see you around," Emmie added, but it was clear from the direction of her gaze which "you" she meant.

Bitterness is a worm that eats away at you, Miss Hadley. That from her grandfather. *The worst thing that could happen isn't what them girls could say to you. It's what they could make you be, make you say back. You don't ever let that bitterness in, you hear me?*

Hadley swallowed hard, tipping her head towards them politely, as she pushed Death towards a ride, aptly named the Hurricane. She needed something to take her mind off the encounter. The excitement she'd felt at attending her first fair in years was fading.

Death stopped in his tracks, forcing Hadley to a halt too. Their arms were still linked. He shot her a slow look that just about curled her toes. *"What did that mean?"*

"Nothing. Those three have been pissing in my corn-flakes for years. And what's with 'Dean'?"

"It was the first thing that came to mind." A frown drew his dark brows together. *"You're not smiling on the inside,"* he finally said, reaching up to brush her mouth. *"Though I can see your smile here."*

She let it fade, the trace of his fingers leaving little tingles across her skin. "It's nothing. Really." But it was nice to have her feelings noticed for once. She'd always been taught not to give folks ammunition to use against her, but sometimes it hurt, keeping it all inside.

Acting impulsively, she reached up on her toes and pressed her lips to his cheek. Death held very still, the hard wall of his body firm beneath the resting touch of her finger-tips. Her heart skipped a beat.

"Thanks," she whispered. Her rosy pink lipstick glistened on his cheek and Hadley flushed as she stepped away.

"For what?"

For noticing. She shrugged though and pointed to the Hurricane. "Come on, let's go on that!"

Dean froze in his tracks. *"That,"* he said flatly, *"is a death trap."*

"I'll hold your hand," she teased. "Besides, wouldn't you know if it was going to fall apart and kill people?"

He had no answer to this.

Hours later, they were sitting on the Ferris wheel with the taste of cotton candy in their mouths. Hadley licked her fingers, glancing from beneath her lashes at him. She hadn't had this much fun in ages.

Too busy tending first her grandfather, and now her gramma. Waiting tables at the diner and falling into bed of nights, feeling like her bones were dipped in lead. She'd had a few friends over the years, but as weeks, months, years passed, they'd slowly drifted away. Started having babies and keeping house. Only Hadley was left behind.

Or maybe she'd left them behind? Losing herself in the drudgery of life, until she'd become little more than a mannequin. Once she'd dreamed of leaving – of travelling the world – but it had been a long time since she'd flicked through the pages of *National Geographic* at the library or looked at the map of Paris she'd once bought on an impulse, and stashed in a journal she no longer wrote in.

A month and a half left. At best. Hadley drummed her fingers on the safety carriage, feeling Death's thigh pressed against hers. He was surveying the fair, his thoughts obscured behind those enigmatic eyes.

For the first time, she examined her life. Maybe Gramma wasn't the only one who was forgetting how to live? Perhaps, if they really only had a few weeks left, she should spend that time with her grandmother? Cut back at work maybe? Live a little herself?

Thunder rumbled in the distance.

"Looks like we're going to get rained out," she noted.

The Ferris wheel circled slowly towards the ground. Sheets of rain beckoned on the edge of town. Hadley and Death hurried out of the carriage, and somehow she found her hand locked through his.

"Time to go!" she called.

Too late.

Rain poured down, drenching them immediately. People fled for safety, but Hadley simply held her arms out and tilted her face to the sky. Letting every little sensation soak in.

When she looked back down, Death was staring at her, as if trying to understand what she was doing. He was completely dry. And then fat raindrops started splattering on his shoulders, leaving little wet polka dots across his white shirt until he was almost as soaked as she. He tipped his face up in surprise, and flinched as a raindrop hit him right above the eye.

"I used to love summer storms as a girl," she said, grinning at him with water dripping down her face and tangling in her eyelashes. "Kinda forgot that for a moment."

"I . . . see."

"No, you don't." But this time it wasn't said sadly. Restlessness surged through her; the kind of feeling that had gotten her into trouble a lot when she was younger. The kind of feeling she'd taught herself to ignore. Like a summer storm itself, brewing in her veins.

A breathlessness. Then the decision to throw herself into that moment.

Standing on her tiptoes, Hadley closed her fingers around his collar and lifted her mouth to his. Death's hands caught her upper arms in surprise, and he sucked in a shocked breath as she kissed him. He tasted of rain and curiosity; of a particular type of innocence. He'd clearly never done this before. She could feel the moment his hands softened on her arms, his lips moving over hers. Tasting. Exploring. Hadley softened against him, flicking her tongue over his.

It started like a slow burn. Everything inside her lit up.

And then the downpour hit with a vengeance, a real *frog strangler*, as Gramma would say.

Grabbing his hand, Hadley flashed another grin at the shocked expression on his face and tugged. "Come on!"

"Where?" he yelled back, over the rumbling warning of thunder.

"The truck!"

Every second step her feet splashed through a puddle. The lights of the fair were dying, carnies waving at them to get out of the way as they ran to shut everything down. The truck loomed ahead, alone in the golden halo of the street lamp.

Slamming the door shut, Hadley looked across at Death. They were both breathless and wet, heating the inside of the cab with their bodies until the windows began to fog over. Water spiked his dark lashes together, and when she laughed, an answering smile tugged at his lips. The first full smile she'd ever seen there.

Her gaze dropped to his wet mouth, the remembered taste of him still on hers. Sliding a hand over his jeans-clad thigh, she crawled into his lap, her thighs nestling on the outside of his. Death sucked in a sharp breath and Hadley ran her hands up the cotton of his shirt, where it was plastered to his chest. Tugged it open. Licked at the rivulets of water that dripped down his bare chest.

A soft groan and then he tugged her face up, capturing her mouth, this time with more urgency, more awareness of what he was doing. *"What are you doing to me?"* he whispered.

Hadley pressed her smile against his throat, rocking her hips forward over his. Her skirts clung wetly to her thighs. Another hissed intake of air and his hands were on her hips, urging her faster, harder against him. It was suddenly violent, the need within her.

Hot, humid damp clouded the windows. Her hands slid down between them, into his jeans and he gasped, staring at her with wide blue eyes before slowly tipping his head back with a groan.

"I want you," she whispered, biting at his throat as her hands worked his body. Fingers dug into the curve of her arse, fisting wet handfuls of her skirts.

"Nobody does," he said hoarsely. *"Ever."*

"I do."

Her knee hit the door as he dragged her up higher, tearing at her panties and filling his hands with her flesh. His hot, hungry mouth consumed her. Awkward and delicious and unbearably sweet. Hadley showed him how to touch her, how to drive her wild.

Together they filled the cabin of the truck with soft, gasped breaths and the heat of their bodies as she took him. Hadley found herself lost in his mouth, his hands, throwing her head back as sensation streaked along her nerves.

This . . . this was what it felt like to live.

6

Tick.

Tock.

No matter where she was, she couldn't seem to stop looking at the clock. Watching as grains of sand trickled through Gramma's hourglass. Each morning was one fewer to count and, though she tried, Hadley couldn't push aside the sick feeling that was building inside her. Only one month with her gramma unless she gave him an answer. And now the days were dwindling. Two weeks. A week. Three days . . .

But she didn't mention it. And neither did Death.

They spoke of life only. Lying on the grass beneath the setting sun, watching as orange stained the horizon. Breathing in the scent of mowed grass and lemonade. A thousand stolen moments between time, which became precious cut-gem memories.

Every day she felt herself slipping further. She wasn't lonely any more. Instead she told the diner she wanted some time off, and spent the afternoons with her gramma, playing gin rummy and hearing the old woman laugh again. After an early dinner, Hadley would put Gramma to bed and steal away. Eager for that breathless, magical sidestep into another world where Death would be waiting, greeting her with a hot-mouthed kiss and impatient arms.

"Tell me about the shadows," she said one night, as they lay watching the sky above from a picnic rug she'd dragged outdoors.

His face shut down, but Hadley rolled over and grabbed his arm. "Please. I know they mean something."

"They can't hurt you."

"Then why are they always watching me?" Especially when he was there, as though they'd followed him from the *Between*.

He sat up. *"I call them the Forgotten. They are the remains of those that can't pass through, but remained . . . Between. Like me,'* he said grimly. *"They are still drawn to death. To me, perhaps. Nothing left but an echo of themselves."*

"There are others like you?" She curled her knees up in front of her.

"Dozens, maybe," he admitted. *"Out of all the hundreds who have accepted this duty."*

"What happens to them?"

"They simply fade. Like I was."

"But you're not fading," she said. He felt so real, so solid.

"Not any more. There are new memories being created. It makes me feel real again."

The image of him as he'd first appeared struck her. Slightly hazy around the edges, his body and face nothing but monochrome darkness. No colour. No life.

"You refused to cross through," she said.

"Once."

"Why?" She gestured at him. "Why exist like this? You said you don't do this out of pleasure, only duty. Why make that choice?"

He shook his head. *"I don't . . ."*

"That's right. You don't remember." Biting her lip, she turned away, then picked up the picnic basket with its remains and headed towards the house.

"Hadley?"

She could feel him watching her as she hurried up the steps to the porch.

"You're angry."

Hadley paused on the top step. "Not at you," she whispered. After all, he'd never made her any promises; never even hinted that he felt that strange, quivering bond she'd been so certain was growing between them. That was all on her, wishing for something he couldn't give. Wishing he'd open up to her, the way she had done to him.

"I didn't wish to cross," he said suddenly. *"There was a woman. My wife, I think. I have only scattered memories of her. Not even her name any more. All I know is that she was lost to me, taken by one who walked* Between. *And I thought, that if I crossed* Between *myself, I would be able to see her again."*

"Did you?" Hadley half turned her head.

"No. She had gone. Moved on. Someplace I could never follow, for I had made this bargain." For the first time, she heard bitterness in his voice as he stepped behind her. *"Once you step* Between *like I did, you cannot move on. Only . . . fade."*

A hand brushed against her neck, sweeping her thick mass of dark brown curls out of the way. Skittering across her skin like little electric shocks. *"All I have left is sadness when I think of her. And anger, that I cannot remember what I should. That even she is being stolen from me slowly."* His voice lowered. *"And perhaps shame, that when I think of her, all I see are your eyes. "*

His lips met her skin, tasting the salt on the curve of her shoulder. Hadley let her head fall back, heat welling up behind her eyes. "I'm sorry that you lost her," she whispered.

"I'm losing myself," he whispered back. Hands fisting in her skirt. *"Except this – you. You're like the sun, you shine so brightly. "*

Hadley turned with a groan, pushing herself up onto her toes to meet his mouth. He gasped, pushing her back against the railing on the veranda as he kissed her. She could feel him stealing her breath, his body wrapped around hers as if he wanted to drink her in.

Then his hands caught her up under her thighs, lifting her effortlessly onto the railing. She couldn't stop herself from shoving his shirt up over his head, breaking the kiss just long enough to remove it.

"I need you, " he whispered urgently. *"I need you. "*

"Then take me," she replied, and lost herself in him.

7

The fifth of August arrived.

Her month was up.

Hadley rang in sick and prowled the house all day, pestering her grandmother until Gramma Monroe told her to quit it. Scrubbing the floors of the kitchen, she waited for him to come, one ear cocked to listen as her grandmother bustled about the sitting room.

The *Jeopardy* theme song blazed to life and Hadley paused. She'd made a deal. If she couldn't teach him why people asked that question, then he had the right to take her grandmother.

No more *Jeopardy*. No more gossip sessions on the front porch. No more of Grams' tea, sweetened so much it made her mouth prune up just thinking about it.

How was she going to cope?

Tears pricked her eyes. It wasn't fair to hold this against him, but somewhere in her heart she did. When he was with her she could forget what he was, but when they were apart the thoughts crept back in. She wanted to ask for more time to find an answer, but knew he'd say no.

And then he would be gone and she would be alone. Alone and hating him for taking her grandmother away, no matter if it was his decision or not.

The hurt of it was like a knife to the chest.

You knew this, she told herself. Wishing that she'd never once kissed him. Knowing instantly that was a lie.

The world grew still, quivering with tension. Hadley looked up from the dishes she was doing, shoving aside the soapy gloves and plates in a sudden panic. In the hall, the clock stopped ticking.

"No." She backed away towards the kitchen door, as if to stop him from entering the sitting room.

Shadows blackened the walls; many more than ever before. Then Death stepped through time, appearing in the middle of the kitchen. He looked grim, hot blue eyes meeting hers and reading in them her denial.

"It's time," he murmured.

"You can change time," she replied desperately. "Time has no rules for you. Does it?"

His lips thinned. *"It's not right for the dying to stay here. It warps them. Changes them in ways you couldn't even imagine. Makes it harder for them to cross. Hadley, you know this is wrong. You know . . . if I could . . . "*

It wasn't fair. Tears stung her eyes as she bolted towards the sitting room. She threw herself bodily between the door and her grandmother.

"Hadley . . . ?"

"You can't have her," she yelled, fists clenched at her sides. "I won't let you do this." Her voice broke a little: "She's all I have."

Slow steady footsteps followed her. Death appeared in the doorway, his broad shoulders filling it. *"Hadley . . . "* He looked sad.

"Hadley May, what on God's green earth are you yelling about?" Grams dragged herself out of the sucking chasm of the Davenport.

Hadley darted a glance between the two of them. "You can't see him?" she whispered. He wasn't *Between* now. He seemed to fill the room, and he'd said that those on the verge of death themselves could always see him.

Gramma Monroe stared from her to the door. There was no recognition in her eyes. "I'm worried about you, Hadley. Are you all right?"

Gramma couldn't see him.

"I—I'm fine," Hadley managed to say. "I'll just go get you . . . some sweet tea."

She pushed past him, wiping at her face as she made her way to the kitchen. Feeling him follow her.

Arms up to the elbow in the sink, she didn't bother looking up when he entered. She just kept washing the tea jug, desperately trying not to think.

"My month's up," she said. "You said you still didn't understand why people always ask that question. Which means . . ." She was too frightened to put it into words . . . *only those on the verge of death . . .*

Wiping at her mouth and leaving suds across her chin, she blinked away the hot spill of tears. "She can't see you. But *I* can." A whisper. A question. "I thought it was because you let me."

"I never said that I came for her," he replied quietly. *"All I said was that you could have a month together."*

Oh, God. Hadley crumpled at the sink, latching on to the counter to hold herself up. She shook her head in denial. Then he was there, arms folding around her. Lifting her onto the counter and letting her bury her face against his chest. Suds dripped down his shirt.

"How?" she whispered.

"It's your heart. A defect passed on through your grandfather."

"No." This was not happening. "But I haven't . . . I haven't seen the world, I haven't done anything." No first love, no babies, no more laughter, kisses from her grandmother, customers complaining at the diner, summer by the creek. Nothing but a horrific blankness where she imagined her future to be.

She couldn't breathe. The pain in her chest grew into a tight hard knot, and then his hand was rubbing at the base of her neck, pressing her face to the side so she could get some air.

Hadley pushed him away as panic locked her body up tight. Somehow she staggered off the counter. Found a paper bag in a drawer and shoved it against her mouth, inhaling the hot taste of her own breath.

Don't think about it. Tears spilled wetly down her cheeks until she was shuddering. But the panic was easing, letting her breathe again.

She lowered the bag helplessly, clutching it in her fist. "What am I going to do? I can't . . . I can't just . . . Is she going to find me?"

"*Hadley . . .*"

Meeting his eyes, she forced herself to hold his gaze. "There's nobody to look after her. I don't know what they'll do to her, where they'll take her. I can't leave her. *Please.*"

A sweep of those dark lashes. "We made a deal."

"And have you learned the answer to that question?" she asked bitterly, her voice rising. "Because, if you want, I could tell you. It's because we're afraid to lose the ones we love. But you wouldn't understand. You'll never understand! Because you're not human!" Shoving past him, she darted out onto the porch and jumped over the fence. Into the cane, towards the creek, her legs and arms swinging and the pain in her chest just growing and growing.

That expression on his face as she pushed him aside. She couldn't stop seeing it. Hadley collapsed against the trunk of an old oak, pressing her lips against the gnarled bark. Shaking all through her body and trying to ignore the sharp pain that had moved to her shoulder.

Seconds ticked past.

"I'm sorry," she whispered, knowing he was behind her. "That was cruel of me."

There was no answer.

Just the breeze, whispering over her skin. The pain vanished, as abruptly as if it had never been, the clamps on her lungs easing up. And then the sensation of his presence was gone.

Whipping around, she found herself alone by the banks of the creek.

But her heart still ached.

8

That night, there was a letter on her bed. Hadley picked it up, running the paper between her fingers.

"She has three months. I will give you this time with her," was all it said.

9

Gramma Monroe died on 17 October.

Moving through a dream world, Hadley somehow survived the funeral and the wake, the whole town turning out to pay its respects. Forcing herself to maintain a polite smile through the endless stream of condolences, casseroles, and folk watching her with curious eyes, whispering behind their hands. She'd finally pleaded a headache and found herself alone in the big house.

Its emptiness echoed so loudly she thought she was going to scream.

As evening began to creep over the horizon, she found herself back at the newly turned grave, tracing the curve of the letters on the headstone: "Death leaves a heartache no one can heal; love leaves a memory no one can steal."

Hadley wrapped her arms around herself. She'd bought a beautiful black lace dress for the occasion. A real splurge. Wasn't as if she'd need the money any more.

A sudden stillness cocooned her. Sidestep into another world.

Not alone. Not any more.

"Is that how you think of me?" Death examined the headstone, hands tucked into the pockets of his jeans.

Heartache. Hadley squeezed her eyes shut and held herself. The truth was, she'd missed him. Spent the last few months looking out for him each night as she locked the house up. But she hadn't seen him, even though she'd known he was there at times. "Thank you."

"*For what?*"

"For giving me the time with her," she whispered.

When she looked, he was staring at the headstone. Not a single emotion flickered over his face.

"*Maybe it wasn't just for you.*" His brows drew together. "Oh?"

Death shifted restlessly. "*You earned your reprieve.*" There was a long-drawn-out moment of silence. "*I . . . understood your explanation. What it would mean to lose somebody. Why people wish to stay. The deal was met.*"

The words left her breathless. Somehow Hadley nodded. She couldn't think on it overmuch or else she was frightened she'd face that same heart-wrenching panic she'd felt the night she realized she was dying.

"I'm ready." She took a steadying breath. These past few months, she'd done what she could of living. Took Grams to the beaches down near Charleston. Even rang her mother once. Said what needed saying.

Didn't make it any easier.

He stared down at her, as though he wanted to say something.

"Don't leave me in the dirt," she said softly.

Death turned away, watching the gray leaves caught in mid-fall from the massive oaks. Dying. Just like her. "*You could stay.*"

"Thought you said nobody could cheat death?"

"*Not there,*" he admitted. "*Here.*" A gesture around him, at the stillness of a world where leaves never fell from trees and sound never echoed. "*You could venture back sometimes. See the world. See Paris.*" For the first time, he looked at her and his eyes were as blue as she'd ever seen them, the stark lines of his face filled with color. "*I could take you to Paris.*"

Hadley's breath caught. "Become like you?"

He nodded. There was something so stilted to the action; as if he wasn't certain what her answer would be.

"Why?"

"You remind me of life," he said. *"When I'm with you, I don't hear the silence. All I see is your smile, that night in the rain . . ."* He glanced at his shoes. *"I know now why people ask that question. And it's you. Because I would lose you. This world would lose you and it hurts. I don't want to be alone any more. And the memory . . ."* Another glance at the script on the headstone. *"Perhaps it would be best if it* could *be stolen. Without you, the silence would be worse, because I would know what it had felt like to live with laughter."*

Hadley's breath caught. Tentatively, she laced her fingers through his. There was an ache in her chest, but not of pain. Not this time.

The shadows haunted the edges of her vision, but she couldn't take her eyes from his, from the melting cerulean blue of his irises. They could not have him. Not whilst she was there.

Life balances Death.

Without it, he would be but a fading shadow himself, too long removed from that which balanced him.

She had done that. Brought the color back, the life in him. His deal with her. It had never been about a question.

Make me understand, he'd whispered, for it was a matter of his own survival, as well as hers. To understand what loss meant, what life meant. To live, for one precious moment.

Bring me back to life, he had asked and she had not understood then.

"We bear this gift but once," he warned. *"You would live in my world and do as I do."*

Caught *Between.*

But not alone.

Could she do it? Be the one to usher others into their deaths? The thought was abhorrent, but then she thought of her grandfather. Of the relief his death had been to him; he who was trapped in a body that had become his own enemy.

Hesitation died. Hadley stepped forward, sliding her hands through his.

"I know I'm not what you want—" His voice roughened.

"No," she cut him off, pressing her fingers to his lips. "You're everything that I want. Of all people, you remind me of what it feels like to truly live. It's crazy, I know, but I feel like I'm breathing for the first time in years."

He swallowed. *"Then you'll stay with me?"*

"I'll stay," she whispered. "But not just because there is no choice. I missed you."

The hardness in his expression softened. *"I—"*

Reaching up on her toes, she pressed her mouth to his.

The kiss lit her on fire, stealing deep within her lungs. One moment of fierce pain – in the center of her chest – and then she suddenly felt weightless. Hadley staggered against his chest; his body was the only thing that felt as though it had substance to it.

Color had bleached from the world, leaving it gray and lifeless. But she could still see the blue of his eyes. The bleached tips of his lashes and the darkened stubble along his jaw.

Reaching up, Hadley slid her hand through his hair and dragged his mouth back to hers.

10

They never did find Hadley May Monroe's body. Just her car, waiting at the cemetery, and the print of her heels in the freshly turned grave dirt.

Some said she ran away. Others said she went mad with grief. And others whispered behind their hands, "Bless her heart, but she were always a strange one. Heard there was a man involved. That Dean. Down Jackson way . . ."

But nobody missed her.

And she didn't miss them.

Instead, she went to Paris and lived a thousand lives.

DATE WITH A DEMON SLAYER

An Accidental Demon Slayer story

Angie Fox

Chapter One

"What do you mean you sent my anniversary present back?" I stared at the silver-haired biker witch. She wore chaps, a leather jacket with fringe and had an obnoxious rhinestone skull do-rag knotted around her neck. Sue me when I felt the urge to yank it tighter.

Yes, my grandmother's gang of witches were . . . unusual. Word had it they'd been a regular coven before a demon had kept them on the run for thirty years. They'd had to move fast, stay on the road. They'd started riding Harleys. Then came the biker nicknames, the tattoos and boyfriends named Lizard Lips. The rest was history.

At the moment, I was tempted to call Ant Eater by her real name. Mildred.

Her eyes widened behind her green-tinted hippie sunglasses as I glared at her. She held up her hands. "I'm telling you, Lizzie, it looked like another box of empty beer cans."

That got a definite frown from the hunky shape-shifting griffin to my right. "The package was addressed to me," he growled.

Damn. I always liked having him on my side. Luckily, I'd been smart enough to marry him. Dimitri stood a foot above the tallest one of us, a wall of muscle and grit. And I'd never get enough of my husband's lyrical Greek accent, even now, with Ant Eater pulling one of her stunts.

"Fairy mail usually requires a signature," I said.

Fae paths were strictly regulated. And reliable. Fairy postal workers could find anyone, anywhere, in two to three business days. Heck, it was the only way to get things while we were on the road.

Ant Eater shook her head. "If you want to return something, you just gotta tell them it isn't for you." She blew out a breath. "I should have looked at the whole *who it was addressed to* thing," she said with a wince, which was as close to an apology as we'd ever get from the scratchy old witch. She shot a glare at the blonde witch closing in on her left. "I was trying to save our asses. I don't care if Frieda collects what she drinks," she said, turning up the volume, "but if that woman doesn't stop ordering beer cans on eBay, we're going to be buried in rusty Schlitz cans."

"Those cans are vintage," Frieda said, as if we were dissing her children. "You show me a 1954 Schlitz that doesn't have rust." She brought a bright pink painted fingernail to her chin. "And if we're cleaning up, maybe I should toss all those bras you have hanging down by the creek."

That got a glare from the other witch. "Do it and you die."

"What the frick, people?" I asked. And when did this become my life?

Yes, I'd run off with my grandma's gang of biker witches. They'd taught me how to fulfill my destiny as a demon slayer. They'd also saved my butt more than once. In return, I hoped I could calm them down a little. I'd been a preschool teacher in my former life. I was used to chaos.

This was a whole new brand of it. And somewhere along the way, they'd gotten me into wearing leather pants. And bustiers.

I wasn't quite sure how that happened.

In any case, we didn't need to be fighting about beer cans. Or dirty undies. I got that riding Georgia's winding back roads could make a person spit dust, but, "No unpacking. We're only stopping for dinner."

Frieda snorted. "Damn, I hope you get more than that."

"That's rude," I told her, ignoring Ant Eater's low chuckle. Although, frankly, I'd been hoping the same thing.

A year ago, on this very night, I married the mostly sweet and always sexy Dimitri Kallinikos. We said our "I do's" at a gorgeous estate on the coast. Of course, the Earl of Hell crashed the wedding, but you know, these things happen.

This year, we found ourselves toning it down a little. Okay, a lot.

As in right now, we were standing in a field off Route 11. We hadn't seen anyone for miles.

It was me, my sexy-as-sin husband and about thirty biker witches, who were busy tossing back beers, making campfires and setting up dartboards against some pine trees by the creek.

I turned to Dimitri. "You want to help me with this one?"

But he'd retreated several steps and was on his phone, tracking my present no doubt.

We were headed out of New Orleans after defeating a power-hungry necromancer bent on world destruction. You know the type. And if you don't? Well, lucky you.

Anyway, when we saw a neat-looking old restaurant, we stopped. Never mind that it didn't open for another hour. Or that the driveway was blocked. No doubt they did that to keep out trespassers. It was no problem to park the biker witches in the woods next door.

The restaurant looked like it had been some kind of plantation house before. I loved the white columns out front, the long winding drive, the brick and iron entrance gates, dripping with lush green vines.

It was perfect for what I had in mind: a date night with my husband. Alone.

Frieda followed my gaze, which had pretty much moved to Dimitri's ass. "You think he got you some sexy lingerie?" she asked.

Little did she know I was already wearing a hot red number I'd picked up in Baton Rouge.

Ant Eater barked out a laugh. "He's got to do something to make up for the dinner." She nudged me. "A hoity-toity place like that is going to serve boring steak and chicken. They won't even have squirrel. Do you know how easy it is to hunt squirrel around here? Your grandma's already caught a half a dozen."

Lovely. We could always count on Grandma to lead the charge.

Then again, the biker witches had agreed to give us a night to ourselves for our anniversary. They could eat raccoon livers for all I cared.

"Just don't get too comfortable," I told them, heading off to join Dimitri. Left to their own devices, there was no telling what the witches would do. "No enchanted animals, no beer can sculptures, and try not to hang your undies in view of the restaurant."

"What part of camping out don't you get?" Ant Eater hollered after me.

Dimitri had ended his call and was shoving the phone into his pocket. He kissed me on the head. "No worries. We're going to have an amazing night. And—" he wrapped an arm around me "—I just arranged for your gift to be delivered after dinner." I loved how he always tried to make things special, even out here.

"I don't know what I did to deserve you," I said.

I nestled against his warm chest.

Behind us, a group of biker witches let out whoops and *atta-girl* cheers.

I leaned my forehead against my man. "Someone must be tapping the pony keg."

Dimitri brushed a kiss over the top of my head. "I think they're cat-calling us."

We weren't even doing anything yet. I felt my lips quirk as I looked up at his handsome face. "You had your chance to run." I was stuck with the biker witches. He signed up for this when he married me.

"Didn't notice." The side of his mouth cocked in a half-grin. "As soon as I saw you, I had to have you."

I leaned up and touched my lips against his. It was supposed to be a thank-you, maybe even a little bit of a tease. But then his mouth slid over mine, and I forgot all about that. I pressed against his solid chest as he deepened the kiss. Mine. His hands slipped down my back, cupped my butt as I ground closer to him.

Oh yes, I couldn't wait to be alone with this man.

"Time out," my grandma called, jogging over to us.

Right. I pulled away. Although Dimitri still managed to keep a hand on my ass. Is that true love or what?

Grandma had her long gray hair tied back in two braids and she was grinning like a mad woman. "Before you disappear," she said, slightly out of breath, "we've got some anniversary presents to give you." She held out a hand as a smart aleck witch named Creely caught up to her. The heavily tattooed witch barked out a laugh as she gave Grandma a recycled jelly jar filled with pinkish-blue goo. Grandma waggled it at us like a tease. "This is to ramp up the passion. Get all wild and crazy. Right?"

"Like we were before you interrupted us," Dimitri said.

"At least we caught you early," Creely said, tossing a red Kool-Aid dyed lock of hair out of her eyes as she reached into her bag again.

Grandma shoved the Passion Spell into my hands as Creely handed her a second jar. This one was filled with greenish-brownish sludge and reminded me of a swamp I'd go out of my way to avoid. Grandma held it up proudly. "Break *this* jar if you want to hold off the passion. Like if you just ordered one of them pricey ten-dollar hamburgers from that restaurant over there and you want to get your money's worth." She handed it to me.

I tested the lid, making sure it was sealed tight.

"Guard that," Creely said, "he's going to try to hide it."

Grandma let out a guffaw.

"Speaking of that restaurant," Dimitri said, eyeing the mansion, "I just saw them open the driveway gate. We should think about heading over."

"Wait." Grandma held up a finger. "One more treat for you tonight." She drew a small baby-food jar from the leather pouch at her belt. It twinkled with a thousand tiny sparks, like trapped stars. "I just perfected this," she said, holding it up and admiring her work. "It's a new sneak spell." She winked, "In case you want to get off somewhere. Alone."

Ah, like we were about to do before she interrupted us. "This is great," I said, looping all three spells into the demon-slayer utility belt at my waist. "Thanks."

"We appreciate you thinking of us." Dimitri gave Grandma a Greek double kiss on the cheeks, which must have surprised her because she started blushing.

He looked at the spells on my belt and his smile wavered. He had to be thinking about my limited success with spells in general. Still, these were simple. And they were good for us. I was sure it would all work out.

"Go have fun," Grandma said, ushering us out of camp. "Pretend we're not even here."

They'd be hard to miss. There was a cemetery between the house and us, but that's not much when you're talking about biker witches. Not to mention the huge bonfire they were putting together.

You know what? It wasn't our problem.

Dimitri offered me his arm. "Want to go?"

I brushed a kiss along his jaw. "I do."

Since a hike through the cemetery wasn't my idea of a romantic time, we doubled back and walked along the road. The old white house almost seemed to glow in the soft evening light. I leaned close to Dimitri. Something told me tonight would be different. Fun.

I was just about to tell him so when I heard an anguished voice behind us.

"Lizzie!" It was my dog, Pirate.

Ever since I'd come into my demon-slaying powers, Pirate could talk to me. It was one of the side effects.

Only those who were in touch with their magical side could understand him, which included Dimitri and every biker witch on the planet.

"Hold up," Pirate said, when I had the gall to keep walking. "Stop. Don't leave me!"

My little dog dashed up next to us like he was on fire.

Pirate was a wiry Jack Russell terrier. He stood about as tall as my shin, but he didn't take that into account when it came to being fierce. He was mostly white, with a dollop of brown that spotted his back and covered his left eye. Hence his name.

"Pirate," I said, trying to be tactful, "this is our anniversary dinner. We can do it without you."

He turned in a circle and sat down on the dirt shoulder in front of us. "I don't understand."

"Go back," I said.

Dimitri gave him a scratch between the ears. "The witches need you to guard their camp."

Pirate cocked his head as we made a detour around him and started walking again. "I get it," he said, following. "You're trying to keep all the steak for yourself."

"Restaurants aren't for dogs," I said, as we passed through the gates and began up the winding driveway.

The old brick and stone had to be original. I was willing to bet the thick, gnarled oak trees on either side of the path were as old as the house. Moss clung to the trunks and dotted the lush grass. It felt like we were entering another world.

Pirate trotted out ahead, nose to the ground. "I think you need me more than the witches do." He sniffed at the packed earth. "This place doesn't smell right."

"It's gorgeous," I said. The pillars of the house were tall and thick. Yes, they'd been painted and repainted over the years, but they were one of a kind, with exotic flowers and creatures carved into the bases and the tops. "Look. A gargoyle," I said, pointing out a carving at the top. A thick white spider's web clung to its wings and stretched up to the antique brass lamp over the front door. It was tarnished with age, but it was still majestic. I wondered just how many distinguished visitors passed through this entryway.

Pirate growled low under his breath. His neck bristled as he stared at a rocking chair on the wide wrap-around front porch.

Dimitri moved up behind the dog. "What is it?"

Pirate remained perfectly still, staring. "I don't know."

I opened my demon-slayer senses. Usually, I had an insane attraction to danger – anything that could attack me, skewer me or chop me in half. I focused my attention on the spot by the chair.

My powers reached out like fingers through the mist. There was a shadow entwined with the chair, possibly a lingering memory or a very weak entity. I expanded my reach and searched inside the house. There was business. Some chaos. Upstairs, I could sense shadows of darkness, pain. But nothing demonic.

"I think it's okay," I said.

The bronze marker by the front door said the house had been built in 1830. I ran my fingers over it as it bled green onto the white brick underneath. "Anything this old is bound to have a few things lurking around."

Dimitri's shoulders relaxed. "Then let's eat."

He pushed open the large black door and we entered a narrow foyer. The walls were covered in rich burgundy paper with gold vines. I watched them scroll past the ornate sconces, up the walls. It reminded me of a garden maze I'd once visited.

Tonight had to turn out better than that little adventure.

A round-faced woman with curly red hair scurried out of what appeared to be a dining room to our left. She wore a pretty green dress and, if I didn't know better, I'd have thought she was one of the patrons. "Welcome to the Peele House Inn," she said, with a fat Southern accent. Her smile faltered when her gaze fastened on my skintight bustier, then my leather utility belt, my short-ish skirt. Then she really stared at my shiny, knee-high black leather boots.

"I got those in New Orleans," I told her.

She tried to recover and failed. "Are you with—" she made a swirly motion with her hand "—*those* people," she said the last part as if it were a secret, "down the road?"

Ah. The witches. They always made an impression.

Our hostess took refuge behind a small wooden stand, which would have been comical except I was pretty sure the woman was actually intimidated.

"Don't worry," I said, eager to let her know that we had not, in fact, brought any beer can collectibles or a pony keg to dinner. "We're not that way at all."

Dimitri wrapped an arm around me and ran a warm hand over my shoulder. "This is what she was wearing when I met her," he said, directing a saucy grin at me. "It's our first anniversary."

The hostess clasped her hands together. "Aww," she cooed. "Happy anniversary!" With new-found energy, she checked her book. "You're the couple with the reservation," she added, as if we'd done something special.

Dimitri nodded. "Slayer. Party of two."

It was how we ordered pizzas and everything. It was much easier than asking anybody to spell Kallinikos.

"I am so glad you came," our hostess said, with a sincerity you could only find in the South. "My name is Marjorie and I'm going to do everything I can to make your night unforgettable."

She led us to the room on the left. It had high ceilings and beautiful blue silk walls. There was already another couple dining at a corner table and a gentleman eating alone. She seated us at one of the remaining three tables, next to one of the big picture windows. "This is one of my favorite rooms. It used to be the parlor," Marjorie said, placing our menus on a table covered in a white linen cloth.

There was a fire burning in the white marble hearth. And, I realized with horror, my dog had followed us inside.

"I'm sorry. He's mine," I said, intending to go after him. Pirate had found a nice warm spot in front of the fire and was curling up.

Marjorie paused. "You know, if he's just going to lie down, it's okay." She gave a small, wistful smile. "We used to have both a dog and a cat here when we were a bed and breakfast."

Pirate planted his head on his paws and arched up his brows in that heartbreakingly hopeful way dogs do when they want to be completely manipulative.

It worked.

Marjorie let out a low cluck. "Aren't you precious?" She left us to go pet him.

"You have to understand . . ." I looked at the other diners, who didn't seem to notice or care.

"We don't want to reward his behavior," Dimitri added.

"Nonsense." She scratched Pirate behind the ears, which started his tail wagging. "I could never say 'no' to a face like that." She ushered us into our seats. "Now I'm going to go get him a bowl of fried gizzards, on the house. You two look over the menus."

I could swear Pirate was grinning as he watched her go. "A cute face and a wagging tail will get you a long way in life," he said happily.

No kidding.

I opened my menu. "They get a decent crowd in here for such a quiet road," I said.

Dimitri was too busy studying the wine list to answer. In time, I forgot all about the other patrons, as well as my dog. We ordered wine. We had lobster ravioli, steak.

I was fawning overly a particularly delicious side of mushroom risotto when Dimitri leaned over the table, grinning at me. "Look," he said, glancing toward the fireplace. "Pirate found a friend."

I turned and saw the ghost of a matronly woman in an old-fashioned dress, complete with a hoop skirt. She spoke to Pirate in soft tones while she rubbed at his ears. He licked at her pale fingers and she giggled.

"Always the charmer," I mused. Pirate had a particular affinity for spirits. And he could make friends with a doorknob, so I wasn't surprised at all when the woman smiled and began talking excitedly.

Dimitri reached for a slice of fresh bread. "I wonder what they have in common."

Pirate's interests were limited, seeing that he was a dog. "It's got to be food," I said, reaching for a sip of wine. "Or smelly things."

"Things that roll, things that make a noise," Dimitri added.

"The mailman." I thought about it. "Did they even have mailmen back when women wore hoop skirts?" It didn't matter, I supposed. I was just glad Pirate had made a friend. The ghost looked as if she needed one as well.

Marjorie returned to refill our water glasses and slip us the check. "Whenever you're ready," she said, as if she were reluctant to interrupt.

I let Dimitri take the black folder. "You know this place is haunted," I said to our host.

"Very," she said, as if it were a grand secret. "Word has it that Hiram Peele himself has been seen upstairs."

I loved ghost stories. Even if most of the ghosts I'd met kept to themselves. "So you called it the Peele House after Hiram Peele?"

Marjorie stood a little straighter, obviously proud of the house's history. "Yes. He's our original owner. Hiram Peele was a wealthy planter and he built this house in 1830 for his bride, a local preacher's daughter named Eva Fawn," she said, with all the finesse of a storyteller. "Men didn't often marry below their station in those days, but it was a true love match and Hiram was very close to her father. They were happy for many years until she died, falling down the grand staircase. He died the next night – in bed, of a heart attack."

Yikes. Maybe that was the darkness I'd felt in the house. "Are they buried in the cemetery outside?" I asked.

"Yes. That's how they did it in those days." Marjorie held the water pitcher in front of her like a shield. "When my husband and I bought this estate, we thought the Peeles' story might bring in the tourists." Her pale skin flushed at the neck. "But—" she shook her head "—it's ended up being a bit much. Right after we opened, a newly wed couple took a tumble down the staircase. Both of them died," she said, her voice catching.

"What a terrible accident," Dimitri said, taken aback.

Color rose in Marjorie's cheeks. "Then it happened again. About six months later."

"Did they? Not make it either?" I asked, stunned.

Marjorie shook her head "no". "The coroner said all four of the deaths were . . . accidental." She made a subtle sign of the cross, but I noticed it. "We don't even like to go up to those rooms any more. I know they said it was a fluke, but my husband and I just couldn't handle it if something else happened."

"I don't blame you one bit," I told her.

She nodded, accepting my sympathy. "It's a shame." She glanced at the dining room behind us. "As you might imagine, we could use the business."

I was about to tell her that it seemed like the other guests were enjoying their meals as much as we did. Only now that I looked at them, the couple dining at a corner table wore Victorian clothes. And had a pearly sheen. The gentleman eating alone had vanished.

After Marjorie left, Dimitri deposited a considerable sum in the bill holder. I was glad he could afford to be so generous. Then again, he was also eyeing me like he had an idea.

"What?" I asked, finishing the last of my wine.

His eyes flicked to mine. "She has private, quiet guest rooms upstairs."

A tingle of awareness warmed me. "Those are closed."

"Exactly." He placed a large, solid hand over mine. "We'd be all alone."

At last.

If we had the guts.

"No biker witches, no camping out," I said, warming to the idea. And ghosts had certainly never bothered me. "A real bed."

Dimitri shrugged his wide shoulders. He was reeling me in. I knew it. He knew it.

"It could be an anniversary to remember," he said, tempting me more than he knew.

I ran my fingers along the edge of my wine glass. "I do still have to give you your present," I mused. "Although you'll have to undress me to get it."

He stood a little too quickly as he reached into his wallet again and peeled off an additional wad of twenties. "We'll add it to her tip, enough to cover a room."

It would be a shame not to contribute to the upkeep of such a wonderful old home.

I stood faster than I'd intended, wobbling my wine glass. "Okay. But just a quickie."

He grinned. "Anything for you."

Oh my God, I couldn't believe we were doing this.

"Come on," I said, standing, taking his hand. "We need to get upstairs and naked." Soon. Before I lost my nerve.

Chapter Two

We waited until our hostess had gone into the back, then we raced up the stairs like we were on fire.

Oh my God. I fought back a giggle and Dimitri smothered me to his chest at the top of the landing. He might be as stealthy as a shape-shifter, but I felt like an ox going up those stairs.

I covered my mouth, but still, my face hurt from grinning as he took my hand and pulled me down the hall. The air was stale. The hallway was narrow, dark, the perfect place to hide.

Dimitri pushed open a door at the end and yanked me inside. The antique furniture was bathed in shadows and dust. It was clear that no one had been up here for a long time. We were truly alone. Free. In an old-fashioned Victorian room. I ran a hand over the carved-wood chest of drawers with its chilly marble top and delicately woven lace dresser scarf.

I couldn't believe I was doing this. I'd never done anything like this. Not in my un-wild, un-crazy teenage years. And certainly not in my responsible twenties.

Dimitri's voice was rough, hungry. "Come here," he said, with the same excitement I felt. He kissed me hard, backing me up against the bed. Suddenly, I was wrapped up in his masculine scent, his strong presence. Him. Lord Almighty, I didn't think I'd ever get enough of this man.

"It's a canopy!" I squealed, as he tipped me down on the bed and went to work on his pants.

I laughed. "Impatient much?"

Wait until he got a look at my sexy red bra and panties.

He shook his head, advancing on me, all alpha male and sexy. "It's been way too long."

Since we weren't sneaking around. Hiding.

Well, technically we were sneaking

"Then come and get it," I said, sliding my hands inside his shirt as he came down on top of me. He was warm, solid. I wanted to eat him up.

I kissed him with everything I had and I swore the room itself started to spin.

He felt heavier on top of me, not uncomfortable, not yet. Still, he didn't usually press down so hard.

I slid my hands up his sides, tried to get around the front of his belt buckle. This was the man who'd fought demons for me. He'd gone to hell and back (literally) for me. And he wanted me.

That in itself was so heady that I felt mesmerized. Captured.

A frantic barking sounded outside the door. Pirate. I couldn't hear what he was saying. He seemed far away.

Dimitri blazed a trail of kisses down my neck, to my collarbone.

I couldn't see the top of the canopy anymore. It was dark.

Too dark.

"Wait." I tried to sit up. Something wasn't right.

Boom.

I felt like I'd been zapped by about a thousand volts of static electricity. The bed lurched. If I didn't know better, I'd think the entire room had spun off into oblivion. "Dimitri!" My fingers felt numb as I gripped his shoulders.

He was a dead weight now, struggling to move. He shoved hard against the bed and fell away from me panting.

Oh hell.

Darkness saturated the room, growing stronger. Heavier.

I didn't know what in Hades was going on, but we had to get out of here. I struggled to get off the bed. My arms and legs felt out of control, like they were asleep, as I forced my way to the door and yanked it open.

Pirate dashed in. "Cut it out! In a jiffy! She says you can't do what you were doing!"

I didn't care what the owner thought. "Help!" I yelled down the stairs. "Something's up here!"

Dimitri would kill me for that if he didn't get his pants on before help got here, but we needed people, noise, anything to fight back the darkness.

Pirate jumped up on the bed next to my husband. "There's nobody down there to call 911," my dog said, eyes wide. "We've been transported!"

Meanwhile Dimitri had gotten his pants up over his hips. "That doesn't make any sense," he said, drawing labored breaths, struggling to get decent.

"You can't do what you were doing," Pirate insisted. "I told her you were just wrestling on the bed. You always do that. But she said, '*Not here!*'"

I braced a hand against the bedpost as electric shivers ran up and down my body. Why weren't we getting any help? "Who the hell are you talking about?"

Pirate let out a heavy sigh. "The lady of the manor. My new friend."

The Victorian ghost from downstairs shimmered into form next to my dog. Her upper half anyway. She stood in the middle of the bed, her gray hair, pulled into a severe twist, shimmering with a light of its own. Her face was drawn tight with fear. "It's too late. He's taken you."

Dimitri rolled away from her. "Who?"

She didn't even give Dimitri a second look. In fact, it appeared as if she were ready to bolt. "The master of the house. He's transported you to another dimension." She cowered, as if she were afraid of being struck. "He rules here."

Bruises blossomed on her cheeks, neck and forehead.

It felt like the air itself was sucking the life out of us.

Cripes. We needed the biker witches. I struggled to the window.

We were at the far end of the hall, toward the back of the house. The witches should be right outside, past the cemetery. I threw open the velvet curtains and let out a choked cry as I saw an empty field.

"Ohhh biscuits," Pirate said, pacing the bed. "She was

right. That ghost transported us. We're in the wrong dimension. I'm in a freaky house with a bad guy."

"Run," Dimitri ordered, struggling to stand.

The ghost let out a keening wail as she sank down into the bed. Her eerily high voice settled low in my gut. "He's coming."

"Who?" I demanded, then changed my mind. "*What* is the master of the house?" We had to learn what kind of a creature we were dealing with. Before it attacked.

"Poltergeist!" Pirate squeaked. "I can feel him. He's right below us."

The ghost brought a finger to her lips. "Shh . . ." Her eyes were sad, her face bruised and bloodied. "My husband." Her eyes locked on the door fearfully. "He's a very pious man. He won't stand for fornication in his house."

"We didn't!" I protested. Not yet anyway.

From the look of her, her husband was a violent ass in life. And if he'd morphed into a poltergeist, that could make him even more vicious.

We needed a plan. Now.

Chapter Three

I forced myself to think. If sexy vibes had caused all of this . . . I grappled for the anti-passion spell Grandma had given me. It smelled just as bad as it looked. I opened the jar and poured the contents over my chest. It hit me with a rush of energy and I actually felt better. More like myself.

I rushed over to Dimitri and dropped a big, wet handful on his bare chest.

"What the hell?" He jerked up. Yeah, it was nasty, but it did the trick. He sat up the rest of the way fast. "What did you do?" he asked, eyes raking over me. "I feel better."

"I put the whammy on any sexy thoughts," I told him, as we both winced at the foul potion. The smell alone would do it.

The ghost drew back, as if even I scared her. "You can't escape him. Don't fight," she whispered as her head began to fade. "Then it won't hurt so much."

Screw that. I felt sorry for her, but I wasn't going to sit here and be attacked.

A dark cloud roiled up from the floor between my boots. Cripes. I jumped back up onto the bed. It seeped through the floorboards and filled the room.

A low growl echoed against every corner of the room. "Fornicators!"

"Fuck!" I said, nearly jumping out of my skin as Dimitri took my arm.

"Let's go," he croaked, helping me off the bed and toward the door.

I reached to my belt for Grandma's Sneak Spell. I broke the jar against the hardwood floors, sending up a plume of glittering purple and silver smoke that felt hot in my lungs and made me cough.

Dimitri looked at me like I was nuts. "That stuff work?"

I fought for a clean breath. "No clue."

Limbs stiff, we lumbered out into the hallway.

"Careful," he said, as we reached the top of the winding staircase. The carpeting was slick with mildew. The banisters were coated in a layer of dust and cobwebs. Lord help us if we pitched down the stairs.

It had been so much fun to sneak up. Now, it could be an easy way for the poltergeist to snap our necks.

I had five switch stars, the weapons of a demon slayer. They were round like Chinese throwing stars, only much more deadly. They could slice and dice incubi, succubi, demons, imps, goblins and Frankenstein's monster, but they didn't work on ghosts. Damn. I really needed the biker witches.

Flames danced in the gas globes below us. Taunting us.

My heart was nearly beating out of my chest and I didn't even realize it until we touched down in the foyer.

Dimitri braced a hand against the wall, gathering his strength, while I pulled open the front door. Dang. The poltergeist had hit him harder than I'd thought. A gust of frigid air blew in, ruffling his hair. "That actually felt good," he said.

Yeah, well I wasn't in the mood for gallows humor.

Poltergeists liked it cold, and it scared the bejesus out of me that the master of the house could control the weather in this . . . wherever we were. It was as if we'd entered the phantom's own particular brand of hell.

"Come on," Dimitri said, taking my hand. He was gaining strength. So was I, as we escaped the house and ran for all we were worth.

The only spell I had left was for passion – fat lot of good that would do us. I had nothing for protection or defense.

We made it to the cemetery at the side of the house. A few hundred feet and we'd be – where? My breath caught in my throat. We were still in the wrong dimension, whatever that meant. Still, we had to keep going. We had to get as far away from the house as we could.

The cemetery had to be as old as the estate itself. Narrow crypts thrust out of the ground, some tilted like they'd been there for centuries. Smaller tombstones crowded the empty spaces in between, their crosses and weeping virgins reaching out to snag my skirt and hose.

Pirate dashed ahead of us, weaving in and out of stones. I followed his rump and stubby white tail until he crashed headlong into a wall of black smoke. It rose up from the earth itself.

Dimitri cursed.

I turned to look behind us and saw another wall rise up.

We were surrounded.

We stood in front of a limestone crypt. A harsh stone cross dominated the roof. Carved angels wept at the corners and the worn bust of a stern, older man stood on a pedestal under the limestone eaves. A faded inscription at the front, black with lichen, read:

Hiram Everett Peele
1796–1857
Eva Fawn Peele
1812–1857
Forever bound

"That's him." I said.

What to do about it was another matter entirely. Grandma would have answers – if she weren't in another dimension. Partying.

Cripes.

Think.

We had to find a way to beat him and then somehow, hopefully, return to the dimension where we lived.

But I couldn't switch star a ghost. I couldn't spell him. Dimitri's teeth and claws would be useless.

"Uh, Lizzie?" Pirate backed up from the grave.

The black fog had begun to take form.

"Get over here," Dimitri told him, as the smoke took on the shape of a man.

The three of us gathered close, as I reached into my belt for the protective crystals I always carried. I laid them out around us in a circle, willing them to hold back the evil that chilled the very ground where we stood.

"This isn't going to be enough," I said. Hiram Peele glowered down at us. His face was cruel. His eyes hard.

The phantom was tall – at least seven feet. Larger than he possibly could have been in real life. He wore an old-fashioned suit, with a thick black necktie and a heavy silver cross. His yellow teeth glowed with an unnatural light as he glared down at us. "Anybody ever tell you? Sin leads to damnation." Fire flickered at the edges of the poltergeist and I could swear I smelled brimstone.

He drew himself up like a demented preacher. "For the whoremongers," he announced, "for them that defile themselves with mankind. Let not sin therefore reign in your mortal body. Cast out your lust!"

I took one step back, then another. "We weren't sinning, we're married!"

He spat on the ground. "No virtuous woman wantonly inspires lust in a man." He advanced on me. "You are a sinful whore."

I hurled a switch star at his head.

It flew straight through and didn't come back. My weapons usually acted as boomerangs. Had the ghost swallowed it? Or had it gotten caught on one of the tombstones.

It didn't matter. The switch star hadn't stopped Hiram Peele.

"What do you want?" I demanded.

He sneered at me like I was a wayward child. "Hold still, you little bitch. You're going to get a good hard beating for the Lord."

Dimitri pulled me close, as if that would stop it, and we braced for the worst.

A thousand sharp pricks of energy slammed into us like debris from a hurricane. It hurt like hell, but I knew it was only a small portion of his wrath. My pathetic crystal ward was hastily drawn, and weak, but it had at least kept most of it back. For now.

Hiram's wrath surrounded us, swirling. Howling.

Pirate stood against the assault, his ears flinging back. "Eva's screaming! She's terrified!"

The winds whipped Hiram's beard and hair. His eyes glared daggers into the black smoke to our right. "Don't you leave, Eva Fawn. You had to go and make friends, didn't you? Now you're going to see what you made me do."

The woman's head shimmered into view, weeping. Her face was a mass of cuts and scars. Harsh winds tore at her hair as she screamed. And with every scream, he grew.

Dimitri gripped me tighter. "Her fear is giving him power."

It was the classic abuse scenario. I'd be willing to bet the sicko succumbed to temptation with his wife and then beat her for it.

She'd given him her power in life and he was using it to hold her here.

"Leave!" I yelled to her. It was obvious she was in pain. "He can't hurt you anymore."

A cut above her eye opened up and blood poured down over her face.

Pirate let out a high-pitched doggie whine.

Shit. I tried to see outside the circle, but the poltergeist was everywhere.

"We have to help her," my dog pleaded.

Impossible. She'd been trapped here for over a century. She didn't have anything else.

The blood poured down her neck, her chest. She shook as her arms and hands came into view.

Yes, she'd crouched by the fire all night. She'd laughed with Pirate. I'd heard her. But I didn't see how a connection like that – with an animal no less – could change a person.

Suddenly, my dog did the unthinkable. He dashed out of the circle, through the hole in the poltergeist and into the arms of Eva Fawn Peele.

"No!" I screamed. Dimitri held me back or I would have snatched my dog out of the air.

As it stood, I'd never seen anyone – ghost or alive – more shocked than Eva when she reached out and caught him.

"I'm here! I love you! I'll help you!" Pirate said, wriggling in her arms, licking at her face, not caring that it was bloody and battered and awful.

I stumbled as the ground shifted. Hiram Peele hollered and lost the left side of his body.

"You got 'em!" Pirate said happily. "Look!" he said as the blood dried from Eva's body.

No, we didn't have him. Eva had just hit him with a bolt of energy. Maybe she had found something else to care about, a loving relationship. Even if her new friend had four legs.

It had to be a shock to the monster, considering it didn't appear he'd seen that side of Eva for at least a century and a half, if ever.

But the shock of the moment had given us one crucial victory.

On the other side of our black-hazed prison, bonfires appeared. Warmth flooded the air and I could see biker witches dancing, casting spells, and basically being their gorgeous, wonderful obnoxious selves.

We were back!

Eva wept, burying her face in Pirate's wiry fur as he snuggled tight against her.

Hiram Everett Peele drew up to his full height, his face a mask of fury. "Drop that filthy animal." He stood over her. "Now."

Eva clutched at my dog, shaking.

Holy hell. Hiram was enjoying it. "Have it your way," he snarled.

The phantom shot out his hand and released a bolt of power straight into Pirate's neck. My dog yelped and fell to the ground.

"Pirate!" I screamed.

"No!" Eva cried.

His small body lay twisted on the grass. He wasn't moving. Dimitri held me back. Barely. Oh my God. Pirate looked dead.

Hiram sneered down at his wife. "Don't look at me that way, woman. This is your fault. You didn't obey."

Pain seared her eyes, mixed with fury. Rage. Her cuts faded away. Her bruises morphed to silky white skin. "No!" Her voice curdled, as she drew out her hands like claws and launched a bolt of rage directly at her husband.

It hit him square in the chest and lit up the night. Needles of her energy pierced my skin as Hiram Peele, master of the house, staggered back, eyes wide with shock. He tried to speak, but no sound came as the light streamed from his mouth, nose and eyes.

He broke apart, lost form as the cloud of smoke surrounding us lost strength.

I ran to Pirate, who was beginning to stir. I took him up into my arms as the phantom that was Hiram Peele was sucked back down into the earth.

Eva Peele stood in front of us. Tears streamed down her face and she looked exhausted. But she only had eyes for Pirate. "Is he all right?"

Pirate lifted his head, although it had to be hard for him after such a hit. "I think I could use a belly scratch."

Eva let out a small, happy cry and stroked Pirate on the head, down the neck. Both seemed particularly pleased when he lifted his little noggin to help her get to the soft fur under his chin.

Meanwhile, Dimitri stood where the phantom had gone down. "There must be a way to ground him for good."

I reached into my utility belt for a biker witch distress flare. It was long, small and had a double set of wings. "Emergency!" I hissed, before launching it up into the air.

It shot up high, leaving a glittery trail, until it burst into a red shower of sparks overhead.

I just hoped the biker witches were paying attention.

Chapter Four

They arrived with pork ribs in hand.

"What have you got?" Grandma asked, ducking past a leaning tomb.

We explained, and in mere minutes we had an army of witches working at breakneck speed.

"Take Two Toed Harriett back into the woods to gather more dioscorea if we need it," Grandma hollered to Frieda, as she poured herbs from her fanny pack into her palm and began mixing them with her fingers.

"That sounds like a disease," Dimitri said.

Grandma made a sign of the cross. "Protective herb. Should be strong enough to plant that abusing asshole back in the ground."

The biker witches had each commandeered a small piece of land and were laying hands on it, chanting and sewing it with herbs. Dimitri brought up torches and supplies from camp. Meanwhile, Pirate had managed to commandeer a discarded rib bone or three. He was looking better. Weak, but happy.

I scratched him on the head. "How's it going, buddy?"

He looked sad. "She says she has to leave."

I looked past him and could barely see the outline of Eva Peele. It was as if she were fading already. "It's her time," I said, to both of them really. She'd earned her peace. "I'll bet she'll always remember you."

"She will." Pirate paused in his chewing. "She's more powerful than she thinks. She just needed the love of a pet to bring her out of her shell."

We both watched as the outline of Eva Peele took on a beautiful golden glow. She smiled. Happy. Then she looked to the clear sky, scattered with stars, and began to rise.

"Thank you," I said, hoping she heard me as she drew higher.

"She knows," Pirate said.

We watched her until we could barely make out a perfectly round white orb as it made its way to the heavens.

An hour later, the witches had completed their work. The night was warm. The haze had lifted and the ground was solid beneath our feet.

Ant Eater walked over and slapped a hand on my shoulder. "Well, the master of the house is pissed. But he's not going to be able to hurt anybody again."

"He's still here?" I asked. I'd half expected them to banish him. Where, I had no idea.

Grandma shook her head, joining us. "He refused to budge. So we locked him up in his grave." She glanced back at the old mausoleum. "As long as nobody disturbs him, he'll be fine."

"I'll let the owner know," I said.

"Want me to go with?" Ant Eater offered.

I shook my head. "Not necessary."

I took Dimitri instead.

He grinned at me, same as he did before, as we walked up to the old mansion. "Let's make a deal. Next anniversary we don't spend it with a ghost who wants to kill us. I don't want this turning into a tradition."

I kissed him on the cheek. "Deal."

As we neared the house, we saw Marjorie standing on the front porch. Her red hair glowed against the heavy bronze light over the door. She raised a hand in greeting. "Is it safe?"

I exchanged a glance with Dimitri as we made over to talk with her.

"What do you think you saw?" I asked her.

She watched me as if she were trying to see into me. "I

saw a bunch of vandals in my cemetery. Until the ghosts by the fire dropped their teacups and bolted for the light."

"Hiram Peele has been put to rest as well," Dimitri said.

"He was the troublemaker, wasn't he?" she asked.

I nodded and relief washed over her features. "This is going to sound crazy, but I could almost feel him leave." She paused. "Do you think it will be safe to open up the bed and breakfast again?"

"It should be." The house felt lighter. Clean. "Bring a priest through to bless the place. And don't disturb his grave," I warned her.

She shook her head slowly. "Now why would I do that?"

"You might also want to hire some help," Dimitri told her. "I think you're going to have a lot more customers from now on."

We'd have the witches whip up a spell to draw some extra customers. Marjorie worked hard. She deserved it.

"Let's head. We're missing the rest of the barbecue," Grandma called, approaching from the cemetery.

Our hostess frowned. "You're with those bikers?" She seemed genuinely confused. "But you're so nice."

I grinned. "They are too. They just took care of your poltergeist problem for you."

"Well darn it," she said, fretting all the more. "Now I wish I hadn't called the sheriff on them."

Grandma smiled and clapped her on the back. "No sweat, we get that a lot." She turned to me. "Ready to go?"

We said goodbye and headed off through the cemetery with Grandma. It looked like the other witches were back at their party already.

"They sure don't waste time," I said, as we made our way through the graves.

Grandma snorted. "Yeah, well when you get up there like us, you don't have a lot of time to waste."

"So are the police coming?" I asked when we'd reached the edge of the field. They were blaring the music again. "You Really Got Me" by Van Halen. Now that the crowd was more spread out, I could also see they were grilling a hog.

Grandma planted her hands on her hips. "Already took care of that. The sheriff is drunk over by that tree. We hit him with a barbecue-craving spell. The rest is on him." She gave me a sideways glance. "Anyhow, it appears we're spending the night after all."

"Good," Dimitri said, taking my hand. "Let's go find your present. It should be here by now."

Grandma let out a curse. "That was for you?" she said. "I sent him away."

"No worries," Dimitri said. He was used to fixing messes. "We have other things to keep us busy," he added, edging me back toward the pine forest.

Grandma hesitated. "You don't want to stick around and celebrate?"

"Lizzie and I have to do one more thing," he said cryptically.

Grandma looked confused for a second, before she started laughing.

He had to be kidding. "You're still in the mood?" I asked. "After all this?"

Not that I minded a romp in the forest with my man, but he'd been through a lot tonight.

He slipped his hand into mine. "Biker anti-passion spells don't last long on me. At least not when you're around."

Damn. "That just totally got me in the mood."

He turned to face me, his sharp features accented by the moonlight. "I love you, Lizzie. I'll always want you, no matter what."

His words soaked through me, warming me like nothing else ever would. "That's the best gift I could ever get."

I reached up and kissed him, contented to know that he was mine. To love, to hold, to grow old with. For better or worse. For the rest of our lives.

RETURN TO ME

Elle Jasper

Ophelia House, Laroushe Islet, Louisiana
Mid-August, dusk

"There's a nasty storm brewin', miss, and dis barge ain't makin' another run this day. You comin'?"

Thunder rolled in the distance, and my stomach twisted into knots as the captain waited for my answer. Doubt clawed at me, made me pause. The wind had picked up, and my ponytail whipped against my cheek. And according to the swirling vicious clouds overhead, a massive storm was in fact pushing in over the parish. That, I hadn't counted on. I needed to make up my mind. Get in my car and return home, or get in the boat. My gaze followed the narrow drift of murky water that disappeared into the shrouded moss-laden trees and around a bend into nothingness. I thought hard about turning back. About not getting on the rickety-looking barge bound for Ophelia House, or participating in the fear study I'd agreed to take part in. Jesus, what had I been thinking? I'd been terrified of the dark for as long as I could remember. Did I really think a two-week revival was going to help me?

But the idea of being fearless, of sleeping for even just one night without a light on, had lured me. No nightmares. No fear. I'd cordially accepted the invitation extended by a Dr Thibodeaux, a prestigious psychologist, according to the state of Louisiana. Inhaling, I stared at the sun-bleached dock between my feet and, as I debated, fat raindrops plopped against the wood in small, dark circles. A cacophony of frogs and cicadas twisted through the humid air that clung to my bare arms and legs. Somewhere deep within the muddy closet of cypress, a bird called out and I looked up. Its hollow cry sounded more like a warning to run, to stay away. *Beware.* Shadows stretched long and awkward over the marsh, like bony fingers reaching, reaching. All of the courage I'd dredged up weeks before left me dead cold. I shifted my weight, looked over my shoulder.

"She's coming, Jacque," a quiet, commanding voice said beside me.

Startled, I looked up – way up – and found the most arresting pair of mercury eyes staring down at me. Not smiling. Not amused. *Confident.* Compelling in a way I couldn't explain, even if I tried. Still, I balked.

"I, um, haven't completely made up my mind," I stammered. Balked, but couldn't look away. "Exactly."

The silvery gaze narrowed. "Yes, you have."

I frowned, glancing over his broad shoulder at Jacque, who merely watched with indifference. "How do you know?"

Only then did the hint of a smile pull at his mouth as he lifted the nylon backpack from my shoulder. From beside my legs he hefted my suitcase, inclined his head toward the barge, but his eyes remained on mine. "Because a storm's coming, and it's getting too dark to turn back."

Just the word *dark* sent shivers down my spine. I felt the suffocating weight of it settle over me, wrap its invisible fingers around my throat and squeeze. I almost bolted right then and there. Then his large hand found my lower back, calloused fingers brushed my exposed skin above my shorts, and without another thought I was stepping ahead of him onto the plank. Onto the boat. Going to Ophelia House.

"Push off, Jacque," the stranger commanded, still looking at me.

"Yes, sir," Jacque answered.

As Jacque maneuvered the vessel through the shadowy waters, I wondered who the stranger was beside me. He'd said nothing more. Hadn't asked my name; I hadn't asked his. He had simply stood, watching the path Jacque took as the barge eased through the moss and cypress, the chug-chug of the engine a vacant echo. A white flash caught my eye, and my gaze followed a snowy egret as it sailed effort-lessly overhead until it landed in the billowy gray-green treetops rising out of the bayou. When I turned back, I was again startled. The mercury-eyed man was gone. I craned my neck, looking everywhere. Maybe he'd gone to speak to Jacque? I rode the rest of the way alone, my eyes ever watch-ful of the fading light.

Then, out of the gloom, Ophelia House rose. As though an image from a dream, it appeared hazy, blurred at first, and I blinked several times to clear my vision. Only it wasn't my eyesight that had failed. A low-lying veil of mist envel-oped the small islet the pre-antebellum structure stood on. As the barge closed in on the dock, I noticed several aged crepe myrtles, laden with Spanish moss, looming on either side of a long path leading to the mansion. The white pillars of the Ophelia's entrance stood stark against the graying purple of dusk. Like the jaws of a contorted mouth, stretched wide. Beckoning.

"Miss?" Jacque asked. He pushed the bill of his white cap further up his wrinkled forehead. "I gotta be headin' back before it busts wide open."

"Right," I replied, and I knew he didn't want to be caught in the storm any more than I did. Home was four hours north, and I wasn't about to drive home at this hour. My body began to move toward the plank, although inside my head I screamed at myself to stop. To go back. Maybe get a hotel room? But I didn't. One second I was stepping onto the dock, my backpack at my feet. The next, almost as if I'd fallen asleep and lost several moments in time, Jacque and the barge faded away from me, into the mist, and too far out of reach to change my mind.

The sun had now dropped completely away, somewhere behind the cypress and oaks and waxy-leaved magnolias, leaving in its wake a purple haze of streaky gray, and the raindrops came faster now. Panic crept up my throat as the wind swept around me, and I grabbed my pack and hurried down the crepe myrtle lane toward Ophelia House. My gaze raked over the top-floor windows, and I noticed one, glowing amber. A corner room. Another low light radiated from the porch. Where was everybody? Odd – no one had arrived to greet me at the dock. No welcoming committee at the entrance. Had the storm driven the others away? What about the stranger? I guess he'd taken the barge back to the mainland with Jacque. I supposed I was the last participant to arrive. But now it was getting dark, a mammoth storm was about to crack wide open, and my heart started pounding so hard I could feel it pulsing beneath my skin. I needed to get inside. Out of the night. I reached the massive front porch, my hand fished my cell phone out of the back pocket of my jean shorts. I glanced at the face. No signal. No calling Beth, or Luke, to come and get me. I felt the breath leave my lungs.

I faced the pillared entrance now, and knowing I had nowhere else to go, I crept up the steps, drew a deep breath, and lifted the heavy iron knocker. I banged it three times. My eyes jerked side to side, watching the shadows stretch, bend at awkward angles, faster and faster, reaching for me, and the wind howled—

The door opened, and a tall figure loomed just inside. "Come inside, Ms Belue," a deep, resonating, familiar voice said. When I looked up, I recognized a pair of mercury eyes. "I've been waiting."

"You," I accused. "*You're* Dr Thibodeaux?" Shock made my face flush as the stranger from the barge – the psychiatrist leading the fear study – moved aside for me to pass. I stepped into the dimly lit foyer. It was either that or be swallowed up by nightfall. Neither choice appealed to me. But I had to pick one, and inside had to be safer than in pitch darkness, riding a tempest bareback. His expression didn't flinch.

"I prefer Damon. Now come inside, we have to batten down."

The heady scent of rosemary hung just inside the entry of Ophelia House, and an elegant yet simple chandelier made of iron and pocked glass cast a fall of tawny light that still wasn't bright enough for me. Hesitantly, I took a long look at Dr Damon Thibodeaux. Six feet five inches, at least. Broad shoulders that stretched the fabric of his form-fitting white long-sleeved shirt taut over an equally broad chest. Shaggy, sun-bleached hair was pulled back at his nape, and loose strands that had escaped brushed his shoulders. An overwhelming sense of . . . familiarity washed over me, accompanied by dread. Neither reaction could I explain. "What do you mean?" I asked.

"This is no ordinary storm, Ms Belue." With a powerful arm, he closed the door behind me. A muscle flexed in his jaw. "Don't you listen to the news? It's a hurricane." He cocked his head, those silver eyes regarding me closely. "You didn't receive the notification of this study being cancelled."

No sooner did the words leave his mouth than the lights in the foyer flickered. My gaze flashed to the man – a complete stranger. I couldn't stay here with him. Alone. "I'm sorry." I reached for the door handle. "I have to leave." Where I was going, and how I was going to get there, were two things I couldn't focus on. All I wanted to do was escape. I pulled my cell phone out of my pocket once more, checked for a signal. There was none. God, what was I going to do?

"Ms Belue," the man said, and grasped my shoulders, stilling me with a firm grip. "You're not leaving."

Panic rose up my throat. "You don't understand," I pleaded. "I . . . don't know you."

A small smile touched his lips, and only then did I notice how beautifully chiseled his features were, how utterly male and full his mouth was. "I hope to change that." The lights flickered again. "But first, help me with the candles." His eyes settled intimately on mine. "I promise, Ms Belue—" he didn't smile "—I won't bite."

Something in that promise made goosebumps rise on my skin. My gaze left his, shot left to right, to the door, to the window. *Shit!* I had no choice. "Fine," I agreed. I stood as tall as my five foot six frame would allow, and looked him square in the eye. "But just so you know, I have friends who know exactly where I am, and what I came here for."

Amusement danced in those mercury depths. "That's good to know, Ms Belue. Now let's hurry before this storm knocks out the power."

I followed Dr Damon Thibodeaux through the massive pre-antebellum mansion, crossed a grand entry room with a dual set of winding steps that led to the next level. We ended up in the kitchen, where Damon led me to a square chopping block in the center. Opening a double-door pantry, he stepped inside, then emerged with various silver candelabras, as well as long candlesticks. Laying them on the chopping block, he disappeared back into the pantry and emerged with several thick pillared candles. Reaching into his pocket, he set a Zippo lighter on the tiled block. "Start lighting, Ms Belue," he instructed. Then he turned to the cabinets, opened them, and pulled out several plates. Silently, he regarded me as he set the pillared candles on them.

With shaky hands, I flicked open the Zippo and started lighting the wax, and within minutes we had no fewer than twenty-five candles flickering. Beneath my lashes, I inspected the doctor of psychology. The very one I'd hoped could cure me of my fear of the dark. Despite the overhead kitchen light still illuminating the room, the sallow hue of the candlelight against his stubbled chin cast his features in sharp planes and harsh angles. Had I encountered him in public, in the daylight, I would have certainly done a double take. He was . . . beyond gorgeous. He was beautiful. Tall, broad, angled and beautiful. But here? Trapped, in an almost two-hundred-year-old mansion amidst a hurricane? Alone? He was both terrifying and alluring. And again, eerily familiar. And I had no idea why. I knew for a fact I'd never met him. Or had I?

Just then, the lights flickered again, and I jumped.

"Grab some candles and follow me, Ms Belue," he said, his husky voice washing over me. "Before we're thrown in complete darkness."

With my heart slamming into my chest, I did as he asked and followed him through a side door that led into a smaller sitting room. A large desk sat against one wall; a fireplace, void of flames, took up another. A long leather sofa, flanked by two leather chairs, sat before a thick wooden coffee table, facing the hearth. A tall bookshelf, filled with tomes, angled the corner. "Set those on the table there." He inclined his head. I did, and we headed out.

On a marble lamp table, I set a lit pillar. Then, I followed Damon up the sweeping staircase. He'd stopped long enough to shoulder my backpack and, as I followed him, I kept my eyes glued to his broad back, narrow waist, and wondered what in the holy hell I was doing in this place, apparently all alone, with Damon Thibodeaux. How did it happen?

Fate? If it was Fate, she was a cruel, psychotic bitch.

On the second floor, we set several candles along the corridor, on tables that hugged the walls. Gilded framed paintings of people from another time stared back at me as I followed and, before long, Damon stopped at a room. He opened the door, stepped inside, and an enormous crack of thunder shook the windowpanes.

I started and gasped.

Just as the lights once more flickered and went out.

He set a large four-tiered candelabrum down on a desk in the corner, and turned to me. "Just in time," he said. The flames danced over his face. "This is your room for your stay at Ophelia House." He set my backpack on a large canopied bed. "Just down the hall, a full bath." He came to stand closer, and he towered over me. His fingers brushed mine as he grasped the remaining pillar candle from my hand. A silver gaze locked onto mine. "Are you hungry, Ms Belue?"

The way the loose tendrils of hair hung at his jaw, the shadows that played across his cheekbones, and the penetrating glow of his stare added to the bundled nerves building up inside me. It was warm, and a sheen of moistness clung to my bare arms. My eyes darted around the barely lit room. "No, Dr Thibodeaux." I looked at him. "I—I can't stay. I can't be here."

Strong fingers grasped my shoulders, and he looked down at me. I could feel a delicious heat radiating off his body, and I was shocked at how I felt inexplicably drawn to him. "You keep saying that, *chère,* and yet you *are* here."

The moment he spoke, called me that Cajun endearment, I felt a rush of dizziness and I swayed under his hands. He steadied me, ducked his head and held my gaze. "Are you all right?"

I closed my eyes and struggled to breathe. "No, I'm not." I shook my head, frustrated. Slowly, I forced my gaze to his. My body shook, and I couldn't help it. "Didn't you read my file, Dr Thibodeaux? Do you even know why I'm here in the first place?"

His gaze sharpened. "I did read your file, Ms Belue. Thoroughly." Silvery eyes dropped to my mouth, then lifted. "You've a crippling fear of the dark, as well as petrifying nightmares. Ever since your parents' death, sixteen years ago." He cocked his head. "Do you understand you're the only study participant at Ophelia House?"

His close proximity comforted and threatened me at the same time. Standing in front of him, his hands on my shoulders, I felt every inch of his six foot five frame. "Yes, I understand."

"And you wish to continue therapy?"

I said nothing – I couldn't. The rising storm, the extinguished lights, the faded glow of candles, the howling wind, all terrified me. But I nodded.

Damon didn't take his eyes off me. "Very well. We'll begin right away, Ms Belue."

"Josie," I whispered, my voice quivering. "Call me Josie."

With the wind howling around Ophelia House, we settled into Damon's study. He'd brought in more candles, and they covered every vacant flat spot available. The room glowed as bright as could be expected with candlelight, and it eased my trepidation enough to at least sit on the sofa and focus on his first exercise. Something I hadn't counted on and wasn't a hundred per cent sure I wanted to experience. But I'd agreed to it and had no choice.

Regression.

"All right, Josie," Damon said. He was kneeling down beside the sofa where I lay. Resting his long fingers against my forearm, his gaze held mine in a firm, unbreakable grip. "Close your eyes now. I'll stay right here."

With a deep inhale, I let my eyes close.

"Concentrate on your breathing, Josie. Soft. Shallow. In. Out."

I did as he asked, allowing his lush, deep voice to wash over me. Lull me into total relaxation.

"As I count back from five, I want you to slowly inhale," he said. "Once I reach one, I want you to briefly hold that breath, then allow it to escape through pursed lips in a long exhale. *Slowly.*" I felt him lean in. "Are you ready, Josie?"

"Yes," I whispered. I felt my pulse quicken. His mouth was very close to my ear, and the sensation of his breath brushing my neck made me unavoidably shiver.

"Five. Four. Three." These he said slowly. Evenly paced.

Slowly, I inhaled, and as I did so my body felt lighter.

"Two."

A little more, my head felt swimmy.

"One."

The exhale seemed to go on and on, through pursed lips, until finally, complete relaxation and peace filled me.

"Blink open your eyes and tell me what you see."

Damon's voice sounded far away. Quiet, as if in another room. But I did as he asked. My lids were heavy, but I blinked, and they cracked open, and I saw . . . my reflection. I saw my ten-year-old self, standing before a full-length mirror. I pulled closer, staring at my familiar image. Hesitantly, I touched my straight black hair, let it slip between my fingers and fall over my narrow shoulder. I skimmed a hand over my tanned bare arms and stared at watery blue eyes too wide for my narrow face. Only then did I notice the mirror itself – aged, hammered copper frame, with a crack in the upper right-hand corner.

"What is it?" Damon's raspy voice carried to me.

"It's . . . me," I answered softly. "Only I'm so young."

"What are you doing?" he countered.

As his words reached me, I peered closely into the mirror at my reflection "Just . . . standing here, staring at—"

At once, a face appeared behind me in the mirror. Horrid, disfigured, a face hidden mostly by shadow and stringy hair. It reached for me, through the glass. "No!" I lunged upward, gasping, and became so conscious of my weighty breathing and thumping heartbeat that it actually hurt. "Damon!"

A gentle pressure against my forehead drew down the bridge of my nose. "Open your eyes."

A clap of thunder boomed across the study as I focused on the face looming over me. No longer was I standing in the mirror, a younger version of myself looking at a scary figure. My gaze was locked solid in the very real present, and onto the very real troubled expression of Dr Damon Thibodeaux.

"Just breathe, Josie," he crooned. "Breathe. Relax."

I sat forward, braced my elbows against my knees and lowered my head. I sucked in big gulps of air, almost afraid each one would be my last. Damon's hand moved in a calming circle between my shoulder blades. My breathing slowed. I almost stopped shivering.

"Now I want you to look at me," Damon said quietly.

I sat up. Turned my head. Looked at him as he crouched on the floor beside me.

"Who was in the mirror with you?" he asked.

Suddenly, I was aware of how warm it was in the study; of the dark wood of the bookshelves, the aged fabric wallpaper a fading burgundy. My eyes scanned the walls, noticing a few portraits of Ophelia House's past. I searched my memory, my brain, looking for the figure in the mirror.

I shook my head. "I . . . can't remember."

"You will."

I turned a fast gaze onto Damon. "How do you know?"

A small smile tilted his sensual mouth. "I just do. Meanwhile—" he glanced at his wristwatch "—you'd better get some sleep. We have a lot of work to do tomorrow."

I thought I'd be okay, really. But as I lay beneath the sheer white fabric of the bed's canopy, doubts flooded me. Damon was a gracious host, and while he still baffled me, in more ways than one, he'd made every attempt to console me, make me comfortable for the night. He'd brought more candles to my room, and it was nearly as bright as if I'd had a big overhead lamp on. But the noise of the storm – the scratching of branches against the windowpanes, the wind screaming through the bayou and bashing the side of Ophelia House – hadn't allowed me to shut my eyes. Not even for a second.

Then, there were images of Damon that kept me awake, too. His features, cut from stone, and those mercury eyes, so mesmerizing. The way he looked at me. No, deeper than a look. As if he could see inside me . . .

Just then a branch smacked the window, and I all but leapt from the bed. Because of the heat, I was clad only in a pair of shorts and a thin spandex sports bra. I was thirsty, scared, and something drew me out of my room and into the hallway. Slowly, I crept, my only companions the portraits on the wall as I made my way to the staircase. With bare feet I padded to the first floor, and although Damon had lit many candles within Ophelia House, some had burnt out. What flames were left flickered as drafts caught them, and odd shadows moved and shifted in the corners. Panic grew, crawled up my throat, and I moved faster, faster, searching for . . .

Him. For Damon.

A stranger. And my only comfort.

The raging storm outside only amplified each peculiar sound in Ophelia. The old pre-antebellum structure shifted with the wind; wood splintered, groaned, creaked. And as drafts caught the flickering candle flames, shadows flailed across the faces in the portraits. Made them grimace. Scowl. Stare. I hurried faster, across the grand entry, the tile cool beneath my feet, which belied the humid warmth of the old house. I headed straight for the study. The door cracked ajar, the dim light flickering inside. I peeked in.

Empty.

Fear grew as I moved away, down a long narrow corridor just off the kitchen. With only the glow of a solitary wax pillar at the doorway, it cast a weak light toward a single room at the far end; it beckoned me. How had I known to come this way? Damon hadn't led me down that hallway before. The clap of thunder, followed by the brilliant flash of lightning, made me move faster. I reached the door, grasped the iron knob, and turned.

Inside, Damon stood facing the window as the storm raged outside. Bare to the waist, his corded arms were braced on either side of the pane, his longish hair loose from the tie that had bound it earlier. His shoulders were so broad they filled the window, and his ribs tapered to a narrow waist where a pair of white cotton drawstring pants slung low over his hips. I could do nothing more than stare, breathless, at the beautiful stranger before me. Lightning flashed, and at the same time he turned. I gasped, covered my mouth.

For a split second, the shadows had crossed his features, revealing . . . something awful. Disfigured. I turned, fled.

"Josanthe!" he called behind me. "Josie, stop!"

I knew not where I ran to; I just . . . ran. My bare feet led me across the grand entry, and without much thought I flew toward the door. Just as I opened it, a force slammed it shut from behind. Damon whipped me around, my back against the double-hung wood.

"Josie!" His raspy voice was stern with concern. "What's wrong?"

Words failed me as I stared up at him, unsure what to do, where to go. Scared to look closely at his face, fearful I'd see the . . . what *had* I seen?

"Your face," I breathed, and closed my eyes. "I saw something. Something terrifying." My brain worked furiously. "The image from the mirror. A monster . . ." Still, I wouldn't open my eyes. I was too scared of what I'd see.

Strong, warm hands cupped either side of my face, tilted my head backward with pressure from his thumbs against my jaw. "Open your eyes, Josanthe," he commanded gently. "And breathe. I'm not a monster."

The heat from his closeness washed over me, comforted me, and, slowly, I opened my eyes. In the hue of amber light his beautifully chiseled face stared down at me, perfect, angled, with the slightest shadow of stubble on the jaw. Without thinking, I lifted my fingertips, rubbed the roughened skin there, just to make sure he was real. That he wasn't a monster. The sandpapery grit beneath the pads of my fingers sent shivers down my spine. I met his gaze, saw the heat pooling in their mercury depths as his eyes raked over my chest, breasts, abdomen, hips . . .

Only then did I remember what I was wearing, and I moved my hands to cover myself. "Why did you call me Josanthe?" I hesitantly asked.

His facial expression didn't change as he looked at me. "That's your name, isn't it?"

The timbre of his voice, the raspy sound it made when he spoke, made warmth spread through my body, made it difficult for me to breathe. Why was I having this reaction to a virtual stranger? Terror? Attraction? Had I lost my mind? Even now, I couldn't take my eyes off him. "Yes," I answered. "But I don't remember telling you that. No one calls me Josanthe. Not since . . ." My brows knitted, trying to remember. When had someone called me that? It seemed too long ago, like, almost never ago.

"It must've been in your files," he said, interrupting my thoughts. "It's a unique name." He lowered his hands to my shoulders, grazed my collarbones with his thumbs. Behind me, a tock-tock of an old clock. The wind shoved and pushed at every crack of Ophelia, squeezing its way in and screaming through the corridors. "Very beautiful. French Creole, is it not?" He lifted my long black hair and let it slip between his long fingers. The contrast stood stark between the darkness of it and his skin. "Native American, as well."

At once, my head swam, leaving me dizzy, and again, I swayed. Unsteady, I closed my eyes, thinking it'd stop the flight of wooziness. I shook my head. Shook it again. Then looked at Damon Thibodeaux.

Familiarity swamped me, seeing him, shirtless, broad shoulders and chiseled abs that delved into a deep pair of Vs at his hips. His hair – I raised my fingers to touch the ends, brushing his collarbone, and the sun-bleached chestnut color fell in soft, messy waves. He kept silent, but I couldn't.

I looked at him. "What's going on here?" I asked. "Have you . . . drugged me or something?"

"I don't drug people. Especially you. Why do you ask?"

"I don't feel so good," I answered, pressing my hand to the crown of my head. "Not . . . right." I began backing away, out of the comforting grasp of his strong fingers – touching me too intimately for a stranger. "I—Something feels strange here. You feel strange."

"You mean familiar."

I pushed my fingertips to my temples, which had begun to pound. "Yes. Familiar. Why?" I shook my head again, and my hair fell over my bare shoulders. A fine sheen of sweat covered me. "We've never met. I've never been to this place." I looked at him. "You're a stranger, Damon. I thought I was coming here to cure my fear of the dark. To stop the nightmares. Get on with my life." I began backing away, fearing this man, this house, my entire existence. "Who are you? What do you want with me?"

Damon held out a hand. "Please, Josanthe. You've no reason to fear me, or this place. I swear to God you don't. You won't be harmed here. You have my word. I'm here to help you. Help you remember."

Terror now grabbed me by the throat and squeezed and, as I retreated, thunder roared overhead. *When I was scared of the storm and shadows earlier, I sought him out. Now, I run away. What's wrong with me? Am I going insane?* "Please, just leave me alone," I begged, and ran as fast and hard as I could through Ophelia House, across the grand entry, up the staircase and down the corridor to my room. Slamming the door, I leaned against the wood, its texture rough and cool against my damp back. Suddenly, I held my breath, listened closely at the door, for any sound, movement, rustling of clothes – anything. It was dead silent. Damon hadn't chased me. I was here, alone.

With the storm raging outside, I crawled between the shimmering white panels of the canopy, curled onto my side, and somehow, amidst crazy thoughts of where I was, who Damon was, and how I'd ended up at Ophelia House, alone, with him, during a *hurricane,* images plagued me until exhaustion took over and I fell into my shallow, fitful sleep. One minute I was aware of my surroundings, the present, even the ominous presence of Ophelia House, then the next I'm . . . *running through a thick copse of oaks and pines, the dead needles on the ground crackling beneath my bare feet. The gown I'm wearing is dingy white, plain, ragged, and ripped open at my breasts. My hair flows long behind me, strands clinging to my damp skin as I weave in and out of the brush. I'm breathless, glance behind me to see if I'm followed, and keep going. Going, going. I make it to the water where a pirogue is tied to a dead cypress, waiting, just as he'd said it would be. I loosen the rope, jump in and, without looking back, I begin to paddle. My heart slams against my ribs, and each breath is painful as I draw it in, but I keep going. I glance down, notice the blood staining a wide arc in my ugly gown. When I press my hand to my side, the pain is fiery hot. I lift my gown and notice the half-moon cut that is sliced through my skin. Oh, God, oh God! I have to get away. Make it across the bayou. Make it to . . . Ophelia House . . .*

"No!" I sat up, my chest heaving with harsh breaths, my heart pounding recklessly and out of control. As I fought to get my bearings, my mind scrambled to remember the dream. But all I could recall was running through the wood. I noticed then that a faded, hazy light filtered through the window of my room. Daylight. I'd made it through the night. Through the storm. Crawling from the canopy, I padded over to the window, pulled the gauzy white drapes back, and peered out. Debris from the storm lay strewn all over; broken limbs, a marble statue, blackened in areas with age, lay tipped on its side. My eyes moved to an enormous oak, and it was filled with dozens and dozens of ravens—

A knock at my door startled me, and I turned. Waited.

"Josie?" Damon's voice sounded from the other side of the heavy wood. "Please, let me in? I have something for you."

I trusted Damon. I didn't trust him. Something lured me to him, and kept me at a distance. It was the most tumultuous feeling I'd ever experienced. Yet my feet moved across the floor, and I opened the door. And as I looked into his silvery eyes, familiarity again crashed over me, making me dizzy. I held on to the door frame. "I don't understand any of this, Damon," I said. I forced my gaze to return to him. Exhaustion – not just from being at Ophelia House, but from the moment the dreams plagued me, so long ago – made me weaken. Made me trust. "Please. Make me understand."

Looking so normal in a black T-shirt and a pair of faded jeans, Damon's mouth lifted in the corner, a hint of a smile. His hair was pulled back again at the nape, but several wild strands fell against his jaw. With his hand, he reached for mine, and I allowed it. Allowed the sensation of attraction, of sensuality, to crash over me. I knew then I wanted him to kiss me, and it surprised me. But he didn't kiss me then. Instead, he placed something cold, hard in my palm, then closed my fingers around it.

His eyes blazed fire when he looked at me. "Shower. Get dressed. I've made breakfast." His fingertips lingered against my skin. "Then we'll begin our sessions."

Slowly, over the next several days, Damon lured me into dreams – places I didn't want to go, never wanted to revisit. I relived my parents' death – the accident that I'd barely escaped. I'd been trapped in the same car with my parents, after the crash. For over twenty-four hours. I was ten. And, ever since, I'd been terrified of the dark.

Or, so I thought. Until one last session with Damon proved otherwise.

The office now felt comforting to me, familiar and soothing. A place I knew Damon strived to help me reconcile my past. It was a dark room, windowless, with dark wood. The sofa I lounged on was a deep chestnut leather. The walls were covered in antique burgundy fabric. The first night – the night of the storm – it had frightened me. Now, somehow, it didn't.

"Okay, Josie," Damon commanded quietly beside me, "uncross your ankles and close your eyes."

I smiled – he had to constantly remind me to uncross my ankles before each session. I did so, then closed my eyes. I rested my hands against my stomach. I breathed.

"Good girl," Damon coaxed. "Now, we begin the count."

This time – unlike all the others – he lifted my hand from my abdomen, his fingers interlaced with mine. "Five. Four. Three."

My heart skipped a beat, then quickened. Wait, this was different. Different than all the other sessions. I wanted to speak, cry out, but I couldn't. I was too . . . relaxed.

"Two. One."

I hear his voice, calling to me as I tear through the house. Flames lick the walls, creep over the wood plank floors, swallow the shabby curtains. The gown I'm wearing is the same one from before, dingy white and ripped, but when I glance down, there is no bloodstain.

"Josanthe! Run!" Damon's voice cries out, followed by a fierce growl of pain. Chanting soon fills the smoke-filled cabin, an eerie echo of a strange, high-pitched voice, of a language I don't understand . . .

Rather, I do . . .

"No!" My heart is slamming so hard now it feels as though it will break my ribs. I run – but not away. I run back through the flames, toward Damon's voice. Toward his cries. Suddenly, I see him, and he's suspended from a heavy rafter, arms bound at the wrists, bare to the waist. His long hair hangs in wet strands, clinging to his blood-soaked body. That haunting, mercury gaze peers at me, silently pleading with me to run, to leave. There is a young Cherokee woman below him, sitting on the floor before a smaller fire contained in a bowl. She rocks back and forth, back and forth, chanting in an ancient language. I recognize her. I recognize the words.

It's a curse.

Suddenly, a white-hot pain sears through my side, and a young man, as black as onyx, stands before me, and I recognize him, too, and the silver blade flashing in the firelight. I glance down, and a sticky red spreads across my dingy white gown. With a final glance at Damon, whose eyes slowly begin to roll back in his head, I run. The pain is so great it leaves me breathless, but I don't stop. I'm in the wood. I'm in the pirogue. I'm paddling—

"Josanthe! Wake up!"

I woke up, violently, and lunged from my place on the sofa. My vision was blurry, everything was a hazy, foggy picture, and I blinked rapidly, trying to clear it. Fear caught my breath and made me pant, and suddenly, I was in Damon's arms. As I was crushed against his familiar body, everything – my past – rushed back in a nauseating wave. Not just my head, but my whole body, my whole being, swayed unsteadily. Damon pushed me just far enough away so he could gather my face in his big hands. He was kneeling on the floor beside the sofa, and his mercury eyes looked so achingly familiar now.

"Tell me," he whispered harshly. His eyes pleaded with me. "Tell me you remember."

I pulled in huge gulps of air to tamp down the nausea, and Damon pushed my hair off my sweaty forehead. Slowly, as I looked at him, I nodded. "I do," I said slowly. "But . . . I don't understand."

"We lived long ago, *chère*," he said, and his raspy voice washed over me. He ducked his head to better look at me, and he brushed my lips with his thumb. "You are *Creole de couleur*, Cherokee and French, from the Cane River." His eyes searched mine. "I was born in Devonshire, England, but my father was French. I came here as a boy, and you and I, we met as children." He smiled then, and the smile was one I knew. "We've loved each other for a long, long time, Josanthe." His features turned murky then, clouded with pain. "As we grew older, our love was forbidden. By both of our families."

My insides shook at his words and, as strange and unbelievable as they were, I did believe them. I'd seen it all happen. In my dreams. I raised my hand to graze his jaw. "You were hanging from the rafters, bound by your wrists," I said slowly, quietly. My brow knitted as I chased the memory around in my head. "It was my aunt and her lover who beat you, cursed you."

Damon's fingertips slowly moved to my side, lifted my tank top, grazed my side. When I looked down where his fingers lingered, I saw a half-moon scar. "And it was your aunt's lover who knifed you," Damon added. His laugh was soft and harsh at the same time. "After your aunt cursed me, she didn't count on my escape. I killed her lover for what he'd done to you. Killed him with my bare hands."

I sat back against the leather cushions of Damon's sofa, my mind whirling from another life. "I got away," I said, staring at my bare toes in my sandals. "You'd secured that pirogue for me. I got in it, paddled away." I looked up at him. "To here. Ophelia House."

A sad smile tilted Damon's beautiful mouth. "You did. You were so brave, Josanthe." An expression of shame flickered over his face. "Even after I joined you, and—"

"I locked you away," I finished. "The curse. Oh, God, Damon," I held his face in my hands now. "The curse." Everything else, between then and now, vanished. One second, I was at Ophelia House, caring for Damon as he healed. The next, I found myself in the present, with people I thought were my parents. The car crash. My fear of the dark, my nightmares . . .

"It was all necessary, Josanthe," Damon said. He stood then, and pulled me with him. "We were secretly wed more than a hundred and fifty years ago. You've always been mine, and I've waited so long. Waited—"

"Until you'd tamed the beast inside you," I finished.

Damon's eyes closed. "Yes."

"And now you fear I no longer want you?" I asked quietly.

Damon's eyes opened, and in the mercury depths I saw sadness, fear. He nodded.

"Fear no more," I said, and pulled his mouth to mine, but I didn't kiss him. "I remember you, Damon Thibodeaux," I whispered against his lips. "I remember everything."

A slow smile pulled at his mouth. "You've returned to me, Josanthe Thibodeaux." His arms caught me below my knees and he scooped me into his arms. "Are you frightened at what I am?"

My hand lifted to graze his jaw. "What you are, Damon, everything that makes you, is everything I am in love with." Emotions pushed at my chest, made my ribs ache. "Even the beast."

"Do you trust me?" he asked. "Knowing what I am, that I tricked you into coming here? To make you remember?"

I kissed him then, a light brush of my lips over his. "I trust you," I whispered, and met his liquid gaze. "I've waited so long for you, Damon. Many lifetimes." I rested my head against his chest. "Please, don't make me wait another second."

Damon carried me through Ophelia House, across the dimly lit grand entry, and up the sweeping staircase. I felt his heart beating against my cheek, and love crashed over me. We were together. Finally. At last.

Upstairs, I slid from his arms and we stumbled together in the shadows, down the hall and into my room, our lips fastened, starved. With a painful slowness, Damon's mouth slanted over mine and he kissed me, his tongue tasting mine, his hands moving over my flesh. Then I found myself hard against the wooden door of my room as he kissed me furiously. My fingers desperately pulled at Damon's shirt, the buttons on his jeans, managing to unfasten a few. I pushed his T-shirt up and, at once, he took over, yanking it over his head and flinging it onto the floor. My heart raced as my palms skimmed the ripped muscles of his abdomen, feeling the scars there, left by my Cherokee aunt and her Creole lover so long ago. My fingers moved over his chest, back down, and I eased my hand inside his fly and over his hardness, which was straining to be let free. His painful groan escaped his throat at my touch, and I looked up, into his eyes. When his gaze met mine, his mercury eyes were dark, glassy, and completely lost in desire. In a love so evident, it all but made my heart burst with joy.

Without words, Damon picked me up and slid me under the gauzy white canopy of my bed. Beneath my tank, he slid his hands up my bare stomach, then pulled my shirt over my head and threw it to the floor. Quickly, his hands grazed my breasts, where he nimbly released the single clasp keeping my bra together, slid it off my shoulders and dropped it on the floor. At the same time his mouth claimed mine, his hands claimed my breasts, and I pushed against him with blinding need, threading my fingers through his shaggy mane, loosening the tie that bound it together at his nape. Our tongues melded, his mouth hungrily taking in mine; I couldn't get close enough, fast enough – as though I wanted to just descend into his skin, submerge into his very being. I wanted him everywhere. On me. Inside of me.

With skillful fingers Damon trailed his hands down my abdomen to the buttons of my denim shorts and, as he released each one, I shivered with need. His hands skimmed my legs, removed my sandals, eased my shorts over my hips, my panties, then he kicked out of his boots, his jeans. Finally, we were both free of clothes. Our heavy breathing filled the hollow, vacant air of Ophelia House. He grasped my face in his hands, looked down at me.

"I've dreamed of you every night of my sorry existence, Josanthe," he said quietly. "Waiting for you, recalling our memories together – they're the only things that kept me sane. Alive. Hopeful." His mouth swept over mine, and the way he tasted me with his tongue gave me chills. He pulled back, locked that ethereal gray gaze onto mine. "I am so in love with you, wife. You've returned to me. Knowing I'm no longer just a man." His eyes shone with that love, too. "You're not running from me."

I kissed him back then, and his sigh into my mouth made butterflies beat furiously inside of me. "I'll never leave again," I assured him. "You're mine forever, Damon Thibodeaux. Beast. Man. All of you." I caressed his jaw. "And we belong here. In Ophelia House. Together forever."

Again, he sighed against my mouth, the action so intimate – more so than any kiss. It felt complete, like worry built up he could finally release. We again melded together, and in the waning light became nothing more than silhouettes and shadows as we stared at one another. Damon's hands slid to my hips, over my backside, his eyes watching me intently, then he laid me against the feathery softness of my bed, followed me down. His hard body covered mine, and he kissed me frantically, desperation in every suck, every lick, every taste, as though he'd longed for me forever, and he'd been starving for me.

I met his hunger, gasping between kisses, suckles, and my hands moved over his body as though discovering it for the first time. His hips were muscular and narrow, and I glided my hands around them, to his backside, and pulled him against me. Damon's hands were everywhere, touching every curve, fingering the half-moon scar on my ribcage and, when his hardness throbbed heavy against my thigh, a groan escaped my throat and I reached for it, and palmed its velvety hard ridges.

He braced his weight above me, arms on either side of my head. "Keep your eyes open, Josanthe," he said hoarsely, his voice raspy and uneven with desire. "See what you do to me."

Breathless, my heart slammed against my chest, as he placed my legs around his waist, then he pushed into me, his thrusts matching my own, and shards of light pierced my eyes as pleasure only Damon could give me racked my body. I watched him, our eyes locked, until finally Damon slowed his movements. He lowered his head and his mouth buried into the cleft of my neck and shoulder. His strong hands grasped mine, interlaced our fingers. Then, after a moment of catching our breath, he lifted his head and looked at me. He stared at me for a long, long time. In shimmering flashes, I saw his face shift in the shadows, and although I couldn't see it clearly, I knew his features moved from man to the beast my aunt had cursed him to become. Only Damon had tamed that part of himself. Tamed it, and waited for me to return. I raised my hand and brushed the damp waves from his brow, traced one perfect lip, outlined his jaw. I found no beast there. Only a man. A man I was in love with.

My husband.

"Welcome home, Mrs Thibodeaux," he said in a soft, raspy voice.

I could do nothing more than smile.

I was finally home, indeed.

"Kiss me, husband," I said to him.

"Gladly, wife," he answered. "Anything you want."

The kiss that followed nearly unglued me; slow and exquisite, Damon took his time tasting every inch of my mouth, neck, collarbone. Then, he pulled away, rolled off of me and tugged me with him until we lay side by side, face to face. The fall of darkness cascaded over the room in a myriad of shadows and planes. A sliver of moonlight shafted through the window, and, for a split second, I again saw Damon's face change.

But when he smiled and his teeth shone sharp white in the darkness, I knew I didn't care. In whatever form he was in, he was mine.

"Nothing will ever keep us apart again," he whispered, and nudged my nose with his. "We'll be together forever." He gathered me in his arms then, my body against his, my head against his chest.

And, we were.

PRETTY ENOUGH
TO CATCH HER

J. D. Horn

I

Every day of his incarceration, Mark Truro dreamed of being outside in the great wide open with nothing overhead but the bright blue sky. Today, he'd watched that sky change from orange to steel, and he felt nothing but exposed as lightning struck around him from every side, gaining in proximity with each strike. Rain descended from above like God had reneged on his promise to Noah. Water rushed like a river two inches deep along the pavement he'd been walking since the piece of shit Oldsmobile the fine families of the Waycross Separate Baptist Church – his parole officer's congregation – had found it in their hearts to give him, had died.

His parole terms allowed him to drive for interviews or work, but driving wasn't working out too well for him so far. The 1988 Delta stunk from the piss of the old lady who had kicked the bucket two years back and left it to the church. From the smell of it, she'd died and driven off to glory in it. The title called its pinkish color "sunset beige". Shit. That was nothing more than tan gone gay. Almost as gay as the pastor who'd made him sit through a half-hour foot washing before handing over the keys. Mark knew he was a handsome man. He used his square jaw and deep-set blue eyes to full advantage with nearly every woman he met and more than a few men too. The way Pastor Selby looked into and avoided looking into Mark's eyes, the way the reverend's soft fingers worked the warm water and olive oil all the way to his upper calf told Mark the good reverend was struggling with his own demons.

Three-quarters of a mile past the point where the car had gone on to join its mistress, Mark found himself with two burning regrets – that he hadn't taken a tire iron to its windshield before taking off on foot and that he hadn't beaten the fairy pastor to a bloody pulp.

Water filled his prison-issue cardboard-soled shoes and spun around his foot like it was trying to find the drain. The tall pines bent in the wind. Mark ran his hand back through his hair to push it from his eyes and shrugged the metal frame of his military-style backpack into a more comfortable position. He trudged on, left hand held out toward the road, his thumb pointed upward. There wouldn't be much traffic in this kind of weather. Anyone with any sense was staying out of God's way.

Only reason he was out here was because gainful employment counted as one of the requirements of his six-month parole. A steady residence was another. McCarthy, his parole officer, had sniffed out a job at Carlisle House that would provide him both. He'd been ordered to arrive right at 9 a.m., no chance of that now. If parole hadn't denied him the use of internet and cell phones, he could've called to explain why he was going to be late. Maybe McCarthy would order out a patrol car to check on his whereabouts and get him the hell out of this storm.

Mark turned at the sound of an engine approaching. A black Shelby Cobra – '68 maybe – moved way too fast for the road conditions, and he stepped back to avoid having the water on the road thrown up on him as the car passed. The sight of curly blonde hair shot by as the driver passed, then downshifted and stopped. For a moment something kept him from moving, but a short burst of the horn woke him.

"You coming or not?" Blonde curls popped out the driver's side window. He gripped the straps of his backpack and took the longest, fastest strides his disintegrating shoes would allow. The passenger side door opened as he neared. He bent over to get a good look at his Samaritan.

"Is that your pussy wagon on the side of the road back there?" Coming from anyone else, it would have pissed Mark off. Coming from her, with her smoky voice and laughing eyes painted dirty with heavy blue eye shadow and thick, smudged liner, it made him grin. Mark felt himself stiffening at the mere sight of her. He didn't answer. "Silent type, huh? I like that in a man. My last boyfriend always wanted to jabber on about his feelings. Well, get the hell in or don't."

Mark pushed the seat forward and shrugged off his backpack. He put it on the folded-down back seat and returned the front seat to its upright position. He climbed in and closed the door. His driver pulled back onto the road without signaling, without even looking.

"Pussy," Mark said.

She looked at him in the rear-view mirror. "Hmmm?"

"Your last boyfriend. He was a pussy."

"Precisely," she said, never taking her eyes off him. She'd probably better keep her eyes on the road, but the rain fell so heavily the windshield wipers were futile anyway. Like driving through a car wash.

She seemed to pick up on his thoughts. "Don't worry, I know this road like the back of my hand. You're lucky I spotted you. But then again, you aren't one to be missed, are you? There's a paper bag under your seat." She signaled with a jerk of her head. "Got a bottle in it. Have a hit and warm yourself up a bit."

"I shouldn't . . ."

"I shouldn't," she mocked him. "Funny, you didn't strike me as a missionary." Her smart mouth, the smell of her, Mark had gone completely stiff below the belt. He leaned over and found the paper bag just to have something to cover his lap. He retrieved the fifth from the bag and opened the bottle, then knocked back a slug, his first since prison.

"Hell, yeah," she said as he coughed. She swiped the bottle from his hand, her skin soft but cold. She raised the bottle to her lips and tipped it back. She returned the whiskey to him. "So how far we going?" Her eyes widened as she pressed the accelerator closer to the floor.

"Carlisle House. Know it?"

"Shit." She rolled her eyes. "How could I not? It's about five miles on down. Why you going there?"

"Job."

"Seriously?"

He nodded.

"Then you'd better have another hit."

He twisted the fifth in his hand. He wanted it bad, but if he showed up smelling of whiskey, he'd end up back in Ware State before what today would consider a sunset.

"Trust me, if you are going to Carlisle House you are going to need a little 'something something' to take the edge off. There's some weird shit goes on there." Lightning ripped across the sky, and a rage of thunder punctuated her statement. She threw her head back and laughed. "See, I told you. Name's Lucy by the way."

"I don't have much choice about it." He focused on the scene passing on his right. Beyond the glass the world continued to melt.

"There's always a choice." She hit his shoulder, and he shifted to face her. "Carlisle House is about five, no, four miles down this road. Florida line is about forty. How about it? How about the two of us, we just keep going? Keep driving until the Keys? Leave all this bullshit back here?"

"You don't even know my name."

"If that don't matter to me, it shouldn't bother you."

It sounded good, real good. He had another taste of whiskey. Then another. She no longer made any pretense of watching the road. She had turned to face him, continuing to accelerate. He glanced over at the speedometer. Eighty-five. Ninety. Ninety-five.

"Two minutes to being an indentured servant. Twenty to being a free man. Which will it be?" And there it was, bouncing at the back of her beautiful, dirty eyes – the crazy he knew had to be there. He said nothing. He didn't have to. She read it on his face. "Fine, have it your way."

"I can't. I don't want to spend the rest of my life running."

"Ain't that what you're doing? No. Don't answer that. I ain't your fucking therapist."

"Maybe I should get out and walk the rest of the way?"

"Ain't nobody stopping you." The car swerved as she leaned across him and reached for the door handle.

Mark shoved her back. "What is wrong with you?"

"Now who's the pussy?" Lucy laughed and let off the gas. The car slowed, but too late to avoid a dip in the road where enough water had collected to send them hydroplaning. Mark braced his hand against the dash, as he watched the molten world around him spin. Lucy howled in delight as she spun the wheel until the car slid to a stop. Mark's heart beat so hard it drowned out all other sound. He reached over and slid the shift to park.

"Damn, I love that dip," she said and laughed again.

His hand shot to the ignition and he turned the car off. He grabbed the keys, slung his door open and got out. "Hey, wait, what the . . ." she started, but he twisted his torso like when he pitched for his high-school baseball and sent the keys hurtling through the air and past the tree line. The keys landed with a satisfying splash.

"You son of a bitch," Lucy screamed and jumped from the car. She ran to the passenger side, where he had already lowered the front seat and started tugging on the straps of his backpack. She slapped him on the back, on the side and tried for his face, but his hand struck out and caught hers. "What did you do that for?" she asked, her pretty, painted face crumbling.

"I might've just saved your life. And if I didn't, at least I saved mine." He shrugged his backpack on and began wading through the ankle-deep lake that had formed at the low point of the road.

"I am going to find my keys," she raged behind him, "and when I do, I am going to run your sorry ass over."

Without looking back, he held up his right hand and waved. "With all this water, you better keep an eye out for snakes . . . and gators." He kept walking, smiling at the sound of her angry splashing and profanity.

The rain slowed, then stopped as Mark walked the final stretch of road. A fancy stone gateway made him suspect he'd arrived at Carlisle House. A small brass plaque on the right stone pillar confirmed the fact. He turned onto the oak-lined drive that afforded him his first view of the grand house. If Mark had been forced to rely more on his wits rather than his looks, he might have stopped a moment to take the house in, admire its perfect Georgian symmetry, the dual chimneys, the dentilled cornices, the Palladian window in the center of the upper floor. As it was, his mind registered three thoughts: big, fancy and money.

He knew he'd been expected, but hadn't thought someone would be keeping an eye out for his arrival. All the same, a plain middle-aged woman dressed in the kind of maid's uniform you'd see in an old movie stood in the open doorway. She wore her dark hair pulled behind her head in a bun. Her expression soured as if she were surveying a fly-haunted trash pile on an August afternoon. The way she looked at him roused his anger, but he forced himself to block it out, put it away for safekeeping.

"Servants' entrance is in the back. Please avail yourself of it," she said and stepped back inside, closing the door behind her. A ray of sun poked through the clouds, causing every surface it touched to give off steam. Mark shook his head and followed the flagstone path around the back of the house.

II

The lady of the house sat in a shadowed corner of what Mark guessed they'd call the library, given the shelves and the leather-bound books lining them. The maid, called Stella, stood on the other side of the room, watching him.

"You must be Mr Truro." A beam of sunlight picrced the window and illuminated the games table that stood before her, the contrast serving only to help obscure her features.

"Yes, ma'am, I am. These all real?" he asked, pointing at the many titles.

She leaned forward, and the light caught her face. Her expression seemed severe at first, but then she scanned her surroundings and laughed. Her beauty struck Mark silent. Granted she was on the wrong side of forty, old enough to be Mark's mother, but she was, what was the term? Well maintained. No, better than that.

"You're beautiful," Mark said, not thinking he'd spoken it out loud.

"I think you should leave." Stella advanced on him as if she intended to drag him from the room. She had a build like a bulldog; Mark wondered if she just might manage it.

"I meant no disrespect, ma'am," Mark said to his host, lost between his desire to remain out of prison, the high strangeness of the morning and the perennial stirring in his boxers.

"I assure you, none has been taken." The lady of the house shooed Stella away and motioned him to a nearby chair. "Sit. Tell me how you've come to find yourself at the grand and reputedly haunted Carlisle House."

Mark moved to take the seat but then remembered the state of his clothes. "I'm sorry, ma'am. I should probably stand. I'm soaked, and that looks like a real nice chair."

"The chair's disposition has nothing to do with it," she said and smiled, the smile fading as she realized her joke had not registered. "Sit. I insist. And no more of this 'ma'am' nonsense. It makes me feel ancient. My name is Morgan. You may call me Mrs Carlisle if you insist, but I'd rather you call me Morgan."

"Yes, ma'am," he said as he hovered over the chair, debating whether any of this was a test he might have already failed. Mrs Carlisle lowered her face so her mischievous green eyes shone on him. "I mean, Morgan." Stella cleared her throat. "I mean, Mrs Carlisle." He lowered himself into the chair.

"Stella, bring the young man something to drink. Coffee?" she asked him. "Tea?" Mark still tasted the whiskey he had drunk. He licked his lips trying to catch any last trace of it. "Perhaps something stronger?"

"Oh, no, I'm not supposed to drink alcohol."

"Well, there are many things to which 'not supposed to' lends a finer pleasure." She leaned back into the shadow, but Mark imagined he could see her just as clearly. Perhaps his eyes had begun to adjust to the light.

"Maybe a little water?" He peered over his shoulder at Stella to see if it was all right to ask for that.

"A little water it is," Mrs Carlisle said. "Stella, bring the young man a little water. I'll have a little water also with a generous splash of bourbon." She reached out her hand and traced a design on the games table. "Sure I cannot tempt you, Mr Truro?"

A pulse in his manhood told him she did indeed have the power to tempt him. "No. No, thank you."

"Thank you, Stella."

"Of course, Mrs Carlisle." The maid left the room.

"As with everything else in Carlisle House, I inherited Stella as well. She began working for my mother-in-law, the true Mrs Carlisle, at least a decade before my husband and I met. You'll get used to her. I have."

"If you hire me, I'll do my best to please her."

"Oh, my dear boy," Morgan said and laughed. "I am the only one around here you need worry about pleasing. And I am already well pleased with you." Her laughter made him think of a beautiful butterfly being pinned in a box. Mark wondered where in the hell he would have gotten such a pansy thought.

"Yes, the books are indeed real, although, admittedly, I don't think a single one has been opened in decades. Many of them are, I understand, first editions. A fine collection, I'm told. They belonged to my husband's family, as did this house and everything in it. So, yes, I am sure everything you see here is real, but I don't pretend to hold any intellectual or artistic appreciation for them. The day we met, my mother-in-law branded me as an uncouth philistine, and I'm afraid the poor dear was right." Her eyes lost their focus, as if she were reliving the encounter. "At least she didn't have long to suffer me. Cancer took her less than a month after the wedding. And my husband John passed the year after that." There followed several moments of uncomfortable silence. "John's brother, Titus, is the last of the real Carlisles, but he doesn't live here with us. He has a law practice in Jacksonville, so he makes his residence there. It's only Stella and myself now. And Royce, of course. He's the one you've come to replace, but you mustn't let him know. As far as he's concerned, you're here as his assistant."

"You're letting him go?"

"No. Never. Royce is a permanent fixture here at Carlisle House. I owe him a great debt. I consider him family."

"He getting too old for the heavy lifting?"

"Too old? No . . ."

Stella returned with a tray, which held a crystal tumbler of bourbon and water and a plastic glass like the ones from fast-food drive-throughs. She held the tray out so Mrs Carlisle could reach her drink. "Oh, Stella, really. Get that ridiculous cartoon cup out of here and fetch our guest a real glass."

"Beg pardon, but this young man is not a guest. He's the help."

"Odd you should feel so anxious to make that distinction," Mrs Carlisle said, freezing Stella with an icy glare.

"It is for your sake I do." Stella took the plastic cup off the tray and held it out to Mark. "And for your sake as well. Do you want your drink or no?"

"Yes, the glass is fine," he said.

"The glass is ridiculous, and you will remove it from this room, from this house, and you bring Mr Truro a proper glass from which to drink, or you will see how quickly I can draw the line between friend and hired help."

"Yes, *ma'am*," Stella said and turned on her heel.

An unreadable look filled Mrs Carlisle's eyes as she watched Stella leave the room. She raised her eyebrows and ran her tongue over her lower lip. "Where were we?"

"You were telling me about Royce."

"Yes. Royce." She lowered her eyes. "I am afraid you may find Royce's appearance somewhat shocking." A vertical line formed on her brow. "He was badly injured. Burned in a fire we had on the property here." She took a breath and exhaled. "He saved my life, then he went back to save my husband's. He was not as lucky that time." She took a sip of her bourbon. "John died in the fire, and Royce very nearly did himself. I was the only one left *unscathed*, at least

physically. Royce is not an old man, but the injuries he
sustained have caught up with him, left him much less
capable than he would have otherwise been at this age. All
this tragedy. So long ago." She raised her head and stared
into Mark's eyes as if she were searching for gold in a dark
mine. "You weren't even born yet."

Another silence descended on them, this one lasting long
enough to make Mark too uncomfortable to keep quiet. "If
you hire me, I'll do my best to help Royce without hurting
his pride."

"You are already hired."

"I got the job?" Mark asked in true disbelief. "I got here
late, looking like, well, in no fitting shape to meet a lady. I
ask you stupid questions, pissed off—er, sorry . . ."

"Pissing off Stella—" she leaned forward and blinked her
eyes like a happy cat "—clinched the deal. However, you
were hired before I ever laid eyes on you."

"Why are you so willing to take a chance on an ex-con?
You don't even know me."

She tapped a card on the table. "I believe I know you
better than you know yourself. First of all, I know you have
a large diamond hidden beneath all that rough." She held
up a card, and for the first time Mark realized she hadn't
been playing solitaire. This was no normal deck of cards.
"I've been expecting you. I have been anticipating you."
She held up one of the cards. "And here you are." She
started to hand it to him, but snatched it back. "Please don't
take offense at the name on the card. It simply means you
are a young man, unmolded. Ignorant, no," she said and
held up her other hand like a crossing guard, "but *unaware*
of your true potential."

She handed him the card, and he examined it. A guy in a
dress walking off a cliff. "I appreciate the job. I do. But this
here. This ain't me. I don't know what you think you
know . . ."

"I know you've met our Lucy," she said and held up
another card, this one marked as "The Chariot".

"Beg pardon, but that girl is crazy. She's going to get
herself killed the way she drives."

"No need to fear that. Lucy is already dead."

Mark jumped from his chair with such force he knocked it backwards. He leaned over to set it right when Stella returned. "Is everything okay here?" she asked, reading the expression of terror on the young man's face. "Mrs Carlisle, I do wish you would put those devil cards away."

Mrs Carlisle ignored the maid and stood, then crossed the room to a long side table covered with photos in silver and golden frames. "He's had a ride with Lucy."

"Don't be ridiculous. The Bible tells us the dead sleep and knoweth nothing. These ideas you get, they aren't coming from any good place," said Stella.

"Lucy is without question deceased. Sleeping she isn't." Her hand hovered over the several photographs then plucked one up. "You've seen this girl, haven't you?"

Mark felt his stomach drop. He refused to focus on the picture, but he could tell it was the same woman he'd shared a bottle with that very morning. "No, I've never seen her. The woman didn't look nothing like her."

Mrs Carlisle turned the photo back so it faced her. A wry smile came to her lips, and she pulled the picture into an embrace before returning it to its place on the table. She glanced over her shoulder at Stella. "Make sure he gets settled in. And I mean properly." Her eyes followed Mark. "Welcome to Carlisle House. Stella will show you to your room."

"Follow me," Stella said brusquely, and Mark jumped to do as she had commanded.

"Oh, Mr Truro." Mark stopped and turned back to his new employer when she called to him. "I see you are a poor liar," Mrs Carlisle said, as a wicked smile twisted her lips. She tilted her head ever so slightly to the side. "I like quality in a man."

III

Mark welcomed sunset. It had been a hell of a day. Between whatever that was this morning and spending the afternoon pulling out tree stumps with the seriously extra-crispy Royce, his muscles were tired and his spirit was weak.

Maybe in time he'd get used to the sight of the man, and the deep scars would stop making his stomach lurch. At least Royce didn't talk much. He'd left Mark pretty much on his own once he'd shown him around and given him his first task. Still, something about settling in at Carlisle House struck him as worse than prison. At least during his incarceration he had a release date in sight. Here, he felt a gnawing sensation this might be his life from now on, his whole life. What if he'd said yes to Lucy – be she crazy, a ghost, or a trick of the mind? What if instead of going all limp-wristed, he'd reached over and put his hand on her thigh? What if he'd pressed her foot harder against the accelerator?

Dirty and discouraged, Mark climbed the back stairs to his second-floor room. He'd have preferred space in one of the outbuildings or at least a room on the main floor, something with its own exit to the outside, so he could come and go as he pleased. That, however, was not on the menu. He reckoned this room was the only one in the grand house suited to his station in life. He leaned into the sticking door – a plane would take care of that – and switched on the brass lamp, the room's sole source of light. The lamp stood on a battered folding table that took up most of the space between the narrow bed and the door. The bed was a twin, the short kind he'd never manage to stretch out on. Along the wall sat a brown leather club chair with a split in the seat that let the padding poke through. On the bright side, this room had its own bathroom. "En suite" Stella had said, as if it were the closing words of a prayer.

He noticed that his backpack wasn't where he'd left it on the floor at the foot of the bed. Anger burned from his loins into his stomach. *Why the hell would anyone here steal his stuff?* He clenched his fists, ready to knock the holy hell out of everyone in this house, when a knock sounded. He grabbed the knob and yanked the door back. On the other side of the door stood Stella holding a full laundry basket.

She flinched at the sight of his face. "The Missus asked me to launder your clothes for you." She pushed past him and sat the basket on the bed. "Don't get used to it. Your position doesn't come with laundry service." She put jeans, a pair of Goodwill khakis, four T-shirts, six pairs of socks and five pairs of underwear, every stitch he had other than the dirty snap button western shirt and mud-covered jeans he now wore, out on the bed. "The closet is small, but I doubt your wardrobe will tax it. And you got the drawers over there." She nodded toward a small chest in the corner. The battered pink lacquer showed it wasn't intended to hold a grown man's clothes.

"You'll need to clean your own room too. You'll find cleaning supplies in the cupboards over the laundry. Vacuum's in the hall closet. Supper's at six. I don't give a damn about what you like or what you don't. If you're hungry, you'll eat."

Mark relaxed in the face of her hardness. Now wasn't the time to show anger. He'd been blessed with the ability to turn his emotions off and put them into a small box at the back of his brain until he could afford to give them a good airing. "I'm sure I'll like whatever you put on the table," he said and flashed her the smile that hardly ever failed him. "Thank you for doing my laundry."

For a moment he thought he had her, but then her mouth pinched into a tight, hard pucker and she tilted her head back to squint at him through her lashes. "Save the charm for Mrs Carlisle, 'cause it ain't going to work on this old lady. I know the type of man you are. I know what you did to land yourself in jail, and I don't buy this rehabilitation bit the liberals keep trying to sell us. Boys like you, you don't change. You can't change. Don't think you're special. You're not the first or the prettiest to stay in this room, and you sure ain't the scariest. The Missus, she's got a taste for your type, but like the others, you'll go when she's through with you. And I'll be the one shutting the door behind you." Then she grabbed the empty basket and left. Mark stood staring at the open door, running his hand over his face as he stifled the urge to follow the old hag and throw her down the stairs. Instead, he closed the door, quietly, coolly, knowing he'd lull himself to sleep tonight thinking up ways to make the uppity bitch hurt.

He undid his shirt a snap at a time before shrugging it off. He popped the button on his jeans, tugged down the zipper and stepped out of them. Clad only in the second-hand blue boxers he'd pulled from a box of cast-offs the Separate Baptist Church kept in a closet at the fellowship hall, he found his way to the bath. He turned on the water and flipped the valve to activate the shower. The water was going to be good and hot when he stepped under the shower head, and he was going to stand under it a good long time.

Mark hated being caged, but he'd adjusted to it. He'd adjusted to the shit food. He'd adjusted to the smell. He'd adjusted to the lack of privacy and to the assholes who wanted to prove something by trying to beat or sodomize him – no one had managed either. He'd even adjusted to the fags who practically begged him to screw them – when he could offer his sex as currency for something he needed, he'd been willing to oblige. He had never adjusted to the short blast of lukewarm water that counted as a shower in prison though. Despite the creepy burned guy and the bitch of a maid, this was the best set-up he'd had in over four years.

He leaned over the sink and wiped away the steam form-ing on the mirror. He hadn't known his own father, but he reckoned he owed his sperm donor for his broad shoulders and large pectorals. His body showed the tautness it owed to workouts in the prison gym. He'd added bulk to his upper body and hardened his core, but he figured he'd still won the DNA lottery. Before prison, he hadn't realized how he could use his physique as a weapon, both against those who wanted to hurt him and those who just wanted him. He twisted to the side to examine himself from that angle, then tugged off the boxers.

The bathroom appeared to have been remodeled at some point within his lifespan. He felt glad of it, because he hated those claw-foot tubs like his grandmother's house had, the way the shower curtain sucked in against you. He stepped over the edge of the tub and pulled the curtain, the proper kind that stayed the hell away from you, closed. He grabbed the cracked, dry bar of gold soap that had probably been sitting on the holder since before they'd invented dirt, and began to lather up. He let the cascade of hot water rinse away the maid's attitude, the freak's nauseating burns, and the bizarre ride that had landed him outside Carlisle House. His mind slid back to the one pleasant point of his day – meeting Mrs Carlisle herself.

Call me Morgan. Not her exact words, but as good a place as any for a fantasy to start. His hand moved over his left nipple and slid down the hard ridges of his stomach. His manhood rose to meet his touch. He closed his eyes, only to have them flash open as music sounded from his bedroom.

He shut off the water and grabbed a towel, drying himself with prison speed. He wrapped it around his waist and followed the sound of music.

"I hope you find the room adequate for your needs." Mrs Carlisle let the last two words linger on her tongue. She sat reclining against the arm of the club chair, swirling a tumbler filled with two fingers of amber liquid. She had changed into a gauzy white blouse. She didn't wear a bra beneath it. He could see her breasts were large and still much higher than he would have expected on a woman her age. Her areolae showed beneath the sheer fabric. "Yes, they are real, just like the books," she said with a throaty, seductive laugh. She flicked her index in the direction of the music coming from an old-style black boom box. The brass lamp had been pushed to the utmost edge of the table to make room for it. "I know it isn't much, but I thought you might enjoy a little entertainment."

He said nothing, letting his continued silence disarm her. She'd come in here thinking she was in charge. He forced his eyes to focus on hers, not on her breasts, not on her perfect legs, and certainly not on the place between them, where he knew as sure as shooting she was wet and ready for him. He wanted nothing more than to spread her legs and slide himself inside her, but if he'd learned one thing in life it was how to bargain.

"You're a beautiful woman, as beautiful as first light on water, but you hired me for a job. I'm grateful for the work, but I think we should best leave it at that." It was a gamble, and he might find himself out on his ass, but if she bit, it meant he could get more out of her than a short-term lease on the space between her legs.

Her eyes flashed, and a knowing smile rose to her lips. "You're better with pretty words than I'd expected. Maybe I've misread you." She took a sip of her drink. "Do you have a *poetic* nature, Mark?"

"Oh, no ma'am, there ain't nothing poetic about my nature." Her words had almost thrown him, but he managed to reel himself back in. "All the same, that don't mean I'm some toy you use to pleasure yourself and throw out with the rest of the trash when you're done."

"I see you've been chatting with Stella."

"She's told me about the others, yeah."

"Stella thinks she understands the world. She thinks she understands me." She took a long draw of her liquor. "Nonetheless Stella is a creature of her environment. She's never really lived, has never even been more than a hundred miles from Waycross. She isn't like us." Her free hand patted a dark red velveteen bag that had been resting unnoticed by Mark on the arm of the chair. "She isn't capable of seeing beneath the surface of things, the way we can." She grasped the velvet bag and stood. "Let me do a reading for you." She moved to the bed and sat down near its headboard. "Here—" she patted the mattress "—come join me."

She sat her drink on the side table and turned off the music. "Better to concentrate," she said.

As she pulled out the contents of the bag, Mark recognized the "devil cards" she had shown him earlier. "I'm not sure I believe in that stuff," he said, unsure why he felt embarrassed.

"Tell me, do you believe in ghosts?"

"Well, no ma'—" He caught himself. "No, I can't say I do."

"Still you rode with one this morning." She pursed her lips and her face hardened. She appeared to be losing patience with him. "Sit. Worst thing that can happen is you might learn something about yourself." He hesitated, but only for a moment. It felt awkward to sit, wearing nothing but a damp towel, but he gave in to her continued stare. She shuffled the cards and placed the deck before him. "Go ahead, cut them." He touched the deck, almost expecting to feel an electric shock or something, but they were only paper. He cut the deck about a third of the way down, and placed the thinner pile on the bottom. She smiled and dealt three cards.

"This," she said as she pointed at the first, "is your past. The five of swords signifies a dishonorable act leading to a loss of freedom."

Tell me something I don't know, he thought, but held his tongue.

"This one here is your present." She touched the center card picturing an angel blowing a trumpet and bodies rising up from the ground. "Don't let the picture throw you." She held it up to face him. "This card is called 'Judgment', but it simply signifies you have arrived at a point where you are being granted the opportunity to reflect. To decide if you want to carry on down the same path you have been, or make a new start. Become the man you can be." She reached out and patted his hand, but it felt like a touch of encouragement, not an act of seduction. "No matter what, I do hope you will take advantage of your time at Carlisle House to do just that." He sensed something softer, more maternal in the way she looked at him. This short display of tenderness affected Mark in a way her blatant attempts at seduction had not.

"Ready to know your future?" She raised her eyebrows, and he saw an enticing glimmer in her green eyes. "Oh, yes, you will enjoy this one. It's known as 'The Lovers'." She handed the card to him. "It seems as if you are certain to have some romance in your future." Another angel, this time hovering over a naked man and woman. She tilted her head to the side and looked at him through the lashes of her lowered eyelids. "Shall we delve a bit deeper into this?" She took the card from his grasp, letting her soft fingers rub along the back of his hand. Now he felt the electricity he hadn't when touching the cards. She returned the card to the mattress and pulled two others and laid them side by side. "Well, well, well," she said as a crease formed on her brow. "I didn't see this coming."

She pointed to the first new card. A woman sitting with a shield at her side. Mark didn't recognize many symbols, but he did recognize the stick figure cross and circle as meaning "woman". "This is the Empress card. You will forgive me if this sounds egotistical, but as the lady of Carlisle House, I believe this represents me." Her lips hardened into a thin, straight line. "And this is the card that unnerves our poor Stella so. The Devil." Her index and middle finger landed on the man and woman standing before the demon's clawed feet. She lifted her middle finger and traced along the chain binding the two together.

"The chain is symbolic of an unhealthy liaison." She paused, evidently realizing he didn't understand. "An unhealthy coupling or union. It appears I have a rival in my efforts to win your *affections*." She picked up the five cards and added them back in with the others before returning the deck to the dark red bag. "The empress wants nothing more than to help lift you up. Your other interest will only pull you even further down than you have been. She is greedy, this other one, living only for the moment." She stood, suddenly all serious, any hint of flirtation gone.

She reached out and placed her smooth, warm hand along his jaw, lifting his eyes to look directly into hers. "I can make you a different man, a better man than you have been. Yes, there have been others with a potential similar to yours, but, in the end, they proved unworthy. I think you might prove a strong enough vessel for the life I hope to give you."

Mark said nothing. He had no idea what to say. This woman was off her rocker, but in the end, he could use it to his advantage. She lowered her hand. "You should get dressed. I dine alone in my room, but Stella undoubtedly has your meal on the table." She clutched the sack of cards tightly and left him there to wonder just what in the hell he'd gotten himself into.

IV

Mark awoke in the night to the sound of pecking against his
window. Figuring it was some damned night bird, he rose
and flicked on the brass lamp, intending to shoo the pest
away. He slid his feet to the floor as another tap sounded.
No sign of a bird, but he jumped a little as a stone struck the
glass. The window protested as he slid it open and leaned
out. The unseasonably warm December air blew against his
chest. "It's all right," a familiar voice whispered in the shadows. "I forgive you. Come on down."

The cloud covering the moon passed, and the moon's
silver light landed on blonde curls. Lucy. "Come on," she
called with more force. He opened the chest of drawers and
pulled out his clean pair of jeans and a – damn it all –
starched and ironed T-shirt. He stepped into the jeans and
pulled the cardboard-stiff shirt over his head.

He was almost ready to put on his shoes when something
stopped him. An unfamiliar type of fear. He'd faced the fear
of the newly incarcerated. He'd faced the hard guys with
their makeshift weapons. He'd faced the fear of being let out
of prison with nowhere to go, with no one who wanted him.
This felt different though. This fear carried the scent of the
unnatural as it crept up along his spine.

Mark leaned back out his window. "Mrs Carlisle. She
said you're dead."

"God, you are an old woman," Lucy snapped, no longer
making any attempt at remaining concealed. "Do I look
dead to you?" She pulled her shirt over her head and flashed
her tits.

"Shhhhh," Mark hushed her. He felt like a natural-born
fool. "I'll be right down." He pulled on two pairs of socks to
shield his feet from the hand-me-down work boots Royce
the scab had offered him. Mark didn't know it for a fact, but
he figured Royce's feet were as damaged as the parts of him
Mark had seen. It made his stomach churn, but he was still
a beggar . . . for now.

He kept his tread as light as possible as he made his way
down the creaky stairs. In a few days he would learn which

would moan under the pressure of his weight and which would keep their mouths shut. He'd have to hope that if Lucy's caterwauling hadn't awakened the house, a few loose boards wouldn't either.

He eased open the door and made a mental note to oil the screeching spring on the screen door in the morning. Lucy had moved back another ten yards or so from the house by the time he made it outside, and she waved to signal he should follow her before running off in the direction of the barn. He moved to follow her, going quickly enough to keep her in sight, but not running. He wasn't going to give her that. There were a hell of a lot of women Mark could see himself running from, but he hadn't yet met one he'd go chasing after. He took his time. He let her wait for him.

He watched as she slid through a narrow opening of the barn's door. He slowed his pace, taking measured steps as a dim light spilled through the entrance. He came to the door and opened it a bit wider, just wide enough for his shoulders to pass. On the ground she'd spread a coarse and dirty blanket. The light came from an electric camping lantern sitting on the floor nearby. Lucy lay prone and naked on the blanket, propped up on her elbows, her knees in the air, legs spread and welcoming. "Ever do it with a dead girl?" she asked and pushed her perfect tits a little higher.

As she arched her back, any sense of supernatural dread Mark's gut had clung to went south with a good portion of his blood supply.

"Well, sugar, do you want it, or have you worn yourself out poking the cobwebs out of the old lady's hooch?"

In an instant his shirt was off and falling to the floor. He undid his jeans and let them fall around his ankles, not even kicking them off before he lowered himself on top of her. She leaned in to kiss him, but he held himself up on one arm, using his other hand to turn her face away as he mounted her. He was bigger than most, and he did what he always did when giving it to someone who'd come begging for it. She felt moist, but so very tight. He thrust it in fast and hard, loving the sound of her sharp intake of breath followed by a cry that he used his hand to muffle. He rode her without mercy, but she seemed to enjoy it, to take pleasure in his roughness. Soon she began bucking up under him, whispering obscenities at him that only made him drive himself deeper.

The world stopped as he released his seed into her. He lay quivering on top of her for a few moments as the sound of his heart blended with her labored breath.

V

"Has she tried her Tarot bullshit on you yet?" Lucy asked, as she pulled her shirt back over her head. "The cards?" she asked when Mark stared blankly at her.

"Yeah," he said and nodded.

"Let me guess," she said, as she bent over to retrieve her jeans. "She's the Empress," she rattled off in a flat bored tone. "You prove yourself worthy, and she will make a big man out of you." She closed the zipper. "So, am I right?"

"Who the fuck are you?" he asked, angry she knew more about what was happening to him than he did. "How do you know what she's been telling me?"

"Language," she said with mock shock. "I know what she's been telling you, 'cause you ain't the first cowboy we've had the pleasure of sharing. And most of them are a hell of a lot more talkative than you are. I've heard it over and over. She always starts out building up your expectations, then after a few months, sometimes only a few weeks, she decides for whatever reason you don't measure up."

"Measure up to what?"

"Listen. It's hard to explain. Suffice it to say the bitch is crazy. She believes all kinds of paranormal shit, like me being a ghost and stuff."

"So?"

"So I think she is trying to bring back the spirit of her dead husband. She's been auditioning young bucks for a suitable body to shove him into." She put her fingers in her hair and pulled them like a comb through her curls.

"That's bullshit," he said and stood, yanking his jeans up.

"Maybe it is, maybe it isn't. You'll see the signs yourself soon enough. She took the last guy for a field trip to the Carlisle mausoleum before sending him packing."

"Mrs Carlisle showed me your picture. At least it looked like you. She is convinced you are this Lucy's ghost."

"Yeah, well, the great lady is also convinced she can stuff her dead husband into your hide. As far as who I am, just 'cause I let you fuck me doesn't mean I'm ready to share all my secrets. Play along with me, and I'll make it worth your while."

"Thanks, but I ain't big into seconds," he lied. His body already urged him to have another go, this time slower if not easier. "What if I don't want to play your game? What's to keep me from dragging you into the house and showing Mrs Carlisle you ain't nothing but flesh and blood?"

"Well, to start with the rape charges I'd be obliged to file against you. Your ass will be back in the pen before sunrise." She took a step back, taking a fighting stance in case it proved necessary. "That's right, you fucker, you have met more than your match, so don't even think of crossing me." She drew a breath and calmed her fire. "Now you've asked the wrong questions, why don't you stop and think real hard about what the right question might be."

He felt his fists clench. Part of him wanted to turn her into the ghost she'd been pretending to be, but he might find a way to turn all this to his benefit. "What's in it for me if I do go along?"

She smiled. "That's right. Now you are thinking." She stopped talking at the sound of rustling in the loft above. An owl swooped down and snatched a mouse from the far end of the barn, catching it up in a bloody rapture. She reached over and extinguished the lantern, plunging the space into full dark.

VI

"She held the title of Miss Georgia, you know, when she first met Mr Carlisle." Royce's words surprised him. Mark had been working at Carlisle House for going on six months, and Royce had never before said anything to him that wasn't directly related to his duties. "Of course that figures back before you were even born."

Mark followed Royce's gaze to where Mrs Carlisle stood before an easel, balancing a palette on her left hand and holding a brush in her right. Art was as important to Mrs Carlisle as it had been to her husband. Over the last several months he and Lucy had continued to meet in secret. At first, sex had been a major component in the time they spent together, but as the novelty of knowing each other waned, Lucy put more and more time into tutoring him about all things John Carlisle. By now he was pretty much an expert in the dead man's habits and tastes.

Mark tuned the radio in his room to a classical music station. Mrs Carlisle rewarded him by leaving twenty-year-old CD recordings of operas and symphonies in his room. At Lucy's prompting, Mark had started asking Mrs Carlisle about the paintings and lithographs lining Carlisle House's walls. She seemed thrilled to take him under her wing, sharing books filled with pictures of paintings and sculptures. Mark feigned interest in the masterpieces as expertly as he feigned his continued ardor after months of careful, vanilla intercourse with her.

From his vantage, Mrs Carlisle stood in profile. A warm breeze played with her hair and caused the skirt of her white chiffon dress to flutter. An expensive-looking white dress struck him as the wrong choice for messing around with paint, but he realized she was putting herself on display. The way she dressed, the way she held herself in the late-morning light, this was the work of art she had composed. The painting was a mere prop. "Mrs Carlisle is still a beauty."

"I'm glad a young man such as yourself can appreciate that." Royce patted Mark's shoulder. Mark forced himself not to cringe at the touch. "She's always been such a fragile person, and she has already lost so much."

Mark fixed his full attention on the older man. He tried to avert his eyes when talking with Royce, but over the last several months he had gotten more used to the sight of him. Even though the late spring had already turned steamy, Royce wore a long-sleeved shirt, long pants and even gloves. A Georgia Bulldog cap covered his head. Mark's eyes went to Royce's face then fell back to the ground near the other man's feet. "What are you trying to say?"

In his peripheral vision, Mark saw Royce's shoulders slump forward. "I'm saying you are a young man, a very young man. We've had a lot of your kind – and I mean no offense by that – through here over the last several years. The others, they came and went, but she seems to be taken with you."

"So what if she is?" Mark watched Mrs Carlisle as she did everything she could to catch the light in a way that showed her to her best advantage. "How is it any of your business?"

"It's my business, because I care about her."

Mark laughed. "Don't kid yourself into thinking you would ever stand a chance with her." He realized the scarred man counted as too easy a target. So easy he couldn't even take pleasure in his own cruelty. Worse, Mark could gain nothing by antagonizing him. "I'm sorry. I didn't mean it." Truth was he couldn't give a shit, but Lucy and he were too close to their goal at this point to risk making enemies.

"No," Royce said, shuffling uncomfortably in the intensifying sunlight, "you're right. She could never love me. Not like this. That wasn't what I meant anyway. What I meant is I have worked for the Carlisle family since I was a teenager. John and I pretty much grew to manhood together, and I don't think I am wrong in saying we were more than employer and employee. We were true friends. John's happiness mattered to me. Look at me," he commanded and whipped off his cap to show his damaged face, the holes where ear lobes once were, the wispy white hair growing in odd patches on his head. "This is a testament to my feelings for the man. If giving my life would have saved him, I would have made the sacrifice without a second thought."

Shit, Mark thought to himself, *this toasted fag was in love with Mr Carlisle.*

But Mark only nodded. "I see that."

"Mrs Carlisle mattered to him, so she matters to me." He returned the cap to his head. "I think she's falling in love with you. I got no problem with that. I got no problem with you, either, as long as you are serious about what you are doing with her. Age-wise, there is a gap of twenty-five, maybe thirty years between you two. It may not matter to you now. Hell, it might even be a bit exciting for you. The woman there, she's beautiful and vital, but none of us can escape time, even her."

Mark focused on her, pretending to take Royce's words to heart, pretending any union between them would last longer than it took to line his pockets with some of her sweet cash.

"I'm not saying you can't have your bit on the side. God knows John had more than a few." Mark's head jerked back a little as he put together the pieces of Lucy's past she had been keeping from him. That explained how his co-conspirator (a word she had taught him) came to look so much like the dearly departed sister of John and Titus. "Mrs Carlisle, she knows how to overlook an occasional straying, as long as she knows your heart belongs solely to her. If you can't give her that, you need to move on. You've finished up the time you have to stick on here. If you plan on leaving, this would be the moment."

"Royce?" Both men stood to attention at her call. She began walking toward them.

"Yes, Mrs?"

She held the brush and palette out to Royce. "You'll see the brush is cleaned and everything is stored away for me?"

"Of course."

"Thank you," she said and rewarded him with a warm smile. "Also, if you two aren't too busy this afternoon, could I steal Mark from you? I'd like him to drive me over to the cemetery."

"There's nothing here that can't wait. You have a good visit and remember me to John."

"I certainly will." She tilted her head, and reached out to touch Mark's sleeve.

VII

Other than when Morgan offered the occasional direction, they drove the ten or so miles to the cemetery in silence. Mark watched her in the rear-view mirror. She had changed from the filmy white dress she had worn that morning into a black one. Her mood seemed to have undergone a similar change. That she struggled with a big decision showed in her distant eyes. She seemed careless regarding the small purse she brought with her, but she clutched a brown paper bag like she worried it would try to escape her at the first opportunity.

"Pull over here on the left," she said. Mark did as she commanded, pulling the car into the shade provided by an ancient live oak. At the point where he idled the car, a path began, which cut through lesser stones and led to an enormous granite mausoleum. Despite its distance from the drive, he could easily make out the Carlisle name carved over its entrance. He set the emergency brake, and hopped out of the car to open her door for her.

The worry in her face melted as he opened her door and stepped aside. "Your bag looks kind of heavy. Can I help you with it?"

She kept a firm grip on the bag, but grinned at him. "*May* I help you with it. We've covered this many times before. When the world judges a man it does so first by his appearance, next by his language."

"I'm sorry," he responded automatically. In truth he wanted nothing more than to take the sack and help her put it in a place where she wouldn't need arms to carry it. "I'm trying to learn. I'm trying to better myself. I don't want you to feel ashamed of me."

Her face softened and her eyes gave off a warm glow. "I could never feel ashamed of you." She shook her head and handed him the bag. "Consider how much you have learned, how much you have grown in a matter of months. You are no longer the waterlogged lost boy you were when I first laid eyes on you. You've made great strides toward becoming the man I've hoped you would become. The man I believe deep down you *want* to be." He offered her his free hand and helped her out of the car. She took his arm as they walked to the crypt. At the mausoleum door, she stopped and retrieved a large skeleton-type key from her purse. She introduced the key into the lock, but didn't move to turn it. "Do you trust me, Mark?"

"Of course I do."

"No, I mean truly trust me." She paused. "Do you trust me with your life?"

Like hell I do. He shifted the bag, trying to weigh its contents and determine what weapons the crazy bitch might have brought along on this field trip. He knew being bat-shit crazy could help make a person strong enough to lift a car, but her delicate frame didn't cause him too much worry. Risk weighed against desired outcome, he nodded to her. "Yes. I trust you. Even with my life."

She surprised him by going up on her toes and landing a passionate – no, loving – kiss on his lips. She tasted of sour mash and sweet mint mouthwash. "I need ten minutes," she said and turned the key. It turned smoothly in the lock, with no sound of protesting metal. The ease with which the lock turned told him she spent a lot more time in there than he had realized. She took the bag from his arm. "Take a short stroll, then come join me."

She leaned into the counterbalanced door, and it opened at the slight pressure. He watched through the small, barred window that opened in on the mausoleum as she sat the bag on a large stone table situated in its center. She opened it and pulled out a black cloth, which she immediately used to cover the opening.

Mark headed further down the path that had led them to the Carlisle crypt. About fifteen or so yards away, he stopped at a grave marked by a stone bench. He checked his beat-up plastic watch and sat. The back of the mausoleum was clearly visible from his seat, and he studied the stained-glass window that took up a good portion of the rear wall. White lilies and a cross draped with a deep blue material. That the name "Carlisle" showed backward told him the colored glass was meant to be viewed from the inside. Seemed a bit of a waste to him.

Ten minutes passes slowly when you are waiting for a crazy woman who may or may not be planning on trussing you up and carving you like a Thanksgiving turkey. He checked the time another twenty, maybe twenty-five times. Strange, he had been waiting anxiously, wanting to get whatever bullshit she had in mind over with, but when his timepiece said it was time to move, his legs felt leaden.

He made his way back around to the mausoleum's entrance. He almost knocked, but thought better of it. If she were prepared to do something weird to him, better to keep the element of surprise on his side. He pressed against the door. It opened easily. Morgan stood naked and vulnerable toward the rear of the crypt. Her hands were held up in the air, a little above the level of her head. Her eyes were closed and her lips moved silently, like she was praying or something. "Come in," she said out loud and opened her eyes.

Mark stuck his head in first, surveying his surroundings before committing to entering. He saw the weight in the bag had consisted mostly of candles. Black ones. White ones. A single red one in a brass holder glowed from the table at the center of the room. "Please come in," she said. He heard the worry in her voice. He could hear she feared that at the last moment he would prove himself unworthy by bolting.

He stepped over the threshold and closed the door behind him. The flickering light of the combined candles played across her face as any sign of worry faded. "I knew it. I knew you were the one." She took a few steps forward until she stood next to the table. She held her arms out to him. "Kiss me."

He hesitated a moment as his eyes adjusted to the light. The single red candle sat in the center of a design he recognized but didn't really understand. A five-point star in a circle. She had drawn it using a substance he well

understood – blood. He knew it was magic, the devil
worship stuff. For a second he almost thought better of
continuing, but she called to him again. "Kiss me." He
realized something in the witch crap turned him on. He
stepped up to face her, and leaned in to place his lips on
hers. "No," she said, reaching up to put her right hand on
the top of his head. She braced herself against the table
with the left.

"Kiss me." She applied a gentle pressure, until he found
himself kneeling before her. He pressed his face against her
stomach and breathed in her perfume. "Kiss me. Kiss me.
Kiss me." Each time she repeated the words, they came
with an increased sense of urgency. She spread her legs. He
lowered himself until the musk of her sex reached him. He
leaned in to answer her feverish demand, and only then did
she release him. He felt himself lost in desire. She had envel-
oped his senses. He bowed there before her in full
submission, a type of ecstasy he'd never allowed himself
before. There was nothing but her. He knelt before her,
oblivious to the sensation of the cold stone floor grinding
itself into his knees. He didn't care about the scent of blood
that had until this moment competed with this feminine
musk. His mind dimly registered a cracking sound before
everything fell black and silent.

VIII

"I don't see how it is you still think you should get half."
Mark leaned back on the rough woolen blanket. "The bitch
could've killed me."

This was the first time he and Lucy had done it together
in months. Neither had to tell the other this was a farewell
fuck. "Well, let's see. First, because it was my idea, and
second, 'cause it should all belong to me anyway. You figured
out yourself I'm the great John Carlisle's bastard
daughter."

"Can a female be a bastard?"

"Cross me, and you will find out." She stood and dressed
with a businesslike speed.

IX

When he'd come to in the crypt, when he saw her standing over him, the bloodied brass candlestick in her hand, when she asked him his name, he knew damn well he'd better answer "John". Over the last couple of months, he'd been pretending her spell had worked, that it was now John looking out through his eyes. Since the visit to the crypt, he'd shared Morgan's bed, a fact that made his last visit with Lucy a hell of a lot more difficult to manage.

His new gold watch showed a little after midnight when he crept through the back door. In Morgan's eyes, he ruled as the man of the house, but he continued using the back staircase, since he had long since learned which would creak under his weight and which held firm. He made his way softly down the long hall to where the door to Morgan's room stood ajar. He eased it open and entered.

"Where have you been?" Her voice came from a chair in the room's darkest corner. He sensed she had been crying.

He felt he had been born to play this scene. He went to her and knelt before her. "I couldn't sleep, so I went for a walk across the fields." Her shoulders heaved as she burst out with a round of heavy sobs. He leaned into her and pulled her into his arms. "I've been thinking," he whispered into her ear. "I've been thinking about us." Her tears stopped cold and her body went rigid in his arms. He loosened his grip and leaned back.

"*What* have you been thinking about us?" She began trembling. "I thought it would be different this time. Now that she's gone."

Mark was taken aback, wondering for a moment if she had somehow picked up on his affair with Lucy. *When in doubt, deny.* "There is no 'she'. There's only the two of us." His eyes had adjusted to the light, and he could see her face smooth at his words. "We know we are husband and wife, but everyone else, they're going to talk behind our backs. Say dirty, unfair things about us. About you. I don't want to spend our lives living in shadow. I want to take you back out into the world. I want to bring life back into this house.

Parties. Big ones. The kinds we used to have. But we won't have a place in respectable society, unless we do the respectable thing."

"What are you saying?" she asked breathlessly, leaning forward toward him.

"Marry me, Morgan."

She flung her arms around him. "What about the Carlisle name? The family name has always been so important to you."

"My brother has no children."

"Well there's Cristina," she corrected him. "But you might not know. She came after . . ."

"I meant male children." *How the hell had Lucy failed to pass on that useful bit of info?* Luckily, Morgan seemed satisfied with her own rationalization. "We were never blessed with children of either sex. Regardless of what we do, the name dies with Titus anyway. How about it, Morgan, will you marry me . . . again?"

"Oh," she said, her voice breaking. Even in this dim light he could follow the tracks of the tears she shed. This time the waterworks were due to happiness. "Yes, my dear John."

Women.

"Yeah, about that. You'd better get used to calling me Mark."

X

A town car had been waiting for Mark at Jacksonville airport, ready to drive him all the way back to Waycross. He wasn't sure who had ordered it, probably the cruise line. Until the moment Mark saw the liveried driver holding up a sign with his name, it hadn't occurred to him he might even parlay Morgan's accident at sea into a payout from the cruise company as well. Seemed as if her tumbling over the railing was going to be the gift that kept on giving.

The driver made no attempts at small talk. Once or twice Mark could almost sense the man gearing up to express his condolences. He obviously recognized Mark and knew his story. The reporters had piled on top of each other to report on the tragic ending to his honeymoon. Pulling up in front of Carlisle House, Mark felt a thrill to realize it now all belonged to him, or soon would. Morgan had made no will. He had made damned sure of that fact before they set foot on ship. He was no lawyer, but even he knew under Georgia law, with no will in place, everything she owned went to her nearest living relative. He was that lucky guy.

The driver stopped the car before the main entrance, and hurried to open Mark's door. Mark suppressed a smile. He could get used to this.

The driver followed behind him carrying the three suitcases, his and the two crammed full of Morgan's crap. Stella opened the front door. "Welcome home, Mr Truro." *No mention of the servant entrance this time, huh?* He ignored her and headed straight to the library, which had until days ago remained Morgan's sanctuary. He made a beeline for the liquor cabinet and filled himself one of the fancy cut crystal tumblers. He downed the drink and a second, then threw the glass into the fireplace, where it smashed into a thousand tiny shards. He heard the town car pull away.

A tall man with steel-gray hair and mustache, thickset but handsome, strode into the room and held out his hand. "Titus Carlisle," he said, as Mark mechanically shook the newcomer's hand. "I am so sorry to meet under these circumstances." Mark recognized him as John's younger brother. Titus hadn't been able to make it to the wedding they'd held right in this very room, but he had demonstrated his goodwill and acceptance of the union by pulling a few strings and arranging for the county registrar to come to Carlisle House to issue the marriage license. A friend of Titus had even come to perform the ceremony.

Mark put on one of his better performances. He even added a twitch to his eye to enhance his stricken appearance. "I . . . I . . ." Mark let his words die away and collapsed sobbing into Titus's arms.

"Dear God, you are a pussy," a familiar voice sounded

behind him. Titus pushed him away, and Mark turned to see Lucy. "Hey, Daddy," she addressed Titus.

"Hello, Cristina."

"What in the hell is going on here?" Mark could feel his pulse pounding in his temples.

Stella came into the room with a broom and dustpan. "Stella," Titus said and laughed. "Leave it. You should finish your packing."

"I've been taking care of Carlisle House for over thirty years, I'm not going to leave it a mess on my last day." She swept up the shattered tumbler and dumped the glass in a can Morgan kept near the desk.

"Go on and finish your packing," Titus said, placing his hand on the maid's shoulder. "The town car is returning for you as soon as he fills his tank." The two fought a silent battle of wills. "I'll see this gets emptied. I promise."

"All right, Mr Carlisle. But I need to say goodbye to your brother before I go."

"As if I'd let you leave without doing that," Royce said, entering the room. He no longer wore his worn work clothes. Instead, he wore a form-fitting black suit and fedora. Stella crossed to him, and he embraced her. "I don't know how I could have survived all these years without you."

Mark collapsed into the same chair Morgan had been sitting in when he first laid eyes on her. "You're John Carlisle."

"That's right." He walked up to Mark and extended his hand. Mark couldn't even imagine taking it. "No? All right then."

"I don't understand any of this."

"Of course not. How could you?" John pulled up a chair and sat directly before him. "I warned you my wife was a fragile woman. I learned that first hand." He wiggled his fingers before Mark's face.

Mark looked over the burned man's shoulder at the woman he had known as "Lucy". She crossed the room and picked up the picture Morgan had showed him his first day here. "It's a trick of DNA I resemble her so. If you look closely, you'll see I'm not nearly as perfect as she was."

"You are every bit as beautiful, my dear niece," John said, glancing over his shoulder at her. He turned back to Mark. "I'm afraid it's my sister's beauty that lies at the root of all this. My wife you see—" he paused "—she grew jealous of Lucy. Morgan made Lucy's life so unbearable she moved out of the main house and into one of the worker's houses on the estate. Even this didn't help. Morgan began to imagine an unnatural liaison between me and my little sister."

His face hardened at the blank expression Mark's showed. "Incest, Mr Truro. She believed I was having sex with my own sister. She set fire to the house where Lucy slept. Lucy died, and, well—" He held his hand up before his face. 'This happened to me while trying to save her. When my dear wife saw my disfigurement, her mind created the character of Royce and decided I had died."

"You should have put her away," Mark said weakly, still trying to figure out what role he played in all this.

"My wife was fragile. She was born fragile. But she was born rich."

"Why does that matter to you. You Carlisles have plenty of your own money."

"That is the well-maintained myth."

"We've been scraping by since the end of Prohibition," Cristina said and laughed. "Isn't that right, Daddy?"

"Well, it's a bit of an exaggeration, but it is fair to say the dowry Morgan's father paid us so that his daughter could enjoy the respectability of the Carlisle name kept us afloat until the old man passed on himself, and she came into the rest of the fortune. But the money came with the stipulation that we never do anything that might impugn Morgan's family name."

"Her dad knew she was nuts," Cristina said, then pouted. "So he put it in writing – should Morgan be institutionalized, and the language around that term was very loose, we'd lose all access to her wealth. We covered up the fire to keep her out of the loony bin. Claimed Lucy caused it."

"You could kill Morgan, but you couldn't lock her up."

"Since you are getting the picture, my boy, we'll toss in the frame for free." Titus crossed to the window and pulled the sheer aside. "Ware County's finest has been alerted you have returned. I'm afraid you've got a lot of evidence against you. I'm sure the jury is going to shudder at the thought of how you used Morgan's weak mind against her. Seducing her. Luring her into an illicit affair."

"The coaxing it must have taken on your part to get a recluse like poor Aunt Morgan to go out on the high seas."

"And to pass yourselves off as newly-weds of all things, a scam you continued to perpetrate even after the unfortunate incident. A little free legal advice – that might prove your best bid for an insanity plea."

"I was shocked, horrified to learn what had been going on right under my nose," John said with a chuckle. "If it had ever occurred to me that such things were taking place, I would have had you removed without hesitation. However, a loving husband often doesn't see what he doesn't want to see. Like I didn't want to see Morgan whoring with the long line of convicts she paraded through her bed."

"Of course the most damning bit of evidence is the new will you had Morgan file before your little *honeymoon* trip. A will setting aside two hundred and fifty thousand dollars for you. Certainly not a lot of money to a generous woman like Morgan, but enough for a loser such as yourself to consider killing for."

Mark sat up, beginning to see a hole he could slip through. "She had no will. I made sure of that."

"Careful sharing that titbit. Definite grounds for premeditation. Yes, there is a will all right. I drew it up myself, and I have correspondence between Morgan and myself where I warned her against informing you of your inclusion in the document."

"Forged."

"Prove it," Cristina said, reaching out to ruffle his hair.

"What can I say, in spite of the glowing reports I'd received from my own brother regarding you and your rehabilitation, I had a presentiment, a bad feeling, about you."

Mark sat back defeated. "Why me? It sounds like you had a lot of chances to pull this off."

"Because, sugar," Cristina purred, "you were the first one pretty enough to catch her and dumb enough to get caught."

LOVE, SUGAR

Tiffany Trent

I hadn't seen my aunt Neveah in many years. I remembered her as a shy, mousy thing, given to sudden outbursts of exuberance about subjects that bored most people to tears. This was, of course, due to her being the head librarian at the local university.

I can't say I was always fascinated, but as I grew older and fell in love with books, especially the making of them, I respected her a bit more and enjoyed whatever bits of wisdom she wished to dispense.

There came a time, though – does it always come? – when our family fell apart, as the elder members passed on and we younger ones had to fend and scrape for ourselves. My mother and father were gone by the time I reached thirty. My grandmother, having survived to see most of her children except Neveah die, passed on a year or two after them.

It was at about that time that Neveah disappeared.

Not literally, you understand. She had moved to be with my grandmother in Tupelo, Mississippi, in her final days. Grandma still lived alone in the antebellum home our ancestors had built there long before the war. I had only visited twice – once as a small child and then again as an adult. Grandma loved to travel and preferred to visit us rather than have us visit her. For some reason, it was hard to keep a clear picture of the house in my mind. It seemed to be constantly changing. It was a giant rambling plantation house, surrounded by live oaks, and was exceptionally creepy.

Grandma willed the house to Neveah, and after that I didn't see my aunt and heard very little from her, except for brusque Christmas cards that looked like they'd been in the attic since the forties and bore a brief signature, nothing more. She never answered the phone when I called.

I was worried about her, but I had my own problems. The annual card proved at least that she was alive.

Then, even the Christmas card stopped.

And one March night, the phone rang.

"Miss Serena," a male voice said. His dràwl startled me. After living so long in Maine, I'd lost all but the faintest traces of my Southern accent, and it had been a long time since I'd heard anyone speak that way.

I held the phone to my ear, entranced.

"Hello? Miss Serena?" he asked again. His voice crackled across the line as if it might fade away to nothing.

"Yes?"

"I'm afraid you're needed here in Tupelo. Your aunt, Miss Neveah—"

"Has something happened?" I interrupted. It was the phone call I was dreading but knew would come at some point. I was her last surviving relative, after all.

"Just please come, Miss Serena," he said. And then the phone went dead.

I hit redial immediately, of course. And just as immediately got the automated message telling me the number had been disconnected.

"What in the ever-living hell?" I muttered to myself. I wasn't sure if I was cursing because of the message or because I'd been disconnected from that voice too soon. The remnants of his accent still hummed in my ears like bees.

Needless to say, I took the first flight to Tupelo I could book. Self-employment has its perks, I suppose. I hung a sign on the door, alerted my online customers, and took off. I wasn't sure whether I was packing for a funeral, but I brought the only suit I still owned just in case. Bookbinders have little need for fancy clothes.

I held on to the sound of that voice on the phone all the way to Tupelo. I went to the house without even bothering to get a hotel. I assumed the voice had meant for me to do that.

The Voice.

I had to shake my head at myself for that, but I didn't have a name to go by. He'd never said and I'd never gotten a chance to ask. I wondered about him – the way he'd said Neveah's name with such urgency and respect, such . . . adoration.

Was there perhaps a compelling reason why Neveah had had little contact over the years? I'd always imagined her in that big, empty house alone and been a little angry at her for isolating herself. Grandma wouldn't have wanted or expected that.

But I was mostly hurt by her silence. I had once, just after I graduated from bookbinding school and was starting my business, come down and helped her with some of the old books in the house. It had been the first time I'd been there since childhood.

It was dark and dusty. The humidity – Neveah was too old-fashioned to go in for air conditioning – had done a number on the library. I scolded her a bit for that, because as a former librarian, she ought to have known better.

"You need to get this room temperature-controlled," I'd said, wiping a finger down a moldy leather binding.

"Everything must stay as it was," Neveah said, almost under her breath.

I'd heard what she'd said, but the way it had sounded I'd tried to get her to explain it.

"What do you mean?"

She looked at me and said, "Just do what you can, but I'm not changing anything in the house. And neither will you, when your time comes."

"My time?" I'd laughed. "I'm never coming here to live, if that's what you mean."

Neveah's expression had hardened. I'd never seen her look so stern. "You will. You won't have a choice."

We'd argued then, which had never happened before. I

suppose that was the beginning of the cooling of our relationship.

Now, here I was, standing in front of Belle Reve ten years later, and I wondered if she was gone.

The winter breeze, warmer than anything I'd experienced since leaving home, stirred the Spanish moss swaying from the live oaks that surrounded the house. I just stood there for long moments, drinking in the sight of its chipping columns and shuttered old windows, hating and loving it all at once. A movement off to my left, over where the family cemetery lay, drew my gaze.

At first, I thought I was in some sort of waking dream because I watched either an astronaut or a ghost walk slowly through the cemetery and out into what looked like a golden cloud. Then I saw the white boxes. Bees.

Ugh. Neveah had allowed someone to keep bees at Belle Reve? I shook my head.

A cough came from the veranda. I whipped around, and realized that a man in a dark suit had been sitting there the whole time. He passed a hand through his thinning hair nervously and stood as I approached. I tried not to let the fact that my heart was on my tongue show in my face as I climbed the steps with my luggage.

He made an unsuccessful attempt to help me, then fell back, as I muscled my way up onto the veranda with my suitcase. Finally, when I was able to extricate myself from the tangle of bags, he stuck out his hand and shook mine limply.

"Bartholomew Levay, at your service," the man said. I noticed, as I hadn't when I'd first seen him, that his suit swallowed him utterly and ironically (or so it seemed to me) and sported pinstripes.

I also found myself exceptionally disappointed and relieved at once. This man was not the one with The Voice.

Before I could introduce myself or ask why he was waiting on me, he said, "I am the executor of your aunt's estate and her lawyer."

Ah. That.

"Care to have a seat?" He gestured at a wicker chair across from the one where he'd been sitting. Though it was

March, all we needed was a tall pitcher of pale lemonade to make the Deep Southern picture complete.

Instead, a frail mosquito indulged me by whining in my ear. I smacked at my neck and sighed.

"I'm very sorry for your loss, Miss Serena. Miss Neveah was quite well loved by those who knew her."

If the last few years of communications had been any indication, I'd guess the list of people who knew her was about as long as my pinkie.

"Mm hm," I said.

"I'm here because Miss Neveah's last will and testament has very specific instructions regarding Belle Reve that must be executed to the letter." His head was sweating. He took out a hanky and wiped it across his bald spot, which had the unfortunate effect of catastrophically destroying his comb-over.

I wanted to giggle, but I knew it would most likely make me sound hysterical.

"Instructions?" I echoed instead.

"You are to inherit Belle Reve and the grounds. I think you already knew that. Miss Neveah mentioned something to that effect."

"I don't want—" I began.

Levay held up a hand. "Forgive me, but it doesn't really matter what you want. You are Miss Neveah's heir."

I folded my arms across my chest. "Well then, I'll just sell it."

"You can't."

"What?" I asked. The mosquito was back. I slapped again.

"You can't sell it until you've spent at least a consecutive month in the house of your own free will." He twitched, as if he'd heard distant gunfire.

"A month?" I really couldn't be away from my business that long. Customers were few and far between. I'd anticipated a week and had several projects on hold with understanding customers, but I couldn't afford to lose a month's salary just sitting around this place. I certainly couldn't move my entire workshop down here just for a month.

"You can imagine how much Belle Reve is worth," Levay said.

"No, I've really no idea."

"All told, nearly a million. Surely you could endure a month for a million?" Levay asked.

It felt like he was bribing me.

"Is someone besides Neveah putting you up to this?" I asked.

He swallowed, mopped his pate again, and shook his head. "Not at all, ma'am. Just pointing out the facts."

I couldn't help thinking of that Voice again, wondering if he might have something to do with it.

"Do you happen to know if my aunt had a . . . companion?" I asked. "Companion", for lack of a better word.

"My clients' personal affairs aren't my business."

Spoken like a true lawyer.

"So the answer is yes then," I said. "Why didn't she just will the place to him?"

Levay looked distinctly uncomfortable, but said only, "I imagine she wanted to keep Belle Reve in the family."

He lifted a heavy key ring onto the table, but his hand hovered over it like a pale spider. "Here are the keys to Belle Reve. You are only to have them if you agree to stay for the required time, and then only when you've entered the house and have gotten settled."

"You want me to agree now?"

His hand fell over the keys and they jangled. "That's the only way I can release these to you. Per Miss Neveah's instructions."

I pushed back from the table and walked toward the edge of the veranda. I leaned against one of the columns, winding my arm around it. I looked out over the live oaks and swaying moss, the magnolias and rattling palmettos. The grounds had always been immaculately kept, and they seemed not to have changed much. I wondered how long it would take for it all to become overgrown and return to the swamp that surrounded it. The thought chilled me deeper than the Maine winters to which I'd become accustomed.

I looked out beyond the cemetery where Neveah would soon be resting along with the rest of my maternal clan. That too would be overgrown one day with no one to tend it. Beyond the cemetery, the golden cloud of bees was zipping in the March breeze. I knew little about beekeeping, but it seemed a bit early for them to swarm. Maybe that wasn't what they were doing. The beekeeper moved among them.

I turned to Levay. "Who keeps my aunt's bees?"

"I beg your pardon?" Levay said. He got up from where he'd been sweating against his wicker chair.

I gestured toward the white shadow under the oaks.

Levay squinted, shading his eyes. The sun really wasn't that strong. "I don't see anything."

"You don't see the beekeeper out there in that cloud of bees?"

"All I see is the cemetery and the old oaks, miss."

I sighed. "You should probably have your eyes checked, then."

He wiped his head down again before he said, "Be that as it may, you still haven't given your answer. Will you stay or shall I move forward with the trusteeship for the next of kin Miss Neveah listed after you?"

I thought about it. The next person in line was my ten-year-old cousin, whose mother had died in a car accident when she was very small. The house would sit for eight years waiting for her, and what would an eighteen-year-old do with this house? Of course, she would sell it! I didn't like to think of myself as acquisitive, but if all that was required of me was to stay here a month, it seemed like I'd be throwing away money I could ill afford to lose on principle. And, as a businesswoman, I wasn't fond of that notion at all.

I took a deep breath. I was suddenly thankful I'd passed up on owning any pets. "All right. Fine. You and Neveah win. I'll stay here the required month. But, mark my words, when that month is up, there will be a 'for sale' sign out by the road!"

Levay nodded and I could have sworn he hid a smile. "As

the will stipulates, you are free to do so once a full month of occupancy has been achieved. But Neveah figured you probably wouldn't want to by then. And so do I."

"Well, we'll see about that," I said. *Twerp*, I added in my head. The moniker fit him perfectly.

For the first time when he looked at me, his eyes were steady. "Yes, ma'am, we will."

He unlocked the front door, and helped me get my bags inside. I wished I'd known about the month-long stay beforehand so I could have packed more clothes. Then, I shrugged. A million dollars would buy me more clothes than I could ever need soon enough.

"See you at the funeral, Miss Serena," Levay said.

I nodded.

Levay handed the keys to me and scuttled off, like the pinstriped cockroach he was, closing the door behind him.

I breathed in the immaculate, humid silence. It was almost chilly inside the house, shaded as it was by the pines and oaks and magnolias. Thankfully, I'd thought to bring a sweater.

I looked up at the curving staircase with its teak and rose-wood embellishments. Weak light filtered through a diamond windowpane high above. I picked up my suitcase and carry-on and started the long march up the stairs.

I wasn't sure what I was going to do with myself here for the next month, but I at least needed to find a place to sleep.

I went to bed without dinner that night. I was suddenly exhausted from the trip and the strangeness here. It was utterly silent in the house and yet that silence seemed full of little noises – creaks, squeaks and groans – I didn't want to identify. I knew I'd have to find a way to rent a car in the morning, unless Neveah's old Buick was still in what passed for the garage. And I could somehow find the keys. I just didn't want to worry with it so close to dark.

The room I'd chosen was in the oldest wing of the house. Not Neveah's room. I wouldn't have been able to bear it. For all that I resented the intrusion on my life and routine, I did miss my aunt. I missed the time we could have spent together, if only she hadn't been so reclusive and I hadn't been so obsessed with my own life. I hadn't known her as well as I should have, and she had been all I'd had left.

I woke up feeling like I'd been crying in my sleep, which was disturbing enough. Even more disturbing was the feeling that someone had been watching me cry in my sleep and had just left the room. The room vibrated with *presence*, for lack of a better word. It had only been a moment. Something lingered in the air. Leather. And honey.

I scanned the room. I'd left the wardrobe slightly open and I stared back at myself from the ancient mirror. I looked like I'd seen a ghost. It was an unpleasant sight. Everything was where it had been and looked no more threatening in the morning than it had when I'd gone to bed. My glasses and pocket change hadn't moved. Nothing was written in blood on the dresser mirror or the walls.

But there was still that feeling. The fine hairs on my neck and arms were still prickled.

I considered speaking aloud, but I wanted to at least try to last the month before I started gibbering and putting scissors in the freezer.

I had luxuriated in the thought as I fell into bed last night that I could sleep as long as I wanted. It looked like it was just after dawn. My stomach reminded me it hadn't had anything since the minimal snack box on the plane yesterday.

It was time to go see if the Buick was still here and get to a grocery store.

I dressed in my usual casual clothes as if I was heading down to my workshop. The thought of having to go into town wasn't exactly my preference. I knew there would be questions and I wanted none of them. I was sure, though, that Neveah's cabinets were bare or else filled with things I had no use for – long out-of-date Ovaltine or digestive biscuits she'd gotten on clearance at Big Lots.

As I went downstairs, my nose tricked me into thinking I smelled coffee. As I got closer to the kitchen, I was sure I smelled it. Coffee and . . . French toast?

I discovered the keys to the Buick on the same old peg by the kitchen door, scooped them into my pocket and rounded the corner.

As in every good plantation house, the kitchen had for most of Belle Reve's history been in a separate building to reduce the risk of fire. But my grandmother had decided by the fifties that she was living in the modern era. She'd renovated a room, one of the house's many parlors, and made it her kitchen. Neveah had renovated it further, adding modern appliances and decorating with that baroque touch she favored.

On the dark granite bar, a plate of French toast, smothered with strawberries and fresh cream, and a steaming cup of coffee waited for me.

Part of me was delighted. But the other part was filled with fear. Was Levay playing a trick on me? I didn't think the little roach was capable of it.

I called his name but got no answer. Then I thought about the presence in my room in the morning.

"Neveah?" I called out. I felt so foolish. I didn't believe in ghosts, not really. But if her spirit were here, would it have made me French toast and coffee? More importantly, would it answer me?

There was only charged silence, as if someone had just stepped out right before I entered.

I hesitated. Then I shrugged. There was probably a perfectly logical explanation for this. Who was I to let good food go to waste?

Accustomed as I was to dry Cheerios (I hated soggy cereal), this was heaven on a plate.

When I was finished, I washed up, poured myself another cup of coffee and decided to peruse the kitchen cabinets to see exactly what I needed in town.

The cabinets were empty. Absolutely and totally. As was the fridge. I couldn't figure out if Neveah had left things this way or if someone had come and completely cleaned out the kitchen when she'd died.

The mystery of how my breakfast came to be went deeper.

"There must be some sort of keeper's cottage," I said aloud, trying to make myself feel better with the sound of my voice. "Food doesn't just magically appear in an empty kitchen!"

The silence laughed at me.

That was it. Determined to figure out what was going on, I clutched my coffee mug and marched outside.

I remembered once I got out onto the veranda that I was still in my socks, and that my shoes were upstairs in the bedroom.

I took a deep breath and looked out onto the morning as it threw its shawl around Belle Reve. A damp mist had moved up from the nearby lake in the night, and the morning sun spangled it with gold and rose. Buildings and trees all had different shapes. I searched to see if any of the buildings looked occupied as I finished drinking my coffee. The veranda went all around the house, and I strolled it slowly, looking out into the mist and wondering whether the person here with me, whoever he or she might be, was friend or foe.

Breakfast seemed innocuous enough, but would I find a horse's head in my bed by midnight? I'd probably watched *The Godfather* and *Single White Female* far too often for my own good.

I took the empty mug inside and set it in the kitchen sink.

When I turned, a bouquet of flowers announced themselves brightly. They had not been there when I'd come in. A card was attached.

"To Miss Serena", the note said in a bold hand.

It was not signed.

"All right," I said to the kitchen, "what the hell is going on?"

Breakfast was one thing. Flowers with a note when my back was turned were another.

But again no one answered.

I dashed upstairs and pulled my sneakers on. I grabbed the mace out of my purse. I was going to get to the bottom of this, but I wasn't stupid.

I went out the front door, determined not to go anywhere near the kitchen. The mist was burning off. I listened, in case the noise of footsteps gave the intruder away. It wasn't that I didn't appreciate the breakfast and the flowers. It was just that the way they appeared without warning or explanation was creepy.

The flowers made me think I should visit the old gardener's cottage first.

It was attached to a greenhouse, and I was both relieved and alarmed to find all manner of flowers growing there – orchids, roses, freesia, herbs of various types, and many more I couldn't identify. Though their growth was lush, they were all very well tended. Someone came here often.

But when I stepped into the gardener's cottage, it was obvious it had been empty a long time. The door hung off its hinges, the roof sagged and had leaked in places. The hearth was cracked and full of detritus from old birds' nests. I remembered playing here as a child. It had been deserted then, but was still functional. No one had lived here a long time. There was no gardener, not on site at least. Who kept up the greenhouse?

I doubted Neveah had. She loved flowers, but her thumb was as black as mine.

Then, I remembered that I'd seen someone in a bee suit yesterday, even if Levay hadn't.

I knew there was a honey shed around here somewhere. I could remember my grandmother showing it to me. Of course it wasn't time to harvest honey, but maybe he kept his tools there.

With my hand firmly on the mace in my pocket, I marched out to the shed.

It looked much the same as when I'd been a little girl. When I stooped under the door lintel and entered, I could smell the sweet gold of old comb and long-gone honey. A bee suit hung on a peg by the door, rotten with mold and cobwebs. The old smoker my grandfather had used was still there, its leather bellows eaten in half by mice.

No one had used these for a long time.

This was making less sense by the minute.

I climbed back out of the honey shed. "Hello? Is anyone there?"

Only echoes and the calls of startled birds.

But there was a strange sense that I'd been *heard*.

I walked back out toward the cemetery where I'd seen the beekeeper yesterday in his clouds of bees. The old live oak spread its arms over my ancestors like a benevolent octopus. When I was a girl, I had climbed up into it often enough until the mosquitoes had gotten too thick to bear. I tried not to see Neveah's freshly dug grave, waiting for tomorrow. Instead, I went to where the hives . . . were supposed to be.

The broken-down boxes I found must have been hives once, but they had long since been abandoned, just like the gardener's cottage and the honey shed. There were no bees, either. Hadn't been for ages. There was absolutely no way that anyone could have been out here working bees yesterday.

I shook my head. I might not last the month after all.

I decided the best thing I could do was get in the Buick and drive to clear my head. I fingered the keys in my pocket and went in search of the old garage.

Though the garage wasn't in the greatest of shape (and neither was the Buick, for all that), I managed to get the doors open and the car started. It probably had just enough gas to get to town.

I was half wondering if I would be allowed to leave, if I was stuck in some clichéd horror movie where the serial killer hiding in the basement brought me flowers before he offed me, but I pulled away smoothly and got out onto the country road with no mishaps.

I wandered Tupelo's streets, not really wanting to go back to Belle Reve. I ate alone in a diner, and though people whispered about me, they seemed to know I was not in the mood for conversation, and miraculously left me alone. I went to the Save-A-Lot for essentials – laundry items, coffee, sandwich bread, peanut butter, ramen. I wasn't going to rely on the friendly ghost or whatever it was continuing to feed me French toast every morning.

The checkout clerk couldn't help herself. "Ain't you Miss Neveah's niece?" she asked, chomping gum like a cow with her cud.

I nodded.

"You stayin' at Belle Reve?"

I didn't really want to answer that, but I also didn't want to seem rude. "Just until after the funeral."

I realized that I meant it. Just one day had unnerved me enough that I wasn't sure I could stay a month for love or money.

The clerk sized me up. "Miss Neveah said that, too, near as I can recall."

I gathered up my sack of groceries and just nodded. I wasn't going to say anything else, but then the clerk said, "Seen something funny, ain't you?"

I swallowed because I didn't know how to explain the fear I felt. "I . . ." I stared down at the garishly colored ramen cups in my bag.

"What's your name, honey?" the clerk said.

"Serena," I mumbled.

"Well, Serena, you may see and experience some strange things up there at Belle Reve, but don't take none of them in a bad way, you hear? Whatever's there's a kindly thing. Don't mean no harm."

I looked up at her, the plum-frosted hair piled high on her head, the coral pink lipstick on her wrinkled lips. I glanced at her name tag. Mavis.

"What is at Belle Reve exactly, Mavis?"

She smiled at me – a thick, syrupy grin that would have given Dolly Parton a run for her money. "Love, sugar. Love."

I grabbed the sack and ran.

When I got in the Buick, I sat there with my forehead against the steering wheel for several seconds, breathing deeply.

Love, sugar.

Had the entire world gone insane?

Driving home, I reflected that Mavis couldn't have said worse words to me. If she'd said an evil spirit or serial killer haunted Belle Reve, I could almost have accepted that. But *love* . . that was the last word I wanted to hear. There was a damn good reason I lived and worked alone.

His name was Eric. I had been in college – pre-med, top of my class – when I'd met him at a carnival where he was working. That night was the most magical in my life. The next night, when the carnival packed up, I went with them.

As such things usually do, after a season of traveling across the northern US and Canada, our romance abruptly ended when I found him in the arms of the funnel cake girl. When the carnival left for Florida, I stayed in the cold north and tried to find the most solitary profession I could. Not writing, because I may have been ignorant in some things, but certainly not in others.

With our shared love of books, Neveah tried to get me interested in being a librarian, but it was the physical art of bookmaking that drew me. I'd always thought I would be a surgeon. Now I operated on books instead of people. I learned and got back on my feet. My family finally started speaking to me again. Neveah was the first to reach out to me, but then we sadly drifted as we both became more entrenched in our lives.

And I was beginning to wonder if there was more to her life than I could have ever imagined.

I briefly considered just driving onward when I came to the turn at Belle Reve. But then I remembered that the funeral was tomorrow, and that, above all things, I'd come here to honor my aunt, the one person who had believed in me back when I'd scarcely believed in myself.

I took a deep breath, grabbed my groceries, and headed into that waiting silence.

I stopped in the foyer as soon as I shut the door. The presence was strong and heavy, the honey and leather smell permeating everything.

I couldn't stand it. "I don't want breakfast and flowers. I don't want coy notes and freakiness. I just want to be left the hell alone!"

I waited, expecting I knew not what to materialize there in the morning light.

But nothing did.

Gradually the presence (and the tantalizing smell) faded. I kept myself busy throughout the day, getting ready for tomorrow's funeral, making phone calls, reading the rest of Neveah's will, pressing my plain blouse and skirt.

That night, I ate ramen from a cup and had the distinct impression that I had gotten just what I asked for. I was very much alone. The silence almost stung.

I went into Neveah's study. It felt criminal to riffle through her things – it was why I hadn't wanted to sleep in her room. The chilling realization came, though, that if I lasted the month, I would have to go through all of it and get rid of it when I put Belle Reve up for sale anyway. Might as well get started.

I didn't know exactly what I was looking for. Something about whatever it was that haunted Belle Reve. Something about love.

I didn't find much of anything in her desk or files. Her effects were mostly ledgers of her accounts. I was shocked that she could survive at Belle Reve on a librarian's pension, but she'd somehow managed it.

It was oddly chilly here at the back side of the house. A fire would be welcome. I went to the hearth, trying to remember how to start one. Everything was close to hand, but ... I peered into the grate. Blackened, half-burned pages fluttered there. I picked them up, and a few phrases in Neveah's hand were still evident. *How I adore him. How I cannot bear to let him go . . .*

The papers crumbled into ash as I held them. Neveah had loved a man. Never once had she revealed this in all the years I'd known her. She had loved someone and she'd had to let him go. Were these words written in her last days? Had she burned them before she died?

Or had someone else?

I shivered and decided that I no longer wanted a fire. Perhaps it would be best just to turn in early. Tomorrow would be a long day. Neveah hadn't wanted visitation nights, but she'd asked for an open casket service at the little church down the road before the final burial here. I wasn't looking forward to it, especially now that I knew the rumors were true. My aunt had had a lover here, but who and how and why she'd never told a soul in her family was beyond me. Though rumors about Belle Reve were evidently rampant around here.

And now I was next in line to be the big gossip among Tupelo's grocery checkouts.

I pulled the prettiest book I could find from a nearby shelf – a gorgeous, leather-bound thing with deckled edgings and such a tightly stitched spine that it made me sigh in envy. It was about the history of Belle Reve during the Civil War, when it had been commandeered by the Confederate Army as a respite for wounded soldiers.

Somewhat grim reading, but anything to take my mind off the present. I trundled up to bed with it under my arm. My feet seemed to echo like drums up the stairs. No. There was no way I could stand living here alone.

The book worked its magic and I was soon lost in the pages of photos of soldiers. One face particularly intrigued me – a kindly-looking man who the caption said had been a famous fiddle player before the war. His name was Samuel H. Fields. He had served under Nathan Bedford Forrest, and had even entertained Robert E. Lee with his fiddle once before he'd been too wounded to stay with the regular army. Like Forrest, he had been a jack of all trades – a planter, a merchant and a beekeeper, as well as a musician.

He was very handsome, as few men seemed to have been in that time period. There was the ghost of a smile on his face, as though the person taking the photo was someone he could not help smiling at. Most photos from that era were dead serious and with good reason. But I had the feeling Mr Fields knew how to have fun.

I wondered idly what had happened to him. Had he left Belle Reve whole and gone on to live his life elsewhere? Had he become a famous fiddle player and traveled the country? I had always loved the fiddle. My final, odd thought before slipping into sleep was that I would have liked to have heard this man play.

I had strange dreams all night and, when I woke to the blaring of my phone alarm, I chalked them up to anxiety and grief and the book I'd been reading before bed. I'd dreamed I was a nurse in Belle Reve back during its respite days, and I'd met a charming soldier. I had vowed to be a spinster all my life and take care of my ailing father. I'd dreamed things I shouldn't have, things I'd not dreamed about for a long time . . . I could feel my face grow hot as my heart sped.

I needed a shower. A cold one.

I hoped the shower would wash away the shreds of my dreams – that and the impending funeral – but the impressions and feelings only seemed to grow stronger in the light of day. If I'd been superstitious or given to New Age woo-woo, I would have thought I'd dreamed of a past life here at Belle Reve. And yet somehow I could tell that the person was not me. I'd worn her face and body in the dream, but I had the distinct feeling that what was happening had all happened before to someone else. I was reliving another's life.

And in that life, she'd disappointed her family and taken up with the handsome soldier. Their love affair had burned so hot, it was a wonder Belle Reve hadn't burst into flames with the heat of it. But what had happened after that – the surely tragic end of the story – I had no clue.

I shook my head as I downed scalding coffee, hoping it would clear my mind. Today was Neveah's funeral. I needed to be fully present.

As I dressed, I thought perhaps I heard the strains of an old fiddle playing a soft dirge somewhere in the recesses of the house. It was eerie enough considering what I'd read and dreamed. But after yesterday's escapade of trying to chase down whomever had left me the breakfast and flowers, I decided to just get to the church and finish letting Neveah go for good.

Everything in the church happened in a blur. The only thing that stood out to me was my first sight of Neveah as I entered the church alone. My aunt looked incredibly, undeniably young. Her skin practically glowed. She had let her hair grow long and, though it was silver, it fell all about her shoulders in waves and curls that should have belonged to a much younger woman. Everyone remarked on what a great job the funeral parlor had done, but I had the distinct feeling that it was something else that had kept her looking so young.

Love, sugar, I heard Mavis say again.

The whispers and chatter fell on me like waves. Another woman fallen to the charms of Belle Reve. Another death that no one could explain. And all I could think of the entire time was how I wished I'd had the chance to say one last goodbye.

I was actually grateful when we returned to the house for the final interment. The crowd had thinned to only those closest to my aunt. The day was warm and drowsy, and the minister's final words were peaceful. I scanned the faces as we bowed our heads for the final prayer.

There was a face among them that I hadn't seen at the church. I peered at the man. He seemed out of place some-how. His clothes and hair were definitely out of fashion. He must have felt my gaze. He looked up, and I gasped. Not just out of place. Out of time.

I knew those eyes, the angles of cheekbones and chin. He wasn't smiling now; he looked sadder than anyone I'd ever seen, in fact. Samuel H. Fields. The Confederate fiddler.

It was all I could do not to leap across the casket and try to catch hold of his lapels to give him a good shake. What the hell was he? A ghost? A figment of my imagination? I wanted to seize him just so I could know whether or not he was real. But he dropped his eyes again, almost as if he was too bashful to meet my gaze for long. I managed to keep silent, though I fidgeted throughout the rest of the cere-mony, which now seemed to last hours.

When it came time to line up and drop flowers on the lowered casket, I found myself somehow right next to him. Our hands met above the freshly turned earth, and I watched as flowers I hadn't seen him holding dropped from his fingers.

"Her favorites," I heard him whisper. That voice. This was The Voice that had summoned me on the phone – rich and low. Our eyes met again. His were filled with deep grief. The grief a lover might feel upon losing his beloved. I shivered as I dropped the rose I held.

Only the tips of his fingers touched the back of my hand, but it was enough to set all my nerves humming.

"I truly loved her," he said. "You must understand that."

"What are you?" I said. My throat was clotted with grief and fear.

Everything, even sound, receded as he looked at me again.

"You are certain you want to know? You made it very clear yesterday that you did not."

I didn't ask him how he'd heard me. I didn't ask whether he'd left the book just where I could find it or how he'd gotten the breakfast and flowers in the kitchen without my noticing. I just said, "I want to know now."

"Now is not the time. But I will come to you when evening falls over Belle Reve." His antiquated way of speaking. I would almost find it hokey if it wasn't for the fact that I knew to him it wasn't antiquated at all.

I nodded.

What I didn't say was that no knowledge he might give was going to change my mind about selling Belle Reve.

We stepped apart and I took a deep breath. It felt like I'd been underwater forever. I looked around and people had moved away in little knots and were murmuring here and there. A few women in colorful hats were approaching the veranda with steaming casserole dishes held away from their bodies with coordinated oven mitts.

I looked back to see what Mr Fields thought of all of this, and then realized he was gone. I had the sneaking suspicion that no one had seen him but me, and that perhaps everyone just thought I was taking my last moments with Neveah alone.

I shook my head. It was going to be a long time until twilight.

★

I spent the day making lists of things. First, a list of the food and those who had brought it so I could properly thank them and return dishes. Next, I began an inventory of the entire estate. That certainly kept me busy. The front parlors alone were so full of knick-knacks and other ephemera that I knew I'd be forever looking up their worth on antique sites.

Of course, I was probably going to hire an estate sale company anyway, but I was sure it could only help if everything was already inventoried and cataloged. I considered what Neveah might think about all of this. Somewhere, I imagined the librarian in her had made her do this already – I just hadn't found the right ledger. Still and all, it kept me occupied. I didn't have to think about what the night would bring.

At 5 p.m., I went into the kitchen and eyed the line of casserole dishes filling the fridge. Listlessly, I chose one, but wasn't sure I could eat.

"Miss Serena."

I spun around, somehow managing to keep from dropping the dish in my hand.

He was standing in the doorway a bit uncertainly. "May I enter?"

I nodded.

He stepped into the kitchen. He was wearing the same old suit he'd worn at the funeral.

"Will you come walk with me? The weather this evening is very fine."

"Let me just get my shawl," I said. Part of me wanted to get it for practical reasons. Part of me wanted to get it to calm my nerves.

He lifted it between his hands. It had not been there a moment ago, I was certain of it.

"I . . . Thanks." In one smooth motion, he wrapped my shoulders with it. He looked as though he wanted me to take his arm, but he just gestured toward the front door instead.

Out we went into the twilight. The herons and egrets were coming in to roost in the lake trees; I could hear their cacophony as they settled in.

We were silent a long while, neither of us knowing how to begin.

He sighed heavily, looking out across the lawn. "I have had this conversation a few times, and every time it gets no easier."

I didn't say anything, but I was thinking about how I'd never had a conversation like it and hoped never to again.

"You probably know most of Belle Reve's history. What's public at least. But there is a secret history that has been kept within the family for generations. Now, as the heiress to Belle Reve, you are entitled to know that history, too."

He searched my face. "You read some of the account of how I came to Belle Reve. I was a soldier. The eldest daughter of the house and I fell in love. Her father refused to allow her to marry me. I died to the flesh not long after his refusal. They said it was infection, but I suspect he had me poisoned to keep me away from Millie. She died of a broken heart.

"I woke to this life – whatever it may be – upon her burial in the family plot. I am not certain, because there was a time when I was nowhere, neither dead nor alive, but perhaps she cursed me in her final breath for the love I had taken with me to the grave. However it was, I woke again, but she did not."

"So you're not a ghost?" I said.

He shook his head. "I am not sure what I am. I can feel things – sensation, emotions, weather . . . things the living can. But I can never die. I have no need of food, but I require energy."

"You're a vampire, then?" I was incredulous that I was even having this conversation.

He shook his head, smiling as if at some inward joke.

"What?"

"Neveah once insisted I watch that Dracula picture with her on the television contraption. He is nothing like what I am."

"And what are you?"

"Love," he said. "Pure and eternal love, Miss Serena."

I would have laughed in his face, but I heard Mavis in my head again. *Love, sugar.*

"I see," I said.

"I think I was sent back to give the women of Belle Reve love throughout eternity. As long as the house still stands and is in the family, then I live and keep this place alive, too."

I looked around at the fading clapboard, the old gardener's cottage, and all the other decrepit buildings. "It seems you've let a few things go over the years."

He smiled again. "Take my hand."

I wanted to refuse him, but I wasn't sure I could. Not for very long. I took his hand. Like a film of dirt being washed from an old window, color sprang to life. The house was painted so vividly that it glowed in the sunset. All the trees and bushes were in blossom. Bees zoomed everywhere. Delicious smells – of pie and fresh-cut grass and all the flowers on earth, it seemed – drifted in the evening breeze.

"This is the true Belle Reve, the eternal home that hides under the old," he said. "And I am its keeper, its spirit, if you will."

I happened to look down and saw that even I looked different. My skin almost glowed. My ugly funeral clothes had been exchanged for a gorgeous gown of the sort I had long since ceased to dream about. And my heart, which had felt so empty, so barren for so long, seemed to have sprouted wings. It was all I could do not to dance for the sheer joy of it.

I was *home.*

"This is your birthright," he said. "This is what you have truly inherited. Would you give all this away for the sake of money?"

It was a loaded and heavy question, and I wanted to say no with all my being, but I had grown wary of men who promised things beyond their power to deliver. True, I'd never met a man who could quite do all this, but . . .

"What's the catch?" Because I knew there had to be one. Why had Neveah died mysteriously and seemingly without cause? She was elderly, but not infirm. She had looked so youthful and full of life, even in death.

He looked down, and I could see that this was also a hard question for him to answer. "I give my life and energy – my love – so that Belle Reve will go on. And you must do the same."

"How's that?"

"You agree to bind yourself to this place and to me, to allow me to take energy from you as needed, and to keep this knowledge secret. In turn, I protect you and Belle Reve. I will show you love such as you've never known as long as your life lasts. And you must promise to pass on these secrets to your heir, another woman in the family, when the time comes."

My life for his love. My life for Belle Reve.

I walked away from him across the technicolored lawn. I was Dorothy just landed in Oz, my gray world suddenly turned into rainbows.

And now I'd discovered the wicked witch in all this – I would have to give everything up that I knew and had fought for to keep this strange world alive.

To his credit, Samuel Fields, whatever he was, didn't push me. He just stood there in the long twilight. He must have summoned up his fiddle, for suddenly he began to play.

The music unwound around me, a slow, sensuous reel. I could have easily danced to it, but I kept my feet firmly planted, convinced it would somehow show my resolve to maintain my self.

I considered my options. Sell Belle Reve and let this all die. Continue to be a lonely spinster. Who knew how long I'd have to live or what might come my way? But I felt fairly certain that if the last few years had been any indication, not much was likely to come at all. I might die like Scrooge, loaded with money but with no one to share it with.

And all this that I loved would pass away.

Or live, however briefly, secure in the place that my family had kept for generations. Secure and loved at last.

It was terrifying, but as the music murmured around me, I knew what I had to do.

I turned.

He ceased playing and moved his fiddle from his shoulder slowly. He watched me with a gentle hunger that undid me more than his music ever would.

"All right," I said. "Show me."

SAVAGE RESCUE

Shelli Stevens

The Sunday morning before Mardi Gras was quiet on
Bourbon Street. At least it was when you compared it to
Saturday evening.

Still groggy from last night, with his arms folded
beneath his head, Terrance stared at the ceiling of his
hotel room.

He'd already been out once this morning to run down to
Café du Monde for some beignets. Bourbon Street had
been almost deserted, with the unpleasant smell of all kinds
of sin being hosed off the sidewalk by some unlucky
employee.

After picking up the breakfast, he'd strolled along the
river, itching to do much more than walk, but knowing just
how damn impossible it was.

Staring at the ceiling fan circling lazily, Terrance
frowned. The urge to use up some vacation time and fly to
Louisiana had hit him hard a couple of weeks ago. He'd
assumed it was just from being in hardcore-work mode for
so long. The idea of coming down to Louisiana – almost
his second home – and partying it up Mardi Gras was too
tempting.

But three nights now he'd partied. Three nights he'd been
left with an unexplainable restlessness. When he'd first
arrived he'd met a pretty, albeit shallow, Southern girl and
they'd hooked up. Her first time with a black man – she'd
told him that little fact mid-orgasm. Which seemed a little
random and unnecessary.

Overall the night had been pretty damn unremarkable.

Then again sex with *anyone* lately had gone that route. He'd figured a trip to NOLA would shake things up for him. Wrong.

His mouth twitched into a small smile as he remembered her parting words that he'd been "an animal in bed". She had no idea. New Orleans might be famous for its voodoo, rumored ghosts and whispers of all things paranormal, but he was pretty sure shape-shifters were under the radar. They did exist here though. They existed everywhere. Most of the world just didn't know it.

Just thinking about it made the wolf inside him itch to come out. His skin tingled with the need to shift, and even now his fingernails started to grow into claws. Clenching his teeth, he used the same discipline he'd used back in high school to keep down a hard-on, and forced the wolf back inside him.

Two days without shifting, and he was going a little crazy. Back in the Pacific Northwest, there were plenty of places to run. Plenty of forests filled with trees. Plenty of ways to indulge his animal side without alerting the clueless human population. Here in the French Quarter, it was a little harder to hide who he was.

So why the fuck had he come here? The partying was nowhere near as amazing as he'd remembered it five years ago, when he'd been twenty-one. It left him empty. Maybe he was just getting too old for the party scene. Except, that damn sense of unease was still there.

His cell buzzed on the table, and he reached out to grab it.

"This is Terrance."

"Morning, Hilliard. Hope I'm not waking your hungover ass."

Terrance sat up in bed, his brows drawing down. Agent Larson, his boss at the P.I.A. – Preternatural Investigation Agency – was calling him this early on a Sunday? While Terrance was supposedly on vacation. What the hell was going on?

"No, sir, I'm wide awake. No hangover." He paused. "Something up?"

"Yeah." The amusement fled Larson's tone. "Would you be willing to cut your vacation short? I need you on something."

Adrenaline, customary for any new case, filled his blood. "Already got a flight booked home today, sir."

"Cancel it. You just happen to be in the right place, at the right time."

The hairs on the back of Terrance's neck lifted. "I'm listening."

"Do you remember Agent Masterson's younger sister? Her name is—"

"Aubree." His sister-in-law's little sister.

The image of her slammed into him. The waif-like teenager with the dark long hair and big blue eyes. She'd stayed with him and his family for a while when she'd been seventeen, and he'd been twenty and in college. She'd walked with a limp, had been pregnant and alone, and was just as beautiful as she was vulnerable.

"Is she in trouble? Is her kid?"

"Unconfirmed, but we think so. Grace hasn't been able to get hold of her sister for two weeks now, and she's got a bad gut feeling. You know how Grace can sense things."

"It's what makes her a damn good agent."

"It is. Anyway, Aubree and her daughter, River, moved to Louisiana two years ago."

His blood quickened, and he looked out the hotel window as if she'd be right outside the building. "They're here? In Louisiana?"

"By last accounts. She became engaged recently to an affluent gentleman – shifter, of course – down there."

Why that news stirred something dark inside him, he couldn't say, but Terrance ignored it.

"Grace wanted to come down herself, but she's due any day now with hers and Darrius' first child. So she's not allowed to fly. She's going out of her mind with worry. So I'm coming to you."

"Keep Grace there. Keep them both there. I've got this." He reached in the bedside drawer for a pen and found a receipt from the night before. "You got a last known address?"

Larson gave him the info and made Terrance promise to keep him updated. Terrance ended the call and set the phone down.

Aubree. Damn. He hadn't seen her in, what, five years? The last time he'd seen her she'd come to a family Thanksgiving shortly after giving birth.

She'd been even more beautiful and looking so heart-breakingly young with a baby in her arms. She always had a small smile on her face, always seemed happy enough despite her circumstances.

His heart was pounding a little faster, and it was from more than just the adrenaline.

The restlessness, the unease, they were both gone. And now he knew with clarity the reason he'd felt compelled to come to New Orleans. To find Aubree.

Sometimes being a shifter meant weird shit happened. You sensed things. The unexplainable. He knew this but it didn't make it any easier to understand why he'd felt drawn to come down here.

Why Aubree? And why him?

There was a steady breeze in the air, but it did little for the uncommonly warm temperature and sticky humidity. The moss dangling from the large Southern oaks swayed in the wind, the leaves a rustling whisper.

Sitting on the second-floor veranda of the large planta-tion house, Aubree stared out over the property. The rows of beautiful oaks, the manicured lawns, the unpaved dirt road, they were all enchantingly Southern and timeworn.

God, but she wanted to hate the centuries-old tobacco plantation that had been handed down through Landon's family. Wanted to hate every inch of land he owned, but she couldn't. It was too beautiful. If she'd been able to shift without excruciating pain, she would've enjoyed exploring the grounds in wolf form.

Louisiana had captured her heart from the first time she'd visited a friend three years ago. It was only two years ago that she'd finally made the move here permanent. And then a year later she'd met Landon. And it hadn't even been a month since the careful illusion had been stripped away.

Which led up to last week, when her whole world had been taken from her.

"Good afternoon, Aubree."

She hadn't heard Landon's approach, and she stiffened in the antique rocker. Squeezing her eyes shut, she struggled against the wave of rage and despondency.

"Is it?" She barely managed to keep her voice calm.

"The sun is warm, the sky's blue. Just lovely out, don't you think?"

She gave a harsh laugh, still not turning to look at him. "The weather. You want to talk about the damn weather?"

The hands that gripped her arm were unforgiving as they jerked her from the rocker.

Her left leg protested the sudden move and she couldn't stifle a cry of pain as she was jerked hard against him.

"I do believe your crude side is showing, sugar. Do you really think this is an appropriate way to treat your fiancé?"

Once, she'd found that Southern drawl charming. The impeccable manners from such a handsome man, who easily resembled a modern-day Rhett Butler. But it was all just a shiny veneer masking pure evil beneath.

"The way I'd like to greet you would be much less appropriate," she ground out.

Anger flared in his eyes, and for a moment she was convinced he might strike her. But then his mouth curled into a cold smile.

"You failed to mention a friend might be dropping by. Who is Clarence?"

She blinked, trying to comprehend his words. She didn't have any male friends around here – Landon had seen to that. And had she ever known anyone by the name of Clarence?

"I don't know who he is." Becoming more unnerved by the accusation in his eyes, she tried to step back from him, but his grip tightened. "He asked for *me*?"

"Yes. He's one of our kind – I could smell the wolf in him."

A wolf named Clarence? The name sounded somewhat familiar, and yet . . . didn't.

"I informed him you were otherwise occupied and offered to give you a message. Not surprisingly, he left none." He sighed, appearing put out now. "But I'll learn who he is. I'm currently having him tracked."

"I don't know who he is, I swear it." Her throat tightened. "Please, Landon, all I want is to talk to River. It's been a week."

He captured her chin in a ruthless grip. "Your daughter is being well taken care of. She probably hasn't even had time to miss her crippled mother yet."

The harsh remark about her permanently damaged leg was easily deflected. She'd developed a thick skin over the years. But to hear it from the man she'd once trusted, had initially wanted to marry and mate with by choice, cut through her.

"I know she does." Her words were ragged.

"You really should get ready," he continued, ignoring her reply. "Our engagement party is due to start in a couple of hours."

The whole idea of an engagement party was an awful joke. The fact that she was being forced to become this sociopath's mate even more horrific.

But he'd left her no choice. She'd tried to leave him, but had failed. And his punishment had been to take River from her, promising not to return her daughter until they were mated.

Where was she? Oh God, every day, every hour that went by was agony not being able to see or speak to her daughter. The fear consumed her. What if River *wasn't* safe? What if Landon had lied? A tiny bit of reason clung, telling her that maybe he was a monster, but he wouldn't hurt his own kind. Especially not a child.

"You will look lovely tonight in that dress I've picked out." His gaze darkened, and moved over her body. "Even lovelier in the lingerie beneath it."

The lust in his eyes was undeniable, and a shiver of fear raced down her spine. Her stomach roiled. He hadn't touched her in months – not since she'd discovered his dark, violent secret. He'd taken his pleasure elsewhere, and she'd been grateful for it.

But there was no denying the promising look in his eyes, and the plans he had for later. The idea of him touching her made bile rise in her throat.

"You won't find me in your bed willingly."

"Willing is overrated, sugar." Amusement flashed in his gaze. "But I have no intention of making use of your lovely body tonight."

The relief was so strong that the tension in her body fled immediately. She released a ragged breath.

"I do believe my business associate will have that pleasure instead."

Her heart stopped for a moment. The look on her face must've pleased him, because his cold smile spread.

No. Oh God, he couldn't be serious.

"You will please him, and do anything he requests of you. Do you understand?"

She shook her head, numbly. He was going to give her to another man. As if she were some part of a business deal.

His fingers tightened around her chin. "This is not up for negotiation, you understand."

"I won't," she choked out. "You can't—"

"Do you want to see your daughter again, Aubree?"

Her heart twisted at his calm, cold words.

"That's what I thought." He smiled. "He's a human, government worker who is aware of our existence and has expressed the desire to fuck one of our kind. You will accommodate him tonight, understand?"

She couldn't reply, had no words. As he let her go, he moved from the balcony toward the door. He paused and glanced back at her.

"Just a few more days, sugar, and we'll be married and mated. Then you'll have your daughter back."

He left her alone again, and suddenly it all made sense. Why he hadn't mated with her or marked her yet. He intended to use her body as currency. Tonight, with his associate. And who knows how many more until they were mated? Because once they *were* mated, he wouldn't be able to share. She would belong to him.

How had her life become such a living hell? How had she not seen this coming – *again*! Her record with men was 0 for 2 now.

More than anything, she wanted to be able to save her own ass and find a way out of this. She wanted to be brave and strong, just like her bad-ass P.I.A. Agent sister Grace. But physically, she couldn't do it – her leg that had never recovered from being horrifically broken as a child. And, as for brave, well, she'd never been so scared in her damn life. But not for herself. For River.

Tonight Landon was going to pass her around like a cheap whore off the street. And there wasn't a thing she could do about it. She knew what Landon and his friends were capable of now.

Nausea swelled inside her, and she pressed her hand to her mouth. She only just managed to get to the restroom, before getting sick to her stomach.

The party was in full swing. From where Terrance was hidden among the oak trees on the property, he could see the masses of formally dressed elite socializing inside the large, white house.

The plantation home was so perfectly Southern, with the large pillars in front and the balconies on the first and second floors. It all looked innocent, and maybe somewhat ostentatious.

But something was up. He knew it both in his gut, and by the response from the evasive man who'd answered the door earlier. He'd tried to give a clue to Aubree by leaving the name Clarence. It was close to Terrance. It was a long shot, but it was all he'd had when Mr Douche-bag had answered the door.

And the jerk had sent people to follow him when he'd left, but they were about as effective as kindergartners at trying to tail him.

Aubree was inside, Terrance would bet on it. And Grace and Darrius had every right to be worried about her. Hell, he was worried too. More so now that he'd been given the runaround.

He'd checked in with Larson and given him the news. He'd immediately been instructed to try to make contact with Aubree. Not that he'd needed the order. Even if this hadn't been a P.I.A. assignment, he would've gone after her. Mostly because she was Grace's sister.

Even as that thought slid through his head, a stab of denial hit. What else could it be? He hadn't seen her in five years. Maybe back then he'd felt a sense of protectiveness toward her – one he couldn't fully understand. But he'd written it off to her being a young, single mom.

It had nothing to do with how pretty she'd been, or how happy and at peace with her life she seemed to be.

Which was damn amazing. The father of her child was dead, thankfully, because he'd been a sadistic asshole. All that was common knowledge for anyone who read the slimeball's file on record with the P.I.A.

She was just a memory to Terrance. His sister-in-law's little sister. Nothing more. He would go in and get her and her kid out. However and whatever needed to be done.

He stared at the crowd inside, seeking any sign of her, but he had yet to catch a glimpse. He spotted the d-bag who'd answered the door earlier – was that her fiancé? He could only assume so. Currently, the guy was chatting it up with a group of men.

There was a flash of red among the black that caught Terrance's attention. He shifted his gaze to the woman and narrowed his eyes. Her back was to him, but he could see that she was slender, with nice, but subtle, curves.

Her brown hair was pinned up in some fancy twist. Even though he could only see her from behind, he could tell she was attractive. So could every man in the room, judging by all the gazes that rested on her.

Was it her? He'd never seen her dolled up before. She'd always favored jeans and T-shirts.

The woman turned just then, glancing away from the group. Even from this distance, he could see extra clear with his shifter side. He took in the glossy red lips and heavily made-up eyes. She was fucking gorgeous. And she was undeniably Aubree.

He struggled to merge the eighteen-year-old girl he remembered with the bombshell he stared at. His blood heated and he gave a small curse under his breath. What the fuck was he doing? Getting a hard-on for the woman he was supposed to be rescuing?

Watching her smiling and socializing though, a prickle of doubt hit. What if she didn't need help? What if she really had just been previously occupied this morning?

And what if she'd just happened to stop communicating with her sister? No. It'd never happen. Everyone knew how close the two were. Even if they lived in different parts of the country, they were in contact of some kind almost daily.

He needed to get in that house and find a way to get her alone. Find a way to talk to her.

As he watched, Mr Douche-bag leaned over and whispered something in her ear. The tension that filled Aubree's body was visible even from where he was standing.

She gave a small nod and then disappeared – with that slight limp he remembered. When the lights upstairs came on, he saw that she'd gone into a bedroom. He knew this would be his chance. He had to move fast.

Several minutes passed as he moved stealthily around the shitty excuse for security, staying in human form for now. He climbed the white staircase on the outside of the house that led to the second floor, keeping his movement as silent as possible.

When he reached the veranda, he found the door unlocked.

It may have seemed a little strange, but he didn't question his good fortune. He slipped inside silently, and closed the door behind him. When he turned to face the room, he went still. The air in his chest locked and his dick instantly became rock hard.

Aubree stood near the bed, facing away from him as she gripped a white, antiquated bed frame. The red dress from earlier was gone, and she would've been naked if it weren't for the scalding red lingerie set she wore. Her hair was loose now, curling down her back and hanging partly over her shoulder across her breasts, no doubt.

From the back, the panties were nothing but a red silk string that ran between the pale, perfect globes of her ass. The bra, a thin band of red that fastened in the back and matched the panties.

Her pale, flawless skin was only highlighted by the silky crimson lingerie. Her spine was delicately curved, her waist narrow and her hips flared, giving her a slight hourglass figure that he couldn't remember from before. Then again, he'd never seen her like this. Nearly naked. Looking like a present waiting to be unwrapped.

All thoughts of why he was here vanished as everything primal and male rose inside him. The urge to stride over and tear the lingerie from her body had him taking a step toward her.

"I didn't expect you this soon." Her uneven words stopped him. Snapped him out of his lust-filled daze.

Confusion mingled with the desire as he stared at her back. She must be expecting someone else, and if she turned around and saw him she'd probably lose her shit and scream.

Which meant he had to act fast. He closed the distance between them and slid one arm around her waist, and his other hand over her mouth.

She stiffened and made a soft cry of fear, before going limp, almost submissive, against him.

What the hell?

He felt it a second later. The wetness of a tear brushing his hand. She was crying.

"It's all right." He kept his tone low, soothing and, before he could stop himself, he brushed a soft kiss that was supposed to be comforting against her shoulder.

The moment his lips touched her skin though, that primal wave smashed into him again. The need to touch her. To turn her around and pull her into his arms and lay claim to her mouth. To her body.

What the *fuck* was wrong with him? He might still be considered a rookie agent at the P.I.A., but he wasn't that green to let a woman throw him off base.

Grinding his teeth together, struggling to keep control, he muttered, "I'm not going to hurt you, Bree."

She went rigid, before trying to turn in his grasp, but he held her still, tightening his palm against the softness of her belly. His fingers teased over the pale flesh in an attempt to relax her.

Whatever you want to tell yourself, buddy.

"You can't scream. Can't make a noise. Do you understand?"

She nodded again, and he could feel her heart beating quicker now. He pulled his hand away from her mouth and slowly turned her in his arms.

She twisted at lightning speed to face him, her gaze running over him in a mix of confusion and then shock.

"You remember me?" he asked quietly. "I know it's been a whil—"

"T! Oh my God, T."

He had a brief flash of gorgeous breasts nearly spilling out of a barely there bra, before they were smashed against him as she flung himself into his arms with a sob.

She was crying, and pretty loudly at that. But the relief at seeing a familiar face was so strong that Aubree couldn't help it as she clung to him.

He wrapped his arms around her, holding her in such a firm, protective grip, she could almost believe everything was going to be all right.

"You remember me," he said gruffly.

"Of course." She'd never forgotten him, or his family and the kindness they showed her when she'd been pregnant.

"I tried to see you this morning. Left a name—"

"Clarence." She shook her head and drew in a ragged breath, bringing with it the scent of him. It brought comfort and an awareness that she didn't have time to try to understand at the moment. "That was you? But I . . . Wait, your name is *Terrance.* That's right. I think the only time I heard you called that was the first time we met, and occasionally by your mother when you were in trouble. Otherwise you were always just T to me."

His soft laugh coincided with the gentle hand that smoothed down her back. Tingles of awareness seemed to follow in its wake, and she arched away from his touch with a slight gasp.

He stiffened and pushed her back slightly so their gazes could meet. Her breath caught at the heat in his dark-brown eyes, and whatever that awareness had been a moment ago amplified.

When she'd first met him he'd been in college. Tall and kind of hot, but now . . . Well, he was still tall, but he was buff and with a few laugh lines around his eyes.

The hairs on the back of her neck lifted and she drew in such a deep breath that her chest lifted in this ridiculous excuse for a bra. His gaze dropped to observe the movement, maybe unconsciously, but then lingered.

Beneath the silk bra she felt her nipples tighten. Confusion and heat raced through her and she shook her head.

"T . . ."

"You need to put on some clothes. Now."

The strain in his voice registered, and so did the fact that she was nearly naked. A blush raced like wildfire over her skin.

"I'm sorry. I—Oh my God." The reason why she was dressed like this came back with clarity.

She pulled away sharply and glanced toward the bedroom door. "He's going to be here any minute."

"Who? Your fiancé?"

"No." Panic swelled inside her. For herself. For him. "I don't even know how you got in here, but if he catches you—"

The door opened before she could even finish her sentence. Both she and Terrance swung their attention to the door. The paunchy, forty-something male with pasty skin paused in the doorway.

His gaze swung from Terrance to Aubree, before widening in shock. "What in tarnation is going—"

Terrance was at his side in a blur of movement,

delivering some kind of blow to the back of the head that had the other man collapsing to the ground.

Aubree made a squeak of shock and backed up another step. How did he know how to do that?

"Not bad for a basketball player," she said weakly.

"Quit basketball after college and joined the P.I.A." He dragged the pasty man around to the other side of the bed so he was hidden.

"Is he dead?" Her voice rose sharply.

"Nah, just out for a while. Hope he wasn't important to you."

"I don't even know who he is." And yet she'd almost been forced to sleep with him. Her head spun and bile rose in her throat, but she made herself stay calm.

Terrance was P.I.A. Which must mean he was here to help her.

"Did Grace send you?"

"She was the one who sounded the initial alarm. She wanted to come after you herself."

Her heart pinched. "Of course she did, but she's too far along in her pregnancy. I knew she'd worry."

"Does she have a right to be concerned, Aubree?" He approached her again, and this time his gaze stayed at eye level.

Her eyes filled with tears and she nodded. "Yes. He'll kill you if he finds you in here, T. You've got to go."

Terrance's mouth thinned. "He?"

"Landon. My fiancé."

His confident smirk didn't do much for. "Trust me, he'll be dead before I will."

"Then he'll have River killed."

That made him pause in his approach. "Where's your daughter?"

"I don't even know." The familiar mix of helplessness, terror and rage filled her. "He has her hidden but won't tell me where."

"Son of a bitch." He shook his head and dropped a few more curses she knew his mom would've smacked him for. "You seem to pick shitty men."

"Thank you for stating the obvious."

"Are you mated yet?"

"No. Thank God."

Was that relief on his face? It was gone as he turned and gestured to the unconscious man.

"And who was this clown?"

"An associate of Landon's." Which was the extent of what she knew.

"And you were greeting him dressed like that?" His gaze burned a trail over her body.

Her face reddened, with shame and humiliation this time, but she kept her spine straight and met his gaze firmly when it finally returned to her eyes.

"I was supposed to sleep with him. Landon threatened to never return River if I didn't."

The dismay in his eyes faded to a soft remorse. Pity. "We need to get you out of here, then you can tell me everything."

"I can't. Please go." The panic hit her again. "I can't leave without River. If I'm gone—"

"Answer me this. If you had your daughter, would you be staying here? Or would you be trying to escape?"

"We already tried. It's why she's gone now. He won't give her back until we're mated."

"You'll get mated over my dead body," he ground out, reaching for her.

She stepped back from him. "You don't know what he's capable of. The things I've seen him do."

"You can fill me in when we're away from here."

"No. I won't go. Dammit, not without River! T—"

His arm went around her, she felt the small prick of a needle. A moment later, the room around her faded to darkness.

"Sorry, honey, but you don't get a choice this time . . ."

Son of a bitch, but he really should've put some clothes on her before he hauled her beautiful unconscious ass outside.

Terrance adjusted Aubree in his grip and quickened his pace. He'd had to disappear out the back end of the plantation, rather than risk getting spotted by someone.

He wasn't thrilled with having to run in human form, but even if she'd been ready to leave with him willingly, he knew she couldn't shift. Not since she'd been in a tragic accident as a child that had left her so damaged that she couldn't shift without excruciating pain.

When he reached the car he'd left hidden on a back road, Aubree still wasn't stirring. He was grateful for the fact, but a small part of him worried that maybe the dose was too much for her small frame.

He hadn't intended to use it on her, but when she'd resisted leaving, he'd known there was no choice. It was clear she was in danger.

Before starting the engine, he pulled out his cell phone and called Larson to fill him in. Five minutes later, he was reassured that Yorioka was on her way from the Seattle office, and several agents from the New Orleans branch were being brought in to locate and rescue River.

Keeping a five-year-old shifter hidden was nearly impossible, and everyone had a price. For the right amount, someone would talk.

He tossed his cell on the passenger seat and started the engine, pulling away from the plantation and past the sugarcane fields.

The drive seemed to pass quickly and before long they arrived at a small cabin nestled among the cypress swamps of a bayou. The place was owned by a friend of a friend. Unless Terrance wanted them to be found, they wouldn't be traced there.

The interior was small, with just the basics. He settled Aubree on the one queen-sized bed and draped the mosquito netting around her, all the while trying to suppress any sexual thought about her. Which was basically like telling himself not to breathe.

Shit, that definitely was not the same boyish, teenage figure he'd remembered from before. Motherhood had only made her more beautiful.

A wave of sympathy washed over him at the agony she must be going through at being separated from River. Maybe it was a good thing she was out for a bit. Less time for her to worry and stress, more time for him and the P.I.A. to try to make things right.

He lay back on the couch and closed his eyes, knowing he needed to catch some sleep while he could. When he woke up the sun was rising.

How the hell had he slept through the night? Was Aubree still out?

A quick peek inside the bedroom showed her still there under the blanket, one hand tucked under her cheek. It looked as if she were genuinely sleeping now, not just under the influence of a tranquilizer.

Relieved and feeling far more refreshed this morning, he jogged out to the car to grab his duffle bag. He returned and settled down on the well-worn beige couch, pulling out his laptop to get to work. A few keystrokes later and he had endless pages of info about Landon Beauchamp.

The wealthy society gentleman was both revered and despised in New Orleans. He was famous for throwing large parties, rubbing elbows with politicians, and always having a young, attractive girl on his arm. Of course no one new what he really was – a shape-shifter. That would've only added to his notoriety.

The most recent article announced his engagement to Aubree. There was a picture of her, Landon and River. Terrance glanced at the child and smiled. She looked like her mother's mini-me. Those big blue eyes and that long brown hair. She was scrawny, but it seemed that she'd outgrow that, if you looked at how Aubree had turned out.

"I had no idea that day."

He swiveled around to see Aubree standing behind him. He hadn't even realized she was awake.

"No idea about?" he asked cautiously, surprised she wasn't freaking out about waking up in a random cabin. About being knocked out, period.

"Who he really was. What he was capable of." She came around the couch and sat down beside him.

She still only wore the lingerie. It could actually be considered overdressed for a shifter, who usually spent a large portion of their lives naked, before and after shifting.

Nudity wasn't something to be embarrassed about. But somehow, that red get up was even sexier than if she'd been naked. It highlighted and yet managed to hide. He should've put a shirt on her before tucking her in to sleep.

He arched a brow. "You going to fill me in on what's going on?"

She settled down next to him. "Yes. Right after I do this."

He didn't even flinch as she punched him in the arm. It didn't hurt, and felt more like a light slap, though she winced and shook her hand afterward.

"You had no right to force me to leave like that."

"You were essentially being held hostage, Bree. You've gotta admit you're relieved to be rescued."

"I am. I can't lie. But I'm so scared for River." Her words broke.

"The P.I.A. has a team searching for her at this moment. They'll find her. I need you to trust me on this. Your daughter will be fine."

She stared at him, searching his gaze. He saw the moment she decided to trust him. To believe that everything would be okay. She gave a small nod, and there was finally a look of relief. Or peace in her gaze. She leaned her head against the shoulder she'd just punched.

A swell of protectiveness raced through him and he slipped his arm around her, pulling her snug against him. To comfort her, he told himself. It was all just to comfort her.

"You have to understand that he wouldn't dare hurt her at this point," he reasoned. "We're on to him and he knows it. He'd be put on trial before he could blink."

The way the tension left her body, he could sense her relief at having someone there for her. And, for some odd reason, it felt natural and instinctive to have her in his arms like this.

"Tell me everything. Most importantly, how you ended up with this asshole."

She gave a humorless laugh. "Not a lot to tell that you can't read online. Landon and I met at a party and fell in love – supposedly. I don't think it was love for me. I was just a little overwhelmed. In awe that someone like him would be interested in me. We got engaged. He was always nice to River. And then . . ."

He sensed the sharp fear radiating from her now so traced his fingers down her bare arm and pressed a kiss to her forehead.

"Go on. You're safe with me now. There's nothing to be afraid of."

She nodded and a shiver racked her body. "He went out duck hunting with the guys one day, and I thought I'd be nice and bring them lunch."

He felt her body tense.

"What happened?"

"They were hunting," she whispered, "but not ducks. They were hunting humans."

Terrance stilled. *What the fuck?* "Humans? As in killing them in their wolf form?"

"Yes. I arrived just as they captured and killed a guy who might've been an older teenager. College aged. They were like on some kind of high from it. Loved the thrill of hearing his screams."

Son of a bitch. This was so beyond anything he'd expected. If this was discovered, it was a guaranteed death sentence from the elders in the community. Their people survived on this earth by the silence of the few government officials who knew, and the fact that shape-shifters agreed never to hurt a human.

"Damn." He shook his head. "Aubree . . ."

"I know. I knew how disgustingly sick it was, and that it went against everything we believe in. When I tried to leave with River, he realized I'd seen him that day." She drew in a ragged breath. "That's when he took her from me. He refused to give her back until we were married and mated. He could control me that way."

He could ensure her silence.

Thunder rolled on the horizon and fit with the boiling rage inside him. If he'd known all this about Landon back at the plantation house, the man would've been dead before the moon rose.

"You're angry," she said quietly.

"Yes. But not with you."

She was silent for a moment. "I should've tried to stop them."

He shook his head. "Multiple shifters in a frenzy to kill? You would've been dead yourself." A growl built in his throat. "And what he did to you? To River? He's a monster. And I should've just killed him when he answered the door this morning."

The savagery in his voice had Aubree lifting her head from his chest. She'd expected some anger, and of course a call for justice, but this . . .

"You make it sound so personal." She'd meant the words to be teasing, but they came out more husky. Questioning.

He turned slightly and his gaze fell to hers. "It is personal."

Her heart quickened. "Why? Because I'm Grace's sister?"

A second went by. And then another. He didn't answer, but his gaze darkened and his pupils dilated. Her breath caught and the air between them seemed to be alive and magnetic.

He reached out and cupped her cheek. His dark hand was large and calloused, nothing like the pale manicured softness of Landon's. But it was gentler. Almost reverent and protective.

His gaze slid to her mouth and her pulse went into overdrive.

"Terrance." She whispered his full name. Didn't call him T as she had when they were teens, when they'd both been so young. They were adults now, and the liquid, hot emotion sliding through her was definitely not childish.

His head lowered, until their foreheads touched, and their mouths almost did. She closed her eyes, dragging in an uneven breath, wanting what was about to happen, and so afraid it wouldn't.

It did. His lips, full and confident, finally closed over hers and she gave a whimper of relief. It was a sweet, soul-driven kiss, and it had been years in the making.

There was tenderness and comfort and a need she could sense he was barely restraining. When he slid his tongue past her lips, she touched hers against his tentatively.

He groaned and gathered her closer. Her heart thudded in her chest and every nerve ending in her body came to life.

For a moment she forgot everything. Everything except him. And then, when he lifted his head to give them both a quick breath, River's sweet face filled her head.

She released a shuddering breath and pushed him away. "I can't . . ."

"Shit, what was I thinking?" Terrance shook his head, his expression darkening. "I'm sorry, Bree. I don't know what the hell just came over me."

She had a fairly good idea, and it was a little bit too much to process right now.

"There's nothing to apologize for."

Terrance stood up and ran a hand over his shaved head. "I'm a little on edge. Haven't run in days."

By "run", he meant shifted. She knew how that could build up in a shifter's system. Drive them a little crazy.

"You should run then."

He swung his gaze back to her, full of skepticism. "Here?"

"We're in some tiny cabin on the swamp. I don't think there are many people around. It's really a perfect place." She smiled slightly. "Just watch for gators."

He didn't smile or laugh in return, just stared at her, before glancing at the door.

She knew how badly he wanted it. "Go. I'll be fine."

After another moment, he strode past her, but not to the door, to the bedroom. He returned a moment later with a shirt and gun.

"You know how to use one of these?" He set the gun in her hand.

"Yeah. My sister taught me a few years back." She frowned. "I don't really like the idea though—"

"If you need it, you'll use it. And this, you're just gonna have to put it on." He tossed the shirt on the couch beside her. "It's one of mine, might be a little big, but it'll cover you."

His gaze, almost unwittingly, ran over her body again and a pained expression crossed his face. She bit back a smile and picked up the shirt.

"So you're going to run?"

"Yeah."

"Good." There wasn't even a tiny pang of envy any more. At this point in her life, she'd accepted her limitations. The wolf lay inside her, but she was dormant in the physical sense. Emotionally and mentally, she still ran free.

Still, Terrance hesitated. "You're sure you'll be okay?"

She met his gaze again. "Go. You need this."

"That's not all I need." He grimaced, and that grim heat in his eyes flared again. "One more thing."

She thought, maybe hoped, he'd kiss her again. But instead he tossed his cell at her. With reflexes that showed the shifter inside her, she snatched it mid-air.

Lifting a brow, she gave him a quizzical look.

"Call your sister."

He turned then, stripped off his shirt and shucked his jeans and boxers. Her mouth went dry at his beautifully muscled brown ass and legs, and she bit her lip to stop a sigh of amazement. His body was a work of art.

She watched as he moved out the door of the cabin, his body already morphing. Fur replaced skin, sharp nails replaced fingers. He disappeared from the doorway. A moment later, she heard the soft padding of footsteps.

A black wolf appeared in the doorway this time, and he stared at her with golden eyes, his gaze somber. He was just as striking as an animal as he was as a human.

Maybe she was losing it, but in her head she distinctly heard him say, *I swear to you, you'll be safe.*

Then he was gone. The sound of his paws against the creaking wood porch could be heard, before rustling and splashing as he moved off through the swamp.

She picked up the phone, scrolled the contacts and found her sister.

When she ended the call fifteen minutes later, her cheeks were still damp from crying and there was more hope in her heart.

She set the phone down on the table and sighed. Folding her arms over her chest – which was now covered by Terrance's shirt – she walked out of the cabin to stand on the porch.

When she'd woken up, she hadn't gotten much more than a glance at her surroundings.

Now, standing on the porch, she could drink it in more. Being outside the cabin awakened her ears to all the wonderful sounds of the bayou. The croaking of frogs, calls of the cranes, and the occasional hair-raising bellow of an alligator. She could just make out the eyes of one such gator who seemed to be just hanging out and watching. Waiting.

Sorry, Mr Alligator, I don't think Terrance has swimming in mind right now.

She smiled slightly and took in the rest of the swamp. Visually it was just enchanting – the various shades of green, from the duckweed in the brown water to the grass and reeds along the shore. It was like being transported to another world. While some feared or were disgusted by the swamps, they enchanted her. Just as Louisiana in general did. She'd grown up in the beautiful Pacific Northwest, but this was a different kind of beauty. One that spoke to her on a soul level.

A flash of light had her glancing up through the cypress trees. She could see the sky had turned an ominous gray, and now she realized that the air seemed notably chiller.

Lightning? The soundscape in the swamp was drowned out by a crack of thunder half a minute later. A storm was rolling in. She scanned the swamp for any sign of Terrance.

The weeds and small trees to the left began to stir, bending and giving way as something large moved through them. She caught her breath and gripped the railing, staring intently.

Then he burst from the growth, racing toward the cabin in wolf form. His fur was covered in mud and his eyes were bright with endorphins.

The moment he hit the first step to the cabin he began to shift back. By the time he was on the porch, he was fully human and fully naked.

Her mouth went dry and her pulse quickened. It was now her turn to keep her gaze focused on his face only. Why was his nudity getting to her? It never had with anyone else.

"There's a storm coming," he rasped.

"I heard. Did you have a good run?"

"Pretty epic. Something about running in the swamps down here." He shook his head, and she didn't miss the awe in his gaze as he glanced out over the swamp. "Love the South."

So did she.

"You called Grace?"

"Yes. Thank you. I needed that as much as you needed your run." He was still standing there. Naked. She cleared her throat. "You should go put on some pants."

Surprise and then amusement flickered in his gaze, and a lazy smile eased across his face. When he took a step toward her, her heart leapt.

His cell phone ringing inside the cabin halted his advance. He gave a soft laugh and stepped past her to answer it.

She exhaled heavily and turned to stare out at the swamp again, her mind running in a million directions as Terrance spoke quietly to someone on the line.

A few minutes later there was another flash of lightning. The storm was getting closer. As the thunder rolled, Terrance appeared at her side again. He held out the phone and she took it, giving him a quizzical look.

"Hello?"

"Hi, Mommy!"

Terrance watched as Aubree pressed a fist to her mouth and slid to the floor. Tears of relief streamed silently down her cheeks as she began to speak to her daughter.

He turned and left, giving her the moment alone she needed. While the good news was that the P.I.A. had successfully located and retrieved her daughter, the bad news was that the storm meant reuniting them was going to be delayed.

River and a couple of female agents were holed up in a hotel in Texas, not far from where she'd been located.

Aubree came back inside a few minutes later wiping away tears.

"Thank you," she choked out. "I don't know how you guys did it, but thank you."

"We did it because we're good. River is one of us, and when the P.I.A. promised to find her, they meant it."

God, but he wanted to stride across the room and pull her into his arms. He curled his fingers to resist the urge. He wasn't sure why he'd lost his mind and kissed her earlier. It had been a shitty thing to do when she was distressed over her daughter.

"Is River doing okay?" he asked.

She nodded. "She's great. Sounded happy and comfortable with the agents staying with her."

"Agent Yorioka is great. I've worked with her on occasion and can vouch for her."

"Well, she's giving my kid unlimited cartoons and room-service pizza, so in River's eyes she's as fabulous as Santa."

His mouth twitched into a smile, but it quickly faded. "You heard the bad news? A storm, complete with giant hail, is heading our way. There's an advisory to stay off the roads."

She nodded. "Yes, and they made the right choice. Why rescue River just to risk their lives driving in this? I can wait a little longer knowing she's safe."

"Not only beautiful, but smart too." Shit. This wasn't flirting time.

But she didn't seem uncomfortable with his words, instead seemed pleased. A flush spread through her as her gaze slid over him, lingering on some places more than others.

His dick stirred and he ground his teeth together, willing it to stay down.

"I didn't get a chance to put on those pants."

"Do you hear me complaining?"

Her husky words made his efforts not to get a hard-on fail miserably. She took a hesitant step toward him and then paused, biting her lip. Uncertainty flashed across her face, but she didn't look away from him. There was a need in her eyes that he was pretty sure matched his own.

Everything in him demanded he close the distance between them and pull her into his arms. Taste her mouth again. Taste anywhere she'd damn well let him.

He took a step and then stopped himself. *No.* Christ, he was a bastard for even thinking it. She'd been through enough. Had he honestly been about to take those few steps that would lead to him seducing her?

"Maybe I should find us something to eat." He cleared his throat and glanced away. "Or we could put on a movie."

The silence had him glancing back at her though. A hint of doubt flickered in her gaze.

"A movie? You want to watch a movie?" She shook her head. "Tell me something. That kiss earlier, was it out of pity?"

Thunder sounded. Harsh and sudden.

But her words had startled him more. "You're kidding, right?"

"Was it to comfort me? Calm me down? I—"

"I kissed you because I couldn't stop myself," he said fiercely, moving toward her now. "Because I had to know how you tasted. How you'd feel in my arms." He reached out and pulled her against him. "I've been wondering since you were fucking seventeen."

Her eyes went wide. "You have?"

"Hell yeah." His gaze dropped to her mouth, rounded in shock. "You have no idea the way I felt about you."

He could've sworn she stopped breathing as she stared at him.

"I had the biggest crush," he admitted, and bit back a disbelieving laugh. "Hell, I think I still might."

She searched his gaze and then gave a small smile. Lifting her slender arms, she wrapped them around his neck.

"Then I think we're a little overdue for this, don't you?" She stood on her tiptoes and pressed a kiss to his mouth. "Make love to me, Terrance."

His control snapped in time with the next roll of thunder,

and he pulled her body flush against his. He crushed his mouth down on hers, the storm inside him as volatile as the storm outside.

She slid her tongue past his lips, and he sucked it deeper, tasting her. Testing her. Commandeering her mouth as his primal side demanded her submission. She gave it willingly, becoming pliant in his arms and making the sexiest, sweetest little moans.

In a moment he'd swept her into his arms and moved them to the bedroom. Before he set her on the bed, he removed the T-shirt and lingerie set.

Her naked curves stretched out on the mattress like a buffet of temptation. Everything inside him was alive with need and want.

There was so much trust and need in her eyes, and the wolf inside him grew instantly possessive. Desire ruled him.

He climbed onto the mattress beside her, draping the mosquito net around the bed and cocooning them into their own little intimate world.

Reaching out, he cupped one pale rounded breast and brushed his thumb over the taut, berry-colored nipple.

She made a ragged sigh and her eyes grew hazy with need.

"Please."

The single word broke him, and he lowered his head to draw the nipple into his mouth. Her cry of surprise and pleasure drew the wolf inside him close to the surface.

He suckled her, loving the softness and hint of sweetness about her. She arched into him, stroking his head and holding him close.

Unable to get enough of her, he switched his attention to the other breast, while sliding his palm down her body, past the gentle curve of her stomach, to the damp curls between her legs.

He pushed one finger past her folds and deep into her, finding her silky hot and wet. His dick turned to granite and he groaned. Her body clenched around his finger and she made a sharp cry.

Lifting his head, he stared down at her. So many years he'd wanted this. Imagined this. And now here she was. Her head thrown back in complete abandon. In submission.

Mine.

The thought raged through his mind. Once and then twice. Becoming a loop as the shocking primal need to claim her rocked through him.

The idea of any man, any shifter touching her again brought up a wall of rage.

Mine.

Unable to process what the hell was going on with him, he lowered his head and claimed her mouth again instead.

Aubree couldn't think. Couldn't do anything but give herself over to him. Her body was on fire and her mind and heart begged to have him inside her, and in a way that went beyond the physical sense.

When he added a second finger inside her, she walked closer to the cliff of release. She clutched his shoulders, clinging to him and kissing him desperately.

One little flick over the right spot and she was there. Crying out sharply, she climaxed and her body quaked through the aftermath.

The haze of pleasure was so strong she was only vaguely aware of him settling between her thighs and easing them farther apart.

His mouth never left hers as the thickness of his erection prodded her sensitive flesh. His kiss grew deeper. More intense. And then he plunged deep into her.

She gasped at the wonderful, sensual intrusion and her hips lifted to take him deeper.

There was no awkwardness. No fumbling discovery of each other's body that seemed to happen with someone new. It was just instinctive and natural. Primal to the core.

He claimed her body and her heart, whether he knew it or not, but without biting her in a way that would make it official. She knew the truth. Couldn't believe she'd never sensed it when she was younger, because he clearly had.

But did he fully realize and accept it now?

It grew harder to think – to process – as he thrust harder and faster into her. Her world existed as the two of them and this moment. As pleasure. She clung to him, letting go mentally.

The intensity between them grew and he choked out her name, burying his face against her neck. For a moment she was certain he would do it. Would claim her. The graze of his canines – sharp and all wolf – against her neck had her heart soaring.

But then he lifted his head again and she saw the fierce control in his eyes. The determination not to let it happen. But the sharp stab of disappointment she felt was soon swept away by her next impending climax. When he reached his orgasm, she was right there with him.

They lay there, who knew how long, with the weight of him on top of her. Her heart was slowing and the realization sinking in. He hadn't claimed her. For a moment, she'd been convinced . . . Had her instincts been wrong? Maybe he'd just acted on unexplored, years-old lust between them?

Terrance lifted his head to look down at her, and she could sense similar thoughts running through his mind.

"Aubree, I—" He froze and tilted his head. She knew they both heard the movement on the side of the cabin. What sounded like the safety being removed from a gun.

"*Fuck*." His nostrils flared. There was a pause. It couldn't have been more than two seconds, but it felt like an eternity, before he buried his mouth against her neck again.

This time his canines sank in enough to mark her and her world exploded in a dizzying white wash of pleasure.

It was over as quickly as it had begun, and then he was running toward the other room. He hadn't even reached the entrance to the bedroom before she heard the door to the cabin smash inward.

"Stay here," he shouted, before disappearing.

Definitely foe and not friend. At the sound of fighting, her mind struggled with the shock of what had just happened. He'd claimed her as his mate. Not when it had been instinctive while making love, but instead when he'd sensed danger.

Seeds of unease planted in her belly and they killed the euphoria she should've felt. As much as she wanted it to be passion driven, she sensed he'd done it to protect her. So that Landon couldn't claim her if something went wrong, because she would've already been mated to Terrance.

Whoever had entered the cabin was no longer in human form. Neither was Terrance, judging by the ferociously violent snarls.

Stay here? Screw that. Spotting the gun on the bedside table, she grabbed it and turned toward the door. The palm that slammed against her chest sent her sprawling backward and onto the floor.

She tried to maintain a grip on the gun, point it toward Landon, who now stood over her, but he'd maneuvered the barrel away from him and now bent her wrist so hard it would snap if she didn't release the pistol.

"Tried to run from me, did you, sugar?" He caught her arms and jerked her to her feet. "You never even realized I had a tracking device planted inside you."

A tracking device? The sounds of fighting continued in the living room of the cabin. Clearly he hadn't come alone but had brought several friends to back him up.

"Now what do you say we skip all the fancy ceremony shit and just make things official?" He grabbed her hair and jerked her head back, exposing her neck. "Pretty soon—*no*. God dammit, no! He claimed you?"

His roar of rage meant she was in pretty deep trouble. Maybe Terrance had claimed her, but they may not live long enough to figure out how they would play out.

"You little whore, I should've just had you killed that day you saw us."

His fingers tightened painfully around her arm, bruising the skin and nearly breaking bone, as he dragged her out of the room and past the fighting wolves. Terrance was clearly struggling to take on four other wolves at once.

She knew he saw her as Landon dragged her out of the cabin, because she heard the savagery of the fight increase, and the whimpers of the wolves that he took down.

"I'd sever your carotid artery myself, sugar, if I could get past the thought of spilling a woman's blood." Landon dragged her down the steps off the porch and toward the swamp. Thunder and lightning only added to the grim situation. "So we'll do this the nice and neat way. I'm going to drown your pretty ass."

With those words barely out, he flung her into the swamp and then pushed her under the water. The darkness washed over and she panicked, struggling to get away from him. To break the surface. She kicked and tried to push his hands off her chest. It was like trying to move a truck off a bird.

The wolf inside her, so usually controlled, began to move past the fear into a rage. For the first time in years, she felt her claws coming out.

Acting on instinct, she used them. Letting go of his arms, she slashed her now-lethal nails across his face. Landon howled in pain and released her.

She broke the surface and gasped for air, barely acknowledging the shock on his face. He probably hadn't realized she could even summon her wolf side any more.

When he reached for her again, eyes crazed, she slashed her claws across his arms.

"Actually, bitch, maybe I'd like to spill your blood." In a split second he'd shifted to wolf, his jaw wide and his canines flashing as he stalked toward her.

Was this it? How it was going to end?

He gave a snarl of rage and leapt. In mid-air, he was knocked backward by a blur of black fur.

Not if I can help it.

Terrance may as well have been in her head, she heard the words so clearly. Terrance and Landon rolled in the swamp, both in wolf form. Jaws snapped and teeth flashed. Blood flew. She couldn't even tell whose.

She ran. Using all her strength, she cursed her slight limp that slowed her down, as she made her way back to the cabin.

After managing her way around the dead shifters, she returned to the bedroom and retrieved the gun.

The battle still raged as she finally arrived back on the porch

All the fear and doubt of having to use a gun vanished in the face of saving her mate.

She leveled the barrel at the two fighting wolves, hoping like hell she had decent aim and wouldn't hit Terrance. Then she pulled the trigger.

Landon splashed back silently into the swamp, blood blooming in his gray fur. Terrance turned toward her, his golden stare full of surprise.

She'd done it.

Giving a relieved sob, she set the gun down and walked down the stairs toward Terrance. As she watched, he shifted back to human and started to make his way out of the swamp.

"Nice shot, Bre—"

Landon rose from the water, in human form again, his features distorted as he moved with shocking speed toward her mate.

Terrance turned, clearly ready to fight again, but before he had a chance, there was a flurry of movement and splashing.

Landon was dragged back into the water by the alligator she'd spotted earlier. Clearly the reptile's patience was paying off now.

"Don't look." Terrance pulled her into his arms so she wouldn't have to see her ex-fiancé being ripped to bits by the gator.

When it was over, there was nothing but silence. And then slowly the sounds of the swamp began to return. The birds. The frogs. Then there was another flash of lightning, followed by a large, terrifying clap of thunder.

"You okay?" He lifted his head and stared down at her, his gaze probing gently.

She gave something between a laugh and a sob. "Define 'okay'?"

He gave a grim smile. "Come on. We'll pack up and get the hell out of here. Send a P.I.A. clean-up crew later to clean up this mess."

★

In a hotel room, just miles from the Louisiana branch of the P.I.A. office, Terrance watched as Aubree busied herself preparing to see her daughter for the first time in over a week.

The storm had passed shortly after midnight once they'd settled into the hotel. A rather nice hotel, and on the dime of the agency, of course.

He watched as she fidgeted with the neckline of the dress he'd bought her this morning. She'd needed some clothes until they could retrieve her things from Landon's place.

Landon would've been sentenced to death for his crimes by the elders in the shifter community, but an alligator had saved them the time and money of prosecuting him.

Aubree wouldn't meet Terrance's gaze this morning. They hadn't slept in the same bed, even after everything that had happened. After they'd become mates. And she was acting as if he didn't exist.

Probably resented the hell out of him for marking her without discussing it. Their lifelong connection was the elephant in the room, and they had to address it before River arrived.

"I'd offer an annulment, but things don't really work that way." His attempt at humor failed when she lost all color and dropped the bracelet she had been trying to fasten around her wrist.

"I know how they work," she said quietly, and bent to retrieve the bracelet.

Watching her dress tighten over her ass, his blood heated once more. He wanted her. Would always want the woman who may as well be his wife in every shifter's eyes. They were mated for life.

"Let me help you with that." He closed the distance between them and took the bracelet from her.

She didn't protest, but said a soft, "I'm sorry."

"For what?" He frowned, struggling with the dainty clasp.

"That you sacrificed your happiness to protect me."

He jerked his gaze to hers. "I don't follow."

"You marked me to protect me. I understand, and it was a huge sacrifice—"

"Bullshit." The word was savage and full of disbelief. "I sure as hell hope you don't honestly believe that."

But he could see the uncertainty in her eyes.

"How would me marking you have *protected* you? Landon went *batshit crazy* when he realized we were mated. He tried to kill you. I instantly put your life at risk when I marked you, Bree," he rasped. "I wasn't thinking about that."

She blinked, tears of frustration in her eyes. "What were you thinking of then?"

"You honestly don't know?" He put the bracelet down on the table near the door, giving up on it. "I was thinking how much you meant to me and have always meant to me. I was thinking that at least if I died, you were *mine* and that sadistic bastard could never have you."

A tear spilled down her cheek and relief shone in her eyes. Maybe she wasn't all that upset about what had happened?

"You *wanted* to mate with me then?"

"Hell yeah I did," he said softly and cupped her face. "Honey, I love you, and it took everything in me to *not* claim you when we were making love. Maybe I'm old-fashioned, but I wanted to talk to you first. Make sure you felt the same connection."

"You are most definitely old-fashioned." She gave an unsteady laugh and then a small, almost shy smile. "And I do feel the same way."

His chest rose as he drew in a deep breath. "You do?"

"Yes."

"Good. Because even if we *were* human I'm not sure I could divorce you, honey." He lowered his head and brushed his mouth over hers. Once, and then twice, until his need stirred in his blood and she clung to his shoulders.

"It's always been you." Her expression was one of awe. "I knew I cared for you and felt this sense of protection, but I didn't know it went this deep. That you'd be the man I loved and mated with."

He grunted. "I think I always had a feeling. When I thought about dropping out of college to take care of you and River."

She gasped. "You didn't think about that, did you?"

"I did, actually. Then told myself I had to be nuts. We'd never even kissed, even if I'd wanted to." He stroked his thumb over her lip. "So I finished school and never really stopped thinking about you. And then the universe brought me down here to Louisiana. Where apparently it was destiny for me to find you."

"To save me and River. And I couldn't be more grateful." Her gaze, full of love and warmth, clouded a bit. "I suppose we should make plans to move back to Seattle."

She loved the South. He could see it in her eyes. Hear the unspoken sadness in her words. "Or we could make plans for me to transfer down to the NOLA office."

Her lips parted. "You'd do that for me?"

"Not just for you, for both of us. I've got bayou in my blood, honey. Ever since I started visiting my aunt each summer when I was ten. I would love to work down here."

"Oh, thank you!" She stood on her tiptoes and kissed him again.

The knock on the door brought them apart.

"Go answer the door and reunite with your daughter. We've got the rest of our lives for the other stuff."

Aubree stood on the porch of their new house, watching River and Terrance toss a softball back and forth. She loved their yard. While it wasn't huge, it was certainly pretty and alive with character. The grassy area was enclosed by a black wrought-iron fence, the branches from an oak tree on the sidewalk dangling over it and offering a bit of shade from the hot summer sun.

It was nice to have some quiet time with just the three of them. Soon to be four. She rubbed her growing belly and smiled.

Only yesterday the house had been full of people who'd flown in for River's sixth birthday. Of course that had been only part of the reason. The group had also wanted to see Terrance and Aubree's new home and wish the newly-weds well.

It had been good to see them all. Grace and Darrius had flown down with their baby boy, as well as Terrance's close P.I.A. friends, Sienna and Warrick. She felt loved and protected by the group. But most especially by her husband and mate.

River dropped the ball and ran toward the house. "Be right back, Mommy, I've gotta go to the bathroom."

She disappeared inside and Aubree turned back to face her husband as he walked up the few stairs to the porch.

"Should you be outside in this heat? Doesn't bug you?" he asked, slipping his arms around her and pulling her to him.

"I love the heat, pregnant or not." Okay, maybe a little more when not, but she loved watching the two of them play and so she put up with it.

He kissed her mouth and touched her belly gently. "You're adorable."

She kissed him back. "And you're amazing. River loves you as much as I do."

"She's a good kid. I love having her as my daughter."

The fact that he'd legally and emotionally chosen to make River his daughter still brought tears to her eyes.

"I'm pretty sure the second kid will be equally amazing." She smiled and kissed him again. "Date night still on for later?"

"Absolutely. Aunt Brandy can't wait to have River over. And I can't wait to get you alone. I should warn you, we may not make it out to a restaurant though," he growled.

"Mmm. I'm not complaining."

Their lips met again, the kiss deepening, until a distinct "Gross, you guys!" drove them apart.

River ran back to the yard and picked up the ball. "Come on, Dad! Let's play."

"We'll finish this later," he murmured, smiling against her mouth.

"Later," she agreed.

As he ran back down the stairs to toss the ball around with his daughter, Aubree rubbed her baby belly and knew the meaning of complete and utter happiness.

IF ONLY TONIGHT

Jessa Slade

In Between Days

I hate being goth in So Cal.

No matter how much powder I use, my foundation turns to paste, then the flat iron that is my giant middle finger to genetics fails me within half an hour and my Blacktastic Starless Night™ hair frizzes into a fright wig. And the sun . . .

It. Never. Fucking. Stops.

I curse the sunlight bouncing off the Pacific – like it's glaring right back at me – while I trudge down yet another hell of palm trees and pavement that is Ocean Avenue. I was an idiot to come back here. They say you can never go home again, and yet Greyhound is always willing to sell those one-way tickets. But I don't belong here, I never did.

Though I haven't found anyplace else either. I guess I belong nowhere.

A mile or so behind me, the cemetery where I just left the only remaining link to my past reminds me there's always one last place to go. Against my will, my breath catches, and I taste a whiff of the Santa Ana the weatherman has been threatening for days. It's thick in my throat, cinders mixed with a metallic tang like diesel.

Or blood.

The hair on the back of my neck tries to prickle, but sweat is matting Starless Night into Bottomless Tar Pit, decidedly *not* trademarked. I stop to hike up my skirt and use the studs in one of my leather bracelets to rip another hole in my fishnets. Anything to get a breath of air on my hoo-ha.

"Show us your tits!"

I hear the catcall over the music flowing through my earbuds. How dare anyone interrupt The Cure? Yeah, I know it's old shit, but you get more cred when you're half-way dead. I tilt my head to squint at the guys in the bronze pimped-out Monte Carlo cruising past. Slowly, I straighten, running my hands over my black velvet hips, into the cinched curve of my waist, up to the tits in question, which I cup with loving tenderness – one of the boys is hanging halfway out the window to look back at me – then I flick my fists up in the constricted OK gesture that silently yet so eloquently says *asshole*. "In your dreams, *pendejo*!"

"Witch bitch!" he screams back.

Did I mention I hate being goth in So Cal?

Which is why I'm cursing again as I step off the sidewalk without looking both ways. The last thing I see is a flash of chrome – like the sun has beamed a solar flare right into my brain – and real darkness comes. At long last.

Just Like Heaven

It's still dark when I blink, my eyelids scraping over my dried-out eyeballs. That's what I get for falling asleep in my stainless-steel designer contact lenses . . . No, wait. I'm not home in bed, and the tinny stench of the Santa Ana is strong enough to gag me.

Except it's not just the devil wind this time.

I touch the back of my head, and my fingers stick. Ugh. Bottomless Tar Pit With Half-Dried Blood Streaks is *not* an improvement. Gingerly, I lever myself to my elbows. Where I'm sprawled, yuccas and manzanitas block my view. God, how far did that car throw me?

My fishnets have new unplanned holes through which I can see my road-rashed knees, and my arms are scratched where the vicious desert plants bit me to hell. But other than that and my seeping head wound, I think I'm not too fucked up.

Not physically, anyway.

Something rustles in the dark brush. Rat or palmetto bug? Or something worse, drawn by the perfume of blood? I don't want to find out. I force myself to my feet. My black platform boots are heavy enough to keep me upright, but my knees are still shaky as I look around.

Standing, I realize it's not quite as dark as I thought. The shadows are charcoal, not black, and there's a faint misty light, the same shade as my stainless-steel eyes. Sometimes the Santa Anas bring a strange fog, as if the ocean is trying to creep back in while the winds aren't watching. The grayish light picks out the rough burlap texture of the palms so the dark trees look wrapped in burial shrouds.

I can't believe I've been laying here long enough for the sun to set, and no one stopped to . . .

Wait. I'm not on Ocean any more. I turn a slow circle, but I can't see the street or the water. Whatever the time of day or night, I should be able to hear cars or at least the waves that never stop.

But there's nothing.

Did the asshole who hit me pick me up and dump me somewhere? My messenger bag is still crossed over my chest, so I swing it around front to dig out my phone. A crack jags a frozen lightning bolt across the screen, but it powers on . . . to no bars, no service, no luck. FML.

I'm still in So Cal, I'm sure of that. At least, I think I'm sure. My first shocked gasp sucked in a lingering dusty heat and the rotten sweetness of fallen jacaranda blossoms. No place else on Earth smells like home.

"What the hell?" The mutter just slips out of me, but it sounds right, so I say it again louder.

The fog swallows my voice, and no one answers, but the rustling in the bushes has stopped. I get the sense something is holding its breath, listening. Not just the invisible wandering creature, but some other, more restless presence.

Suddenly reluctant to stay, watched by unseen eyes, I take a hesitant step forward. My left ankle aches, but the tight laces and buckles of my boot hold it firm.

Sometimes the ass you need to kick is your own.

I hobble another step forward and, as my angle of view changes, I realize that the palm trees are arrayed in two parallel lines. A pathway. But it doesn't look much used. The Bermuda grass is dense and spongy and I leave a clear track of footprints behind me. But mine are the only ones.

Even though it doesn't seem very promising, I follow the path. If no one has found me yet and the sun has set, I'm on my own.

But then, that's always been the case.

When the palm path finally opens up, I am too exhausted to do more than stand and sway and stare at the Mission Revival hacienda crowning the low hill. In the soft gray light, the pristine stucco arches of the front arcade curve like the rib bones of some giant moon-bleached whale carcass. Across the second story, small windows flank a series of balcony doors, all dark, as if a row of beings with empty eyes and gaping mouths were peering over the balustrade.

Centered above the front door, a bell gable rises into the weirdly overcast night, but there's no bell in its heart, just another empty arch framing the ashy sky.

I hesitate again. It looks as if no one's home. Maybe I can break in and try to find a landline phone. Maybe I can get a view around from the hilltop, see if there's another house nearby. Or at least someplace I recognize.

I limp out onto the lawn that skirts out from the concentric tile steps leading to the front door. The moment my foot hits the grass, matted like dreadlocks, I hear that rustle again. Shit, something is following me.

I whirl around, gasping as my ankle twists.

From out of nowhere, there's a guy standing behind me. Even in the crappy light, the blond waves of his hair gleam a little, as if the Pacific sun – invisible at the moment – is shining through a secret passage to ruffle his locks. Though we're outside, my gut clenches in claustrophobic panic, and the reek of the Santa Ana suddenly reminds me of high-school hallways where no amount of scrubbing can remove the taint, too close, too confining, the lines of lockers and empty doorways stretching into dull eternity.

When I stumble, he starts to reach out, but stops himself. My faithful shit-kickers catch me anyway, and I flinch back. The chains around my waist chime a warning that I repeat aloud, "Don't touch me!"

"Hey, easy." He holds up his hands, fingers outstretched like stars. "I saw you coming. Are you lost?"

The Perfect Boy

He's a golden boy. You find them everywhere in So Cal, buffed and burnished, until it stops meaning anything, just a shiny penny you think you're lucky to find as a kid and step over when you're older and wiser by, like, a day.

I can't believe I ever fell for that look.

He's taller than me by a lot, but most guys are. His chinos are slung baggy around his lean hips, and his T-shirt is tight enough to show off his surf-ready musculature. Through the thin white cotton, I can just barely see the shadow of a tattoo circling his bicep, though the design isn't clear. He's barefoot, which is crazy because Bermuda grass is coarse and cruel. That happens sometimes to things that bake too long under the hot sun.

I drag my gaze back up to his sunny-sky-blue eyes when he takes another step toward me, a worried furrow in his brow as he studies my various bangs and bruises. My achy skin prickles at his close attention, and I wish I hadn't put the extra holes in my stockings.

"You were hurt," he said. "I'm sorry."

Once upon a time, I would've killed for someone like him to look at me and care. But not any more. I glare at him. "Are you the one who hit me?"

"What?" He stops in his tracks. "No. I didn't—"

"Then why are you sorry?"

The furrow turns into a scowl. "Because no one should end up here just because they didn't want to be wherever they were."

"Here?" I echo. His cryptic explanation makes me even more guarded than before. "Where did you come from?"

"The house." He gestures behind me.

"I thought nobody was—". I glance over my shoulder "—home. Huh."

The hacienda is ablaze now, every window and door and the arcade on both sides glowing with a yellowish light. Only the upper gable where the bell would have been is still dark, and the Santa Ana fog twists restlessly through the white arch.

"Come on," says Golden Boy. "The mistress is waiting to meet you."

"Mistress?" I echo doubtfully.

He doesn't respond.

Just because I'm dressed in a leather corset doesn't mean I'm into anything kinky. But it's not like I have a lot of options. Reluctantly, I shuffle along beside him, feeling particularly short and drab next to his shining shelf. Shit, I thought I'd left this pathetic insecurity behind. "How did you know I was out here?"

"The mistress told me to look for you." His mouth turns down. "She knows everything."

I'm momentarily distracted by the curve of his lips. He doesn't have the tight mouth of many blond Anglos. In profile, his top lip is lush, slightly overreaching the lower lip in a reverse pout.

Which only reminds me how long it's been since I was kissed. I booted my last fuck-buddy a few months before I boarded the Greyhound. He'd used the words "get" and "over" and "it" one too many times for my taste. But if he'd had lips like those, maybe I wouldn't have cared so much what words were coming out of them.

"What's your name?" I ask, keeping it casual.

Coz maybe I'm willing to fall for that golden look one more time.

He glances down at me. Whatever he sees on my face causes one corner of that mouth to tilt upward again. "I'm Wyatt. And you are . . . ?"

"Alma." When he starts to speak, I cut him off. "Here's the thing, Wyatt. I'm not sure how I got here, but I just want to go home, wash off the blood, drink too much of something made from liquefied agave as revenge for being cut up by those fucking yuccas, and then I'm going to sleep like I'm dead."

Wyatt recoils. It's not obvious, but he moves so gracefully, as if the ground is water under his feet, that I can't help but pay attention to his body. Though he keeps his gaze fixed on the house, his blue eyes are half shuttered, and unreadable shadows lurk behind his lashes like the mysterious tattoo on his arm.

Maybe he thinks I'm rude, or maybe he thinks I'm a drunk. Whatever. I'm not a pretty little princess, and I've got places to be.

Except I don't, not really. The cemetery, to say goodbye, was my last stop. But I'm not going to tell Golden Boy that.

We leave the grass for a terracotta walkway that leads up to the front door, which is wide open. I squint, but my eyes, which have gotten used to the gloom, can't see past the yellow light coming from within. Flanking the front walk are potted palms, and the glare behind them makes their frayed bark shiver like they are on fire. The walkway splits to circle around a central fountain. Wyatt walks to one side and I take the other, glancing at the stone figurine in curiosity.

It's an angel holding an urn angled above her head. Not so unusual, except the urn has been cracked open and the angel's wings hang limp and defeated from her shoulders, trailing down into the water.

Or where water would be. The fountain is bone dry. Only a rusty stain marks the angel where the shattered urn has dripped, from her breast down her skirts to the basin below. She looks as if she has stabbed herself with the broken remnants of the stone and is standing in a pool of her own blood.

"Alma."

I jerk my head around to see that Wyatt has gotten ahead of me. He waits with one bare foot up on the first step. The faintest Southern drawl of his Dust Bowl ancestors – some slow Okies, maybe, whose dying wheat swapped their children for golden-haired changelings – makes my name sound strangely sweet in his mouth.

"You can't go back," he says.

I *know* that, and yet the way he says it makes me stiffen. There's a darkness lurking at the bottom of his blue eyes that makes me think he knows more about me than he possibly can, and I'm about to show him exactly what I *can't* do – take *can't* as an answer, for example – when a figure appears in the yellow light of the doorway.

For a confused moment, I think the angel has come alive. But then the woman steps farther out into the courtyard, and I see what my bumped head mistook for wings is actually her long pale hair. The silvery waterfall of her hair glides past her hips, perfectly silky, perfectly straight. I'd thought the word *kinky* earlier when Wyatt mentioned his mistress, but this hair has never had a hair out of place.

A crow taking a crap on the fountain angel's bowed head wouldn't have been more out of place than me standing here among these fair beauties.

"Welcome." Even her voice is beautifully smooth. I get the impression she is older, but she is slender, and her face – moon round and pallid in a way that I'll never achieve, not with all the foundation and powder in the world – makes it impossible to guess her age. "I am Bianca, mistress of this house. Please, come in."

Wyatt glances back at me, a peculiar appeal in his eyes. I wonder if she's hurting him. She's his mistress, after all, so maybe he likes it. He's a big boy, with the broad shoulders to prove it, and despite his bare feet, he could walk away if he wanted, right?

"I just need to make a call," I say.

"Of course you do." She smiles, her dark eyes bright.

Wyatt doesn't move until I pass him on the steps, then he follows us silently into the house.

A breath of the fog swirls behind me, chilling my scratched arms. For a second I think I hear whispers, quieter than the chime of chains around my waist as I pass beneath the terracotta medallion set into the stucco above the lintel. There's a phrase etched into the tile, the house crest, I guess: *Las Ombras del Sol.*

"My kind of place," I mutter.

Despite my low voice, Bianca looks back at me with another smile. "Indeed." Her eyes are very dark, so dark I can't see where pupil meets iris, which looks odd on someone so pale. Like the hacienda looked when I first saw it, seemingly empty.

Bianca's skirts whisper across the tiles, and my boots thud with reassuring toughness, but Wyatt is still silent behind us. But, of course, he is barefoot.

Though Bianca is triggering my weird-o'-meter, my focus is still on Wyatt. Something's bothering me about his bare feet, but I can't quite . . .

Then it hits me. When I first turned and saw him standing behind me out on the lawn, the sharp tufts of grass were crushed by only one set of footprints: mine.

As if he had appeared out of thin air.

Sleep When I'm Dead

I'm not interested in mysteries, I just need to make a damn phone call.

I stop abruptly in the middle of the foyer. Bianca pauses with her hand on the wrought-iron newel post of the grand staircase leading upstairs. With the dark wood floors and exposed beams and stark white plaster walls, I feel like I've fallen into an old black-and-white movie. The only color comes from the sickly glow of the Moorish-style chandelier – wrought iron, big as a medieval gibbet – suspended two stories above our heads. Yellow lights flicker behind the glass; they must have lit candles when the power went out and the house went black. Seems unnecessarily dangerous to me, there could be a fire. But then, I don't mind sitting around in the dark.

With precisely polite enunciation, I say again, "I just need to make a phone call."

Bianca tilts her head. "To whom?"

I open my mouth to be much less polite but realize I've got nothing to say.

Whom, indeed?

Tears prickle in my eyes like the saw-toothed edges of the yuccas that stabbed me, and my stomach churns at the pathetic little gasp that comes out of me.

If *mi abuelita* were here, she would hug me close to her bosom and say, *Pica la abeja, mas dulce el favo.*

The bee stings, but the honey is sweet.

That was always her response when I said life sucks. She believed it even though her only daughter died before she did, even though her only son disappeared back into Mexico never to be heard from again, even though all her grandchildren are fucked up in myriad ways. And I'll never hear it from her again.

She was the one I called when life was too hard and sharp and cruel, and now she is gone.

Bianca flicks one finger toward me. "No matter. You can't call out when the devil winds are blowing. And who knows how long the lights will stay out this time? Perhaps you can try again in the morning."

Wyatt makes a soft sound, like a protest, and Bianca pins him with a glance. "Since you are here, Wyatt, please take our guest to a room where she can rest."

He nods once, a jerky motion more like he's getting his face out of the way of a blow. He starts up the stairs without looking at me.

I don't want to go, but I'm feeling dizzy. Maybe my head was banged worse than I thought. Maybe I just can't take any more tonight.

From the second floor, I'll be able to see farther. The Santa Ana fog won't last forever, and I'll be able to find other lights. Then I'm out of here.

Unless the power stays out.

I'm not going to think about that. Not now. Just like I can't think about how Aba's flat headstone sank into the dirt, already half lost under the ragged grass.

I follow Wyatt upstairs, pausing on the upper landing just long enough to glance back. Bianca is watching us, unmoving. Two young women appear through the doorway that leads to one of the front arcades. They turn their heads to look up at me, the twinned gesture eerily identical, especially since they are both wearing white sundresses similar to Bianca's. One of the girls is as blonde as Wyatt, and although the other has slightly darker hair, they might as well be matching Malibu Beach Barbies.

"Who are they?" I ask Wyatt.

"They stay here too." He continues down the hall.

Not really an answer. The dark wood and white plaster feels even more claustrophobic up here where the hall is narrow and the windows are small to keep out the heat. Wrought-iron lanterns set high on the walls flicker with the same wan light as the chandelier, but the frosted and crazed glass makes it impossible to see the candles inside.

The pulsing light is giving me a headache, and though I'm uneasy about the mood of this place, I'm still grateful when Wyatt pushes open a small, dark-stained door. The metal bands and studs that decorate the heavy wood give me pause, but the room beyond is gorgeous.

A simple white bedspread covers the big iron poster bed, looking whiter than white under pillows of bold Zapotec patterns. The side tables flanking the bed are the same dark wood as the rest of the house, but delicately shaped, and there's a hint of perfume coming from the dried flowers arranged in matching vases in the same Zapotec hues but muted.

There's even a round corner fireplace decorated in cheerful bright tilework, though there are more flowers rather than flames in the hearth. A backless divan is pulled up in front of the fireplace, the cushioned arms flared open as if summoning me to sit my weary ass down.

Instead, I go to the window. The glass pane is set deep enough that I have to lean into the window well, but it opens at my touch. A curl of mist brushes a cold touch over my fingers.

"You should keep that closed," Wyatt says. "The dust blows in on the wind."

I look across the tile roof. The rich red is corroded to the same rusty color as the angel's bath by the gray sky. My window is above the front line of palms that marches out into the darkness like an army advancing on . . . nothing.

There's nothing out there, no lights, no sound of traffic, nothing. I tilt my gaze upward. The Santa Ana fog has obliterated any trace of moon or stars. Or sun. For a stubborn child of the night like me, this should be heaven, but instead the stagnant light unnerves me.

I glance at Wyatt. "What time is it?"

"I don't know." He crosses his arms over his chest, which strains his T-shirt over his wide shoulders and bunches up his biceps. No watch around his wrist, I see, and I still can't make out the tattoo.

"Is it . . ." I'm not sure why I hesitate. "I was knocked out when the car hit me. Is it late night or early morning?"

He is so quiet he seems to bring the world to a standstill, and I finally hear a noise from outside . . .

A scream. Faint, not because it was far away but because it sounded as if the screamer had simply run out of breath.

I jump. "What was that?" That wasn't a coyote howling or a squeaking bat. Or any other animal.

"Doesn't matter if it's day or night," Wyatt says.

I whirl to face him, thoroughly sick of his non-answers. "I asked you a simple fucking question." I snap out each word like I'm spitting cactuses. "Where am I?"

His tone is as flat as the gray light outside. "Las Ombras del Sol."

"Yeah. Shadows of the Sun. I saw that above the door. But where—?"

"Even the brightest sunlight casts a shadow." His mouth twists, distorting his full lips into something grotesque. "The sun always shines in Cali, so I guess that's why these shadows never fade."

I stare at him, my breath hitching in frustration. All those wretched years when I wished one of the cute boys would talk to me? Yeah, never mind if they're going to talk like this. "Are you loco or something?"

"I wish," he says. "I'd take crazy over being dead."

I freeze, but my knees start to shake, as if the cold fog has stolen my bones.

He advances on me slowly – on those bronzed bare feet that left no marks in the grass – and I match each step with a retreat. "This is *no* place," he says. "And there is *no* time. Not any more. It's run out. Like the water in the fountain. There's nothing left, just dust and wind and fog."

I back up until the hard edge of the window bites at my spine. "Okay, look, I love gloom and doom as much as any goth girl, but—"

"Then you should feel right at home," he drawls. "Which is a good thing, since we're never leaving. I'm trapped here, like the others. Like you now, Alma."

He's too close and I'm too confused. The kind of confused that makes me angry, that made me run from home when I was way too young to be on my own. And I came back too late to try again, to make some sort of peace. Everyone who might have helped me make sense of the path I've found myself on is gone.

Including this golden boy, apparently. Or so he says.

But I'm done running away.

I push away from the window and meet Wyatt halfway, up in his face, though I have to go on tiptoe to glare at him.

"I'll leave any time I want," I tell him. "No one can make me stay." I say it with conviction, even though that reality has been the cruelest curse of my life.

"You're one of us now," he says again. Because of the difference in our height, he's looking down at me, but his blue eyes are terribly gentle. "You can never leave."

"Just watch me." I go to flatten my palm on his wide chest to push him away.

But my hand disappears straight into his heart.

I gasp, half expecting a gush of blood around the studded bracelets on my wrist. He stiffens. Our gazes lock. I'm sure my stainless-steel contacts are about to pop out of my shock-widened sockets, while in his blue eyes there's a sorrow dark and fathoms deep.

"I died, Alma," he says, his voice soft again with that lingering hint of the Old South, but he's close enough I should feel his breath. And I don't. "I'm a ghost. Like you."

I make a gurgling sound. It sounds like a laugh, and for a moment I'm sort of proud of myself. But obviously *I* am the crazy one to be seeing and hearing much less believing all of this. My knees finally give out and even my big black boots can't hold me upright.

Wyatt reaches out to catch me, but his hands go right through my chest. My heart races at the phantom caress – did that happen to him when I touched him? – then my head hits the edge of the windowsill, and my own private blackness claims me again.

Watching Me Fall

When I wake this time, I'm in the white bed, the Zapotec blanket tucked around me. Lying here, I can see the small window. It frames the same steel-gray sky as before, like a reminder that I might somehow escape through it, but there is nothing more beyond.

Because Wyatt says I'm—

I bolt upright in the bed. My corset is gone, my spiked jewelry too. I'm wearing only a simple white shift. I touch the back of my head, where my hair is clean and tumbles in loose waves around my shoulders. Somehow, the black dye has been stripped away, leaving the natural dark brown that isn't anywhere near tough enough.

At my commotion, a figure rises from the divan in front of the fireplace. It's one of the blonde girls I saw the night before with Bianca. I hadn't noticed her sitting there, she was so still. She stares at me from across the room.

I'm freaked out, but I'm not going to let that stop me. "I have no idea what the hell is going on, but get me out of here." The appeal whines out of me, lacking the demand I had intended. I sound desperate.

"I can't." She stands with one hand on her cocked hip, her head tilted as she studies me. "The mistress told me to prepare you."

The breathless quality in her voice reminds me of everything I hated about girls from the valley when I was growing up. Worse, it reminds me of the scream I heard earlier. It was her, I'm sure. "You can come too," I tell her. "We have to . . . We just have to leave."

She angles her face to the gray window. "Anywhere we go, we'd still be lost. That's how you got here."

I study her perfect blondness, which reminds me too much of Golden Boy. "I'll be lost in my own damn way, thanks anyway."

She looks back at me and smiles faintly. Somehow, that smile is more awful than the scream. "You are not one of us."

Just great. So apparently even dead girls have cliques?

I shove back the blankets to get out of bed – my head still aches a little, but I can kick her skinny blonde ass even without my boots – until there's a hesitant knock and Wyatt peers in.

Our gazes lock.

I shrink back, clutching the Zapotec blanket to my breasts. I'm usually never shy. Ever. But I've never stuck my hand through a dead guy's heart before either.

Fuck. When did I start believing these psychos?

Oh, about the time our hands went right through each other.

Wyatt looks at the other girl. "Is everything okay in here, Jewel?"

She glides toward him. "No, Wyatt. Everything isn't okay." She stops toe to toe with him. "Don't touch her again." She yanks the half-open door out of Wyatt's hand and shoots one last look at me. Then she deliberately walks through him out into the hall.

The impossible merging of their outlines makes me feel sick to my stomach. But it seems even worse for him; he shudders and sags in the doorway, pale under his tan.

Despite my shock, I feel the urge to go to him, to soothe the anguished look from his face. The impulse makes me mad since stupid is the first thing that should be cured by being dead. So I just glare at him from under my annoyingly mascara-free lashes. I've been stripped of everything that made me what I was. "So your girlfriend seems really, uh, sweet."

"She's not my girlfriend. We . . . we can't do that sort of thing any more."

"Be possessive and vicious and make vague moaning noises? That seems like exactly the sort of thing ghosts do."

The somber set of his lips softens. "Well, when you put it that way . . . " He makes his way across the room and sits in the divan facing me instead of the fireplace. He stares at me and his sun-kissed color returns. I guess golden boys never fade, and I have the awful thought I will always be haunted by the things I couldn't have, the things I couldn't be, from back when I was too stupid to even know what I wanted.

I gotta stop wondering about this stuff or I really will go crazy, but I have too many questions. I'll start with the basics. "So I'm really dead? I mean, I'm dead, really?"

His hands tighten on the edge of the seat, making the muscles in his arms bunch. "Yes."

"And you're dead."

He nods.

For a second, my mind reels and I can't breathe. But I guess ghosts don't need to breathe. Still, the sensation of choking scares me and, as always when I'm scared, I get angry so I don't have to be scared. I frown a challenge at him. "Why didn't you just walk through the door instead of knocking? And how can you sit there without falling through the floor?"

He rolls his surfer's shoulders in a shrug. "I don't know. Sometimes being dead isn't all that different from being alive."

For some reason, that depresses me more than anything I have ever heard in my whole entire life.

Wyatt raps his knuckles on the scrolled wooden detailing on the divan, a hollow noise. "So many things seem the same. But the candles in the lanterns never burn down, and the sun never rises." He turns his face toward the window, but his gaze stays fixed on me. "When we try to touch one another, first it burns, then it freezes, then . . . nothing. It's awful, worse than any torture. And we can never leave."

I hug the blanket tighter, as if the bright colors can ward off the chill sinking into me. "Is this . . ." I think of all the defiantly depressing music I've sung along with over the years, and I'm embarrassed when my voice breaks. "Is this hell?"

"I thought so at first, but . . ." He shrugs again. "I think it's worse. We died, but we haven't crossed over. Because of her. She keeps us trapped in this halfway house, away from the light."

By "she", I know he doesn't mean the bitchy Malibu Jewel who was in the room a few moments ago. He means Bianca, mistress of Las Ombras del Sol.

The memory of her blank black eyes makes my skin crawl, and I clamber out of the bed.

Wyatt rises too, though he stays far enough away from me that we won't accidentally touch. "Where are you going?"

"Out," I say. When he starts to object, I wave my hand. "Away from here." The pretty flower arrangements now look more funeral than festive, their perfume tainted with the stench of ashes.

Wyatt sigh and then nods. "Fine. Come on."

Considering he said those words to me before and I followed him into the house of the dead, I'm probably an idiot for listening to him again. But when he heads out into the hallway, I'm right behind him.

My room was near one end of the hallway. In the center of the house, above the central stairway, is another wrought-iron staircase, this one circular and leading up into the darkness. I hang back a little to give Wyatt time to start up the circle. With the tight curve of the stairs, his ass is almost in my face. It's a cute ass for a dead boy.

I can't believe my taste in men sucks every bit as much as when I'm dead as it did when I was alive. Golden boys and goth girls never mix, not in my life before, and obviously not now.

Wyatt throws back a trap door that blocks the top of the stairs and climbs up into the bell tower.

He stands back as I clamber out, not trying to help me. He'd said that the ghostly touch is torture, but that's not what I'd felt when he tried to catch me before. My whole body had tingled, and not in a bad way at all. Though I'm not going to mention that, obviously.

Instead, I prowl around the periphery of the small, square tower. The adobe walls are cut into four arches opening out into the four directions. Paler curls of fog trace the eerie pearl-gray sky all around us. Wyatt tucks himself out of the way, leaning that cute ass in one of the windows, watching me, his blue eyes darker than usual under his half-closed golden-lashed lids.

He's not touching me now, but my skin still shivers a little. Without my velvet and leather and spikes, I feel naked. I *am* naked under this stupid white shift. I cross my arms over my chest and glare at him to show him I'm not intimidated by his stare. "What are you looking at, *chulo*?"

"You," he says. "You have pretty eyes when they aren't barricaded. And I like your hair this way."

Oh sure, *now* he answers my questions without riddles. I have boring brown eyes, and it takes all my willpower not to wrap one of my wayward ringlets around my fingers. Fuck, I might even giggle. Having ringlets often results in giggling; it's like the corkscrew shape drills into your skull and lets the brains leak out. Which is why I much prefer the weapon-like straight edge of an asymmetrical A-line. Except even my choice of hairstyles has apparently been taken away.

So I ignore his comment and direct my attention to the sky. "I know we're still in So Cal. I *feel* it, but I thought for sure I'd see something from this high. Other houses, traffic on the 405, something."

"There's nothing. Except . . ." He shifts on the wall, making more space beside him. "Come over here." He holds his hand out, not to touch me, but an invitation nonetheless, and it makes my heartbeat race in a way I would never have allowed if I'd been alive.

The Empty World

I dither for a long moment. There was a time when this was everything I could've wanted: a boy who walks with the sunlight in his hair, smiling at *me*. But I got over that pathetic desire. I don't *need* the boy or the sun or the smile. Gah. This really is hell. But since I'm told I can't escape . . . I join him in the arch, hitching my hip up onto the ledge so I'm sort of facing him but looking outward too.

He points. "There. Do you see it?"

I look. "Palm trees like severed heads. Gray sky. Gray fog. No stars." My voice is starting to rise with something like panic, so I chomp down on my lip.

His finger never wavers. "Farther. On the very edge of the horizon, as far as you can see."

"There's nothing." I realize with a chill that I'm repeating him. *There's nothing.* But for all the nihilistic songs I've sung along with, if there is breath vibrating between vocal cords to make the notes that hang in the silence, then there is *something.* Suddenly, I think I see a faint shine. "What is that?"

"I think it's the ocean." He shakes his head, a thick blond lock falling across his eyes. "No, that's not true. I don't think that, I just wish it was."

It's just a sliver of light, thinner than the trail of a shooting star. Considering I spent my life – what there was of it – courting shadows, that elusive glimmer fills me with a ridiculous joy.

And a tidal wave of regret. I'd played at darkness before. Is it to be my existence now?

My eyes burn with the threat of tears. I *never* cry, not since I realized crying only works for pretty princesses. Ugly girls can only get mad. But I've welled up twice since I came back here. What is happening to me?

. . . Oh. Right. Dead.

I fix my gaze on that teasing splinter of light until the tears dry. "Have you ever tried to get there?"

"Once. Just after I . . . came here. I don't know how long I walked. A long time, but I never got anywhere."

There's a lot he's not saying in that pause. I use the lingering burn in my eyes to try to laser my way into his shuttered gaze. "How did you die?"

Despite my insistent focus, he looks away. "The same way we all did. By killing myself."

I choke on a hard breath. "I did *not* kill myself."

"That's what I said too. At first. Sure, I knew the storm surge was heavy, and the advisory said the riptides were gnarly, but it was my last day before I went back to med school and I wanted to surf."

Surprise rips me out of my anger. "Med school? You?"

He rubs his forehead and sighs. "See, this is why I told everyone I didn't want to be a doctor, even though it was a long, proud family tradition. Being a doctor obviously wasn't for me."

My cheeks are hot. How much do I hate when people make assumptions – even true ones – about me? And I just did it to him. "Sorry," I mumble.

"Why are you sorry?" The mocking note in his voice reminds me how I'd snarked at him earlier about whether he'd been the one to hit me. "You didn't force me to do something I didn't want to do. I did that to myself." His upper lip curls, a rogue wave with a rough break. "I said something epic, like, 'Surf or die!' and . . . I was a surfer who drowned. How sad is that?"

I think of how I stepped off the curb without looking, thinking of death. "You made a mistake," I tell him. "A bad decision is not suicide."

He finally looks back at me. "I guess that depends on what was in your heart when you decided."

I had most assuredly *not* decided to die! After visiting Aba's grave, I'd left the cemetery and decided to walk back to my busline because I needed some time, when I realized there was nothing and no one left for me . . .

When I hear the echo of my words in my head, it sounds pretty damning.

Wyatt must see the dawning horror on my face. "All of us here had a moment where we thought, for whatever reason, life wasn't worth it. And then we ended up here." He reaches toward my hand clutching the wall where we sit, though he doesn't touch me. "Honestly, when I first saw you, all in black and white, I thought maybe you'd been dead longer than I have."

I jerk back, furious just at his proximity, which feels too much like the last time I tried to touch the light . . . and failed. "Right, because even a dead golden boy is worth more than a goth girl."

He withdraws his hand and snorts. "That's not what I meant, but you already had enough clouds hanging over your head to put these shadows to shame."

I. Will. Not. Cry. I stare at the distant crack of daylight. If she was still alive, my Aba would laugh. I've worked so hard to guard myself against the stingers of life's bees, built up layers of armor no one can breach, and now I want that tiny honey-gold glimmer like I've never wanted anything before. "Wherever that light is, I'll get there."

Wyatt pushes to his feet as if he's going to block my way. "I told you, it's impossible." He paces one step then back. "I shouldn't have shown you. I just wanted . . ."

"What?" I ask acidly. "Wanted to get my false hopes up?"

"No. I wanted you to not feel so alone."

There's another crack, like that bit of light, somewhere inside of me, and I don't know what to do with it. "Come with me," I tell him.

The words are out before I can decide if they are a good idea or another damning one. I suck in my breath – as if I can recall my offer before he rejects it. Everyone gets rejected, I don't know why I take it so personally, but I always have.

"Alma." He rakes his fingers through his hair, leaving harried furrows. The gesture makes his sleeves roll back, exposing the tattoo on his bicep. I shouldn't be surprised, it's a stylized sun and standing wave. No color, though, just bold, black lines: the simple, clear, everlasting expression of his love, nailed into his skin. The hiked-up T-shirt also exposes deliciously tight abs from pulling himself up onto a surfboard over and over.

I shake my head. "How can someone willing to walk on water be afraid now?"

He drops his arms, hiding his belly and the tattoo. His expression is blank. "When I tried to walk out, the mistress came after me."

"Is Bianca a ghost too?"

He shrugs and shakes his head at the same time. "The others say *bruja*."

I translate flatly, "Witch."

"I don't know what she is. I told you when we touch – the ones who killed ourselves – it hurts us. With her, it's different."

But it hadn't hurt when he touched me. I feel heat in my cheeks and elsewhere at the memory. Isn't that proof I didn't want to die? But if my touch hurts him, does that mean he did? I refuse to believe one bad moment deserves this entrapment in nothingness. I guess it's true a golden boy can hurt too, but no matter what was in his heart, he should be free to make his choices, whether to catch another wave or walk away. How can I try to convince him, though, when I've gone through life thinking the world is fucked and I was already half gone? So I don't interrupt him when he continues.

"Our mistress keeps us here, the suicides who can't move on, and she takes something from us." The muscles in his arms are clenched tight where he wraps them around his own body.

I want to reach out and soothe the taut pressure, but I won't risk hurting him. "What does she take?"

He lifts one shoulder in a stiff shrug. "Jewel says it's our life force, but we're dead. Maybe if I'd finished med school I'd know more, but I think it's something else. Our . . . our souls, I guess. When the mistress comes for me, I look into her black eyes and I see forever." He shudders. "That sounds like something from a love song, but it's *my* forever she is eating."

"Eating?" A surge of queasiness makes me swallow. "She eats ghosts?"

"Until there is nothing left of us. Even then, we can't leave." He gestures out into the unchanging gloom. "That fog drifting around the house? After she finishes with them, it's all that remains of the ones who came before us. Sometimes you can hear them screaming, but it's only whispers now."

I sag back into the tower arch, dizzy with vertigo. It's a long way down, but I suppose it's silly to even dream of jumping. Without my big boots, though, I feel like I'm floating away from everything I knew.

Or maybe that's just because I'm a ghost.

"I didn't want this," I whisper. "All the black was just to keep anyone from seeing too much."

"I know," he whispers back. "But I see you."

His words rip me open like I'm the sheerest, rotten silk. "I think you are the only one, ever." I keep my voice low, but I still hear the wet waver of emotion in my throat. I want to stop myself, be silent again, but I feel I owe him an explanation.

Or maybe I owe it to myself.

"I'm sorry I didn't believe in you," I say.

He gives me a wry smile. "You didn't believe I was a ghost? That seems reasonable, actually."

"No. Well, yes, but I mean, I didn't believe you were a good guy. I'm sorry I called you Golden Boy like it was a bad thing."

"Who hurt you, Alma? Before tonight?"

"No one." I hesitate, hearing the lie. "Everyone. I don't know. I didn't have it any worse than anyone else. But when my parents divorced – I know, *everyone*'s parents get divorced – there was just something about the way Dad left."

"He didn't look back?" Wyatt guesses. He stares out into the darkness. "I wish I'd looked back before I lost everything I loved."

For a second, I'm so grateful that Wyatt thinks I was something valuable enough to actually lose. But I shake my head and say, "He *did* look back, but . . . it's like he didn't see us. At all." Or maybe he had, and it – we – just didn't mean anything to him. I'm not sure which is worse. "It wasn't even really a surprise. Mom had been sick for a while, and they'd been fighting even before that. I'd tried to be such a good girl, so I was never the thing they'd fight about, but after he left, my mom died, as if she just couldn't take it any more. And I was done with being a good girl."

Wyatt snorts softly. "Somehow this doesn't strain my imagination at all."

My face heats a little, but I find myself smiling. "Yeah. I thought of the worst thing I could do in a good Catholic family."

He quirks one eyebrow. "Convert?"

"Get pregnant." At his gasp, I look down at my hands, ashamed. "There was a girl in school who'd had a baby, and she talked about how she looked down into its eyes and she saw . . ." I shrug awkwardly. "She said she saw what love was, a love that would never leave her. So I went to the biggest man-whore I knew: the captain of the football team."

"A golden boy," Wyatt said with an exaggerated sigh. "Just so you know, I surfed because I've never been able to catch anything ball-like."

I raise my eyes to his. "Why couldn't I have met you before?"

His clear blue gaze is soft. "Would we have even bothered with a second glance?"

I know he's right. And I realize most of the blame would have been mine. "I went to a pool party after a game. He'd been drinking and gone into the bushes to piss. I followed him and . . . and I took off my bikini top. And he . . ."

Wyatt's hands clench into fists. "Did he hurt you? I wish I wasn't dead so I could kill him."

"No! No, it wasn't like that. He didn't even touch me. I might as well have been invisible."

Letting out a shaky breath, Wyatt lets his fingers unfurl as if there's nothing left to hold on to, not even his anger. "You wanted a golden boy, and I would've given anything to be brave enough not to give a fuck. And yet we both ended up here."

"I've always hated irony," I growl.

He reaches out again as if to cup my cheek, not touching, but leaving not even enough space for the drifting vapor to come between us, so close this time I feel the almost-touch like a luminous glitter in my veins. No pain at all, only something beautiful, something enchanting. Something . . . I've never felt before.

His blue eyes widen, and his lips part as if he is about to speak.

Or kiss me.

Burn

A scream rips through the mist, leaving streaks of nothingness through the gray. I flinch, thinking the lost ones are protesting this moment trembling between Wyatt and me. Maybe they know nothing good can come of it, like everything else in my life.

But the fog parts to reveal a jaundiced yellow glow through the arch on the other side of the bell tower. Wyatt rushes over and looks down toward the back of the house.

"Oh no," he says. "Not yet." He whirls to me, his hands raised like a wall. "Stay here."

I want to grab him, to show him our touch doesn't have to be pain, but now is not the time. "What's happening?"

"Bianca. She shouldn't need to feed again so soon. Snaring new souls drains her power, and bringing you here must have exhausted her. She's been taking Jewel lately, but if she does it now, Jewel will fade."

I remember the hopelessness in his eyes when he told me about Bianca. But what I see now is the wild fury that must have been in him when he charged that last wave. And I'm afraid. Afraid of death in a way that would have made me scoff before and should be impossible now. "What are you going to do?"

"I can distract the mistress. I've done it before."

"You mean she'll feed off you instead." I clench my hands into fists because I can't grab him. I wonder how many times he's done this, saving others when he couldn't even save himself. I bet he would've been a great doctor. "What if she drains you?"

For once, I want the pretty lie, blowing sunshine up my ass, but he only closes his eyes for a moment. "I'll whisper sweet nothings in your ear," he promises.

Then he's gone, the trap door left yawning behind him like a dark, silent cry.

I race to the arch where Wyatt had looked down.

The back of the house is a courtyard. Ranks of concrete planters holding spiky desert plants, which always look half dead, march around an empty pool. If the pool had been blue under the hot sun, surrounded by bronzed goddesses, it would have been a perfect fever dream of fifties Southern California. But from my angle, I see wraith-like figures hiding behind the concrete urns, pale and hunted. The flagstones look like huge shards of broken glass, shining slightly, and at first I think water is seeping across the stones into the pool. But no, it's the ever-present fog, slinking into the low spot and swirling like dry ice.

Bianca is the star here. A dark star, for all her flowing white gown. Jewel is on her knees in front of her mistress, her head bowed so her blonde hair makes a shroud around her face. Bianca grasps her hair, tilting the girl's head back. A stream of light – translucent gold – flows like honey from Jewel. My eyes, grown accustomed to the gray, are too stunned to see if the light comes from Jewel's mouth or eyes, or maybe her heart. But even I, from up here, can feel the warmth, the energy.

The life.

Jewel's golden light begins to fade, taking on the jaundiced hue of the lanterns. Then even that begins to turn gray. The outline of her body is getting wispy, as if she's leaking into the shadows to become another wraith, one step away from joining the drifting fog.

"Stop!"

Wyatt appears from a doorway below me, striding barefoot across the broken-glass pavement. The mist sends dreary fingers to lap at his ankles. If their touch hurts, he doesn't pause to show it.

"Let her go, Bianca. She can't satisfy you."

I swallow at the grim determination in his voice and the strong set of his shoulders. This is no easy-going beach bum; this is the man who might have one day challenged death itself with a scalpel and science to back him up. Here, he has none of that, but he seems to glow with the light that faded from Jewel.

Bianca faces him. Her eyes are black pits, bottomless with a hunger no light can fill.

She spreads out her hands toward Wyatt, letting Jewel crumple to the flagstones.

Can a dead girl die again? Her head is angled awkwardly toward me, as if her empty eyes still see. My breath is stoppered in my throat, silent, and so I swear I hear her whisper, "You are not one of us."

And I don't want to be.

I rush down from the tower, whirling down the spiral staircase, grateful for once I have no tight-cinched corset or heavy boots or chains of any sort to slow me.

I burst into the courtyard, leaving streamers of mist to spin like dust devils in my wake.

Bianca holds Wyatt in her embrace, her arms sunk halfway through his body. She is already stealing from him – stealing the life he lost too soon – and he is fading before my eyes. His head is canted to one side, his blue eyes closed, and her mouth is poised above his neck.

She startles when she sees me, and her lips draw back in an ugly hiss. My heart stutters, as if it's tripping over every point of her serrated yellow teeth.

Without even thinking, without breaking stride, I snatch one of the lanterns hanging beside the door and charge.

I'm on the *bruja* in another three steps, the lantern swung hard behind me. I unwind with dervish intensity, putting all my fear and fury into the mighty blow.

The lantern passes through Wyatt in his translucent state. It slams full force into Bianca like a fiery wrecking ball.

Glass shatters. The wrought iron shrieks as it bends. And the power inside explodes with arrows of golden light in all directions.

Not candlelight. The same light as came from Jewel.

Oh God, is every flickering light in the place an imprisoned soul? How many have been lost here, and for how long?

I try to duck but I'm off balance and the arrows pierce me . . . and speed onward. The lurking wraiths I'd seen from the bell tower leap from their hiding places with wordless cries like a hundred doves, their arms outstretched to receive. The arrows find their homes, spirits given shape.

More lanterns explode and more arrows are released until the courtyard is aglow with golden shooting stars. The hollow ghosts fill with light until they begin to float upward, rising out of reach, each one a small glowing sun, bright and warm as honey lit from within.

I'm dazzled with the energy, the life.

The love.

"Alma."

Wyatt's whisper in my ear brings me back to earth just as Bianca tosses him aside and rushes at me, her fingers curled into talons tipped in poisonous yellow.

"You want to let them all go?" Her hiss is like palm trees rattling in the Santa Ana. Like a thousand killer bees. "Then you'll be alone here and you can take their place!"

Her claws aim at my face, to slap, to strangle, to sever the threads binding me to a life I'd fled. Her mouth stretches impossibly wide, her jaw unhinging to reveal row after row of serrated needle teeth spiraling straight down her black throat.

For a timeless instant, I stare into that void. What is she? A witch? A vampire feeding on the lives we hadn't finished living? A greedy fallen angel who stole these lost souls instead of ushering them into the light? A thieving monster, without a doubt.

But how much worse was I, who'd had what she wanted and yet didn't think the sweetness was worth the scars?

I catch her wrists, forcing her to stop. Her black eyes widen as if she hadn't really bothered looking at me before or wondered what kind of wandering soul she'd snagged this time. She sees me now, though.

And I'm not sure which of us is more shocked.

I am holding her.

Which means I'm not dead. I'm not a ghost who can't touch or be touched. Somehow I stumbled into this house of nothing, but, as Jewel had warned, I'm not like the others.

I'm not dead.

Bianca tries to wrench away, but I tighten my grip on her wrists. "It's over," I tell her. My voice trembles, but my bare toes curl on the paver stones, holding me steady. "They aren't yours to keep. Not any more."

As if to prove my words, more souls are streaming from the hacienda's windows to find their emptied shells and then flickering upward in dancing flames.

"They'll be lost without me," she snarls. "They're nothing but shadows."

From the top of my used-to-be-dyed-black head to the soles of my missing boots, I resent her derision. "What better than shadows to point the way to the light?"

"Their light is mine!" She screams and darts her fanged mouth at me, impossibly quick.

I stumble back. Wyatt said she might be weakened, but I've never had to fight off a witch before. Actually, it's embarrassing to admit, but for all my tough-girl ways, I've never fought anyone. Except myself, of course.

My heart is pounding with adrenaline – big, painful thuds that shudder in my chest – and I let her go rather than be bitten. Though my distraction is giving the ghosts time to escape, I don't know what else to do. But I know I want to live.

Bianca darts at me again. Her flowing skirt seems to flap like leathery wings.

I dodge, spinning away from the pool.

Out of nowhere, Wyatt looms up behind her, still pale but ferocious as the whitecaps of an oncoming tsunami. "You want the light, mistress? Then you can fight for it, same as the rest of us."

She whirls to lunge at him, mindless in her hunger, and reaches for the last flickering vestiges of him. He is almost translucent; it's impossible he could stop her from draining him entirely. But he stands unflinching, except for the slight incline of his head, his hazy blue gaze locked on mine.

From behind, I grab her white gown and her long pale hair. Her shrieks pierce my ears. Under my fingers, something slimy and bristly squirms, but I refuse to let go.

Until I fling her toward the pool.

"Surf's up," Wyatt murmurs.

Like the mosh pit at a heavy metal concert, the gray mist of dissolved ghosts raises a thousand fingers to catch her.

Passing her farther in, it seems almost gentle. Until it drags her down.

She claws for the edge of the pool, and this time her screams are not rage, but terror.

The vapors close over her head, pouring into the black pits of her eyes. The golden light that belonged to these ghosts is gone forever, and now the shadows she left with no place to go have found an emptiness they can call home.

When eddies of scarlet stain the mist, I finally look away.

To Wish Impossible Things

The last of the freed souls rise, untroubled by the mayhem here in Las Ombras del Sol, and their glow lightens Wyatt's hair until my eyes ache. I blink hard and this time the tears trickle down my cheeks.

"Hey." He reaches out to caress my cheek, hesitates, then I feel his shimmering touch, like floating in the Pacific, warm and soft and uplifting. Wonder makes his eyes brighter than his hair. "I can feel you. And it feels . . . right."

"I'm not a ghost." Saying the words, another matched set of tears courses down.

"I can't even start to tell you how happy that makes me." His voice thrums with sincerity. Of course it would. My Golden Boy. He saved me, from Bianca's teeth and from my own darkness.

He is so luminous I have to glance away. But when I blink through the tears, the flickering remains, I turn to track the new radiance. "Oh no, the house is burning! Some of the broken lanterns must've had candles after all."

The bell tower is filled with gold and purest white and a hint of bloody red.

"It's not burning." Wyatt stands close behind me. I can tell by the shimmery feel, alluring as the touch of summer on my skin. "Look. The sun is rising. Finally."

This place steeped in everlasting night is seeing its first dawn, and I feel the wonder slowly flooding into me. "But it can't . . ." Obviously I'm wrong, as I've been wrong about a lot of things.

With ghostly hands, he turns me to face him again. "It is, because of you. The girl who walked in her own shadows brought the morning too."

Knowing the incandescence of him is only reflected daybreak should make me feel better, but it doesn't. It makes him look alive. And reminds me he's not.

He thumbs away more of my tears and my pulse quickens at his touch. "Good thing you aren't wearing eyeliner right now."

"Jewel knew I wasn't one of you. I'm . . . I'm still alive." Even though for awhile I think I'd forgotten what that meant. "When she took care of me after I passed out, she must have figured it out."

"And she sacrificed herself to Bianca so I would intervene."

"So then I would come after you," I finish. "But she's free now."

He tilts his head to smile down at me. "Why *did* you come after me, goth girl?"

I open my mouth to tell him off, but instead I kiss him.

It's awkward, since he's a ghost and mostly incorporeal and I'm alive. But first kisses are always awkward.

Still, I make the most of it, because from now on, I'm always going to find the sweetness through the stings. I spent so long staring into the shadows, I'd never looked up to see what was beyond. But now I've seen, and I won't forget. I close my eyes so I can concentrate on the subtle sensations. I feather my fingers through his hair and catch a faint tang of ocean wind as I breathe my life, my light, my love, into his mouth.

When I sink back to my heels and look up, there's a color to his skin that has nothing to do with the rising sun. Who knew ghosts could blush?

He touches the tip of his tongue to that lush upper lip. "Ah. That's why you came after me."

His kiss rouses something in me that is too much like the hunger I saw in Bianca. I shudder; I could've been like her, trying to steal life and love rather than risk my own. So I remind him: "You're free too."

"I know." He tilts his head in the other direction, sending the shock of hair sliding into his eyes. "Do you hear that?"

"Choirs of angels summoning you to heaven?" I ask miserably.

"No. Sounds like waves."

I hear it then, a thrumming hush like a pulse. "Where is this place, really? What do we do next?"

"I don't know, Alma. But I know I'm with you."

I stare at him. My heart aches with a fragile hope. I always preferred leather and steel because this feeling is just so delicate it terrifies me. "Don't you want . . ." I swallow around the lump in my throat, but I have to say it or I'm no better than Bianca. "Do you want to go with the others?"

He meets my gaze dead on, unfaltering. "I want to be with you."

The sun rises into the frame of the bell tower and floods across the courtyard. The pool glistens blue as a sapphire under the open sky. Reflected sparkles glitter on the tips of the yuccas like diamonds.

But I still see darkness in the corners. I can live with that, though. I always have. Aba was right to say the sweetness of life is worth the stings. The one can't exist without the other.

"Not all the shadows have moved on," Wyatt says. "When Bianca consumed the souls entirely, the ghosts couldn't leave with the others. They still need a place to be."

"This is their place," I say. "And ours." I touch his lip and smile at the tingle in my fingertip. "I'd love having a golden boy to brighten my nights." I turn to face the sun. "*Las ombras* have a new mistress now."

CURSED

A Coveted story

Shawntelle Madison

Chapter 1

The brochure quite loosely used the words "quaint Southern charm" about Bright Haven, Georgia. I turned the trifold piece of paper upside down just in case I missed a disclaimer on the advertisement. Before we stopped for gas on the outskirts of town, we'd passed a kudzu-covered, lopsided *Welcome to Bright Haven* sign and two abandoned bungalows.

My husband gave me a wry grin as he pumped gas into our SUV. "Natalya, stop worrying."

Worrying? *Pfft.* I was a werewolf. My vision worked just fine, and based on what I saw as we drove into town, there was little to excite me. The 800-mile trip from Jersey to eastern Georgia should be the beautiful wedding we never had when we became mates a year ago. A chance for us to experience saying our marriage vows in a more formal setting.

Once he finished filling up the SUV, Thorn got in and leaned over to kiss my forehead and his warm lips left an impression on my heart, too. I couldn't resist smiling. He always knew what to say at the right times.

"You'll be fine," he said softly. "We'll be fine. They promised us our renewal vows would be an event to remember."

I needed something good to remember. On the night we became mates for life, I had to fight my way into our pack and prove my place as alpha female. Now that we were together, I wanted so much more with Thorn, but at a pace I could manage. A family someday, maybe even a chance to feel normal – which was rather hard for me already since I had an obsessive-compulsive disorder. For the past couple of months, he noticed I hadn't felt the same about kids.

The need to be optimistic tugged at me. A rather hard task when I was a professional worrier.

A few weeks ago, Thorn received an invitation from a pack alpha who briefly stopped in South Toms River where we lived. The invite included a weekend stay at a romantic Southern bed and breakfast. For someone like me who wasn't fond of strange places, I wasn't keen on the idea – until Thorn gave me the brochure. The place was an antiquarian's paradise with over ten antique shops. Like an antique junkie waiting for her next fix, I immediately packed our bags – while leaving plenty of space for whatever goodies we planned to bring home.

So now that we drove down Main Street deeper into town, where Uncle Barker's Bed and Breakfast was located, I wondered if maybe there was a misprint on the brochure and maybe this pamphlet was for another town. Grand, live oak trees along the street blocked most of the overcast November sky. Water from a recent rain shower dripped down the Spanish moss hanging from the trees. Those things I expected. What made me wary were the boarded-up shop windows and the cars with flat tires along the curbs. There weren't many people walking around either. Only a lone woman in a long overcoat walked her dog, her face obscured by the dark-blue scarf on her head. Something about her slow gait pulled me in to stare.

The narrow street opened to reveal the center of town and a glorious stone building surrounded by trees. I leaned against the window to look closer. Columns of dark red and white bricks peeked from between tall pines and cypress trees. As more of it became visible, I noticed there wasn't much to see – what was left of the building was nothing more than old, charred wood and stone collapsing in on itself from time. A part of me wanted to explore the land as a wolf. To see and smell what lay hidden from human eyes, but the human side of me didn't want to touch the emptiness that lingered.

"Is that what's left of the old Bright Haven Fortress?" Thorn asked.

"Yeah." I wiped off the fog accumulating from my breath on the window. "According to the brochure, it was burned down and rebuilt three times. Once by the British, then the Union Army, and the third time was an accidental fire from the drunken mayor during a Fourth of July celebration in the twenties."

"I guess the town was determined to keep the place," he replied. "Talk about bad luck. Wow."

Not far from the fort, we pulled up to our destination. The red and green glow from Uncle Barker's Bed and Breakfast sign lit the interior of the car. I opened the door, and a gust of wind brought humidity into the car.

With a nod of approval I said, "Now this is what I call Southern charm."

Compared to the other homes we passed, the expansive three-story structure looked like Santa's sleigh crashed into the side of the house and the cheerful contents from his bag were discarded everywhere. A grin filled my face. Christmas lights covered every curved corner on the yellow and lime-green house. There were still a few weeks until the Christmas holiday, but these folks knew how to throw on some cheer. The huge wreath on the door practically beckoned us to sing carols.

And yet, there was more. An abundance of jigsaw-like architectural details fit together in white arcs over the white railings on each floor. The century-old batten used to build the house whispered its age to me based on the cracks in the paint and size of the single live oak in the tiny front yard. This was the kind of home I wouldn't mind living in as Thorn and I grew old. We were only in our early twenties, but I was drawn to these types of places. They had history. Someone loved this house enough to repair the growing flaws over the decades.

With a skip in my step, I opened the slick, wrought-iron gate. My mate caught up with me by the time I swung my arm to knock – only to have a man open the door before I could.

Arm in mid-air, I stared at him with wide eyes and he did the same, perhaps flabbergasted that we each surprised the other. His large brown eyes blinked a few times before a smile broke out on his face. "You must be Mrs Grantham," he said with exuberance. His barreled chest gave him a deep, smooth accent. "I spoke with your husband on the phone. I'm Jackson Cason, the mayor of Bright Haven and the owner of this establishment."

"Call me, Natalya, please." I extended my hand, and the older werewolf shook it. I almost repeated his name, but something told me I'd stumble over it. I mouthed the name and verified the double "son".

He nodded and smiled, his mouth hard to see under such a bushy blond mustache and beard. The mayor had the strangest, most expansive eyes – like two bronze coins reflecting in the dim light of the foyer. The enticing smell of freshly baked cookies and coffee drew me inside.

"This is a nice place you got here," Thorn said first.

"Thank you," Jackson replied. "Our pack is pleased you came at such short notice."

Thorn shrugged. "My mate and I have had a hard year. The opportunity to relax and enjoy the time here was welcomed." He glanced at me from the corner of his blue eyes and I couldn't help grinning.

"You're right on time for dinner," Jackson said with a hearty laugh.

Thorn glanced at me again. "Again. My wife."

"Our pack leader is already here. His wife Mary Ann wanted to prepare our meal," the older man said. "Something about how my food tastes like I'd wrangled up a half-dead croc and served its head on a plate."

"I'm sure you do just fine," I said to be polite.

The outside of the house was grand, but the inside hadn't seen a broom or a duster in a while. A layer of dust covered an ornate china hutch that extended across the wall.

Tarnished silver plates and dusty Wedgwood china filled every shelf. My heart broke to see them in such poor shape.

The Friday evening shadows in the room grew longer as the faint light from outside darkened, and shortly, hard rain beat against the windows.

"We got in just in time," I managed over the rumble of thunder.

"This nasty November weather has gotten worse lately." Jackson gestured for us to follow him into the dining room. A lone dark-haired man sat at the head of the long table, which was covered with a white tablecloth. He sat with a straight back, his chin jutting, as his sharp iron-gray eyes accessed every move we made. His scent was strong even from the doorway. This was the local alpha. The tiny hairs on the back of my neck prickled, but I ignored the feeling as Thorn rested his hand on my hip and pushed me toward a seat.

"Natalya and Thorn, I'd like for you to meet our pack alpha, Calvin Braxton Cunningham. Most of the boys around town call him Cal."

Calvin cocked a grin, revealing the hint of an incisor. "Thanks for coming, Grantham." His low timbre voice was Southern-smooth like a double shot of Kentucky bourbon.

My mate nodded, his gaze never leaving Calvin's as he pulled back a chair for me. They stared at each other for a moment like werewolf males always did. A dance of sorts, where they virtually circled each other to sniff out their vulnerabilities. Thorn did this countless times in front of me, but today just seeing them engaged in the staring match made Calvin seem like a predator hunting its next prey. The alpha's eyebrows lowered and his smirk stretched his prominent cheeks. He didn't need cologne with all the cockiness he exuded.

Neither of them looked away, but Calvin spoke first. "How was the drive?"

"Uneventful. Just the way I like it," Thorn said smoothly.

"Good." The mayor brought in a bottle of Scotch with a few shot glasses. "Let's get this dinner started before Mary Ann brings out the food, shall we?"

Twenty minutes later, we were surrounded by delicious cuisine. Mary Ann, the pack's alpha female, was a sharp-tongued redhead with ruddy skin. She marched out tray after tray of steaming delights: a bowl of green bean casserole, fragrant corn bread, fried chicken, and sweet potato pie.

"And that's just the first course," she boasted.

She knew how to keep hungry werewolves satisfied.

Thorn and I dug into the feast, not holding back from generous servings.

Mary Ann tried to pour me another drink with a smile, but I declined.

"Just one." I rarely drank. As much as I liked to have fun, I preferred having my wits about me. Especially with a man like Cal around. He kept drinking and couldn't keep his mouth shut.

"Have you ever been down here before?" Calvin asked Thorn.

"Not really. I've stuck to the north-east. This year has been different though." He glanced briefly at me with a smile. "But due to pack problems, I've stayed close to home. Now that things are stable, I've enjoyed traveling more."

"This town has run into hard times recently, but back in my time, it was in its glory."

"Here we go again." His wife rolled her eyes and tried to give him another serving of pie, but he pushed it away.

Calvin poured Thorn another shot of Scotch. "Oh, hush, woman." He tipped back his own drink in a single swallow and then kept talking. His voice showed not a single sign that the liquor touched his senses. "This year, I'll be one hundred and seventy-five years old. If I'd been born a year or two sooner, I'd have a leg up on the ol' mayor here."

Jackson nodded. "You're still a crusty old fart in my eyes, boy."

Calvin continued. "Back then, this land was different. All the electronics and gadgets we have today have made the landscape into something I don't recognize any more. I miss the good ol' days. I'm assuming you haven't explored all the sights around here? You ever been to a plantation before?"

Thorn shook his head.

"You should see one if you get the chance. Over the years, they've gotten a bad rep due to Southern *traditions*. But they hold good memories for some." Calvin appeared wistful. "Even during wartime."

"So you were a soldier?"

"I'm still a soldier, Grantham. Even the good mayor here did his part for the Yankees. Either way, there will always be an enemy to face."

I squirmed in my seat until Thorn took my hand under the table.

Calvin continued. "My first real taste of fighting was in General Sherman's March to Sea back in 1864." His long fingers played with the rim of his shot glass. "My regiment was on their way to offer reinforcements to Fort McAllister, but we never made it. Those Yankees burned countless homes and plantations." Then his fingers froze and he gripped the glass tight enough for his knuckles to turn white. "After that, we hardly had access to any food. We had to *take* what we needed."

"And how did you do that?" I asked. I had a feeling he didn't buy what he needed from peddlers by the side of the road.

His sneer was prickly. "There was this plantation near Savannah that was fortified by the Yankees. I was more than happy to join a few other hungry boys. Like I said, we took what we needed from them. Food . . . and otherwise."

Thorn's grip tightened until my hand ached. Lightning flashed outside the windows, and my shoulders tensed as thunder boomed to shake the house, even rattling the dinner plates on the table.

Calvin smirked. "Once or twice, I ran into slaves steal-ing away from other plantations. Once I caught this old woman trying to run away. She had the nerve to put up a fight, too. What I remember the most about her was what she tried to take with her – this strange statue made from some kind of wood I'd never seen before. She kept saying she needed to protect it. To bury it to keep it from the likes of men like me. A bunch of hogwash. I took it from her – I knew it must be valuable – and her eyes had been fierce, like she had a fire inside her that a man like me couldn't extinguish."

"What did you do to her?" I murmured.

"What do you think I did to her?" He let his final words hang in the air.

I wanted to say that he probably killed her. I wanted to stay that he probably returned home a hero without worrying about what he'd done. Yet when I opened my mouth I realized I didn't want to say anything at all.

"Well, you might've fought with those Johnny Rebels, but it's a good thing we hadn't met in the field, 'cause I would've shot your crazy ass down," Jackson said with a laugh and licked his fingers. What was left of his fried chicken was nothing but naked bones.

Calvin joined his laughter. "You were a lot skinnier in those days, friend. You could've taken me."

"Mmm-hmm. I would've whipped your ass good."

The joviality lifted the somber mood at the table. I tried to smile at Thorn. Calvin was just the alpha of these parts, after all. We were here for us and not for him.

Chapter 2

The next morning, I took my time waking up. Tonight was the full moon, after all, and all of my senses escalated to dizzying heights. Safe in the dim lights of our second-story room, the rain and wind continued with a dull cadence outside. Light taps from a branch outside beat against the window over our bed, its shape casting ghostly shadows on the walls. We had the largest suite to ourselves.

I curled up next to Thorn and rested my head against his back. He smelled so good. During the full moon, most werewolves smelled like tantalizing pre-packaged sex. Thorn was no different.

He rolled over until he leaned over me. "Awake already? I bet you spent the night with dreams of old dusty vases and vintage Christmas ornaments, didn't you?"

"Not really." *Yes, I did.*

His hands slipped down my sides, and he lowered his head for a long kiss. "We could stay here in bed. And get ready for tonight."

His lips rained kisses along the nape of my neck, his breath soft against my skin.

"I want you," he whispered.

My body hummed every time he said those words. Over a year ago, our relationship had been tumultuous since he was forced into an engagement with another woman, but now he was mine. He rolled over on top of me, the evidence of his arousal pressing into my thigh. His black boxer shorts doing little to hide it.

His lips trailed across my chin until he met my mouth. Kissing Thorn was like paradise: his mouth was sunshine, his hands on my skin were cool ocean waters, his caress was a never-ending sunset. As our kiss deepened, his warm hands snuck under my shirt, kneading my skin until he cupped my breast.

A moan escaped my mouth into his.

"Mine," he said against my mouth. "I want to claim you as mine again and again tonight." He urgently tasted my lips as his fingers trailed down between us. His fingertips brushed against my heat, and my body trembled.

"There are so many things I want to do to you after we hunt." He gave me a wicked grin. "Don't even think about sleeping."

He tried to pull up my shirt, but I tugged it back down. He knew what having sex right now meant. No matter how hard it would be to say no to Thorn today, he had to understand how I felt about starting a family.

"How about we wait until tonight?" I suggested, but he knew what I meant. I was brushing him off yet again.

He sighed. "My hand is getting tired of doing all the dirty work."

"Thorn! Stop being crass." I couldn't resist laughing. Just imagining Thorn Grantham servicing himself brought heat to my cheeks. "We have sex all the time."

"Am I asleep when it happens?"

With a gentle shove, I pushed him out of the bed. "All we'll do is sleep tonight if you don't take a shower so we can go shopping."

As he got into the shower though, I couldn't resist frowning. This was what we always did when I dodged his advances during the full moon. I couldn't keep doing this to him. To us. I shuffled my feet, looking for reasons to feel like I was ready. But how the hell did someone who swam in doubts every day come to terms with how they'd be as a parent?

I loved Thorn with all my being. I had risked my life to go overseas to find a spell to lift a deadly curse that would've taken him from me, but some things, like what we faced today, still seemed insurmountable to me.

The cool rain pelting my face didn't stop me from my shopping trip. Jersey winters laughed at what the Southerners called a "winter chill". I'd traipsed through snowdrifts for a sale before, and a bunch of wind wasn't gonna keep me from perusing antique shops and getting my rocks off feeling up old antebellum-era tables and delicate afternoon tea sets.

The antique shops we visited blended into one, but their smells were out of this world. The richness of the old wood. The faint touch of vanilla and lavender on a cotton and lace bonnet. As I browsed the aisles, I ran my fingers against everything from bureaus from the early 1800s to ribbon-wrapped jars of jams with fresh strawberries inside. Every clerk had a smile for us, asking if we were newly-weds on our honeymoon.

The most interesting shop though was a tiny business right next to a crumbling Piggly Wiggly grocery store. A covered porch extended from the front, protecting from the rain an elderly gentleman, who tipped back and forth in a creaky rocking chair. As grocery store shoppers passed, they'd nod to him, but he just kept on rocking, not paying them any mind.

As we passed him to enter the tiny shop, he murmured, "You should be careful digging holes when you don't know what you'll find."

His paper-thin voice was so whispery it barely registered over the pitter-patter of the rain on the tin roof.

"Excuse me?" I asked.

But the old man didn't respond, merely continued the steady motion of his rocking.

The storefront for Lilly Mae's Antique Emporium was only a narrow bay window with a headless, barely clothed mannequin, but on the inside, the shop extended far into the back and a few select lights here and there illuminated the space. Curiosity tugged me inside. The air here was far stuffier than most of the other shops. Almost as if every morning the doors were shut for years and only reopened for inquisitive souls like me. A good sign.

The sounds of shuffling from the back storeroom reached my ears. A shadow grew along the wall until I spied an older woman wearing an ill-fitting, dark-brown dress waddling our way. "Can I help you?" A fog of jasmine enveloped me. The werewolf had dabbed herself a few too many times.

I smiled at her. "Not yet. I'm visiting from out of town to see if anything catches my eye."

She nodded, adjusting the black wig on her head. Bits of her white hair peeked from underneath. Instead of leaving us to browse, she hovered close as if we'd eventually need help. Not far from me, I spotted a strange black box with shiny tools inside. One of them appeared to be a long metal pick. The other one was a hammer. A shudder ran through me when I read the words *"Transorbital Lobotomy Kit"* in cursive on a tiny card next to the box.

Thorn cocked a grin as he found a spot to hold up the wall. He'd probably read the news on his smartphone until I was done shopping.

"Is your friend from around here?" the woman whispered. Discretion was a Southerner's best friend. The other best friend was gossip.

"No, *my husband* isn't," I said.

"Your husband? He's handsome." She paused for a moment as if in deep thought. "I have a granddaughter I should introduce him to."

Thorn chuckled when he heard her.

"How *sweet?*" What else could I say? *Look, Granny, he's married. As in taken. So send your granddaughter and her basket of goodies to some other hungry wolf.*

The elderly werewolf continued to follow me as I looked over the jewelry cases. It was rather hard to enjoy the craftsmanship with her tailing me.

"He looks so familiar," the woman said from close behind me. "Does he have kin around here?"

"Not that I know of."

"I wish I could remember where I saw a face similar to his. Anyway—" her voice strangely brightened "—you two should be careful. There's a rumor that the town is cursed."

My hand froze on the edge of the container I was holding. "Excuse me?"

Thorn's head slowly lifted.

"I refuse to live in town but I come here every day to operate my shop." Her gaze floated away for a moment before she met my eyes again. "Haven't you taken a look around this place? The buildings? The way a darkness has settled around the corners of every home?"

The need to humor her was obvious. A moment before, she wanted to introduce a married man to her granddaughter – if she had one. But she had a point. It was like a ghost town. That was what concerned me the most.

"The town is run-down, but that doesn't mean it's cursed," I said. Magic was something I didn't trifle with – in any form – but I wasn't going to let the senile ramblings of an old werewolf ruin our weekend.

"Now I remember." She moved in close enough to violate my personal space, so I took a polite step back. "Is your friend's last name Grantham?"

"Yes, it is." Thorn joined us.

From our past conversations, all I knew was that the Granthams emigrated from Europe to the United States long before my family came. I listened for many hours to my grandma Lasovskaya talk about her journey from Russia to the US, but Thorn never revealed his family history.

The old woman chuckled, briefly reaching out with her thin fingers to touch him. "I've seen a face like yours on a photo from an album. Those men were Union soldiers, a bunch of handsome boys in blue. The one who looked like you had the name Oswald Grantham."

After hearing that name, Thorn perked up. "Where can we find this album? Do you have it?"

"Oh, no." She shook her head. "The pack alpha bought most of my Civil War memorabilia a few years ago. He's batshit crazy."

Thorn and I exchanged a look. Now that was definitely the pot calling the kettle black.

"If you ask him, he might dig into his collection and let you know more about the man in the picture," the shopkeeper said.

Thorn nodded, and we thanked her for her time.

As much as I wanted to hear more, the shadows in the shop were stifling and I suddenly had to get back out on the street.

Chapter 3

Sunset approached far faster than I'd expected. After a quick dinner at a local diner, we returned to the bed and breakfast to get ready for the ceremony. As hints of the moon rising touched me, my skin hummed from the oncoming change. In a few hours, I would be hunting beside Thorn as a wolf. The monthly ritual was our time alone in our natural forms.

Thorn dressed in a white shirt and black formal slacks while I put on a long white gown made from the softest chiffon and silk. I didn't have anything nice back at home, so my aunt Olga was kind enough to loan me one of her pageant dresses from back in the day – the late eighties, to be honest – but her kindness was appreciated, so I accepted the dress with grace.

"It's classic, Nat," she said with a swirl of her fingers. "This dress never goes out of style."

Thorn didn't complain. The garment clung to every curve I had, and based on the hungry look he gave me, I did the dress justice.

"So . . ." Thorn drew my body against the hard lines of his. Damn, he smelled so good. "Do we start the mating ritual before the ceremony or after?" His lips trailed along my jawline, sending delicious sparks in their wake.

I had to swallow past the lump in my throat. "They want us down in the fortress before sunset."

He drew me into a kiss and his large hands rubbed the bared skin of my back. Warmth spread from each stroke. Our kiss deepened, and I couldn't resist moaning. He tasted amazing. All I could do was clench his wide back and hold on for the ride.

"We can start early on the baby-making if you like. I wouldn't mind getting you out of these clothes twice." His low voice melted my insides, but the reality of the situation also pressed against my mind. I was Fertile Myrtle tonight – whether I was ready or not.

I froze.

"You know how I feel," I whispered.

He continued to hold me close, but I sensed a wall crash down between us as he sighed.

"And how *do* you feel?" he managed, probably trying not to sound too upset.

He tried to kiss me again, but I added some space between us. As much as I wanted to dance the horizontal mambo with Thorn, I wasn't ready for pregnancy. There were too many reasons that I didn't feel like rehashing with him.

Also, I was a stickler for time. The clock read five thirty. We didn't have time to make out like two horny college kids.

He took my hand. I sensed his blue eyes on me, but I didn't want to look at them. To remember all the beautiful things he told me the last time we had this discussion:

I choose you as my consort.

You're perfect in all the right places. Our baby would be the same.

Your mental illness hasn't kept you from overcoming the challenges in your life.

I had faced many challenges, including dealing with an obsessive-compulsive disorder, but bringing a kid into this world was a game-changer. A life-altering event that even my willpower couldn't swallow whole. Just hearing Thorn say those things wasn't the same as believing *without* a doubt. Something I wasn't sure I could do.

Instead of tugging him into my arms to surrender to desire, I pulled him toward the door. It was time for the ceremony. Dealing with the next major step in our lives was best suited for after the wedding vows and the light of the morning.

A wide, dirt path took us from the sidewalk toward the Bright Haven Fortress ruins. The sun peeked from the horizon, and a purple haze bled through the trees, giving them an ominous glow. Thorn held my hand as we walked without words toward the columns.

Maybe he was mad at me. When I squeezed his hand, he didn't squeeze back. That was a first for Thorn. He was rarely perturbed by what I threw at him, but I guessed everyone had limits.

As much as I wanted to see his side of things, it was hard. Living as a werewolf wasn't an easy existence. A rival pack attacked ours over a year ago. There were enemies within our ranks who searched for any opportunity to bring us down. How could I possibly protect a baby in that situation?

He looked at me and must've sensed my thoughts. "You have the largest family I've ever seen." He chuckled. "You'd never be alone. You're never alone when you have your pack and the people you love around you."

The trees obscuring the ruins came into the view and, with them, the lights from torches inside the hollowed-out building. To my left, I spied headstones in the growing darkness. Most likely from the soldiers who never survived the countless attacks. The dates stood out in the carved, moss-covered limestone. 1733. 1878. To think Thorn and I would live for centuries if we took care of each other was mind-boggling at times.

The sounds of voices bounced around the open space inside the ruins. A sizable crowd had gathered, including a few recognizable faces from our shopping trip. The older werewolf from Lilly Mae's Antique Emporium waved at me. And she wasn't alone either. She pointed to a young woman, most likely her single granddaughter, and winked at Thorn. A few women huddled around a long table, setting up a wedding cake and appetizers. One man continued to light torches in the circle they formed around us.

"It's almost sunset," Jackson said with enthusiasm. He led us toward a single stone block near the front of the fortress. "We should get you two taken care of . . . before the sun goes down."

"Sorry," I murmured. "We needed to talk for a bit."

"Not a problem. How about we get started?" He glanced to Calvin, the pack alpha, and his wife Mary Ann who waited for us. "Our alpha wanted to say a few words before your ceremony began. He'll be sure to be brief."

I tried not to laugh. The last thing we needed was for everyone to shift into werewolves and have a bunch of dogs ransacking the food table. The twinges of the change should've hit me hard about now, but I felt fine. Maybe I had enough control to last through the ceremony. Thorn could always control his shape-shifting until the last minute.

Calvin stepped forward. "These are the Bright Haven Fort ruins. As both a boy and as a man, I've seen the honorable structure in its glory days and now I see her in her wreckage. Precious moments like your vows tonight remind us that what was once tainted can become clean again. Through the ceremonies we hold here, we can only hope you two see past any differences you have and agree that a united front is better than a divided one."

I sensed Thorn's deep blue eyes on me, but I couldn't hold his gaze. So far, I hadn't done too well on the united front part.

Beyond Thorn's back, I spotted what was left of the sun as it sank toward the horizon. It glowed against his back, giving him an angelic halo. I snorted and tried not to think about the devilish things he planned for me tonight.

"You're not a part of our pack," Calvin continued, "but the bonds between you and your mate can be declared anywhere with a dominant pair present. Please speak your minds."

Thorn faced me, and I swallowed the well of feelings that sprang. A smile spread across his face and, for a moment, it was just us. His hands in mine. The breeze ruffling his hair. The deep scent of old stone and thick Spanish moss.

Not far from me, I caught the nervous gaze of the mayor. His eyes kept flicking to the alpha pair. *What had him so twitchy?* A disturbing sense of unease crept up my spine.

"The first time we did this, you were tired, I was tired." Thorn had my attention again, and I was pulled into his words, remembering. "You'd fought for your life that night to become my alpha female. No matter what would've happened, you would have always had my heart. I choose you for all the things that make you perfect for me." He reached out a hand and wiped something off my cheek. I hadn't realized I'd started crying.

"Now that we're making strides in our relationship, I wanted to give you the moment you deserved—"

Suddenly, a shriek filled the ruins. Followed by another. Thorn's grip on my hands tightened and he pushed me behind him toward the center of the fort.

"What was that?" I said.

"It sounded human," Thorn replied.

Beyond the ruins, someone raced across the field in the murky darkness. Then two more shadowy people ran past on our right. The sounds of their footsteps and rapid heartbeats filled my senses. Beyond them, I noticed the sun had set. Darkness prevailed and leached toward the columns beyond the fortress.

Instead of backing toward Thorn and me in a defensive formation like any group of werewolves would, the wedding party members glumly stood there looking at us.

Had the drinking started too soon? Had I missed something?

"We'd hoped you'd finish the ceremony first, before things got complicated," Jackson said slowly.

"Complicated?" Thorn said, the growing tension thinning his voice.

Uncontrollable laughter, followed by the sounds of shattering glass came from farther away.

The mayor sighed. "Many years ago, someone cursed our town and the people who live here."

Dread kicked me in the gut. So what the shopkeeper said was true? Had something happened to all the humans?

He took a step away from us and appeared crestfallen. "Things around here have gotten pretty bad."

"No shit," I whispered.

"We need to leave," Thorn said firmly.

"Please don't go," the alpha female said. Calvin continued to stand as silent as the stone walls around us. "We need help from werewolves who haven't gone mad. None of us trust each other any more so we've invited so many couples. They came and ate our food, but none of them succeeded in removing the curse."

"Maybe because you brought them here under false pretenses," I spat. The desire to leave grew, but something told me to stay put and learn the real deal. "Give it to me straight."

Thorn trembled at my side, his anger building.

"Look, look. Here is where things stand—" the mayor began.

"Stop feeding them bullshit, Jackson," Calvin said. He looked me square in the eyes, and I did the same to him.

"Not long after the Yankees took out this fortress during the Civil War, one of our ancestors tainted this town with a curse," Calvin began. "Ever since then, no werewolf living in town shifts into their natural form during the full moon. As time has passed, everyone has slowly gone mad, but during the full moon every month it gets worse. Overnight, all the pack members fall into complete madness – destroying property and terrorizing the human population. When the sun rises the next morning everything resets back to how it was before." He let out a long sigh. "The town hasn't been the same since we've been cursed."

The mayor held his head down, avoiding our hard stare. "The Granthams won't help us like the others. They'll run away."

"They *will* help," the alpha implored. "They have no choice."

No choice?

My gaze snapped to Thorn's. Icy fear slithered up my back and wrapped around my throat like a tightening vice.

Then I sensed it – or perhaps the better term was that I *didn't* sense it. Between the cries from the crowd around us, the town beyond the fortress had gone silent. The song from the wind whistling between the columns muted. My heartbeat's rapid pitter-patter faded away, too.

Even worse, the moon's siren call for me to shift into wolf form never reached my ears. The itch to shift was gone. With growing horror building into a heavy iron block in my stomach, I stared at my husband.

"We're cursed, too," he gasped.

Chapter 4

Everyone faced each other, no one moving until a man shrieked like a night owl as he streaked butt-naked across the field. Another woman, not a single stitch of clothing either, made a beeline for the refreshments table and landed on top of it.

With a gleeful expression on her face, she shoved hand-fuls of wedding cake into her mouth. Then she flung a fistful of cake at the mayor. With a wet plop, a healthy dollop of icing struck the side of his face.

Two dark-haired, half-naked men advanced on us from the right. One diverted his path to pounce on the alpha. Calvin rolled out of his attack, tossing the pouncing man into the fortress wall. Thorn and I stood watching the madness like fools until he grabbed my hand and we silently decided to make a run for it. I ditched the heels and ran barefoot out of the ruins.

"Where are we going?" I already sounded breathless as we reached the street. My lungs burned as he led me around a corner, but we kept running. All the lights from the houses were out. There was no one on the streets – except the members of the wedding party who were chasing us, of course.

The need to look behind me tugged at me. For so long I'd depended on my ears to hear pursuers, but now I didn't trust myself. When I glanced over my shoulder, I was stunned and gripped Thorn's arm.

"They're closing in on us," I yelled.

Thorn noticed broken glass on the sidewalk so he hoisted me over his shoulder and kept running down the street.

"This isn't a smart move," I belted out.

He put me back down once we reached a dark alley. We hid behind a filthy garbage container. I ignored the rising disgust, but it threatened to overtake me.

"This is so gross," I hissed into his ear. This wasn't the time for my obsessive-compulsive disorder to kick in full strength.

I closed my eyes and took a deep breath. In through the nose and out through the mouth. *I'm okay. I'm okay. I'm okay.*

"Why aren't they coming after us?" I whispered, trying to think of anything except our predicament. My anxiety had skyrocketed since we became locked into our human form. The wolf in me, the part that didn't care about the trivial things humans cared about, was silent.

"They can't hear or smell us," he replied.

We exchanged a look. "Those crazy bastards are as human as we are."

He nodded and rubbed his arms.

I noticed the cold then, too. Normally our warm bodies never noticed temperatures a few degrees above freezing, but right then, I couldn't help but feel the icy breeze that swept down the alley and went up my dress. Wow, that kind of cold was something humans felt all the time. What a bummer.

"We need to get our clothes and coats." A look of determination crossed his face. "You stay here where it's safe and dark. I'll hurry back to the B. and B. to get our stuff. Once I get back, we'll get the hell out of this place."

I grabbed his arm. "I'm not staying here by myself."

He sighed. "Things are different now. You're different—"
He stopped then added, "We're *both* different. The sooner
we get to safety the better."

I couldn't stop my bitter retort. "You mean I'm even
weaker now."

"I didn't say that, Natalya."

"But didn't you think it?"

He held my face between his large hands. "I didn't think
it. If you really used that smart head of yours, you'd know,
I'm the weaker one right now. I may look like I've got my
shit together, but right now I'm pretty messed up inside."

I had calmed myself through controlled breathing.
Attending group therapy for my anxiety taught me a trick
or two about coping with stress.

"You're not going alone," I said. "We need to stay
together."

He finally nodded, relenting.

He took my hand and led me out of the alley back into
the street. We took things slowly, aiming for stealth like any
good hunter would do. We darted from building to building,
car to car, until we reached the outside of Uncle Barker's
Bed and Breakfast. The flashy Christmas lights were turned
off, and now the beautiful building had a dark presence.
Thorn and I considered going through the front door, but
we noticed two half-naked folks lounging on the veranda.
One was pulling the wires out of the Christmas lights while
the other one plucked the heads off the orchids in the
flowerbed.

I shook my head. It was a damn shame they had to ruin
the prettiest part of the house.

The only option left was to try the back of the building or
climb in a side window somehow. Each floor had a balcony.
With some hard work, we could get to our second-floor
room. We approached one of the trellises that reached up to
the second floor.

"Will it hold your weight?" I asked Thorn.

He checked and nodded.

Then he gestured for me to go on up first. Under normal
circumstances, a quick leap to a second floor could be done

without a thought but now we'd been cut down a peg or two in terms of strength. I grabbed the side of the trellis and barely got a few feet. It was embarrassing to say the least.

"Give me a boost," I hissed.

"How?" He grabbed me around the waist and heaved me up as far as he could. "I hadn't realized you were this heavy," he said with a chuckle.

"You are so dead when this is over, Grantham."

Somehow, we managed to climb the trellis and enter our room through the unlocked balcony door. The house was silent. Far too silent, I thought. Usually a furnace or the fridge faintly hummed. This never-ending silence, where all I heard was my own breathing and the rustle of clothing as I took off my dress and pulled on some jeans, was disturbing.

All I had left was a rising sense of dread. Some of these townspeople seemed harmless, but I worried that they'd lost all sense of themselves under this curse and might get violent. They seemed to have ransacked the town and left it in the state it was in now. They'd destroyed their own town themselves.

Thorn clutched the car keys in his hands. "We need to go."

"Wait a minute."

"What's wrong?" he asked.

I wrung my hands together. "What if this is permanent?"

"Calvin said that only the *townspeople* are like this. The minute we leave this place, we should go back to normal."

"But we don't know *for sure*. Right now we know we are cursed. But what if we go back home, we go loco and we harm *our pack*? We could end up hurting our families. To me that isn't worth it."

He searched my face as if an answer would come, but it didn't. He gathered me into his arms, and I sensed his fierce need to protect me fighting with his desire to do the right thing. A pack leader always protected their own. Even to the death. Running away was a potential solution, but it might not be the right one.

Families still lived here. All those men, women and

children needed our help. One thing I'd learned from my family was to do the honorable thing. And that meant staying.

One look at my face and he sighed.

"So what now, wife?" he asked.

Chapter 5

"Calvin said at dawn everything resets, that everyone goes back to normal." I rubbed my face with my hands, hoping to keep my wits about me long enough to figure out a solution. "So we need to find the cause of the curse. Didn't the shopkeeper *and* the alpha say that the town's problems began when the fort was rebuilt a second time after the Civil War? And that the decline slowly occurred *after* the pack alpha returned home from war?"

"That sounds about right. Do you think Cal could be behind all this?"

"What can cause a curse? Most curses come from injustice, don't they? An event occurs where a wrong is committed . . ."

Then everything came together. Almost like an audible click in my noggin.

"Remember the story with the woman and the strange figurine?" I asked.

Thorn nodded.

"What if she was a witch? And she cursed him?" I asked.

"That sounds possible," Thorn said. "But how do we find it?"

"Oh, that's easy. Guess who is the town heirloom collector? Or should I say 'fellow antique junkie'?" I added.

Thorn scoffed. "I wouldn't put the two of you in any group together."

"You have a point there."

A sound from down the hallway made Thorn freeze. He glanced at me, pointed to the doorway, and then pointed to his ears. I still expected him to use body language – as a wolf everything was subtle, a glance of the eyes, the way his body would shift toward a place where he caught a sound. Thorn might've been human now, but a part of the wolf still swam underneath his skin. Without a sound, he moved to the door and pressed his ear against the old wood to listen.

He whispered something, but I didn't catch it. A few seconds later, he waved me toward the window.

This lack of enhanced hearing took some getting used to.

From the balcony, Thorn climbed down the trellis first. He dropped our bags into a heavy fog that slithered across the ground.

I flashed him a look – why did he grab our bags?

His smirk practically screamed back at me. "Do you wanna stay here after we save the day?"

He had a point there.

As I started to follow him, I immediately had doubts about how I'd get down. Leaping to the fog below wasn't the smartest idea. Not when it was so thick I swore it might swallow me into the swampy earth below. I angled myself off the balcony's edge, using a death grip on the railing until I found solid enough footing to climb down the trellis. Thorn waited with his arms stretched wide.

We found a quiet corner while I looked up the alpha's address on my cell phone.

"Do you expect to find him in the local Yellow Pages?" Thorn asked.

"I seriously doubt the alpha who was alive during the Civil War period will live in one of these tiny run-down places. If I was him – and I believe he thinks like me – he will live in the oldest house around here with enough space to satisfy a hoarder." As I scanned the cell-phone screen, I found what I was looking for and presented my findings with a smug expression.

Thorn just shook his head.

I could get used to this being right thing.

Calvin's place was on the outskirts of Bright Haven, to the north of town. We'd passed the long driveway to his home on our way to the ceremony and hadn't even known it. Cypresses covered with thick Spanish moss obscured the driveway, and the limbs extended toward the narrow road. The dirt path was riddled with puddles and plenty of potholes. Thorn drove the SUV up toward the house. As we pulled in, he turned off the lights.

"What are you doing?" I tried to peer through the fog into the darkness, but I couldn't see much.

"Do you want him to see us?" he replied.

"What good will sneaking up on him do if we run into a tree?"

Thorn slowed to a crawl for the rest of the way until we spotted an expansive two-story home. There weren't any cars in the driveway and the place was dark. Maybe Calvin and his wife were still trying to clean up the mess in town to keep the other pack members safe.

Stone columns, moss peeking out of the cracks, lined the edges of a pebbled walkway that led to the house. A large owl dove from one of the trees toward the house. It perched on the rooftop and peered at us as if we were prey.

I tried to listen, to *feel* for whatever could be coming for us, but it was damn near impossible. How did humans live from day to day without getting taken out as a species?

Thorn took a step on the porch, and the wood groaned. It hadn't seen a fresh coat of paint in years. The chairs, which appeared so welcoming from a distance, had cobwebs clinging to their corners. A pitcher, filled with gunky water, sat on the ledge.

Lemonade, anyone?

We didn't expect to see inside, but the ornate oak door was wide open and creaked in the breeze, inviting us in. The floor in the foyer sighed and creaked with each step. If we expected to make a quiet entrance that opportunity was blown. My gaze took in the chandelier, lit from the moonlight bleeding through the doorway.

When the shopkeeper said Calvin loved to collect memorabilia, she wasn't kidding. Along the wallpapered walls in the foyer, I spotted shelf after shelf after shelf of guns, sharp weapons in cases, ornate vases and other dusty antiques.

But no statue or wooden relic so far.

From the foyer, we ascended an elaborate staircase to the second floor. There was a sitting room on our right, and a dark hallway straight ahead.

I glanced into the sitting room and gasped. From one end of the room to the other, animal heads lined the walls. Elk, bucks, an elephant, too. Yet it was the five heads displayed in the center that made my skin crawl.

The mounted heads of five wolves stared at us with glassy eyes. With each step I took, I felt their gazes following me.

According to the laws that governed werewolves, hunting regular wolves was a forbidden act. They were intelligent kin to be respected unless they openly attacked. To hunt them was like hunting your own kind.

Not far from me, Thorn clenched his fists. "Let's go," he whispered. "We've got a job to do."

But we decided to head up the next staircase before we left. We wanted to find Cal's personal belongings. The carpeted staircase remained quiet and we plodded up to the second floor.

This whole house had such strong bones, I thought. It was a shame that dust had covered the paintings of beautiful women in nineteenth-century attire that adorned the walls.

From the top of the stairs, Thorn suggested we try the double doors.

Calvin's master bedroom, unlike the rest of his house, was maintained to perfection. Candles pushed away the room's shadows. The poster bed was beautiful, taking up the far right side of the room, while his sitting area to the left had the seating to accommodate a quiet evening for two. The television tray with its crackers and cheese messed up the scene somewhat though, I thought.

Thorn walked to the opposite end of the room to check out the closet. As I took a step into the bedroom, I spied our prize on a white pedestal along the opposite wall: a dark wooden statue, over a foot in height, heavy at the bottom and curving upward into the form of a ripe pear. A plump bosom down to wide hips.

An African fertility goddess.

As I took in the relic, I could almost see Calvin standing above that poor slave, the butt of his rifle raised to slam it into her face. He was dressed in his gray Confederate uniform and wore the smug expression he had during dinner. A man like him – one who took what didn't belong to him and harmed the defenseless – didn't deserve such a prize.

Suddenly, a hand circled my throat from behind and pressed a knife to my throat.

"You're a smarter gal than I thought you'd be," a low voice drawled in my ear. "Keep quiet, bitch."

Thorn was still searching in the closet. He hadn't heard a damn thing.

"Natalya, I think—" Thorn turned and saw me and Cal, the knife digging into my neck.

"Ah, ah, ah . . ." Calvin flashed the knife as Thorn lunged at him. It glinted against the glow from the candles. "Stay back unless you want a demonstration of how slowly she'll heal now."

Thorn froze, a menacing growl building in his throat.

Cal laughed. "It's been a long time since I've been able to do that."

Thorn's blue eyes darkened. "If you hurt her . . ."

"If I hurt her, you'll do what? When I learned about your name, I wondered if you were as cowardly as another Grantham I met many, many years ago. What was his name again?"

"Oswald Grantham?" I supplied.

Thorn flashed me an exasperated look.

"Yep, that was the boy's name," Calvin said. "A newborn pup had more spunk than Oswald. A flea could knock the man's ass over faster 'n his fist."

Thorn's jawline twitched, but nothing else moved. The light was dim in here, but I could've sworn he'd hunched over a little, almost as if he was trying to shift.

"I'm quite impressed. Only one other alpha made it to my house. His grandfather had fought with me at Fort Sumter. A brave man he was, but when you stripped away the wolf, all that was left was a husk of a man." Calvin pushed me hard to the floor. "Are you weak?" he asked Thorn.

"Why don't you come and find out?" Thorn growled.

My knees hit the floor hard, the pain reverberating up my

leg. As much as I wanted to sit there and recover, this asshole rubbed my fur the wrong way.

"He's not weak, and neither am I." I stood and threw a right hook across his chin. The moment my fist connected with his jawbone, I knew I'd made a mistake.

Crunch!

"Son-of-a-bitch!" I shouted.

Now that was new. Pain from throwing a punch.

I clutched my hand and took a step back as Cal laughed. He rubbed his chin. "Not bad."

"How about this?" Thorn swept forward, ramming into Calvin. He rained punches into Calvin's right side. I expected to see the alpha's face contort in pain, but he sneered and sidestepped behind Thorn. With smooth movements, he slammed his fist into the middle of Thorn's back.

"No!" I rushed at them, as Thorn groaned and fell to his knees, clenching his lower spine. Before Calvin could land another punch, I careened at that crazy bastard, swinging again – broken hand be damned. I bared my tiny human teeth at him. My puny punches didn't do much damage, and it showed. Calvin flung me to the floor again. My head hit the hardwood with a thud, the world around me shifting like I was riding upside down on a tire swing.

Calvin took a defensive stance as Thorn came in hard with a right hook followed by a left that made contact with Calvin's face. Blood ran down the alpha's split lip and already the signs of bruising marred his face.

Using his right shoulder, Thorn rammed Calvin into the far wall and knocked over the pedestal. The relic crashed to the floor and rolled toward the fireplace near the seating area. I crawled after it as they fought behind me. The two men stumbled, Thorn in a headlock as they rolled to the floor.

"Thorn, what are you doing?" I called.

"Getting choked to death!" he spouted.

Thorn roared and managed to raise Calvin on his back. My husband's face blossomed red from the lack of air, but, with a final push, he backed hard into one of the solid wood bedposts. Meanwhile, I scrambled to the relic and managed to get a good grip on it.

I tried to stand on steady feet, but the world wobbled. I swallowed back the nausea and advanced on them. Thorn's eyes were rolled up in the back of his head. Calvin refused to let him out of the chokehold.

"See how you like this!" I raised the statue high, and brought it crashing down on Calvin's skull. He staggered a bit so I hit him one more time. With a heavy thud, my husband landed hard on the floor as Calvin released him. Calvin collapsed on top of him.

I released a long sigh. "I hate dogpiles."

Getting Calvin's dead weight off my husband was difficult, but I managed it. Thorn was breathless and a bit dizzy, but he'd survived.

I touched his poor face. On any other day he was perfection: chiseled cheeks, the kind of face-stubble a woman wanted to touch. Right then, he was a hot mess of blood, bruises, and cuts.

The man I'd fallen in love with.

"How bad is it?" He stumbled over a few of the words because his lip had swelled up.

"You look perfect. We should take a couple selfie." I fished for my camera, but he backed away.

His laugh was throaty as he took the statue from me. "So what do we do with it?"

That was the sixty-four-thousand-dollar question. "What did that woman want to do with it? Before he took it from her?"

Thorn glanced toward the ceiling as if searching his memories. "She wanted to bury it."

"Let's try that," I said with a groan. What I wouldn't give for some painkillers.

"Are you sure?"

"Can you think of anything else?"

He sighed. "Where should we bury it?"

"The way I'm feeling right now, if there was a flowerpot with dirt, I'd be game."

"Backyard, it is."

We got down the stairs – without falling – and managed to reach the landscaped front yard.

"If we hide it here, won't he find it in the morning?" I asked Thorn.

"How about the backyard, near the woods?"

Once we found a good spot, we got to work. Side by side, we used our hands to dig a hole in the rich mud in the backyard. I should've gagged from all the worms and filth, but right then, I was too weak and tired to care. I was alive with my husband at my side and there we were, like two fools, digging into the Georgia clay to bury a statue.

As I placed it into the two-foot hole we'd dug, the heavy wood warmed my hands. I ran my fingers along the marble-smooth curves, wondering what powers the statue held. Was the woman truly some kind of spellcaster, maybe a witch? After encountering amazing people and seeing the impossible become possible, just holding this figurine and making what was wrong right again made me feel like for this one moment in time I could withstand anything.

Like my future with Thorn.

"Whatever grievances you have," I whispered, "I hope this will make amends." And, I added, "We beat his ass pretty badly."

Thorn left my side as I began to cover the hole. "What are you doing?" I asked him.

"I need to make sure he doesn't find it. We need to leave our scent all over the place." Thorn dug countless holes and refilled them as I finished burying the figurine. As the reddish-purple sun rose on the horizon, a world of scents opened up to me. The wind brought a bouquet of seedling wildflowers. A chorus of birds and insects greeted me.

I believe we had lifted the curse.

I was hot from working so I shrugged off my coat. Then I caught my husband's scent. Every now and then, he glanced at me, even winking at me once. The night of the full moon was now over, but we'd survived the night together. Even at our weakest.

By the time we left in the SUV, Thorn's face looked a lot

better. I'd snapped a quick picture when he was at his worst. Once we were on the road, he voiced his concern.

"What's the purpose of taking my picture?" he asked.

"When are you ever going to look like that again? You're always so *perfect*. And anyway, a photo like that is album material. Wedding album material."

"Don't be surprised if that picture goes missing. I could never live that down with the pack."

"So you'll tell our future children their dad was too much of a punk to stand showing his weak side? Even for one night?"

At my words, his face softened. "Future children?"

I took his hand, and our fingers intertwined. "After tonight, I think I'd be open to talking about it more."

"Why the change of heart?"

"I don't know, really. I think it was when I saw Calvin choking you. As a human, you're so vulnerable. So much more than you were all the times you risked life and limb for me. I don't want to let go of you or what we have. Even at our weakest, we pulled through." Raw emotion welled up inside me, but I tried to push it away and failed. "Together. We did it together."

"Those are the best vows I've ever heard, sweetheart."

He drew my hand to his lips and kissed it. I laughed.

"What's so funny?" he asked.

"A few hours ago, that kiss would've hurt like hell." Happily, my fist had started to heal quickly since we'd left the town behind.

"So you're saying the human thing isn't for you?"

"Give me butt-naked transformations, howling at the moon, and obnoxious pack behavior any day. This living as a human thing is not for us."

Suddenly, he pulled over to the side of the deserted road. He turned toward me after he killed the engine. "And what about mating?"

"The full moon is over, you know."

"I don't need the full moon to want to make love to my wife." He closed in on me, leaning over the seat. The scent of his desire filled my nostrils and caressed my body.

"Aren't you tired from all that fighting?" My voice was already breathless.

"When we get back to Jersey, we can sleep all we want. For now, I got some catching up to do."

He kissed me, enveloping me in his arms, and I knew I wouldn't have it any other way.

WAERD AWAKENINGS

Amanda Bonilla

One

"Can you hear me? Stay with me. Can you tell me your name?"

The slow drawl of the paramedic's voice echoed in Shelby's mind as if he called to her from the other end of a long tunnel. The last thing she remembered, she was speeding through Battery Park, past the pride of Charleston, South Carolina's historic mansions, in a car that definitely did not belong to her. His face swam in and out of focus as he pressed a stethoscope to her chest. Funny, it didn't feel cold against her skin. In fact, she couldn't feel anything. He lifted a penlight to her face, and a bright light flashed in her vision before he switched to the other eye and repeated the process.

She tried to answer the paramedic's simple question, but her jaw wouldn't work right and her tongue felt swollen and filled up her mouth. Her eyelids were weighted, difficult to keep open. Strapped down to a stiff board, she couldn't move. And her neck was encased in some sort of plastic collar that held her head in place. Sweet Jesus, what in the hell happened to her?

"What's going on?" Shelby tried to ask, but the words came out thick as though she spoke around a mouthful of marbles. A mask had been placed over her nose and mouth, and she tried to jerk her arm free so she could pull it off. "Where am I?"

The paramedic didn't respond.

"Are you taking any medications?" He came at her with another bevy of questions. "Do you have any allergies? Do you know what day it is?"

Oh, she was medicated all right. If he considered coke and vodka medicinal. Her mind swirled with disjointed images of the accident. It had happened so fast . . . The paramedic sounded even farther off now than before, a voice shouting from the other end of Charleston. His voice grew fainter as he continued to ask questions, but the words didn't make sense anymore.

Maybe Shelby's wish had been granted when she slid behind the wheel of her car and intended to put this bullshit life behind her once and for all. That had been her goal, to escape the pain of living. Shelby felt herself float away, totally weightless, no longer tethered to the board beneath her. *Free.* If this is what it felt like to die, it just proved that this feeling was what she'd been after all this time.

The ultimate high.

Shelby sped through the Battery, past the historic million-dollar homes and the crepe myrtles and magnolia trees, heavy with sweet pink blossoms that smudged into a riotous blur of color. Common sense pushed past the drug and alcohol haze, urging her to pull over. Stop. No way. She wasn't going to stop or even slow down. In fact, she wasn't going nearly fast enough. Shelby punched her foot down on the Porsche's accelerator, and the car lurched forward, just as wired and ready to go as she was.

The tires squealed in protest while the back end of the car threatened to come around. Steering into the skid, the car straightened out, and Shelby gave a triumphant whoop. What a rush! She was tired of this life. Tired of pretending. Her mind raced with too many thoughts to process, but a comforting truth seemed to blink like a neon sign in her consciousness: she wasn't getting out of this car alive.

Shelby thrashed, gasping for air as she struggled to sit up in the bed. "Help!" Her back arched off the mattress as the word tore out of her raw and aching throat. She pulled at the tubes delivering oxygen up her nose and alarms blared from the machinery monitoring her heart rate and pulse. The room was dark and smelled of dust and old, musty things. Ancient oaks swayed in the breeze outside of the high window, the Spanish moss dangling from the branches performing a graceful dance in the wind as heavy rain pelted the glass and bounced off a tin roof. Shadows seemed to press in around her, like hellspawn clawing at her skin. Before she could scream again, a nurse rushed through the door, followed closely by a uniformed guard.

"Calm down, Miss Monroe." Shelby stared wide-eyed at the militant-looking nurse standing over her. The woman reset the machines before pulling a syringe from the pocket of her scrubs.

"Where am I? What the hell is going on?" Shelby railed in response. Panic-fueled adrenaline rushed through her veins, giving her that crazy boost of strength and energy only mothers are supposed to have when a car lands on their toddler or some other shit. A burst of strength she experienced *every single time* she felt threatened. She swung her fist high, catching the nurse in the side of her face. The woman reeled backward, and Shelby screamed again, "Where am I? Why won't you tell me what in the hell is going on?"

The nurse wiped at her bloodied nose as she lunged out of the way of Shelby's backswing and motioned to the armed guard. "Help me hold her down."

Shelby thrashed her head from side to side and arched off the bed like she was possessed, but even with her crazy strength it didn't do her a damn bit of good when the guard rested his considerable weight on top of her, pinning her down. A primal scream worked its way up her throat as she wriggled beneath the big, burly bastard holding her. "Why are you doing this? Where am I? Goddamn you, tell me what's happened to me!" She'd kissed her ass goodbye the second she got behind the wheel of the stolen Porsche. Death wasn't supposed to be like this. It was supposed to be peaceful. Calm.

The nurse plunged the needle into the IV connected to the back of Shelby's hand. Icy cold chased through her veins as the drugs took hold. Her limbs became heavy, her mind foggy and thick. "I'm not dead . . ." She cleared her throat, tried to shake the fog from her mind "Am I?"

"No you're not, Miss Monroe," the nurse said, matter of fact. "But until Thaddeus decides what to do with you, you might just get your wish."

Shelby shifted in the bed, wanted nothing more than to scratch at the skin pulling uncomfortably at her forehead. But her goddamned hands were secured to the bed with leather restraints, and so she nuzzled her face against the pillow in an effort to ease her discomfort. Her entire body ached, but the pain was nothing compared to the guilt that shredded her soul like tattered bits of cloth ravaged by the wind. She'd been reduced to a mass of raw nerve endings exposed to the open air. She could have killed someone pulling that crazy bullshit stunt. For all she knew, she had killed someone. Why else would she be in this place, strapped to the bed like some kind of murderer?

A bullet to the head would have been a better plan, Shel.

"That sedative they shot you up with was enough to put down a horse," a voice said from beside the bed. "And you're just a tiny little thing. You must've hit Sylvia pretty hard for her to knock you out like that and tie you up, to boot."

Free of the oxygen tube in her nose, Shelby flexed her hand, the IV now gone and nothing but a cotton ball and a strip of tape to mark where it had been. Her head lolled toward the sound of her visitor's voice – it reminded her of cool lemonade on a too hot day – and one eyelid peeked open to find the blurry outline of a man beside the bed. Jesus, he was ancient.

"Sixty-nine isn't ancient, darlin'. I like to think of myself as well seasoned."

Had she said that last bit out loud? Shelby's mind was so cottony from the sedatives, she had no fucking idea. But if the old man had answered her, then she must've said it out loud, right?

"Not necessarily," he said.

Okay, this was straight-up trippy. She studied him for a moment, from his old-timey-looking get-up – the suit too formal to be anything other than a lawyer – and the shiny black cane with a silver topper that looked like some sort of arcane symbol, the meaning probably fading into history with its creator. His dark gray hair was streaked with white at the temples, giving him the same archaic appearance that made her wonder if he'd stepped right out of a history book. Creepy.

"Funny, I don't remember signing up for adopt-a-grandpa day." The words rolled off her tongue smoother than she'd anticipated. And by the way her tongue stuck to the roof of her mouth, she knew with certainty that she had, in fact, spoken out loud this time.

"Aren't you a fiery little thing?" The old man's slow, old-South accent rolled over her like molasses. "You'll be a barrel of fun."

Rather than answer, Shelby let her head rest back against the pillow. She wasn't in the mood for Grandpa Munster's cutesy banter. Who was he and why was he even in the room? "If you're here to offer me legal counsel, you're barking up the wrong tree. I don't have a cent to my name."

The old man chuckled. "Oh, you're quite right, darlin'. You haven't got a pot to piss in. But I'm not here for that. When you steal a car, you go all out, don't you? From what I understand, it isn't every day a state senator's car disappears right out from under him. And I heard he's riled up about it. He'll probably lean on the state prosecutor, get as many charges racked up against you as possible."

Wow. Grandpa was a veritable ray of sunshine, wasn't he? Shelby didn't bother to face him as she responded, "Look, I don't know why you're here, but I'd suggest you get the hell out my room before—"

"Before what? Before the white coats come back to dope you up again? Hell, you might like that," he interrupted. "By the way, I've never been partial to Grandpa. Grandpas are so . . . .*old*. Frail. I'd like to think I've got a little virility left in me. Call me Thaddeus. Or Thad."

Freaky. How in the *hell* was he doing that? Hadn't the nurse mentioned someone named Thaddeus? Right before she shot Shelby up with some grade-A shit. What else would cause her to hallucinate like this? "Fine. Get the hell out of my room, *Thad*, before—"

"Let's just can the tough girl act, what do you say? Last time I checked, you were strapped down to that bed like Hannibal Lecter so I doubt you're going to do anything to me if I don't *get the hell out*. I'm going to let you in on a couple of things right now, Shelby Monroe. First of all, you're in a lot of trouble, missy. And second, that lovely sedative Sylvia shot you up with is the last narcotic that's ever going to make nice with your bloodstream again. There are four guards posted outside of this room, to protect you. The police are looking for you, and if they manage to track you down, they'd love nothing more than to haul you off to jail. You have a choice to make, my dear, and you've got until tomorrow morning to make it. I can help you out of this abysmal mess you've gotten yourself into, but you may well prefer an orange jumpsuit to the sentence I'm about to deliver."

Shelby's head came up off the pillow, and she turned to look Thad in the face. His soft, green eyes showed a spark of compassion, but something was hidden behind that kindness. Whoever Thad was, he'd seen some things in the course of his life. Bad things. And this innocent-looking grandpa definitely had some secrets. The many wrinkles lining his face were proof enough that he was a man who wasn't afraid of anything, and his body, though trim and lithe beneath the gray of his suit, showed that, despite his age, there was still a fair amount of strength left in him.

"Where am I?" Shelby asked warily. "And why would there be guards here to *protect* me?"

"You're in a private facility," Thad answered as if where Shelby had been taken was totally inconsequential. "And the guards are here to make sure that nothing happens to you – or anyone else – while you weigh your options and make your decision."

"Decision about what?"

"About your future, darlin'. I've never been much for beating around the bush, so I'll come right out with it. When the Sentry finds a rogue Waerd, the decision is usually made to put the rogue down. Immediately. You're a dangerous lot. Untrained. Unfocused. With little to no restraint. Like a wild animal that can't be domesticated. So, I could leave you here, wait to see what the authorities decide to do with you. Or, I can kill you now and save us all a lot of trouble. But I consider myself a gamblin' man and I don't see any point in letting your potential talent go to waste. You've made your bed, so now you can lie in it. You have a choice, and it's a far cry better than most people get: maybe go to jail for a few months or a year and serve your sentence, or I can do as the Sentry asks and put you down right here and now. You can die like you wanted to when you got in that car. Or, you can put all of this nonsense behind you and pay your penance to me. It's that simple."

Holy cats, was he for real? Shelby's stomach did a flip as anxiety pooled in her aching muscles. God, she needed to stretch. This was a scene right out of a goddamned horror movie. Private medical facility, armed guards, a mysterious man threatening to kill her before offering up a deal. She'd be sold as a sex slave and shipped off to some foreign country or chopped into tiny bits and her organs harvested before the sun set. Hell, maybe he was the devil. Her mama always said that the devil came in the guise of gentleman, making offers you couldn't refuse.

"Are you always so melodramatic? Do I look like a human trafficker?" Thad asked. "Or the devil?"

"How are you *doing* that?" Shelby swallowed down the fear rising up her throat. "I didn't say a damned thing."

"You don't need a voice to speak to some people." A knowing smile curved Thad's lips. "You're quite the broadcaster. It's a good sign. As for me, I'm just an old Southern gentleman who likes to help his neighbors. I want you to come work for me, plain and simple. You're useful, Shelby. Important. No matter what you might think to the contrary right now. So, that's your choice. Work for me or the Sentry will put you down. No loopholes, no fancy contracts to sign. You just say yes, or you don't."

Who in the hell was this Sentry? Some drunk-driving advocacy group? Sort of like the militant arm of MAAD? It was true, Shelby had wanted to die in that crash. But the thought of being *put down*, as Thad put it, sent a rush of fear through her bloodstream. "What would I be doing?"

Thad stood from his chair and ran a weathered hand down the front of his pristine suit jacket. Wasn't he hot in that damned thing? The South Carolina humidity was unbearable this time of year. "I think you've had enough excitement for one morning. I'll send Grady over around lunchtime with some food. You don't want to eat what they're serving here. No flavor."

"Grady?" Shelby asked.

Thad smiled. "Oh, you'll like him, darlin'. Now, you'd better get some rest. We'll talk soon."

The door closed soundlessly behind him and Shelby let out a deep sigh that did nothing to banish the anxiety pooling in her stomach. She rolled her wrists and ankles as best she could in their restraints. Her circulation wasn't great and both her fingers and toes had begun to tingle. Thad's visit had been disturbing to say the least, but now that he was gone, Shelby was left alone with his admonitions and her own crushing guilt.

Maybe she'd died in the crash after all and this place was purgatory. Thad had come to her with a choice, but the question was: which option elevated her to heaven, and which delivered her straight to hell?

Two

Grady walked through the doors of the old rundown mansion the Sentry used for their regional facility with enough food to feed at least half of Charleston. Thad's wife, Grace, always made too much. But her fried chicken was even better the next day, so if the rogue hunter Grady was here to evaluate didn't eat it, he'd just take it home and have it for lunch tomorrow.

The trek up the stairs to the third story was agonizingly slow. From the outside, the Sentry building appeared to be an abandoned, run-down plantation. The grounds wild and unkempt with gnarled, live oak trees draped with Spanish moss, untended flowerbeds, ivy that all but swallowed the building and weeds that sprouted from the old cobblestone driveway.

Grady rolled his neck and tried to ease a little of the tension creeping up his shoulders. As the Master Bearer for the southern Charleston territory, Thad took a pragmatic approach when it came to wrinkles in the Sentry's carefully woven infrastructure. Waerds were found at birth, taken in by the Sentry and trained to be the force that protected the world from supernatural threats. Rogue Waerds – those who'd slipped through the cracks – were dangerous and volatile. And usually too old to be introduced into this life. The Sentry was all about protecting their secrets. More times than not, the Sentry covered their bases by silencing rogues for good.

Whereas Waerds were taken from birth, Bearers like Grady were inducted to the Sentry's service at all stages of life. As empaths, they could handle the burden of emotions that came from the revelation that there was more to this world than met the eye. Grady had been found by Thad when he was thirteen. He knew others that weren't called to serve the Sentry until much later. Some already in their forties. But emotional strength was their business. It was the Bearer's job to make life in the Sentry easier for the Waerd. But would this Shelby see Grady as a comfort or a threat? Thad had offered her a choice, but truth be told, it wasn't hers to make. This was a test. Grady was here to vet her, so to speak. If her emotional and mental state proved she was stable enough to train, she lived. Failed? Then Thad wouldn't think twice about putting her down.

At any rate, he hoped to hell that Shelby Monroe was hungry. Grady hated eating while someone sat there and watched. And if he didn't pick up his pace and get his ass to her room, he was going to be tempted to sit on the floor and dig in right now.

Grady stepped onto the third-floor landing and passed a small desk at the head of the creaky old stairs, giving Sylvia a flirty wink as he passed the private nurse's station. Yep, Syl was dedicated. Damned good thing, too. That woman was a tough old bird, and anyone with an ounce of sense would know it was best to stay on her good side.

Grady turned the corner and headed down the hall, the ancient hardwood creaking under his feet as he made his way to the last door on the left. He'd read the file Thad had thrown together on Shelby so he knew enough about her. The info hadn't been too hard to come by, considering she had more than a couple of arrests under her belt: mainly possession, disturbing the peace, and one for obstruction. As a rule, Waerds were never raised by their birth parents. Shelby's had died in an automobile accident when she was a freshman in college, right around the time she began to act out.

While most of her classmates had come away from their college experience with a diploma, Shelby had nothing but an appetite for cocaine, booze, reckless behavior and a general disdain for authority. He snorted. Waerds were a force of nature. Anyone who tried to control them paid dearly.

The Sentry's Southern roots went all the way back to early colonization. Before the Revolutionary War, hell, before Charleston was even a settlement, the Sentry had been here, policing supernatural evildoers and keeping innocent souls safe from harm. The Sentry was older than the South itself. And to exterminate a Waerd was no small thing. The fact that Thad was going to such lengths to prevent it spoke volumes about the woman Grady was about to meet and it piqued his curiosity. Just what was it about Shelby Monroe that had Thad so eager to see her saved?

As he turned the knob on the door, Grady realized that Thad hadn't told him anything else about the girl aside from, "She's right up your alley. Prettier than a magnolia blossom in summer with the hot temper of a saint in hell." And the assumption that he'd find her attractive didn't mean much because Thad had fallen under the assumption long ago that

Grady liked anything with tits. Which he guessed was sort of true. He hadn't yet found a woman who could make all of the others pale in comparison. He swung open the door and stepped inside the room. Shelby's energy buffeted his skin like cool summer rain. It threw him off balance and before he could gain his bearings he swayed on his feet. No wonder Thad wanted to get his hooks into this one.

A smile tugged at his mouth. She was lying completely still, strapped down like a wild animal. A lot of power for someone so tiny. Jesus, she couldn't weigh more than a buck ten and that was a generous estimate. Knee high to a grass-hopper, too. He gauged her height at maybe five and a half feet. Shit, he had an assault rifle in the armory back at Thad's house that was almost as big as her.

"It's not polite to stare."

Her voice wasn't what he'd expected. That slow easy drawl was like warm embers glowing in a dying fire, just waiting for the kindling it needed to spark to life. He bet she was feisty when she was angry. He liked feisty women.

"I brought lunch," Grady said as he pulled up a chair next to the bed. "Hope you're ready to eat, because I'm so hungry, my stomach thinks my throat's been cut. I'm Grady, by the way." When she gave him a dubious look, he added, "Thad told you I'd be coming by, right?"

She didn't utter a word. Just looked him up and down. Grady didn't let it bother him. He set a small black satchel on the floor beside him and opened the picnic basket Grace had sent containing plates, silverware and food. He'd been sized up by nastier creatures than this one. And besides, he enjoyed the way her life force pulsed against him as she studied him. Like thousands of tiny hands giving him a full-body massage. The sensation was almost sensual as her power brushed up against him. Caressing his flesh. And so, *so* distracting. She didn't have a clue, either. She had no idea *what* she was.

"Shelby, right?" he asked as he spooned a large heap of mashed potatoes onto her plate.

"Untie me and you can call me whatever you want," she responded, a sweet smile curving her full pink lips.

Yep. Feisty. He couldn't help but smile. "Not a chance. Don't know if I can trust you yet." He popped the lid off of a Thermos and poured some of Grace's home-made country gravy on the potatoes and then pulled a still-steaming biscuit from a smaller bag. "One biscuit or two?"

Look," Shelby drawled, resting her head back down on the pillow. "I get it. The old man was the bad cop, so you're obviously here to be the good cop, commiserate with me, agree that Thad is batshit crazy, blah, blah, blah. I'll spare you the effort. Just get down to brass tacks and let's get this over with."

"I'll just give you one biscuit," Grady said. "You look like a white meat girl to me, so I'm going to be a gentleman and give you the chicken breast. But I'm warning you, stay away from the wings. Those are mine."

Grady watched her from the corner of his eye as he finished serving up her lunch. He'd known way too many Waerds just like her: snarky, full of attitude with a chip the size of Texas on her shoulder. And Thad's instincts were spot-on. Shelby would be the perfect Waerd to fill the empty spot left by Grady's partner, Althea, who'd gone on to bigger and better things. Shelby definitely packed a punch in the power department. Hell, she might even be trainable. But that was still left to be seen.

"I'm not hungry," Shelby said. Her voice quavered, and Grady paused as a wave of pain radiated from the center of his chest outward, stealing his breath. *Idiot*. He'd been so focused on being charming – the good cop as Shelby pointed out – that he'd failed to acknowledge the fact that she was still recovering from a few injuries, no matter how minor. He came around to the bedside table where he'd laid out their lunch and approached the bed. Waerds possessed preternatural healing. Superior strength. They were harder to injure than a regular person, but sometimes it was easy to forget that people like Shelby could actually be hurt.

Her body had been beat up pretty good in the crash. Cuts and bruises marred her creamy ivory skin, and her upper lip was a little swollen. Her eyes – deep blue and fathomless – looked a little glazed over. Even bruised and scratched, she was incredibly beautiful. Breathtaking. It was a miracle she'd come out of the accident alive, let alone without any broken bones. But then that was the thing about Waerds: they didn't break easily. Injuries healed faster than they should, bones and organs withstood severe trauma. Did she ever wonder about it? Or did she just consider herself lucky?

"Where does it hurt?" he asked.

Her gaze slid to the side. "Everywhere."

Grady chuckled. "That doesn't give me much to work with. Where does it hurt the worst?"

She cocked her head. "You some kind of doctor or something?"

"Or something," he said. "Are you gonna tell me where it hurts or do I have to guess?"

"My head is killing me. That drill sergeant nurse said I have a pretty bad concussion. And I feel like someone put all of my major organs in a blender set to frappé . . ."

Her voice trailed off, and a fist of regret squeezed Grady's heart. Thad hadn't been exaggerating that Shelby was a strong broadcaster. Her physical injuries were nothing compared to the emotional damage. Her pain was like a beacon, calling out to his soul. Bearers and Waerds were two sides of a single coin. All of the emotions she hid from the world were laid bare to him. He could see into her soul. It called to him. And only a Bearer could accept the emotional weight a Waerd carried.

He made a mental note to sit down with Syl and go over Shelby's chart. See if they'd done a CT scan or run any tests. He'd need to know the full scope of her physical injuries before he could do any real good. But for now, he'd rack up a point for the home team and take a step toward earning her trust. "Hold still for a minute, okay?"

Shelby glanced down at her wrists. "Does it look like I've got a whole lot of mobility here?"

Grady smiled. Her sass was definitely growing on him. He reached out slowly, like one might approach an injured wild animal, and gently brushed back a lock of her long, straight blonde hair. He took a deep breath while he allowed the energy within him to build and, as it pooled in his stomach, he trembled just a little. This was the hardest part: controlling the power that wanted out before it was time to release it. He wasn't as strong as some of the other Bearers. It took an immense amount of concentration to focus his energy. Just before the tremor in his hand graduated to violent shaking, he cupped her temple in his palm.

Shelby gasped, and Grady knew she felt the pulsing heat that flowed from him. It snaked in wiry tendrils from his stomach, outward, and rushed through his limbs, searching for escape like water sucking down a drain. His eyes locked with hers, and a spark ignited between them, the connection that would be so vital, fusing them together. They'd be two halves of one whole. That was, if she made the right choice. Her death – the loss of so much potential – would be a tragic waste. The Sentry needed this woman, there was no doubt in Grady's mind. And in that moment, he realized that he'd do anything to make sure she chose them. *Him*.

Grady slumped as the last of the healing energy drained out of him. The process always exhausted him and left him feeling like he'd just donated a gallon of blood. Lowering himself into the tattered wingchair beside her bed, he closed his eyes for a brief moment. His arms and legs were tingly and weak, like his blood sugar had just taken a nosedive. Even his fingers seemed too heavy to lift. Damn. Now he *really* needed to eat.

When Grady finally looked up, Shelby was staring at him, eyes wide with disbelief, jaw slack. "What . . . in the *holy hell* . . . did you just do to me?" Her voice was breathy. The sound was like a caress, igniting his every nerve ending.

Grady reached out and snatched up a plate from the nightstand. "Sorry, but I've got to get some food in me." He grabbed a chicken leg and bit into it, taking half the meat off the bone in one bite. "You feel better, now, right?" he said after he swallowed.

"Better?" Shelby exclaimed. "I could get up and run a marathon right now! I've never . . . the way it felt . . . the *rush* . . . How in the world did you do that?"

"How 'bout first we eat, then talk," Grady suggested.

Shelby huffed out an exasperated breath. "I told you, I'm not hungry."

Grady cocked a brow. "Come on. Thad's wife's cooking will make you swear you've died and gone to heaven. No one can say no to Grace's home-made fried chicken."

"I can," Shelby replied. "Especially when I'm incapable of feeding myself."

Grady flashed his most charming smile. He'd manipulated the conversation, steering it back where it needed to go. Trust. "Promise you won't take a swing at me?"

She gave him a look. "What makes you think I'd do that?"

Grady winked. "I heard some things."

"What sort of things?"

"Oh, don't you worry about that, slugger. You just feed that pretty little face of yours while I do the talking."

A tremor of nervous energy skittered up Grady's spine. He'd hit a nerve with that last bit. Man, she was a strong projector. Her emotions lit him up like a switchboard. He wondered what set her off. Did she have an eating disorder or some shit? Or was it the reference to her pretty face? He knew from her file that her previous relationship had been on the dysfunctional side. And only someone with super-low self-esteem would have behaved as self-destructively as she had. The fact that she thought so poorly of herself that an innocent comment would send her emotions into a tail-spin made his heart ache.

His shoulders hunched from the weight of what she was feeling, his skin suddenly tight and prickly. The urge to escape, to leave life behind entirely overwhelmed him. Her emotions were too strong. Too powerful. Grady wasn't sure where his own ended and hers began. The utter despair coursing through him threatened to bring him to his knees. He'd never been so affected by a Waerd before. He wanted to pull her tight against his chest and hold her. Comfort her. And then punish every single person who'd ever hurt her.

"I'm feeling generous today," Grady said as he rose from his chair and moved to the foot of the bed, "so I'll untie your ankles too. You've got to be damned near numb."

"I am," she said with a sigh, and he knew she wasn't just talking about her body. "I really need to stand up and stretch."

Carefully, he pulled back the sheet covering her feet. Grady's fingers brushed the bare skin just below her ankle and a pleasant rush of sensation zinged through him. God, it felt good. He looked up to find her watching him, the expression on her face somewhere between pleased and perplexed.

"You make me feel funny," Shelby whispered.

That made two of them. His insides were bound into tight little knots. Grady cleared his throat and released one buckle, and then moved to her other ankle to repeat the process. When her legs were free, Shelby released a luxurious sigh that sent his blood racing through his veins. Goddamn, it was an erotic sound. He watched her flex and point her toes and then roll her ankles. Grady stuffed his hands into his pockets to keep from reaching out to touch her again. He was hopelessly addicted. He'd rub the aches and tension from her feet, her ankles, her thighs if she'd let him. Physical contact was essential to Bearers. It was more than a base desire or craving. It paled in comparison to need. And Shelby's life force was a siren song he couldn't resist.

"God, that feels good," she all but moaned. "I can finally feel my toes again."

Something inside of Grady wanted to crow and strut around like a proud rooster for doing something that made her feel good. The pleasant energy radiated from her like sunlight, and it soaked into his pores.

Their eyes met again, and she bestowed upon him an honest, blinding smile that rocked him to his core and turned his bones soft. "Now," Shelby said, "how about my wrists?"

Three

Shelby waited patiently as Grady unbuckled the restraints on her wrists. It gave her the opportunity to study him from beneath lowered lashes as he gently worked the straps loose. *Wow.* Standing over her was a man gorgeous enough to be a demi-god. Waves of golden-brown hair brushed his eyebrows, making her itch to reach out and brush those locks to the side. The angles of his face could have been chiseled from marble. His eyes were a bright hazel that only added to the appeal of his well-muscled body and slightly tanned skin.

Something aside from his looks made him stand out from every other man she'd ever met, though. She couldn't quite put her finger on it. Shelby had never believed in new-age hippie shit like auras, but Grady had it. A brightness, like the sun, which he carried within him. Warm. Compassionate, but at the same time strong. Her stomach clenched tight and low as his fingertips brushed the inside of her wrist and a delicious shiver danced across her skin. She could lose herself so easily in Grady's touch. He paused as if he'd felt the way her skin ignited from the contact. What the hell was going on? Who *was* this guy?

"So, is this place one of those progressive, alternative treatment facilities or something?"

Grady raised a brow in question as he set a chicken breast on her plate. He positioned the plate on a tray that he sat on the bed and took a seat next to her on the wide mattress. "I'm not sure I know what you mean," he said a little too innocently.

"Oh, come on, what you just did to my head? What do you call it . . . energy healing? Chakra therapy? Don't tell me you're one of those weirdos who dances around with vipers and uses his faith in the Father, Son and Holy Ghost to get the job done."

Grady laughed. It was such a wonderful sound. Genuinely good-natured. Warmth bloomed in the center of her chest, in a part of her that had been cold and dead for a very long time. He pointed toward her plate and gave her a stern look that was clearly playful. "You eat, I'll talk."

"Okay, but you have to eat, too. It bugs the hell out of me to have someone just sit there and stare at me while I'm eating."

The bemused look Grady gave her in response was so intense Shelby had to avert her eyes. She used her lunch as a distraction and dug into the mashed potatoes. *So good.* She hadn't eaten an honest-to-God home-cooked meal in ages. Since she was kid. Her mom had been the best cook . . .

"What are you thinking about right now?" The question was completely guileless, and Grady's tone was soft, sweet in her ears.

"Why?"

"You're sad."

Her heart stuttered in her chest at Grady's revelation. Tears stung behind her eyes as she tried to banish memories she'd spent years burying. Shelby had never been very good at coping with strong emotions. That's why she'd turned to drugs in the first place. Booze, weed, coke, whatever she could get into her system. The problem was none of it ever did any good. The high was too short, the effects of the drugs burning through her system too fast. And no matter what she smoked, snorted, or swallowed, she'd never formed an addiction to any of it. She'd never overdosed, but not for lack of trying. She was so screwed up, she couldn't even be a proper addict.

Grady studied her, the look of awe on his face unsettling. She felt like a tiny particle being magnified under a glass. "You can't tell what I'm thinking?" Shelby said at last. "That guy, Thad . . . I'm pretty sure he could."

Grady leaned toward her, so close that she could feel the heat from his body. His eyes burned with an intensity that set her on edge, and a strange electricity sparked between them. It called to her and something deep within her, something hidden, answered.

"I don't want to play games with you, Shelby. I don't want to manipulate you or mislead you just to convince you to make the choice Thad wants you to make."

Holy cow. She was sweating like a whore in church. When had the room become so warm? Shelby's breath quickened, and she passed her palms down the simple white nightgown someone had seen fit to dress her in, more to give her hands something to do than to wipe the clamminess from them. No, the drugs had never done a thing for her, but this man, Grady, affected her in a way no drug ever could. She was

strangely drawn to him, *needed* him, and she couldn't fathom
the hows or whys of it. As if she might suffer from with-
drawal the moment he walked out of the room. She wanted
nothing more than to reach out. Touch him. Feel the heat of
his skin on hers. "What *are* you?" she whispered.

Grady gently swept the pads of his fingers across her
jawline. The rush, almost sensual in its intensity, had no
comparison. Like when he'd laid his palm to her temple
earlier, her body flooded with warmth and emotion swelled
in her chest. "I'm a *Bearer*," he murmured. "And you,
Shelby, are a *Waerd*."

Shelby cocked her head to the side as if adjusting the
angle of her ears would change the words that had come out
of Grady's mouth. A Bearer. And a ... "W-air-d?" She
drew the word out slowly, testing the feel of it on her tongue
and the sound in her ears. The word rang with familiarity,
though she didn't have a clue what it meant.

"A Waerd is a warrior. Sort of."

"A warrior." Shelby's tone went flat.

Grady smiled and her heart skittered in her chest.
"Waerds keep humans safe from the things that go bump in
the night. They're hunters, defenders, protectors. I know
how all of this sounds, and if the circumstances were different, you would have grown up knowing what you are and
what's expected of you. Our world, it ... it's not the world
you know."

"There's only one world, Grady," Shelby said. "And so
far, I haven't seen anything to convince me otherwise."

His answering expression was so close to pity that it
twisted her heart. "Thad and I belong to the Sentry, an
organization that's been around, well, damned near close to
forever. If the human population ever finds out what lurks
in the shadows – creatures associated with the worst nightmares – can you imagine the chaos it would create? We
collect arcane knowledge, artefacts, magic ... and we keep
the populace safe from the untold evil that stalks them."

Shelby's mind spun as she tried to process Grady's
words. Evil? Creatures from nightmares? This guy was off
his nut! He *had* to be kidding.

"So, what?" she asked. "You're saying that demons, ogres and trolls really exist? They guard bridges, make evil bargains, steal babies for their supper and possess the souls of innocent church-goers?"

Grady shrugged as if they were talking about a subject as mundane as the weather. "More or less."

"And some paramedic just happened to pull me from the wreckage of a totaled car, called it in and said, 'Hey, I think we've got a Waerd, here. Whaddya want me to do with her?' And here I am, ready to be delivered to some esoteric organization that fights evil on behalf of innocent humans. I may have a concussion, Grady, but I'm not that addled. Nice try."

"The paramedic didn't have a clue what you are. He only knew that there was no logical explanation for why you didn't die in that crash." Grady paused and gave her a pointed look. "You should have died, Shelby. Your injuries were more consistent with a fender-bender, and you wrapped that Porsche around a tree at over ninety miles an hour. Your heart rate didn't even break fifty beats a minute when they checked your vitals. Waerds are special. You aren't normal. You can't be with what you'll have to go up against. Most demons heal within seconds of being wounded. Others have super strength. Speed. They can breathe fire or toxic gasses; some can freeze your blood with a simple kiss. You have to have a genetic leg-up if you're going to stand a chance at fighting an otherworldly creature. And even if the MD at County hadn't been sure about you, I am." He reached out and circled her wrist with his thumb. Shelby's breath hitched. "I knew what you were the minute I walked through that door. Your life force is *so* strong. It's like a beacon. Power just shines out of you."

She searched his eyes for any hint of deception. Lies could slip easily enough from the lips, but the eyes always revealed the truth. Windows to the soul and all that. She'd always had a strange intuition. The ability to sniff out a lie when someone was bullshitting her. But in Grady, she saw nothing but truth. *Wow.* "You're saying that you know I'm one of these Waerds, because you're a Bearer and you could *feel* it?"

Grady leaned in so close that his cheek brushed hers, and her heart kicked against her ribcage as a riot of butterflies took off in her stomach. "You're anxious right now." His warm breath in her ear caused a pleasant shiver to travel from her head to her toes. "Curious. You're a little scared too, but that's not the strongest emotion you're feeling right now. Buried under all of those other emotions is a sadness so heavy you can barely carry the weight of it."

How did he know? The sorrow, the loneliness she felt every day was breaking her down. "Yes." Her lips brushed Grady's cheek as she spoke and the tears she'd held in check finally spilled over her lids. "How did you know?"

Grady pulled away from her, cupped her face in his hands and brushed the tears from her cheeks with his thumbs. "Bearers are empaths and healers. It's our job to bear the weight of the Waerd's emotional burdens. It makes you a more effective hunter and a stronger protector. Let me show you. I can lift that weight that's crushing you."

Thunder crashed, shaking the windows as the storm picked up in earnest, as though echoing Shelby's emotions. Rain pelted the windows with renewed vigor and she closed her eyes as another rivulet of tears trailed down her cheeks.

How could any of this be real? She'd always felt like an outcast, though, hadn't she? Wishing she could melt into the status quo and become part of the societal hive mind, only to realize that no matter what she did, she'd always be apart, watching, like some sort of outsider. The drugs, alcohol, and now grand theft auto – one stupid, reckless mistake after another. They were all failed attempts at distracting herself from the pain of loneliness and detachment that had been eating her alive for so long.

She opened her eyes and looked at Grady. Their gazes locked, and she felt a connection arc between them, chasing through her veins. "Show me."

"I don't have to touch you for this to work," Grady said, tentative. "But it helps to make a stronger connection if I do."

Shelby shifted on the bed so she fully faced him and took his hands in hers. Every nerve ending on her body flared, tiny bubbles of pleasure feathering against her skin before they burst. A slow smile curved Grady's mouth and his lids drooped almost imperceptibly. "Ready?" he asked, his voice lazy.

She nodded her consent, because she knew her own voice would sound slurred, as if intoxicated by his nearness. Something tugged from her center, and she felt a whoosh of sensation, like the creation of a vacuum, and all at once the emotional burden weighing on her lifted and she felt lighter. Free. This was what she'd been looking for all along. Not the ultimate high, not the oblivion of death. This feeling. Him. *Grady.*

"Oh my God," she murmured. "Grady, I can't believe how—"

The words died on her lips as Grady's mouth covered hers in a tender kiss. Tentative at first, his lips caressed hers as if seeking permission, and when she didn't object, he parted his lips, deepening the kiss.

Shelby needed to end this – now – before they were both swept up in the moment, but his mouth on hers felt so good. Not just good but *right*. She couldn't bring herself to pull away.

As if someone had flipped a switch, the sense that her emotions were being funneled from her body began to ebb and in its place she was flooded with sensation: her skin sensitive and warm, her body aching for his touch, her nipples hardening against the thin fabric of her gown. She sensed a push against her mind, spongy, resisting at first, and then giving in to what had to be Grady's personal thoughts. Images flashed like snapshots in her mind. She saw herself, laid out on the hospital bed, naked and writhing in Grady's arms. Another flash and this time he worked his way down her body, leaving a searing trail with his mouth as he tasted her flesh at her throat before working his way lower, past her stomach, ending between her thighs. Shelby moaned into Grady's mouth as the erotic onslaught continued, this time an image of him rolling her on top of him as she threw her head back, her hips moving in a maddening rhythm as she rode him. A thrilling, electric energy raced through her veins like quicksilver, and desire consumed her. The need to have Grady hold her closer, touch her, taste her, consume her, became a singular thought that she couldn't ignore. A craving she'd do anything to satisfy.

Addictive.

Four

Holy hell, what was he *doing*?

Never once, in all of the years that Grady had been a member of the Sentry, had he allowed himself to indulge in his physical attraction to a Waerd. Oh, it happened. The male/female pairing of Bearers and Waerds made for complicated relationships that were more often sexual than not. Grady prided himself on his ability to draw a line, though. He'd worked with his previous Waerd for five years before her promotion and nothing had ever happened between them. But one look at the feisty blonde in this bed and all bets were off. He could only imagine what Thad would do if he walked into the room right now.

But as Shelby's tongue slid against his in a sensual dance, he didn't give a good goddamn if the entire hospital staff walked in on them. God, she felt good. Her life energy funneled into him, nourishing him, replenishing everything he'd given to heal her. The thin gown was all that stood between his hands and Shelby's bare skin, and as she pressed her body against his, her nipples rubbed against his chest, driving him out of his mind with desire. He bunched the gown in his fists, more to ground himself and to keep from tearing it off her than anything.

Thad had warned him that something like this might happen someday. The life force of Waerds called to Bearers because they were two halves of a whole. One couldn't work without the other. But he'd never met a Waerd in fifteen years of serving the Sentry that affected him the way she did. He wanted her. No, fuck that. He *needed* her.

Shelby continued to rub her breasts against his chest, pressing her body hard against his, and all rational thought whooshed from his mind like someone had turned on a high-powered fan inside his brain. Easing up on her knees, she maneuvered her body until she nestled between his legs and Grady couldn't suppress the groan that worked its way up his throat.

Her fingers threaded through his hair, her nails gently scraping his scalp. A chill raced across his skin, settling between his legs where his erection strained against his fly like it was suffocating and desperate for air. Shelby's mouth slanted against his and she tasted so damned good, he wanted nothing more than to find out if she tasted this good everywhere. He could just picture her arching her back, thrusting her hips up to meet his mouth, as he kissed and tasted that secret part of her . . .

"I don't know how you're making me feel this way, Grady." She pulled away just far enough to murmur against his mouth. "But I like it."

Her words were like icy sheets of water meeting his skin. "What are you talking about?" He put his hands on her shoulders and gently urged her away so he could look into her eyes. "Shelby, do you think I'm influencing you in some way?" He'd never been able to push a thought or feeling into a Waerd's psyche before. Thad and some of the older, stronger Bearers could do it, but Grady's own power was considerably weaker.

"Say my name like that again," Shelby said in a sweet, cajoling purr, which made him want to do anything she asked of him. "All slow and sweet like a hot August afternoon. I like the way it sounds."

"Wait."

"No waiting. No thinking. Please, Grady . . . I need this. I need *you*." Shelby nuzzled Grady's collarbone, tracing a line with her tongue up his neck to his ear. She took his ear lobe in between her teeth and sucked. Her mouth was warm, wet. Oh yeah, he wanted more of that. *Wait a sec*, his damn common sense piped in. *You just met this girl. You don't even know her.* This wasn't like him to be so ruled by his base desires. But the connection fusing them together gave him permission to ignore his better judgment. The way Shelby's energy called to him told him that he already knew everything he ever needed to about her. He might have only met her mere minutes ago, but his Bearer's soul had known her *forever*.

His desire became an animal instinct overriding rational thought. Grady gently lowered Shelby down onto the bed, his breath mingling with hers as he kissed her hungrily. Shelby shifted beneath him, spreading her legs and, as Grady nestled between her thighs, he marveled at how perfectly they fit together. His erection brushed up against her core, and he felt her heat through the thick fabric of his jeans, sending him further toward the edge. He'd never wanted anyone as much as he wanted her. The hem of her gown rode up her thigh, skirting one bare hip, and Grady ran his hand up her exposed flesh, under the gown and over her ribs. She arched into him, moaning as he cupped her breast and feathered his thumb over her nipple once, twice, and again until it rose to a stiff peak.

She broke their kiss, and a sweet, whimpering sound escaped her lips. Her hands passed down over his pecs, continuing their exploration of his body until she reached the hem of his T-shirt. Grady helped as Shelby tugged at his shirt, using one hand to strip it from his back. He tossed it somewhere behind him and closed his eyes in ecstasy as her mouth moved over his neck, across his collarbone, and his stomach clenched tight when her tongue flicked out over his nipple.

"Shelby," he murmured, as she kissed and licked his bare skin, her fingers loosening the button on his jeans. He held his breath as she tugged his zipper down and pulled his erection free.

"Touch me, Grady," she said, now bordering on desperate. "I want to feel your hands on me." She stroked his shaft, her grip just tight enough, and Grady shook with need. "Do it. Touch me."

His fingers slid over her slick core, and it was all Grady could do not to come right then and there. Shelby continued to stroke him, moving up and down his shaft, as he circled her stiff bud. She thrust her hips into his touch, moaning, her body shuddering with each pass of his fingers. She was so ready for him. He ached with the need to fill her, to join them in every way possible.

"I want you, Grady. Please, I can't wait. I have to feel you inside of me." Her tone was desperate, pleading, and Grady kicked at his jeans with enthusiasm, working them down to his ankles. Jesus, this wasn't exactly a romantic first encounter, but as an empath he was afforded the benefit of knowing his partner's feelings at all times. White light sizzled across the night sky, thunder cracking immediately after the lightning's passage. Grady swore he could feel the electricity sizzle over his skin, heightening his pleasure. He knew that Shelby felt it too and she didn't have any objections to what was happening between them.

"You're sure?" he murmured next to her ear. It would kill him to stop now, but he would if that's what she wanted. "We can stop. We don't have to do this." But didn't they? Something bigger than both of them guided them now, as though some mystical force they were powerless to fight brought them together.

"Yes . . . we . . . do . . ." Shelby answered between pants of breath. "Grady, the way you're touching me feels so good. I've never felt like this before. It's like I can feel what you're feeling, too, and it's wonderful. Take me. Now."

Shelby wanted Grady so badly she thought she'd go mad from it. He'd brought her so close to the edge, and it wouldn't take much for her to tip and fall into an ocean of ecstasy. This was crazy, impetuous and more than inappropriate. She knew that. And even so, something deep within her knew him and welcomed him as if she'd waited her entire life for him. The need to join with him in the most intimate way possible went beyond mere sex. It was soul deep. Primal. A demand that she couldn't ignore. Grady wanted her just as badly. She could feel it. Though he'd played the gentleman and told her they could stop at any time, they both knew it was far too late for that.

Grady rose up on his forearm and positioned himself at her opening. She rolled her hips up to meet him and gasped as he entered her, stretching her, filling her completely. He seated himself deep within her and Shelby marveled at how they fit together so perfectly. Her body accepted his like they were made for one another. And when he began to move inside her, oh God, the pleasure – both hers and his – consumed her completely.

Grady's pace picked up and his ragged breath in her ear sent a thrill through her body. He was going to come, she could feel it as his body tensed and trembled against hers. She'd never in her entire life felt so close to another human being. And, yes, she was about to come with him, too. So close . . .

Waves of pleasure lapped at her body, the orgasm sweeping her up in a frenzied state of passion she'd never experienced. Grady called out, her name on his lips, as he thrust hard and deep, his passion fusing with her own pleasure and emotions to add to the perfection of this moment. If she had in fact died in the crash, Shelby knew that she'd gone to heaven. Because the man resting in her arms, his body limp and sated, could be nothing less than an angel.

Five

The sound of an alarm blared through the PA system, ringing in Shelby's ears. Grady pulled away from her, a look of mild panic ghosting over his impossibly gorgeous face. The peaceful aftermath of their union shattered by the shrill electronic siren. Grady sprang into action, throwing his clothes on and rushing for the door. He eased it open, just a crack, and looked to his right. Slamming the door shut, he turned to face her, his expression settling into steel-hard resolve, as if he had just made a very dire last-minute decision.

"Security breach," Grady said by way of explanation. He took in her disheveled state, pausing at her bare feet and then at the gown all but hanging off her shoulders and gave a resigned sigh. "Nothing like trial by fire to see what you're made of."

Security breach? Trial by fire? He wasn't saying what she'd thought he was saying . . . was he? "Grady, you don't expect me to—"

"Yeah," he said, as he dug through the black bag he'd brought in with the picnic basket, "I do." The timing was shitty but it was necessary for Shelby to face her test. Grady just hoped she would come through it with flying colors. "The facility has security in place, but as far as I know, you're the only Waerd in the building. We have to do what we can to protect the staff and anyone else. Have you had any combat training? Do you know how to use a gun?"

Shelby's brain put on the brakes and shot into a tailspin. "Combat training? Jesus Christ, Grady! No, I haven't had any combat training! I can't even hold a glass steady half the time and you want to know if I can use a gun?"

She had to guess that Grady had forgotten why she was here in the first place and that she'd been strapped to the bed not thirty minutes ago, nothing more than a prisoner.

Hellloooo! She'd been coked out of her mind and heavily sedated, and that was just in the past twenty-four hours. And for some reason, he thought it was perfectly logical to expect her to charge into battle against God-knows-what, in her bare feet, no less? What was she going to do? Throw a vase full of flowers at whoever was wreaking havoc inside the building? Yeah, that'd help. Sure.

"Shelby, I need you to try to calm down." Grady pulled something from the black bag that looked suspiciously like a dagger. "Your emotions are making it hard for me to focus."

He reached out and slapped the weapon into her palm. Yep, definitely a dagger. "Grady, I know you're convinced that I'm some sort of superhuman warrior or something, but I'm not so convinced. I don't know how to use this," she exclaimed, brandishing the dagger like it was some sort of magic wand. "So how in the hell do you expect me to—"

The sound of panicked screams followed by a deep roar echoed down the hallway, shaking the three-story mansion to its foundation. Shelby crouched down, as if making herself smaller would save her from the chunks of ceiling plaster that rained down from above.

In her palm, the silver dagger began to warm, heating to the point that it was almost uncomfortable. A soft, white light encased the silver blade, and Shelby held it away from herself as if the damn thing might explode at any second. She *had* to be dead or dreaming. Coma, maybe?

"You might not believe me," Grady called, as he crossed the room to the door, "but you can sure as hell trust that dagger in your hand. The blade is charged with magic and it's reactive. It only works when used by a Waerd. Just by holding it, you flipped the switch to the 'on' position." His tone was curt, down to business. "And yeah, I'm sorry to throw you into the deep end like this, but there's a big motherfucking brimstone demon barreling down the hallway and killing everything in its path. So I suggest you put your doubt on hold and save your questions for after we've killed it, okay?"

Without another word, Grady pulled a gun from the bottom of the black bag, ejected the clip and checked it before slamming it back into place. He gave her a look. A silent order to follow him, no questions asked. Then, he threw open the door and ran out into the hall.

Holy crap! Shelby thought frantically, as she looked around the room, wishing that the floor would open up and swallow her whole. *Shit.* Shit, shit, shit, shit, *shit!* She didn't have faith in anything. She trusted no one. How could she possibly just run after Grady and charge into battle against something that sounded like it could tear her to shreds with its fingers? Not to mention that her recent mind-blowing orgasm had her legs feeling like cooked spaghetti noodles. Instinct tugged at the back of her mind, and one foot moved in front of the other, answering a command that she hadn't consciously given. Moving her forward. After Grady. Toward danger.

To protect him.

Another eardrum-shattering roar echoed down the corridor, throwing Shelby off balance as she chased after Grady.

Instinct had effectively taken control over her body, a strange autopilot function that had her ducking and weaving through the long hallway like some sort of demon-slaying commando. Shelby's bare feet slapped on the linoleum floor as she navigated the debris littering the hallway, Grady just ahead of her. She was definitely having an out-of-body experience. Some woman who wasn't her had shimmied under her skin. And this woman had no problem whatsoever charging head first into a deadly situation.

The entire third floor looked like a combat zone. Light fixtures dangled from exposed wires in the ceiling, spitting sparks on piles of debris. She tried to ignore the terrified screams of those still escaping. She knew that most of the occupants of this floor could be dead or dying. Deep grooves lined the floor, individual claw marks that were as wide as Shelby's forearm. *Jesus Christ.* Damn thing had to be the size of Godzilla to cause this amount of destruction.

This is crazy! There's no such thing as demons and you're not a demon slayer! But her instincts ignored her common sense. Another roar tore through the air, followed by a rumble not unlike thunder, which knocked Shelby completely off her feet. It was a wonder the house was still standing.

"Look out!"

Grady's warning shout came on the heels of a black, mountainous form rounding the corner toward her. The brimstone demon didn't look like anything solid enough to wreak the kind of havoc it had. Shelby's jaw hung slack as she took in the sight of the nine-foot-tall demon whose skin looked to be composed of nothing more than black, billowing clouds. Red, beady eyes shone out from a featureless face, and sharp teeth, dripping with blood, leered at her as it advanced. She gagged as the demon's sulfuric odor all but burned her nostrils.

This is what hell must smell like. With a lunge and drop, she managed to roll out of the way of a massive fist swinging toward her. It pounded into the floor, the impact causing her to bounce a good three feet off the ground. She landed in an unceremonious heap, limbs flailing, her long gown twisted tight around her waist.

The demon threw its head back and roared its frustration, smoke and flames billowing from its maw of a mouth. If it didn't shake the building off its foundation, there'd be a pretty good chance the demon would burn the place down – not to mention everyone left inside – with nothing more than a few gasping breaths.

"Grady! What do I do?" Shelby shouted. The demon roared again, swinging its fist, this time at her head. Grady shouted back, but his voice was muffled in the cacophony of the demon's thunderous tirade. The dagger burned in her palm, as she deftly rolled out of the way, reminding her that she had a magic weapon at her disposal.

Time to put Grady's faith and trust to the test. Shelby's own speed astounded her as she launched herself at the demon. The beast was cumbersome, and its size worked to Shelby's advantage in the narrow hallway, as she rolled between its knees and struck out with the dagger. The blade cut through the demon's flesh. Good Lord, it felt as though she were cutting through smoldering embers. A thick substance resembling molten lava flowed from the wound. It plopped and sizzled as it hit the floor, splashing up onto Shelby's arm.

"Holy shit!" she cried out, as the demon's blood burned her flesh. She quickly used the hem of her gown to wipe it away as best she could without smearing it and making the burn worse. The demon swiped a giant, clawed hand at her, and she just stood there like an idiot as she waited for the killing blow.

Shots rang out over the din of destruction, and Shelby caught a glimpse of Grady through the smoke and fire now licking up the walls. Another alarm joined the already overwhelming noise and, a moment later, the sprinkler system turned on, drenching the entire floor in a spray of water. Bullets peppered the demon, bits of charred, obsidian skin flaking from its shoulders and chest. Molten lava blood splattered the walls, adding to the fire, eating holes through the flooring and exposing the second story beneath them.

Chaos didn't even begin to describe the scenario playing out like a twisted nightmare before her waking eyes, and Shelby watched in terror as the demon changed course, barreling toward Grady with murderous purpose.

The urge to protect him overwhelmed her. She'd never felt like protecting anyone since her parents died, but something sparked back to life inside of her, a determination and compassion that she'd thought left her a long time ago.

She had to kill the demon before it killed Grady. But how? Sweet Jesus, she was a wreck. Emotions swirled within her: panic at the sheer impossibility of the situation, fear for Grady's safety, embarrassment over the fact that her bare ass was more than likely exposed by the short gown, and strangely enough . . . excitement over the prospect that she was capable of so much more than she could ever comprehend. Completely unable to focus her thoughts, the emotions overwhelmed her, too much for her to handle.

And, just like that, she felt the glorious vacuum. Somehow, Grady had managed to make that strange connection between them and funneled from her all of the troubling thoughts and emotions that clouded her ability to think. To react. In its place, she was left with a void. An apathy that allowed her to focus on one thing and one thing only: death for the demon.

The clarity of mind amazed Shelby. Without her emotions to weigh her down, her mind worked in an efficient line rather than twisting and knotting around worries, morals and doubts. The dagger weighed nothing in her hand, becoming an extension of her arm, and, as she charged the brimstone demon, her course of action was clear. In the black depths of the beast's chest, his heart glowed bright red, pulsing with life. She knew that if she could plunge the dagger into that evil thing's heart, it would die just like any living, breathing creature – human or otherwise.

As Grady continued to empty rounds from his gun into the demon, Shelby sized up the logistical issues – like how she was going to reach the demon's heart? She needed at least two feet of a boost to get the job done, and any of the furniture that would've given her height enough to reach the beast's chest was destroyed.

Lungs aching from her labored breath and her heart beating a frantic rhythm in her chest, she continued past the staircase. The south wing of the house was beginning to crumble in a cloud of black smoke and flames, as Shelby sprinted down the long hallway toward the demon, determined to stop it before it could hurt Grady.

Up ahead, she saw a small office area. A couple of tables still stood upright. It was as good a place as any to corner a nine-foot-tall demon that could breathe fire and bleed lava. Her body hummed with energy, and she sensed the connection between her and Grady arc like a bolt of lightning. As if he knew what she'd been thinking, he turned and took off toward the alcove, dodging the swinging fist of the demon before squeezing off a couple of shots. When he threw the gun and turned to run in earnest, Shelby assumed he'd exhausted his ammunition. It was now or never. If she didn't kill the brimstone demon, Grady was as good as dead.

Shelby pushed her body harder than she ever had, willing her legs to carry her fast enough to get to the table that Grady was rushing toward. Bits of broken glass dug into her feet, and she slipped on the wet floor and her own blood as she ran. But the physical pain barely registered. She was as numb on the outside as she was on the inside, but two thoughts goaded her forward. *Kill the demon. Save Grady.*

She trained her gaze on Grady, determined to coordinate her path with his. He dodged the demon, zigzagging a path toward Shelby. Just inside the doorway, Grady dropped to the ground in a skid. At that precise moment, her body working in tandem with his, Shelby leapt atop a table at the same time Grady found cover beneath it.

The brimstone demon's steps faltered. Which prey to attack first? It was all the hesitation Shelby needed. With both hands wrapped tightly around the dagger, she drove the blade into the demon's chest. Magic pulsed around her, the dagger all but singing with power, as she jammed the cutting edge as deep as it would go. The demon threw its head back and bellowed to the sky, flames shooting toward the ceiling like the exhaust from a rocket. Shelby twisted the blade and felt tissue tear as she jerked the dagger free. The fire died in the demon's mouth, its breath stalled, no longer billowing smoke. A weak, mewling sound wriggled from its chest and it crumpled to the floor in a heap.

"Jesus." Shelby collapsed on the tabletop, exhausted. Her limbs shook violently, and the blade tumbled from her hands and bounced from the tabletop to the floor. Water from the sprinkler system rained down on her, and her hair stuck to her face in soggy, black strands, obscuring her vision. Grady had been right all along. That man, Thad, had known it, too. There was no choice to be made, not really. She'd just killed an honest-to-God demon, with a magic dagger no less. Shelby knew what she was now, and somehow, despite how unreal this moment felt to her, it all made sense.

"Waerd," she whispered and slumped to the ground beside Grady. In a rush of movement, he scooped her up in his arms and held her tight against him. She knew if her emotions had been present, her chest would have swelled with affection. Trust.

"Sugar, you're a wreck," he murmured against her ear. "Don't worry, Shelby, I'll heal you. I'll take care of you."

She liked the way her name sounded when Grady said it. "I guess you know this means I've made my choice, right?"

"Oh, yeah?" Grady asked. "Just for the record – what do you choose, Shelby? Jail? Death? Or life?"

Shelby reached behind Grady's neck and brought his face to hers. "I choose life," she said before brushing her lips against his in a gentle kiss. "I choose *you*."

Six

Shelby stared out of the window of Grady's beat-up Chevy S-10, the green blur of the trees passing by like an Impressionist painting, while the sweet scene of magnolia in the summer sun washed across her senses. So much had happened over the course of one week. Her entire life had been torn apart and then rebuilt.

"I've never been to a real honest-to-God plantation before," Shelby remarked. Grady reached over to give her hand a reassuring squeeze and her bones all but melted from the warmth of power that radiated within her. Magnolia Plantation was tucked away behind ancient oaks with vast grounds that seemed to go on forever. One of the few private plantations in the state, Thad and his wife Grace had inherited the whole kit and caboodle from Thad's great-great-granddad or something. According to Grady, it was a legendary Sentry stronghold. And many Bearers and Waerds before them had called the grand house home.

Grady had told Shelby that her power astounded him, but she knew the truth: it was Grady who had the real power. Starting over in this new life should have been a terrifying prospect for Shelby. Before Grady, something like this would have had her climbing the walls with anxiety, looking to score anything she could get into her body, whatever drug would distract her from the crippling emotions she was too afraid to face.

"You'll like Magnolia, Shelby," Grady said, interrupting her thoughts. "Sure, it's tucked away, but it's hardly boring. The property sits on the intersection of two ley lines, magical highways that attract a lot of supernatural activity. It's the perfect place for a Waerd to train and see a lot of action . . ."

His voice faded to the back of Shelby's mind as she focused on the ornately carved sign up ahead that marked the turn-off to the plantation. Closing her eyes, she let the sound of Grady's voice lull her as he continued to talk about the plantation's history, Thad and his wife Grace, the Sentry, and what she could expect when they arrived. But she wasn't worried or even a little afraid. The calm settled on her like a heavy quilt protecting her from the cold night air. She wondered if Grady even realized to what extent he affected her. In such a short time, he had become her shield, the protection she'd been seeking most of her life from the crippling weakness of her emotions. Grady had quickly become her drug of choice and she was hopelessly addicted.

Thad had given Shelby a choice – join the Sentry and serve them as a Waerd, destroying evil and protecting humanity, or be put down like a rabid animal that couldn't be trusted around people. There was a time that she would have gladly let the Sentry do just that, but thanks to Grady – and even Thad – Shelby finally felt like she had something to live for.

"Grady," she said lazily, "are you going to teach me how to shoot?" Maybe she could make up for all the mistakes of her life if she worked hard, learned as much as she could and dedicated her life to protecting innocent people. It was work she'd be happy to perform as long as she had Grady by her side.

His laughter sent a thrill through her body as his power called to her. The connection between them was strong, and she knew he could feel the pleasant shiver that traveled over her skin when he spoke. She leaned against his shoulder and let the sound of his voice lull her as she drifted off to sleep. "I'm going to teach you how to shoot, how to fight and how to hunt." He brought her fingers to his lips and kissed each of her knuckles. "And I'm going to do my damnedest to make sure that you fall hopelessly in love with me before Thad manages to convince you it's not a good idea for Bearers and Waerds to have a relationship outside of work."

Thad is already too late, Shelby thought as she began to doze off. *I'm already hopelessly lost to you, Grady. I need you. I'll need you forever.*

Grady turned off the highway into the private drive. Shelby had agreed to stay at Magnolia with Thad for the duration of her training, and Grady was planning on making himself at home there too.

The connection between them was so strong. At times Grady had a hard time adjusting to the feeling that Shelby wasn't just sitting beside him. Part of her was *with* him. Inside of him. Her power mingling with his own. The intensity of their connection was something that could potentially cloud Grady's focus, but he would never let Thad know that. First and foremost, he was a Bearer and his loyalty rested with the Sentry. But he could see the possibilities that he'd never considered laid out before him when Shelby was near. A real life. A life that didn't exist to serve the Sentry's needs. Love. Happiness. He could see himself turning his back on everything he'd sworn loyalty to for her.

He'd do anything for her.

As Shelby slept beside him in the passenger's seat, Grady replayed the events of the past couple of days over and again in his mind. Thad had a plan in place when he'd sent Grady to the Sentry facility. Shelby was strong. Stronger than any Bearer he'd ever known. There was a reason Thad had been appointed as a Guardian – the highest ranking a Bearer could achieve – by the Sentry and it wasn't because of his gentle Southern charm. There was only one step above Guardian in their hierarchy, and the Watchers who governed the Sentry trusted Thad completely. Thad was all about the cause. One hundred per cent dedicated. And nothing stood in his way when Thad wanted something.

In fact, he hadn't made a secret of just how badly he'd wanted Shelby on board. "Don't come back without her, Grady," he'd said. And, like a good little soldier, Grady obeyed. Shelby had passed her test with flying colors. She'd barely needed a nudge before instinct had taken over, guiding her to be the warrior she was born to be.

As Grady pulled up in front of the impressive facade of the 200-year-old plantation house, he noticed Thad standing on the front porch, waiting. He brought his truck to a stop near the front steps and killed the engine. He looked over at Shelby, so beautiful and peaceful in sleep. Sheets of blonde hair spilled over one slim shoulder and her long lashes rested against her smooth, porcelain skin. Grady closed his eyes for a brief moment as he reached out with his senses, easing his way into Shelby's psyche. She was peaceful in sleep, untroubled, and unburdened by any guilt or sadness. And as long as he had anything to say about it, she'd stay that way.

"Shelby," he said, as he gently rubbed up and down her arm. "We're here."

She stirred beside him, stretching like a contented feline before opening her eyes. She looked up at him, the haze of sleep still clinging to her, and smiled. His heart beat a mad rhythm in his chest as a rush of power flooded him, chasing through his veins like fire.

"I still don't know how you're making me feel this way, Grady." She leaned toward him, close enough to murmur against his mouth. "But I like it."

Grady wrapped his arms around her and kissed her, his lips teasing hers until her mouth parted. He wanted nothing more than to stay right here and kiss her until she was breathless and begging him to take her somewhere private. A blast of anxious energy skittered up Grady's spine, reminding him that Thad's watchful eyes were taking all of this in, and he reluctantly pulled away.

"Are you ready for all of this?" he asked, as he reached for the door handle.

"As long as you're here with me," Shelby said. "I'm ready for anything."

"I'm here," he replied. A rush of pleasure, her pleasure, made his chest swell with emotion. "For as long as you want me."

"Good," Shelby said, as she pushed open her door. "I'm holding you to that, Grady."

"Deal." As Grady got down out of the truck his eyes locked with Thad's. He gave Grady a knowing smile that worried him. *She's right up your alley,* he'd said to him in this very same spot the day he'd left for the Sentry facility.

Thad couldn't have been more right. Grady more than liked Shelby. In fact, as he gazed hungrily at the woman waiting for him to join her so they could walk together toward the house, he realized he was looking at the woman who *absolutely* made all of the others pale in comparison. A woman he wanted to spend the rest of his life with.

And he had Thad to thank for it.

ABOUT THE AUTHORS

Jill Archer
Former lawyer, writing instructor and adjunct professor, she is the author of the Noon Onyx series, dark fantasy novels including *Dark Light of Day*, *Fiery Edge of Steel* and *White Heart of Justice*. She grew up in western Pennsylvania and spent summers and holidays in south Louisiana. She now lives in Maryland, just south of the Mason–Dixon line.
www.jillarcher.com

Sonya Bateman
Author of the urban fantasy novels *Master of None* and *Master and Apprentice*, she also writes thrillers and paranormal romance under the pen name S. W. Vaughn, including the popular Skin Deep erotic trilogy and the House Phoenix thriller series.
www.sonyabateman.wordpress.com

Amanda Bonilla
Lives in rural Idaho. She's a part-time pet wrangler, a full-time sun worshipper, and only goes out into the cold when coerced. In the summer, she can be found sitting by the lake, enjoying the view from her dock. Amanda also writes contemporary and romantic suspense under the name Mandy Baxter.
www.amandabonilla.com

Angie Fox

New York Times bestselling author writes books about biker witches, demon slayers and things that go bump in the night. The *Chicago Tribune* calls her books, "Fabulously fun." Angie is best known for her Accidental Demon Slayer series and for the Monster MASH trilogy.
www.angiefox.com

J. D. Horn

Author of the Witching Savannah series published by 47North, which includes *The Line*, *The Source* and *The Void*, was raised in rural Tennessee, and has since carried a bit of its red clay in him while traveling the world from Hollywood, to Paris, to Tokyo. He studied comparative literature as an undergrad, holds an MBA in international business, and worked as a financial analyst before becoming a novelist.
www.witchingsavannah.com

Elle Jasper

Nationally bestselling author of the moody, Savannah-set Dark Ink Chronicles, as well as ghost romances written as Cindy Miles.
www.ellejasper.com

Erin Kellison

New York Times and *USA Today* bestselling author of the Shadow series, the Shadow Touch novella series, and the Shadow Kissed series, all of which share the same world, where dark fantasy meets modern fairy tale.
www.erinkellison.com

Laurie London

New York Times and *USA Today* bestselling author of the Iron Portal and Sweetblood series, hot paranormal romances about bad boys and the women who tame them. She writes from her home near Seattle.
www.laurielondonbooks.com

Shawntelle Madison
Urban fantasy author of the Coveted series, featuring were-wolves and other supernatural creatures.
 www.shawntellemadison.com

Bec McMaster
Writer of award-winning romance novels featuring red-hot alpha males, kick-ass heroines and edge-of-your-seat adventures. Her London Steampunk series is available from Sourcebooks.
 www.becmcmaster.com

Jessa Slade
Despite being born a child of the sun in Southern California, she loves to write from the shadows. In her award-winning paranormal and science fiction romances, dark heroes win the day . . . and the night.
 www.jessaslade.com

Shelli Stevens
New York Times bestselling author who not only writes sexy contemporaries but action-filled paranormals. She lives in the Pacific Northwest where she cheers on the Seahawks, and enjoys the beauty of the region. Rain or shine.
 www.shellistevens.com

Dianne Sylvan
Author of five novels of the Shadow World urban fantasy series and two books on Neopagan spirituality, she is also currently writing the popular Agency series (available via the Amazon Kindle store), a paranormal adventure/romance. The remaining books of her Shadow World will be self-published, beginning later in 2014.
 www.diannesylvan.com.

Tiffany Trent
Award-winning author of fantasy and science fiction novels for young adults, including the Hallowmere series and the

steampunk novel *The Unnaturalists*. She has published several stories for adults in other Mammoth collections.
www.tiffanytrent.com

Shiloh Walker
Award-winning writer of romantic suspense, contemporary, paranormal romance and urban fantasy, also writing under the name J. C. Daniels. She's also a mom, a wife, a reader, and she pretends to be an amateur photographer. She published her first book in 2003.
www.shilohwalker.com